HIDDEN

HIDDEN

JOHN WOODBERY

Indigo River Publishing

Indigo River Publishing
3 West Garden Street, Ste. 718
Pensacola, FL 32502
www.indigoriverpublishing.com

First edition, 2020
Printed in the United States of America

ISBN: 978-1-950906-71-0 (paperback), 978-1-950906-73-4 (ebook)
LCCN 2020935573

Edited by Joshua Owens and Regina Cornell
Cover design by Robin Vuchnich
Interior design by Nikkita Kent

Special discounts are available on quantity purchases by corporations, associations, and others. For details, contact the publisher at the address above.

Orders by US trade bookstores and wholesalers: Please contact the publisher at the address above.

With Indigo River Publishing, you can always expect great books, strong voices, and meaningful messages. Most importantly, you'll always find . . . words worth reading.

This book is dedicated to the author's law school professor of ethics, who said, "If you are not sure whether or not you have a conflict or an ethical problem, you have a conflict or an ethical problem."

CONTENTS

PART I

THE QUEST

1

First You Have to Get There

The campfire was dying a natural death in the muggy heat of the evening, and good riddance, too. The team, headed by Montana Blake, were safely tucked inside their mosquito nettings for the night. It was hot in jungle country, making even breathing miserable, and the mosquito—with the real risk of malaria or dengue fever—added the possibility of terror to the day's encounters. The nettings were the only real defense, however unpleasant due to the heat, against the hordes of blood-sucking mosquitoes that swarmed around like enemy fighter planes.

This was a different kind of war Professor Blake was waging. Horatio Averill "Montana" Blake, PhD, was a full professor of anthropology at Fangleer College, located in the North Florida Panhandle community of Hedley, and never failed to let anybody around him know it. While Fangleer was a small college by ordinary standards, it was huge in academic reputation in the fields of science and culture thanks to the reputations of men such as Dr. Blake.

"Montana" was the nickname hung on Horatio early in life since he came from the western state and nobody, except a parent steeped in family name tradition or eccentricity like his, would have named a child Horatio, much less called him that. The childhood nickname "Harry" had long since faded out of use. Anyway, he liked the moniker because it sounded romantic or daring, attributes in which he liked to think he excelled.

Montana's accomplishments appeared in research and the publication of books and articles in learned scientific journals on the Stone Age people. He'd had the good fortune to stumble upon such tribes in an expedition to the Pangria tributaries of the Rio Ucayali in the Andean Mountains of Peru, and one of the many headwaters of the mighty Amazon. Of course, to get to the delightful climate of the Andean highlands where the primitive tribes had the good sense to make their homes, you had to traverse miles of mosquito- and crocodile-infested river-bottom country, like where the expedition was now sleeping.

Montana was on a search mission to study, photograph, and maybe even touch a certain Stone Age relic that could very well end up making trouble, but he never thought in such terms since whatever goal he happened to be pursuing at the moment was everything to this overachiever. His excited ego pushed risk aside without a second thought.

His goal was to actually see and photograph the relic hidden safely away in the hands of a shaman of the Musquaeli tribe he had had the good fortune to meet on one of his many scientific expeditions and which led to five articles in respected anthropology journals. He had heard and written about the little relic over and over in graphic detail, but had never been allowed to even see it, much less hold it in his hands. He had even squeezed speculations about it into one of his several tomes on basic anthropology. Getting his hands on the actual war god of the Musquaeli and—in the fantasy of his vivid imagination—finding a convincing way to get it away from the shaman without risking the destruction of the way of life of the Musquaeli people was what he would like to do. He could rationalize that it would be museum bound and not a part of his private collection. And this would probably signal his last trip to this particular tribal area. The feat, if he could pull it off, would lift his status in the scientific community even higher. That was all that really mattered to Montana.

The Florida Museum of Science and Natural History, heavily endowed by a private foundation of one of the railroad developer families in Florida, was paying for this particular expedition and had all rights to any discoveries, although no one on the grant review committee really expected to see such tangible rewards for their grant dollars.

Montana had actually been close to seeing the little stone idol once. It was reputed to be carved or created, depending on which tribal member you asked, from a piece of rare obsidian, and an ugly little black devil, as it was described to him. According to the warriors who had been privileged to actually see it, it had tiny red jewel-like eyes that seemed to follow you wherever you stood in its presence, like a hall of portraits in a medieval castle, and it seemed to squat in a stealth-like stance, ready to pounce on you, the enemy, or anything else that displeased it.

Montana got the impression from Urchuwa, the Musquaeli shaman, that the war god was rarely pleased with anything. An actual source of spiritual power or not, it was a scary little thing to the Musquaeli tribesmen, and since warring against neighboring tribes competing for desirable space in the jungle was their forte and necessity, they guarded it gratefully. They believed the idol had special powers that made them invincible in the many conflicts, with only the victorious conflicts bragged about or at least remembered, it seemed, and the others safely relegated to the dustbins of forgotten memories.

Montana, like most westerners, believed this "war god" business was a mere superstition typical of what you would find as a common belief in ignorant peoples, but he was wise enough to give Urchuwa the benefit of his beliefs and carefully watch for the opportunity to see the little relic and maybe even think up a way to relieve the tribal leader of this superstitious burden.

Montana had stretched his academic interests to include mastery of the Quechuan language that was close enough to the unusual dialect the Musquaeli actually spoke, to at least understand a smattering of the conversations his two guides used in the delicate negotiations that were necessary on each visit. The Indians' speech sounded to Western ears like a melodic high pitch, which made you think the male of the species had never had the characteristic voice change that all other male humans had during adolescence. Montana was unsure if this voice characteristic was natural or acquired; he had never heard them speak in a lower pitch, but there might have been a secret lower voice pitch, or even a different dialect, reserved for private occasions.

Everything he'd ever heard them say had been in the songlike dialect, but he held open the idea there was a time and place for something else. He didn't trust anyone in his dealings with the Indians, or practically anyone else, and reserved the capacity to decide for himself essentially what they were saying. This was especially true as far as these two former Musquaeli warriors were concerned, the two having been captured as young men, forced into slavery, and domesticated enough to safely hire out as guides on his expeditions. They could be trusted in normal daily affairs and even in basic communication with their former tribesmen. But Montana always expected the worst and believed nobody, except himself or possibly his able assistant, Elliot Drake, could be trusted in a scrap.

Elliot Drake was a man of many skills, and his experience as a mercenary in many unmentionable theaters of war was unknown to most. He had literally been a gun for hire with little regard for what the objective happened to be. There was one episode in his "career" as a professional soldier that he refused to reveal to anyone. A prince or potentate in North Africa had hired Elliot to assemble a team of professional fighters to slip into a neighboring country and assassinate the teenage heir to the throne of that kingdom. With the heir gone and the king having become impotent, the king would become more cautious in his negotiations with his neighbors on such things as oil-reserve lease rights. The employer in this case paid Elliot well because, after the assassination, the oil rights obtained in delicate negotiations between the two leaders turned out very favorably to the employer.

Elliot's team had successfully penetrated the palace in the still of night and made its way to the royal sleeping quarters. Elliot's memory, if he allowed himself to bring it into consciousness, was vivid and painful. His operatives had posted themselves at all the entrances, and Elliot entered the bedroom alone where the young man was sleeping. Like all plans for a perfect crime, the problem was in the unanticipated details.

The room was dark except for a small nightlight at the base of a lamp by the large bed where the potentate's teenage heir was sound asleep, snoring all the while. Elliot's weapon of choice at that time for these clandestine assignments was a .32 caliber Berretta with a silencer screwed on to the end of the barrel. He carefully and silently moved around the end of the bed to make a clean and deadly shot to the base of the target's skull. As he maneuvered into position and placed the weapon a few inches away from the victim's head, he heard—or, more accurately, felt—a motion on the floor next to the bed. He swiveled his head around and saw in the dim light, to his surprise, the small form of a human sleeping on the floor, curled up in a blanket of some kind.

What the hell? Who could that be? Can't have any witnesses to this assignment, can I? he thought. On closer inspection, he concluded that the form was the body of a small boy considerably younger than the target. He immediately considered all the possibilities: a younger brother unknown to his employer, a visiting friend, or another relative; and if so, should he take this one out too? He made this evaluation without removing his weapon from the intended victim's head, but clearly struggling with the decision. As he did so, the form turned over and he found himself staring into the eyes of a beautiful boy child of about five years with a look of terror on his face and his mouth already starting to open to scream. *Can't risk it, have to do it, damn!*

And then he fired the Beretta into the terrified face, snuffing out the life of the innocent, unintended victim. He then turned, finding the original victim unchanged and, more importantly, not wakened by the little snapping sound the silenced fired round had made, and completed the grisly task he had originally been well paid to accomplish. Quickly checking the carotid artery of both victims with a slight pressure to the side of the neck to confirm death and mission accomplished, he swiftly left the royal bedroom, rejoined his assistants, and safely left the premises.

Within hours, Elliot's team was on the way to a safe exit from the country and on to the next assignment, whatever it turned out to be. There were always more assignments for this talented crew. But Elliot was somehow never the same after that night.

The guilt of having taken the lives of the heir and whoever the other boy had been, and especially that part of the bargain for which he had definitely not been prepared emotionally, weighed heavily on Elliot, though the healthy fee he earned assuaged it somewhat. He just put it out of his conscious mind and over time rationalized it into acceptance. The expedition with Dr. Blake was a far less rewarding one for Elliot financially, but he saw little chance this expedition would cause the guilt to raise its ugly head. Time would tell.

The two ex-warriors whom Elliot had recruited for the expedition were a little past their prime according to Musquaeli standards since, by the time of maturity, most of their men either died from disease or found the wrong end of an enemy spear. But the guides were still able to heft a spear or run all day on the jungle trails. Wanei was a little taller and more muscular than Estova, but both men were in excellent shape and generally reliable, with Wanei the better translator of the two.

"Wake up, sir. Daylight will be here soon, and the fires have burned out. The boys must have fallen asleep on duty," Elliot said as he gently nudged Professor Blake into wakefulness.

"Uh-huh, yeah, I'm awake. Get them up, Elliot, and stir that thing back to life; we'll need it for breakfast," Montana said as he rolled over on his sleeping pad to catch another forty winks. This was a lean and mean expedition, designed this way by Montana because he trusted Elliot to back him up on this delicate mission in a way many other hangers-on, such as the graduate students and wannabe-famous teaching assistants who often tried to sweet-talk their way onto one of these excursions, could not be trusted. Elliot unzipped the mosquito netting, crawled out of the tent, and found Wanei and Estova sound asleep under their own mosquito netting, the dying fire low on their list of personal priorities. The Indians had some immunity to malaria and dengue fever, but they had lived on the plantations long enough to appreciate the comfort that the light netting shield provided against the bites of the little buggers.

After a light breakfast of tinned ham and dried fruit washed down with boiled coffee, they broke camp and trudged up the river trail in search of the access into Musquaeli land. Montana typically put one guide on the front and the other bringing up the rear for safety and to serve as the "ears" of the expedition. Wanei and Estova, like all Musquaeli, were trained from birth to read the danger signs of the jungle, whether of animal, human, or plant variety, and could be relied upon to alert the team to any danger in time to prepare for it. They were especially keen to read the signs, directly or indirectly, that their former tribe's people were approaching or being approached.

"The access" was the name Montana had given to the hidden path, the only one you could take up the waterfall on the Pangria. It fell two hundred fifty odd feet from a rock precipice above, where the tributary of the Rio Ucayali launched its powerful deluge into the river valley below. He had discovered it, or more accurately one of his guides had, when he had been led underneath the powerful waterfall at his insistence to explore the caves underneath. The path served as a way around the otherwise inaccessible mountain face but was hardly one you might think of taking on a stroll in the jungle. It was basically vertical in direction to permit the elevation gain necessary to make it to the sacred Musquaeli plateau. There were roughly hewn steps, one after another, that would be difficult at best for even well-conditioned travelers. The presence of vine and root handholds at key points up the path were the only thing that made it passable, and not even that for those out of shape, undisciplined, or unmotivated. Since Montana and his team were veterans of the trek, they knew to pay the price of preparedness with regular trips to the local gym back home and had no difficulty making their way successfully, albeit laboriously, up the access.

The Musquaeli relied on the mountain face as a barrier of sorts to keep foreigners out of their sacred territory, but used the access route for their own purposes as circumstances demanded.

"Thunderfall there up," spoke Wanei in his poor English rendition, gesticulating in the upriver direction through the dense undergrowth surrounding a bend in the Pangria where the waters were still languid and no one but the two Musquaeli could yet hear the falling water.

"Okay, I hear you. Close it up, boys. If Wanei can hear it, the falls and access can't be far ahead," Montana said. He renewed his scanning of the river and jungle because this meant they were nearing dangerous territory. He checked his nine-millimeter Berretta semiautomatic pistol, always worn in a very visible holster to let the Indians who would undoubtedly see him before he saw them know that he meant business. The Indian spears could be deadly, but the Musquaeli were frightened by the big bang firearms made and had seen too many of their warriors die from the "smoke and punch," as those who could speak a little English would describe a killing shot from a foreigner's handgun or rifle.

Still, Montana knew these Indians, and once safe contact was made he could peacefully go about the business of exchanging gifts for information about their lifestyles and culture that his scientific expedition's sponsors required. If by chance he did see the war god relic, photograph it in its secret hiding place, and make it safely out to professional acclaim, so much the better. He had even had the foresight to bring along a canister of molding plaster to make an impression from which a facsimile model could later be constructed.

Montana only hoped the Musquaeli natives, if they saw him first, would recognize him as the "Big Doctor," a term he insisted they call him, and not think him to be some other foreign intruder that they would dispense with unwittingly.

After the team reached the foot of the waterfall and conferred briefly to plan the ascent, with the pack loads evenly allocated among the team members, but with lighter loads given to the guides to aid them in climbing freely, Wanei took point and they started the laborious process. Wanei made the ascent seem easy as he took one step after another like a spider navigating its web. Montana and Elliot struggled mightily to keep up, with the occasional misstep, slip, or near fall even with the handholds available. "Damn!" "Oh hell!" and similar expletives could be heard with every miscue by any reasonably perceptive jungle resident above or below.

And there was someone listening. The Musquaeli happened to be at war with a neighboring tribe, each vigorously contesting possession of the sacred canyon whose ridges flanked one particularly beautiful segment of the Pangria tributary that lay in the area each tribe claimed in their competing territories.

Practically anything else could have triggered the latest war, such as revenge for some perceived affront to the dignity of their side, a pig that had been raised and fed on one side of the ill-defined border being speared by a hunter from the other, a woman from one side captured as a slave by the other side, or even a shadow covering the moon when it—according to one tribe or the other—should not be there, in the direction of the hated tribe. It didn't take much to trigger a war between these tribes. And life expectancy—if they thought about such things—was short indeed.

It had been like this throughout the living memory of the most ancient tribesmen; the Musquaeli had never known things to be any different. The war was being waged on a front far away from the sacred waterfall, but the rear entrance to their sacred lands, as it were, was always protected from entry by a token security team, just in case of an unexpected attack from the rear.

These rearguard men were either the younger and untried, not really warriors yet due to inexperience, or the older men who were scarred too much from many battles and not strong enough to be trusted with front-line duty. But since this culture sat delicately balanced on a teeter-totter of the opposing moral attributes of shame and honor, nothing was worse than to be on the shame seat, regardless of the innocent reason or cause. So every assignment—rearguard duty included—presented the chance to make it back over the fulcrum to the seat of honor. This situation was a powerful motivator, and the two lonely and frightened warriors guarding the trail above the waterfall that day were brought to full attention at the first sounds of the expedition's noisy and clumsy ascent up the access trail.

"Cum a lei? Do se le'ah," said the taller and younger of the two men to his much older companion, a veteran of many campaigns.

"Cou se ah do me'ah uh, dei teano. Les soo et ah cramique?" said the other in answer.

The rough translation of this exchange in English with a Western colloquial slant would be something like "Did you hear that? Something's coming up the mountain trail." "Of course it is, you idiot. What else could make such a racket?"

The older and more experienced warrior of the two gestured to the other that he would position himself with a view of the top of the access trail and signal with his spear, friend or foe, by the agreed and customary method. The other left quickly, and within minutes the stakeout and signal positions were in place.

Wanei was the first to appear above the trail's spout, like a jungle mouse crawling out of its hole. First, the slightest movement caught the sentinel's practiced eye; then came the realization that something out of nature was appearing. Soon the sentinel recognized the telltale signs that someone had appeared from the secret access route, stopping and listening like any sensible Musquaeli would and then moving slowly and with much care before turning back to the top of the spout and signaling the all clear to his companions behind.

To the sentinel's surprise, he recognized Wanei, the point man of the Blake expedition, as the same Musquaeli guide who as a boy had been captured by the foreign devils and taken into slavery. On two or three occasions Wanei had led some of the foreign devils—with the permission of the great chief—into the sacred lands of the Musquaeli. The sentinel had been a mere boy when the feared foreigners, with their smoke-and-punch sticks, had stormed the Musquaeli village, located then in the lower reaches of the Pangria, before their migration to the safety of the sacred reaches above the waterfall. But he remembered the terrible tragedy and Wanei, a boy of similar age at the time, who was a distant relative of his and who he came to know much better after several of the scientific expeditions that the Big Doctor had made into the region.

The Musquaeli did not fear the expeditions because the scientific inquiry that meant so much to Montana meant absolutely nothing to the Musquaeli. They eagerly accepted the gifts the white foreigners brought. Although they understood what a trade meant, since the information the anthropologist was taking was of no value to them, the foreigners were simply generous fools working so hard to get into the sacred lands and taking nothing. This was fine by them.

The older warrior stood his ground as Wanei and Estova stood out front, ready to interpret or fight if need be, until Professor Blake and the remainder of the team reached the top of the access route and filled in behind, with their weapons at the ready. The weapons were not necessary on this trip, and Wanei relaxed as he discovered that the older warrior of the tribe serving as a rear guard actually recognized him. At first Wanei had some difficulty in remembering who this was in front of him, but after a short exchange between himself and the other man, he relaxed his guard as the telltale signs of friendliness and trust were readily apparent.

"Kem sei leah, Wanei? Uen seia recuneshe las heli solei gunertishhes, Efstei Culaam, mea shenu," the older warrior said.

"Keashi culaamseka, Efstei, dii keesta," Wanei replied. Then he turned to translate the exchange for Professor Blake.

"He remember me from last visit. Efstei Culaam is name. We may even have tribal roots same, but no danger lies here," Wanei explained.

"Good job, Wanei, but no matter; take us to their leader, wherever the camp is," Montana impatiently demanded.

Wanei held up his hands in a cautionary manner. "Much must be learned before village may be approached, Big Doctor, but Wanei will try," he said respectfully.

Montana rolled his eyes disrespectfully as though he had no time for such niceties, but gestured with a "go ahead" signal that let Wanei understand he had reluctantly agreed this time but not to make a habit of it.

Wanei and Efstei began what sounded to Montana like a dialogue entirely too long and involved for the simple task of negotiating an access to someone in authority so that he, the Big Doctor, could re-establish contact with the shaman of the tribe and get on with the business at hand—his business, anyway, which was all he really cared about.

He could follow the substance of what Wanei was saying and some of the replies with his fairly complete grasp of the Quechuan language, from which the dialect the Musquaeli spoke was derived, but many of the details escaped him. Much of the exchange was taken, wisely on Wanei's part, to find out the state of affairs of the tribe, whether they were at war or at peace.

He could tell by the tension in Efstei's demeanor that things were far from peaceful or routine. Efstei took quite a while to explain to his distant relative that the tribe was at war with the hated enemy from up the river bordering their territory and that only he and his young companion were standing guard over the backdoor entrance to the tribe's territory, which the Blake team had penetrated.

It was a credit to Wanei's skills as a jungle diplomat that Efstei could be persuaded to open up and disclose the perilous nature of current conditions. Montana slowly, if impatiently, began to understand the delicate nature of these negotiations. However, he saw an opportunity that might just develop in his quest for the war god if the tribe was preoccupied with the war itself and, most importantly, if the war god was back at the village or hidden somewhere nearby and not on the front lines of combat, where theft by the dreaded enemy might occur.

Based on his past dealings with Urchuwa, the tribe's respected shaman, Montana, in his usual confident manner, was sure he could locate the little statue and find a way to steal it from the tribe. The fact that such a theft might disrupt the well-being of the Musquaeli, whether their little war god was as powerful a force behind their survival as they believed or a simple superstition as he knew to be the case, was of little importance to Professor Montana Blake.

And if he was able to steal the thing and make his escape, it mattered not to Montana that this would be the last trip to *this* Stone Age tribe. There were always many other such groups to find, explore, manipulate, and exploit; and losing the right to use these people mattered little to the Big Doctor. After twenty minutes of the exchange, Wanei signaled to Professor Blake that the way was clear for the expedition to trek upriver to the main village site on the serene and picturesque banks of the Pangria.

2

THE HOME FRONT

Montana's team made its way dutifully following the two Musquaeli warriors and their own guides as the trail meandered toward the main village alongside the Pangria in as picturesque a setting as any Hollywood director would have demanded for a '50s-era Tarzan movie. The Pangria above the falls was preternaturally calm compared to its turbulence at and below the falls as the water cascaded in fits and starts relentlessly toward its eventual joinder with the mighty Amazon.

The village was strategically placed in a clearing along the banks of the river, but hidden from view unless you happened to be looking for it. The dwelling huts were clustered around a center area that was free of vegetation and hard packed from countless footprints making a steady drumbeat of daily-living activities, but the area was visible to all the villagers so that nothing happened in the communal area of the village that would escape anyone's notice.

The huts that made up the housing units of the village were constructed with limber poles bent like barrel staves, interlaced with tough reed fibers, and coated with river mud baked by the sun into a hard shell. The method had hardly changed since the invasions of the conquistadores. They were functional, if not beautiful beyond a prosaic way, and protected the Indians during the nights with frequent rain squalls. The houses permitted the storage of meager personal possessions, but were used for little else since the climate did not favor lounging around inside except when a downpour made the heat a tolerable alternative to getting soaked. The Musquaeli were a primitive hunter/gatherer people well adapted to their jungle environment. They lived by foraging on plants, roots, and wild game, which took them on extended treks into the jungle, rain or shine.

Except for the noise of children at play and women working, the village was quiet when the expedition arrived. The activity stopped, however, as soon as the noise from the trudging expedition, with the clank and clatter of jostling equipment, was carried in the gentle jungle breezes as effectively as a telegraph system in modern culture. The Musquaeli were so attuned to their environment that any change in the atmosphere by sound, smell, or wildlife activity could be detected by even women and children long before outsiders would have noticed such an arrival in their own noisy, clamoring world of modern societal interactions.

The expedition was led into the encampment and shown an area where they could set up their own camp under a thatched structure supported by poles but open from the sides, allowing for maximum cooling breezes to flow through. A message would be sent to the front to get further directions from the chief of the tribe. Efstei Culaam, the older of the two rear guards, had assumed this responsibility after a careful instruction to his younger assistant to keep a close eye on the strangers.

Not every adult male was away at war, however, and Montana was surprised and astonished to learn that his old "friend" Urchuwa, the shaman of the tribe, was still in the area of the camp and not away at the battle zone like the others. He wasn't hanging around the village twiddling his thumbs, though, but was engaged in the very serious business of interacting with the tribal gods, personified in the little black war god, for favor of their side in battle. The "interacting" took place in an area sanctified by tribal traditions and safely away from the din and clatter of daily life. Montana had been to this sacred place once before, but understood the importance of respect for protocol and had to wait until he was properly summoned by the holy man, at least if he came pretty darn soon.

He would never presume to just wander over there and announce his presence in the camp, but he would not sit around all day waiting for the shaman to take his good, sweet time to come seeking an audience with him. However, there was no doubt in his mind that Urchuwa either was or would soon be aware of his presence in the village. Because absolutely nothing took place in the immediate area that the holy man was not aware of very quickly, and the arrival of a noisy foreign expedition to the village would make its way into his inner sanctum no matter how important his "interacting" process was.

The team did not have to wait long. Almost as soon as they had set up their camp in the designated assembly area, a hush settled over the village, like what happens in an old, abandoned house when a group of young boys trying to prove their bravery think they hear a ghost coming, inspiring the courage to be the first to bolt out of the place.

Within a few minutes, the tall, majestic Indian walked quietly into the clearing just behind the expedition's encampment. All eyes—villagers' and foreigners' alike—were fixed on this magnificent example of human kind, Indian or otherwise. Very few humans are gifted by birth and environment to present such a physical specimen as Urchuwa did. His tall stature, by Indian standards, was so different from any Indian the expedition team had ever seen, but it was more than his unusual height, broad shoulders, and supple musculature that captivated their attention. He had an air about him that spoke volumes beyond his mere appearance.

Though having not yet spoken, Urchuwa had a certain charisma about him that drew people to him and persuaded them—without objective reasons—to trust this man. There was almost a glow about him that made his dark Indian skin radiate, not with light as such but with an aura that defied physical description. Montana and Elliot looked at him, then at each other, and nodded knowingly as if agreeing with each other's thoughts about his presence.

They would soon learn that what they were observing was the afterglow from the trance-like state the shaman had been immersed in from his sessions with the war god. Real or imagined, it had the same effect no matter who saw it, including the Big Doctor himself, who was moved to mutter under his breath in Latin, "Mirabile dictu," or in English, "Strange to say, wonderful to report."

"Urchuwa, friend, come again." Montana, gesturing to himself, spoke slowly in English, knowing that the shaman could under normal circumstances understand him and was proud of his ability to do so. It never occurred to Montana that, as an outsider visiting with a war going on and himself plotting against the best interests of the Musquaeli, it would have been more diplomatic to communicate in his broken version of the Quechua language and show his willingness to ingratiate himself with the tribe. But Montana had no diplomatic or, for that matter, interpersonal social skills to speak of, and for him it was no time to start learning them.

The tall Indian stood his ground, silently surveying the scene before him as if he were emerging from another world. He took it all in as though sitting in an optician's chair and having different combinations of filtered lenses flicked in front of his eyes, waiting until the version of reality he saw with his eyes lined up with the one he could form in his mind. Time was not an important criterion to him because the world he had just left was a timeless place where past, future, and present merged into one spiritually clear version of that reality in order for him to see clearly what the war god wanted his tribe to do to succeed in battle.

Nothing else mattered to him at this moment. He tolerated this intrusion partially out of curiosity and partially out of a cautious need to help his tribe survive in every circumstance. Perhaps these foreign strangers' powerful smoke-and-punch weapons could somehow be employed on his side. He recognized the large foreigner from prior expeditions and stood as if pausing for dramatic effect, although such techniques as a modern actor might employ would never have crossed the mind of any Musquaeli, even their shaman.

"Us quelia umtra lesti, Gesto Wa? You come here back, Great One?" Urchuwa said, first in Quechua and then in his fairly accomplished version of English, demonstrating his superior language and diplomatic skills. However, the subtle rhetorical technique of using sarcasm to belittle your opponent to demonstrated effect without crude or offensive words was not usually in the moral repertoire of these simple yet complicated people. And this was a very exceptional Musquaeli Indian, at that.

"Of course I'm back, you fool," Montana said with a gracious smile and a little bow of simulated obeisance, choosing his words carefully as he realized from his understanding of the language that there was no Quechua equivalent to *fool* and that the tone a person used had more significance than the actual words used with these people.

"You come, ugh, time bad. War take Musquaeli place. Spirits come, time be better," Urchuwa said with the confident tone of one who had just finished connecting with the spirit world and had a message of hope from there about the tribe's present prospects in the war. Montana could never understand that connection or its effects in this life.

"We understand your tribe is at war. How can we help?" Montana said slyly, looking for an opening to worm his way into the Indian's confidence and hoping for the opportunity to separate him from the object of his affection and obedience, and the goal of this expedition. What he had offered could be seen one of two ways, but the shaman must have thought only of the aid the smoke-and-punch weapons would bring in the upcoming battle and never even considered that the Big Doctor had thought of anything else. As it turned out, both were right and both were wrong, as events would reveal. But, regardless of perceptions, a deal was struck that was to have far-reaching consequences.

Early the next morning, Urchuwa led the white foreigners and the guides, with their weapons and baggage, upriver toward the battle area that was forming. The conflict was taking place near the disputed territory of the Musquaeli, in some of the deepest, darkest areas of the forest. It was also one of the most sacred because of its unusual geographical shape.

The river flowed through a deep canyon flanked by parallel ridges with a narrow, flat protuberance at the top of each plateau just wide enough for a few men to stand on, some 150 feet in elevation above the canyon floor. The sides of the canyon sloped concavely but gently enough down to the valley to allow jungle vegetation to cover them to some extent, before bottoming out seventy-five feet or so on each side of the river on the canyon floor. On the opposite end, a rough, convex slope faded into some long-forgotten turn of the river's history, forming a test-tube shape from an aerial view, open on one end and closed on the other.

It was as if some giant had found this little mountain and scooped out the middle to let the river run through it. In fact, it was possible to see it this way because there was a small mountain to the west of the canyon towering above the whole scene and accessible by a difficult switchback to the top. When this view was gained by strenuous effort, the mystical tube that had attracted the Musquaeli to the area and inspired them to defend it to the death as one of their most sacred places revealed itself.

The plateaus at the bottom of the tube sloped artistically but in a slightly convex manner down to the canyon floor. The interplay of these sloping surfaces dropping down into the valley from the sides and then climbing up before falling again to the river at the "opening" at the bottom of the tube on the valley floor would have given a calculus professor a severe challenge to compute the angles. But it left a narrow opening just wide enough for the river to flow through, with a path along each side, before opening into a wider area of the river where a beautiful small lake had formed, flanked by dense jungle vegetation right down to the edge on either side.

The river also turned east just at this point, which allowed the sun to fill the corridor with blinding light each morning. The Musquaeli never tired of watching this oddity of nature. To their eyes, it possessed a mystical quality, making it seem as though they were being scrutinized by the gods, with nothing hidden from view.

Musquaeli who had paddled to the middle of the lake outside the outlet end of the tube and gazed back into the canyon during the morning sun had, from time to time, recounted descriptions of the view a man might have had standing between two gigantic and beautifully green-covered female breasts. Montana had a theory that this was why the Musquaeli considered the area sacred. The male of the species everywhere seemed to be captivated by a woman's breasts, with possibly some psychological longing for a time when nurture and nature were intertwined in the mother–man-child relationship, according to Dr. Freud's insights.

However, no such desires had ever been expressed among the Indians, or even consciously thought about, as far as anybody knew; but that is the nature of psychological desire: to be hardly ever understood or recognizable and talked about unless just a figment of the imagination of men too smart for their own good. The front end of the tube began just as suddenly and majestically as it ended, as the two plateaus gradually sloped up on each side from the valley floor.

As far as any outsider reports that had been published, no geologist had witnessed the geographic phenomenon, so it remained just as much a mystery to Montana and his team as to the Indians, who never really thought about such things. It was just the way the gods had made the earth, and no other explanation had ever been necessary to these deceptively simple people. They just enjoyed it.

The expedition arrived around dusk in the area of the forest that contained the Musquaeli base camp, a short distance downstream of the lake at the end of the canyon. They hoped to get there just in time to set up their field tents and store their supplies before the blanket of total darkness draped them completely.

As soon as they were within hearing and smelling distance of the camp Wanei and Estova recognized that something important was in the works. Wanei stopped for a moment and lifted his nose into the evening breeze to sniff the air like a hound. He slowly turned his head, cocked slightly, from side to side as if trying to sense any subtle shift in the forest's sounds or smells and then signaled to the Big Doctor to come forward for a talk.

"Arrive soon at camp. Dark be soon. Must hurry," Wanei said, trying to encourage his leader to get the expedition team to hurry.

"How in the Sam Hill do you know that?" Montana asked, more for his own benefit, knowing the Indian would have no idea what that old southern expression meant. But figuring the Indian had some way to read the signs of the rapidly darkening forest, he told the rest of the team to get a move on. In fifteen or twenty minutes, even the outsiders could see the obvious signs of foot traffic and broken plant life that one would normally expect when humans were around.

By the time they arrived at the campsite alongside the Pangria, darkness had begun to blot out the little afterglow visible from the sun, with giant trees casting shadows. The curiously shaped mountains beyond the lake were still visible as they stood at the camp near the water's edge. The water on this broad stretch of the Pangria was still as it emptied out of the magic lake, and with the fading light blocked by the tall, imposing trees, it was transformed into a blackened mirror reflecting nothing.

Neither Montana nor Elliot saw anything unusual about the camp to signify that a war zone was nearby, and based on all outward appearances, both felt this was just another disorganized and quiet Indian village that could be dismantled and moved in short order. There were only a few warriors in the camp, and these men were preoccupied with preparations for the evening meal or other unknown tasks and hardly seemed like warriors at all. Of course they were warriors, or they would not have been this close to the action. And their blowguns, spears, and hatchets for making war were safely set aside within easy reach should the call for reserves be sounded by the jungle-coded drum telegraph or swift-footed messengers calling them quickly to the front.

The only structures visible in the camp were a few crude work tables and benches made of small but sturdy hand-rubbed tree limbs tied together with vines. The center of the camp was swept clean, forming a convenient gathering place for the assembled fighting tribesmen, and packed hard from many such gatherings. A few thatch-covered lean-tos were made the same way to give the resting warriors a place to lie down for an evening's rest with some shelter from a late-night rain squall. One larger covered area of undetermined purpose was set apart from the center of the camp, and that was about all there was to the encampment.

The river's edge at the campsite was at the rim of the lake just outside the entrance to the magic canyon. A beach of sorts, suitable for the canoe landing, in front of the encampment would have made the scene quite picturesque if the war-making purpose of the encampment were not hanging over the scene with such an ominous air of expectancy in the minds of the Indians present. This was the scene Montana, Elliot, and their guides found as they trudged noisily—by Indian standards—into camp and began to set up for their stay.

3

A Council of War

The first sign of change that was significant enough to interrupt the white men in the hustle and bustle of making camp was a silence that settled over the jungle around them. Even the huge river frogs populating the eddies that normally made this time of day a cacophonous din of unharmonious hollering ceased their lustful bellows.

Elliot was the first to notice. In a former life—as he liked to call it—he had served a substantial stint in the US Army Rangers, with experience here and there in jungle warfare and covert tactics off and on the payroll of some government or other when his price was paid. And, like most combat veterans, he avoided talking about it. The memories were just too painful.

He had another memory, another reason not to mention his past even to himself, though this painful memory had been manageably submerged except for an occasional nightmare. Long ago he had come to realize he had much to atone for from his past, and he was gradually coming to terms with it emotionally. This expedition had seemed a perfect place to work out the demons hidden in the deeper recesses of his soul, because he had not expected much in the way of combat on this trip. The setting was different here and consistent with his expectations, but every self-respecting combat soldier, especially a platoon commander like Elliot had been back in those days, knew to pay attention to such things and never forgot it.

"Listen up!" Elliot said, raising his hand like a fourth grader telling everyone he was going to the comfort station whether the teacher liked it or not.

"Oh, what for?" Montana said, busy directing the stowing of the camping gear.

"Something or someone is coming. The noise. Get it?"

"What noise? I don't hear anything," Montana said with some annoyance on being interrupted.

"That's just it, sir: there isn't any. The frogs shut up for a reason. Someone's coming, I'm certain of it."

Debate became meaningless as the first warriors from the front silently made their way into camp, hardly noticing the white men as they gathered around Urchuwa, who had seemingly appeared from nowhere in the center of the open space. He needed no outward symbol of authority or special markings or costume to draw them to him, even if they didn't know who he was, which all of the warriors did of course, as the afterglow of the spiritual trance was still lingering about his visage, like a fading neon sign above a gambling casino in Las Vegas flashing its message, "Come over here, come over here!"

It was apparent to even the outsiders that a council of war was beginning. The warriors stood in a rough semicircle around the shaman with their spears and hatchets at their sides. Urchuwa listened as each of the warriors reported from his own perspective on the strength and position of the enemy they had faced. European wars had been fought in more or less open territory with the power of modern weapons being the deciding factor in the outcome in a squad-sized fight or larger. This kind of war was vastly different because spears don't have much range, and in the jungle it was impossible to see your enemy until he was on top of you. By then it was too late unless you were extremely quick or lucky. The warriors had been spaced out to protect the sacred valley from enemy incursion, and the enemy tribe had been just as determined to make that place their valley.

The fighting to the present had been basically one-on-one hand-to-hand combat. The chatter of the warriors reporting to Urchuwa was incessant.

One of the fighters chattered excitedly in Musquaeli, which was complete gibberish to the white men. But Urchuwa took it all in stoically, having the security of his trust in the spirit session he had experienced in the presence of the war god. He realized that the men had every reason to be concerned, but he was bringing them hope and confidence. They just didn't know it yet.

The shaman patiently listened until all of the Musquaeli warriors had finished their accounts of the fighting so far, and then paused for what seemed like an eternity to Montana and Elliot before he began to speak. He explained to his men that he had full confidence in their ability to fight for the honor of the Musquaeli tribe and protect the sacred valley, but that he was pleased to announce that he had good news for them. Not only had the war god sent his blessings but the white foreigners had agreed to bring their smoke-and-punch weapons to aid the noble Musquaeli in this vital battle.

He quickly translated this to Montana and Elliot, who nodded in agreement. A sound that may have been a rendition of a cheer rose from the throats of the Musquaeli men as they jumped up and down with excitement. Urchuwa then gave instructions as to how the battle was to be fought the next day. Each man was to take his station across the open end of the entrance to the valley and fight with courage, one-on-one, against the enemy, taking comfort in the knowledge that the war god was empowering them to victory, and with the white foreigners backing them up. The warriors reacted enthusiastically. Above the din of the celebration, Wanei did his best to translate Urchuwa's message for Montana and Elliot.

Elliot stood alongside Montana gazing at the scene, taking in the last light reflected off the waters of the lake, and looking to the small mountains standing beyond, with the magnificent cleavage before him. "I wonder what's beyond those giant teats up there and upriver. Where is this battle line supposed to form? Wanei, is there any way I could get up there and see the whole valley from above it?" he asked.

Wanei nodded his head and said, "High peak spot, sundown side there," and pointed to the west of the right breast.

"Can you see the whole valley from there, Wanei?"

"Yes, valley get small quick fast on climb. Bird like see, you can," Wanei explained.

"Sir," Elliot said, looking past Wanei and Estova, and ignoring the continuing celebration by the warriors, "this battle plan I'm hearing is long on ego and vainglory and short on tactics. You lose one man in it and that enemy tribe will come streaming through here like crap through a goose. It's a plan all right, a disaster plan, I'd call it, sir."

"Good point, Elliot," Montana said.

Urchuwa understood enough of the exchange between the two white men and, being a bit smarter than the average Indian, stopped to ponder what they had said.

"First light tomorrow, Big Doctor, we take this man for look-see up there," and he pointed with a dramatic gesture to the west of the right-hand mound to a tall peak barely visible in the dying light.

The next morning at dawn, Elliot, Wanei, Urchuwa, and two warriors boarded one of the canoes by the lakeside and paddled their way across the magic lake into the face of the blinding morning sun and through the entrance of the canyon beyond, where the rounded slope on the inside end of the canyon came to a stop at the river's edge. There they left the canoe where one of the warriors found a barely visible trail that left the shore, switching back and forth up the slope until the little group crested the peak on the right-hand side of the canyon.

From this peak, the going was easier as Urchuwa and the two warriors led them down a well-used trail that ended on the opposite floor of the canyon. The high observation point Urchuwa had mentioned was now visible to them. The men paused to catch their breath before starting up a very narrow and steep mountain trail, mostly of rock and roots, which would have been a challenge to most amateur mountain climbers. When they reached the peak, an amazing sight was displayed before them.

From this vantage point, one could see the full spread of the valley, just as Urchuwa had claimed. It was truly a bird-like view that allowed one to take in all its features and study them carefully. Sure enough, there was the undeniable test-tube-shaped valley, created over the centuries by the erosion of the Pangria carving its way through the porous rock, like so much butter by the scoop of a deft and artistic giant, with a hole at the bottom spilling its contents into the mystical and beautiful lake.

Beyond the opening end of the canyon was a relatively flat area that extended across both sides of the canyon, heavily forested with a moderate growth of jungle vegetation as far as the eye could see. The tall forest that was common to this area didn't seem to grow well alongside the river there and the plain—covered with low, dense jungle vegetation—was parted by the Pangria into what appeared to be the cups of two giant hands flanked on both sides by the normal giant forests. Elliot, the experienced combat soldier, could see right away the potential benefit and the danger.

If the shaman's plan was followed and the Musquaeli warriors were strung out across the open end of the canyon to fight one-on-one to bar the entrance to the sacred valley, one break in the line as he had imagined it from the ground level would be even worse when seen with his own eyes from up here. There would be nothing to stop the assault and the Musquaeli village would be doomed.

"I've seen enough," Elliot said, and diplomatically asked the shaman if he thought maybe it was time to return to the war council with the valuable information his showing of this vantage point had revealed. Urchuwa, being not only smarter than most but just a little bit vain as well, quickly lapped up the faint praise and agreed.

"We go!" he said emphatically, and made the steep descent with Elliot and the others silently following his lead.

4

THE PLAN

As the warriors gathered around Urchuwa, Elliot, and the others, Montana eased his way into the excited gathering and assumed his normal position of prominence as though he were somehow responsible for the plan that was about to be developed. Elliot noticed his arrival and signaled him over for a brief private conference before they addressed the group.

"Sir, there is an opportunity here. I think we can help these people."

"Okay, Elliot, what's up?"

"That's just it, sir—up! That's exactly what I mean, sir. From that eagle's nest vantage point over yonder," he said, pointing toward the peak they had just climbed. "There is real danger for our people in this thing, but an opportunity also."

"Explain yourself, son. You're not making sense."

"Yes, sir, I'll explain." Elliot turned to find a stretch of level sand and, using a convenient stick, quickly sketched out a rough overview of the canyon peaks as a passing bird might see them. "You see, sir, this valley is rimmed by two long humps on either side of the river, with an elevation of about a hundred and fifty feet. The whole canyon is shaped like a test tube, sort of, something like that anyway, long and guarded by these two long, parallel ridges. Our chief here wants to string his men across the open end and fight it out man-to-man, mano a mano, and let the best spearman win. That's the danger, sir. One break in the line and the enemy spearmen get wind of it and come doubling back at the break like a German blitzkrieg, and there would be hell to pay. If I was the chief on the other side and saw that setup, that's what I would do—take our men on cheek-by-jowl with a reserve shot of spear-chuckers ready to capitalize on any breakthrough and pounce on it or—better yet—into it, like a leak in a water balloon. Before you know it, Moscow is into Berlin and flooding through the Brandenburg Gate, or vice versa into the Kremlin, if you get my meaning, sir."

Montana had never considered himself a military tactician and had never seen the need before now to create the illusion that he was one. But necessity is the mother of invention, as the old saying goes, and the Big Doctor's ego was in fast need of a transfusion since he sensed that Elliot was about to make an important recommendation that would reduce him to a mere spectator in the eyes of the shaman. That would never do. He needed to find a quick way to get some credit for it, real or imagined.

"Now see here, Elliot, are you about to tell me that you have seen some advantage from that trek I sent you and the boys on up that mountain trail? That's what I would have expected, son. Now tell me which of several plans you think I should choose, and I'll decide which one is best."

Elliot had not been born yesterday and quickly saw what his boss was driving at. He thought about it for a quick minute and said, "Well, sir, there are really three plans we could try. You will see which one is best, as always." *Now let me see . . . How do I do this and let him pick the right plan? Make him think he picked it, the military genius that he's clearly not! The third one will seem best because it clearly is, if I spin it just right.*

"Sir, first we could take the Urchuwa plan with an improvement, say, make a double layer of spearmen backed up with our guns. Second, we could align the men alongside the river, using the river as a kind of defensive barrier as the men fall back, compressing their strength where it counts, down here at the end of the test tube, where those sloping little hills will provide a psychological barrier, with our guns stationed here," Elliot explained, pointing to the lower mounds overlooking the opening out of the valley as shown on his crude drawing in the sand. "And third, we could start with Urchuwa's plan, but weaker or thinner I mean, inviting the breakthrough that is bound to come. When it happens, our men feint a retreat, if we can convince them their honor is not about to be sacrificed. They beat it back here, to the bottom of the valley opening, but with intent," Elliot continued, again pointing to the bottom of the test-tube-shaped valley on his crude sand drawing. He paused for the question he knew was coming.

As if on cue, Montana jumped in. "Elliot, that doesn't make any sense, man. Why give up the strength of the line—their fighting pride—like that?"

"Because we use that to our advantage, sir. We position half the men on these sloping hillsides, both sides I mean, hidden in the dense undergrowth, and just when the enemy warriors think they've won and have our men on the run, they come running like hell down those slopes and attack each flank simultaneously. The shock of that will put a twist on them, sir. But you know best, sir. Whatever you think we should do," Elliot said.

Montana saw that the third plan was best, just as Elliot had planned he would.

"I like number three, Elliot, with one change. Urchuwa takes a cohort of his best men and plugs the test tube at the gap and saves his supposed spiritual power for the final thrust, the counter attack, just when your flank attack rolls the enemy back onto it. You take one flank and decide when the counterattack begins, and I will stay here, at the plug, with the shaman. We will each have our rifles and pistols as scare factors. Yes, I think plan three is best with those changes, so that is what we'll do, Elliot, my boy," Montana said.

Elliot whistled under his breath as he realized that Montana had not only adopted the plan he expected him to, but made a change to it that gave the plan the imprint of his own ideas and bragging rights if it succeeded. But it remained essentially Elliot's plan in case it failed. *Not bad, really not bad*, Elliot thought. *Maybe the old man sees more than I thought!* The Big Doctor had adroitly maneuvered his way into the appearance of true generalship, or was it something else?

All the while, Urchuwa was listening to this little theater of stratagems with his best language skills at play and understanding most of it. However, Montana had to take center stage anyway to tell him about it all again in his best rendition of the native tongue. One way or the other, everybody that mattered got the plan, and Urchuwa proceeded to give orders to the men to place them in position for tomorrow's expected battle. The most important thing for him was that he would be at the center of the point of the counterattack with the reservoir of strength from his session with the war god still ruminating within him, just in case the strangers didn't know what they claimed to know about fighting his kind of battle. With the extra reserve of spiritual strength the war god had given him, in his mind there was no way he could lose.

5

Algorithm for Armageddon

The most famous of all battlefields in the future will take place, according to Bible prophesies, on Mount Megiddo in Palestine. Although not really a mountain but a crossroads for access by historical invasions into the Holy Land, Mount Megiddo had nothing of exceeding importance to the people of that land by comparison to the scene of the coming battle for the security, sacristy, and safety of the Musquaeli people. Everything important to them was riding on this battle, and they knew it. They could not lose and retain their hutches, women, honor, or even their lives. To lose this battle meant losing everything, even their identities. Each warrior spent many anxious moments that night in concentration, fear, and expectation.

Long before the next morning's sun would illuminate the activity of the Musquaeli warriors making their way to their assigned positions in the valley, the contingent that would set the bait of the trap across the open end of the valley formed up in single file. They had their spears at the ready and filtered out of the camp into the darkness. Shortly afterward, in the same predawn darkness, two other files of warriors made their way around one side of the sacred lake and entered the canyon to divide and position themselves on the two slopes of the canyon's gently sloping, verdant walls.

Elliot, with Wanei and Estova in tow as interpreters, accompanied this group, intending to lead one line with Wanei up the left side of the valley and send Estova up the right side with the other to wait for him. First, he would supervise the placement of the men of the first column. He had marked it all out in his mind from the previous day's surveillance of the battle scene. He would then join the second group on the right side of the sloping valley wall and position them, and from there he would remain in command and give the flank attack signal.

Elliot had never led a jungle engagement with primitive warriors armed only with spears before, but he had plenty of experience positioning troops to set a classic ambush: using a feigned withdrawal down the center of a battle line to invite the enemy troops into the trap and then swooping down on them with a flank attack from both sides. He instructed Wanei, who followed him with the left-side contingent, to tell all that they were to hide until the signal was given for the attack at just the right moment by the firing of his pistol from his vantage point on the right wall of the canyon. The sound of the dreaded smoke-and-punch weapon combined with the shrieks of the counterattacking warriors as they swooped down on the attacking force would theoretically cause a panic in the enemy ranks and weaken their resolve to fight just as the simultaneous flank attack closed in on them. If all worked according to plan, the enemy warriors could be surrounded from three sides and eliminated with extreme prejudice.

Once Elliot was satisfied the warriors on the left valley wall were strategically placed, hidden in the dense undergrowth, and understood their instructions, he and Wanei moved around to the open end to make sure the "thin red line" across the open end of the valley was drawn as planned. The men were placed in position, and once again they were instructed on how they were to absorb the first assault before falling back in the appearance of panic to lure the enemy warriors into the trap. Those warriors who did not suffer a breakthrough were to follow behind to close the trapdoor behind the attacking enemy warriors. Elliot then instructed Wanei to remain at the center of the line to remind the men that there was honor in this maneuver and that by retreating they were doing a courageous thing and not giving in to an act of cowardice as it seemed. Elliot proceeded on around to meet up with Estova to position and instruct the right-side contingent in a similar fashion.

Meanwhile, Montana joined Urchuwa with his cohort at the plug and positioned himself on the high side of the left little mound, where he had a view of the valley and all that was about to happen in it. The trap was set.

6

Cataclysm

The valley extending out of the sacred canyon was especially quiet that morning, as everything that makes noise in the jungle is especially sensitive to activity within it, and in this stretch of jungle there was plenty of activity, however stealthily enacted.

The enemy warriors made their way into the valley with the fear and trepidation that normally accompany soldiers heading into battle. There were no illusions in the minds of these veteran warriors. Hand-to-hand, or more accurately spear-to-spear, combat brings out the best and the worst of human kind. Every person who lives has to consider that someday he will die and pass through whatever conception his culture has about death and existence thereafter.

The lead enemy warrior paused as he entered the flat and heavily vegetated terrain, listened, and sniffed the air for any telltale signs that the dreaded Musquaeli enemy was up ahead. He, along with his compatriots, had already noticed that the birds had become silent, and the occasional monkey or tree sloth normally visible or audible in the canopy that bordered the valley floor had ceased all activity as well. The seasoned advance team for the enemy tribe knew in the fibers of their being that the battle was just ahead. They just didn't know how far.

The lead warrior, their chief, lifted his hand, and the columnar file behind him immediately stopped. He thought about what lay ahead for a few minutes, and the warriors behind him knew their role was to simply wait until he was ready. He moved his head very slowly from left to right as he examined the scene in front of him. He paused briefly at one point, then continued his methodical but almost imperceptible swing to the right before pausing again, nodding slightly to himself, and then continuing to scan until he had reached the end of the jungle horizon in front of him. He turned to the file of men behind him and gave the "come to me" signal. They gathered around silently until all of the advance team could hear him speaking only in a whisper.

"Ke soo lah eh se, res eft gin son yu." (The enemy lie up ahead, from there to there.) The warrior pointed from left to right. "Go se thus! Dis den gon hu! Den go sun?" (Look there and there. See the glint of spear points, slight move only? There! See it?) "Bednu su gen se, ris den ghu!" (Send a runner for the main body of warrior men. We commence our attack! The line is thin; we must not wait for backup.)

Two of the warriors spun in their tracks and quietly sped off to summon the main body and carry the word that the chief would lead the attack against the line of Musquaeli warriors he had seen spread across the sweep of the entrance to what this tribe also considered sacred ground. It would be a few hours before the main body would arrive, but the chief was going to commence the attack without them, confident he had identified every enemy warrior and that they could win.

With an instinctive move and himself in the lead, he directed the advance team to form a kind of wedge that would strike just about in the center, where the Pangria parted the entrance to the valley. This meant that roughly half the defenders were separated by the mystical stream. And if the enemy attackers could overpower a man at the center and pour through the breach, it would be difficult for the faked retreat in Elliot's plan to be pulled off. The enemy chief of course had no idea about this. And then, if the main body made it up in time, Elliot's plan, which had seemed so brilliant the day before, would quickly turn into a disaster for the Musquaeli. But the invaders were not expecting a couple of things that were about to be introduced to their system of warfare.

The attackers spread out in their wedge formation, and the chief signaled a general advance across the front. He had ordered the wedge to land just between two of the Musquaeli warriors his keen eye had identified from the glint of the early morning sun on the sharpened blades of their spears.

The attack began, and the lead warrior engaged in a frontal assault against his opposite. The victor would be determined by who was stronger, more courageous, or the luckiest.

Unfortunately for the Musquaeli warrior, pitted against the Goliath of the enemy troops, he soon lost his footing and suffered a spear thrust that reached between two of his ribs and unlocked the door for him to the spirit world.

Wanei, who was stationed near that central point, saw the Musquaeli warrior go down and signaled the remaining men to fall back as planned in the fake retreat, not running but fighting in a kind of rearguard action while falling steadily back toward the riverbanks on both sides and into the canyon. The retreat allowed the defenders to bunch up at the front so that the enemy warriors on the attack would have to face two men instead of one as expected. Ordinarily they would have expected more resistance, and should have suspected that the retreat in front of just their advance team was a sign that something ominous was coming. But it never occurred to these men, as their blood was up and victory seemed imminent.

As the Musquaeli warriors retreated into the magic canyon with the enemy warriors in hot pursuit, Elliot surveyed the scene, trying to decide just when the double flank attack should begin. Something about the number of attackers involved didn't seem right, but the retreat had been pulled off just as planned and the moment seemed right to him. He lifted his pistol and aimed the weapon as best as he could at one of the attacking warriors and fired. Although it missed the running warrior, the shot had the desired effect, and the emotionally charged Musquaeli warriors on both sides let out their version of the rebel yell, charging down the slope at a full run.

The enemy chief, though flush with his first victory in the battle, was suddenly shocked by the dreaded smoke-and-punch weapon's discharge and the yelling of the counterattacking troops, so he signaled a retreat of his own. However, just at that moment the main enemy body arrived on the scene of the rapidly disorganizing battlefield.

7

Opportunity Knocks

Montana Blake stood at the foot of the little mountain-like mound on the left side of the valley at the canyon's end. He couldn't see anything from there, but he could hear the clash of spears and the screams of fighting warriors as they hurled themselves at each other at the opposite end of the canyon.

Although climbing up on the midget mountain permitted a better view of the battle, there was a risk of exposure to the combatants. Urchuwa and his cohort were positioned around the base of the opposite mound, but Montana had restrained his desire to know what was going on at the front since the plan was to stay hidden until the trap was fully sprung. This bit of strategy was not an impediment to Montana. If he needed to know something, no plan—or even common sense— would stand in the way of his immediate desire, so he climbed cautiously up the midget mountain and surveyed the battlefield, deep in thought.

Even if it is truly my plan today, I have to see what's ahead so I can get it done. Just like when my scientific materialist father thought he could force me to adopt that philosophy. I guess I did fall for his plan and become one. But I stuck it to him by including that chapter on faith in my dissertation thesis in grad school. He never forgave me for that. But forget about that; nothing stands in my way. My plan is at stake here, so I have to be where I can see everything that happens. I will get it done!

From his new vantage point he saw the attack on the Musquaeli line and their valiant withdrawal into the magic canyon as planned in Elliot's strategy. But what he could also see—even before the flank attack that was soon to follow—was the mass of the main body at the far end of the valley approaching in two long lines of warriors. Montana was no military strategist, but he could see that the flank attack was likely to come too soon and leave the whole defense vulnerable to a double envelopment when the main body arrived after the flank attack had been launched. What would happen then, as he could only imagine it, was a stalemate with an unpredictable outcome.

As he stood there taking in the scene of the battle, thoughts went through his head with amazing rapidity, even to him. *Well how about this? Some plan this was; it's likely to blow up in our faces. What if our guys lose? How will I manage to get it then? If I left now—that's it! No one's guarding it, not even Urchuwa. What if I brought the little thing up here, closer to the action? Wouldn't that help these fools? And if it didn't, who could fault me for running with it if the trap falls apart? That fool thinks he has the magic power; what an idiot! Well, I'll see if proximity means anything. It won't, but at least I will have tried, won't I?*

Without further hesitation, Montana made up his mind and slowly turned away from the battle. He slid down the little slope, picked himself up, and headed back toward the Indian settlement alone and with one purpose in mind. He had to get the little bugger and bring it to the front, at least until he could see who would win. Then, after the battle was over—whoever won—he somehow had to manage to steal away with the little war god as he, Elliot, and the two guides headed back to civilization.

While Montana quickly headed toward the Indian settlement to gain his nefarious if somewhat rationalized ends, Urchuwa had a different idea. The shaman could tell by the sounds of the battle and the occasional shouts of his warriors that carried their way on the currents of the shifting wind that desperate measures were needed.

Right about this time, Elliot signaled his premature flank attack and the general melee began. Just as Elliot's men wrapped up the invading advance guard in their enveloping flank attack, the main body of enemy warriors arrived at the front and joined the attack. Urchuwa, as if prescient or guided, chose this moment to act.

The valley of the Pangria reverberated with the sound of the conflict, which had lost all semblance of plan or purpose. It had become a general engagement with every man fighting as the enemy warrior in front of or behind him attacked. Within the chaos, there was no hope for the desired result. Urchuwa gathered his thoughts and summoned every ounce of courage and conviction within him, then climbed to the top of the right-hand little mountain.

He stood on the top with his arms outstretched and made himself visible to every warrior of the Musquaeli fighting for the life and honor of the tribe. His position all but invited some ambitious enemy warrior to disengage himself from the hand-to-hand combat, run with reckless abandon to get into range, and hurl his spear against the spiritual leader of the opposing tribe. But Urchuwa was confident that the war god's spirit was within him, and was absolutely fearless, without any regard for his life.

The Musquaeli warriors could see their leader standing fearless and exposed on the pinnacle and gained some inestimable reservoir of strength. And then, as if by magic, momentum, or spiritual power emanating from him, the tide of the battle seemed to shift. The enemy warriors noticed it as well, and even though they had gained the momentum of the unexpected timing of the arrival of the main body, they could clearly see that the tide had turned.

Meanwhile, Montana had returned to the village, which was deserted as the women and children were either hiding in case the battle turned out badly or were closer to the front to cheer on or pray for the safety of their warrior husbands and fathers. He had no difficulty finding his way to the trail that led to the shaman's sacred cave, where all the important spiritual intercession took place, for he had been given the privilege to visit it on prior occasions.

His problems were two: time and location. He had to quickly find the idol and return to the battlefield in time to see how he was to play the delicate game he had chosen. He had been to the shaman's secret hideaway once or twice before, but he didn't know where the little idol was hidden. It was not the kind of artifact that even primitive Indians would leave out in plain view; it was too precious for that. But it had to be somewhere, right?

Montana stood in the center of the small cave and asked himself, "If I were a shaman, where would I hide the thing?" Nothing obvious came to mind, and for Montana to imagine he was Urchuwa or that he could think like him was a bit preposterous. He nervously scratched his head and turned his body in a complete circle, trying to think as he searched. As he pivoted in his panoramic search, his left heel sank into a depression in the floor of the cave that he had never noticed before. On closer inspection and after digging a bit around where his left heel had sunk, he discovered an opening in the floor of the cave. The opening was covered by a large stone plate that, by its position below the dirt layer covering the floor of the cave, was almost undetectable. After clearing the dirt away, Montana could see that the stone plate had to be there for something, an opening to a secret chamber perhaps? With some effort, he thought he might be able to lift the plate to discover its purpose.

With the excitement of having discovered something that held the possibility of great reward, he exposed an opening in the floor of the cave. *This has to be it! Hot damn! This is my lucky day*, he thought, and proceeded to use a spear he'd found leaning in the corner of the cave as a pry bar, lifting a corner of the stone plate until he could grab it with both hands and expose a series of crude steps leading down into a lower chamber under the floor of the shaman's cave.

He reached in the utility pack he always carried and produced a working flashlight to light his way deep into the secret cave. *It has to be here somewhere*, he told himself as he swept the lower chamber with his light, looking for his prize.

And there it was, sitting in what appeared to be a shrine over in the corner, lifeless, as he expected it to be. The room was dark, but as Montana shone his flashlight on the little war god, its red eyes seemed to glow as if it was inexplicably alive in some sense. Montana stood watching it for a second, dismissed the question that had flitted across his mind as mere nervous speculation, then grabbed the idol. He placed it in his utility pack and climbed out of the lower compartment.

Before heading back to the battlefield to see what had happened in his absence, he gently replaced the door and restored the dirt that had previously covered it, careful to erase all of his tracks and any other evidence that a stranger had invaded the sacred space of the Musquaeli shaman.

8

THE TURNING POINT

By the time Montana returned to the battlefield, the fighting had turned from a matter of tactics or planning into a general melee. The Indians' method of fighting in these conflicts had reverted to its traditional, ancient form, one man against another, with individual and tribal survival at stake.

Elliot charged down into the flat area on his side of the Pangria with his pistol blazing. *This is a hell of a note,* thought Elliot. *That's the trouble with plans: you never fully anticipate what the other guy will do or just what pure, unpredictable circumstances will bring. But we are committed now, and ours is not to reason why but to do or die,* he concluded, and led his counterattacking men into the breach.

The initial shock effect of the smoke-and-punch weapon of the foreigner had run its course, and the adrenaline raging through the blood of every warrior in the contest had driven fear to the outer reaches of their minds, where it no longer had an effect except for the five or six enemy warriors that were killed before Elliot's ammunition was exhausted. From that point on, he was no more a threat in the battle than any other Indian warrior, probably less. He had grabbed a spear from a fallen enemy and did the best he could in the hand-to-hand fighting, but lacked training or experience in that kind of fighting.

The first enemy warrior Elliot encountered had not fully figured out what was going on, and Elliot had a slight advantage from his angle of attack. He managed to deflect the warrior's spear with his own as the enemy swung around to his left, too late, with a thrust that lacked force or conviction. Elliot made a blow with the shaft of his spear, a classic infantryman's rifle shove, and the counterthrust caused the warrior to lose his footing and fall. As quickly as his battle-honed reactions permitted, Elliot brought the spear point back across the warrior's body, slicing an awful gash across his back, then rammed the business end home just where the heart could be reached from behind and sent yet another warrior into the spirit world.

Unfortunately for Elliot, the chief leading the enemy attack saw this encounter and, with the skill of countless engagements, planted his feet and heaved his fighting spear across the small open space, and the spear point pierced Elliot's body just below his last rib on the right side. The force drove his body back, and he landed flat on his back. As Elliot pondered in those brief seconds the mystery of the end of life, the attacking warrior rushed over, saw Elliot's life was slipping away—no longer a threat—and retrieved his spear for the next engagement, leaving Elliot for dead.

Elliot lost consciousness the moment the large spear point struck him, but as his life slipped away, his consciousness returned. Everything seemed clear for once in his life. The pain was terrible, for sure, but its significance receded into the background. It was as if a sound-control mixer at a rock concert were dialing in or out various aspects of his experiences and had decided that pain was an unnecessary distraction right now.

Elliot lay there, alive to some extent but dead in others, while his consciousness was the actor on the stage receiving all of the lighting and the attention of the other players. His grasp of the present, the memory of his past life, and decisions about the future were all that remained of his existence.

It was as though the essence of who he was rose mysteriously from his dying body and hovered over the scene of his death. He felt—if that's what it could be called—a strange state of peace he had never experienced in his entire life. None of the other combatants could see him, or this part of his existence anyway, but whatever sight means to the dying soul, he could see and understand all that was happening over the battle scene.

I'm a goner, that's for sure. Look at that spear wound; no way could I have survived that. So I'm dead then. Is that it? If so, how can I see? This is all new territory, Elliot. Whatever Elliot was, or what was left of him at this point, he could no longer see the remains of his earthly body or the battle. He faced a tunnel of light. A figure approached him, or he approached it, and his consciousness or whatever he was stopped.

The figure spoke: "You enter the spirit world, my son. What do you desire here?"

"I have no right to desire anything because of what I have done."

"Do you not know that I am aware of all of your actions, including the murders you committed long ago?"

Elliot sank into immediate despair, for he had never been able to shake the personal condemnation that his acts deserved, and which should have earned him the condemnation of others if there was any justice in the world, which he really doubted.

"I deserve nothing but condemnation for that," he said, not having to hear what "that" was to understand of what the spirit being spoke.

"I have another purpose for you, my son, that is not apparent yet. But you must wait until that time before we see whether my love is greater than choice or its consequences."

"Where do I, or whatever I am at this point, go for now?"

"Do not become concerned with where and when and other earthly concepts that no longer apply in the spirit world. It will all be made clear to you, my son."

"But who are you, Lord?" was about all Elliot's consciousness could muster.

"Continue at peace for now, my son, and all will become clear to you." Both apparitions vanished from each other, and all was dark.

Urchuwa remained on the right-side midget mountain, fully exposed but having none of the effect on the battle he expected. Never before had the power of the war god abandoned him. He was baffled as to why his preparation for the battle in the spiritual exercises he had experienced the day before was no longer having its desired effect.

Montana stood at the base of the small mountain on the left side of the battlefield, but could see nothing. In desperation and throwing caution to the winds, he climbed up the little hillock to get a better sense of how the battle was proceeding. When he reached the summit, he could see that all of Elliot's plans and the shaman's supposed spiritual strength had accomplished nothing. The warriors fought across the valley on both sides of the river, but he could get no sense of who was winning. In any event, the Musquaeli warriors had not dominated and conquered, so, in Montana's opinion, they were losing. How it would eventually end up was anybody's guess at this stage of the battle.

Montana stood there, in his exposed position, and briefly pondered exactly what he should do. Not feeling courageous, and expecting an enemy spear or arrow to find its way into his chest at any minute, he turned away from the battle and climbed—or, more accurately, slid down—to the plain as rapidly as he could. When he recovered his balance at the bottom, he started to head away from the sounds of the conflict. He wanted to put some distance between himself and the danger so he could decide what to do, but a strange sensation he didn't understand brought him up short.

He wasn't sure at first what it was, but it wasn't more than a few seconds before he realized that his utility pack was vibrating. It was hardly noticeable at first but seemed to grow in intensity. When he moved in the direction of the shaman, the vibration increased. This puzzled him at first because he had never believed there was anything to this war god business except native superstition or the product of excited imaginations.

Even the idea that there might be supernatural reality beyond his beloved philosophy of scientific materialism was so foreign to him that he refused to even consider it. But now he wasn't so sure. He had seen the glowing little red eyes of the idol when he had found it in the hidden room, but had dismissed it as his own frightened imagination or just a reflection of his flashlight beam on the glass beads that were planted in it for the semblance of eyes.

There was nothing in his utility pack that could possibly vibrate, and certainly nothing that could vary in intensity depending on the direction of his movement. *Could there be something to this spirit business? Could a little stone idol that was clearly carved from ordinary obsidian actually have in it some mysterious force that could vibrate or, worse yet, have some control over the behavior of these primitive people? Goes against everything I ever believed to be true. The world just isn't made that way, is it? Someone outside in charge of things? Someone to surrender to besides me? Never! The Indians certainly believed it, especially Urchuwa. That guy certainly has a way about him, I'll be the first to admit! But spirits that vibrate stone? That's absurd, isn't it? That chapter I put in my doctoral thesis about faith just to spite my father. Ha! I never believed that stuff, but what is this vibration business? How could it be real? Yet I feel it, darn it!*

Unfortunately for Montana, there was no one around to answer his monumental question. *Let's see. When I moved toward the shaman, the vibration increased; maybe I need to get it into his hands and the battle might yet be won. Could it make any difference now? Elliot's dead by now or soon will be, he's no spear-fighting warrior, and he's out of ammunition by now for sure. I haven't heard a shot for a half hour. If I hang around here in a losing cause, I might be next and my mission would be a failure. Can't have that now, can I?*

The distance to Urchuwa's position would take about ten minutes to cover if he walked slowly, giving himself time to think. Montana started that way, thinking that he had a loyalty of sorts to the people of the Musquaeli tribe, who had befriended him over the years and helped make his reputation as an anthropologist. As he walked, the vibration in his utility pack increased to the point that its vitality as an object capable of communication, in a mechanical sense anyway, whatever was causing it, could no longer be doubted. He didn't understand it, but reality was reality, and he was a realist even if vain and self-directed.

Urchuwa was oblivious to what had been going on with Montana and had no idea that the war god was anywhere but in its shrine in the secret compartment underneath his crude temple. But he could sense that something was changing. He could feel it. His arms, which had been held outstretched for some time now as a symbol to his warriors to fight on valiantly for the honor of the tribe, were no longer a struggle to hold up. More importantly, the strength he sensed was increasing, and rapidly at that.

As a shaman used to the effects of the laws of the spirit, he was wise enough to know that understanding how things worked was less important than acting on them with belief. So trusting to what he believed to be true, that the war god was empowering him in some way, he began to shout encouragement to his fighting men in the field. And the men, on hearing this and sensing that the spirits were with them, began to fight harder. The momentum shifted in their favor, and the enemy warriors found themselves falling back.

If you could have seen this scene from above with the knowledge of all the participants engaged in the battle, you would have correlated the change in momentum in favor of the Musquaeli with the movement of the war god in Montana's utility pack in the direction of the shaman's position. But no one on the field of battle could have had this perspective, especially Montana. He was struggling with the challenge to his Western idea of scientific materialism, that every physical phenomenon had a cause-and-effect relationship explainable by the laws of nature and the undeniable principles of physics undergirded by the immutable laws of mathematics. Men of his philosophical stripe may not have had an explanation yet for every observable physical phenomenon, but they had been convinced since Sir Isaac Newton that a physical cause would eventually be found and that one need only wait until somebody discovered it. Even the newer developments in quantum mechanics had shaken the confidence of his cohorts in the scientific community. To these men, as well as to Montana, any explanation that tried to explain phenomena by some other rules or laws, such as "the laws of the spirit" or religion, was simply out of court from the start.

As it seemed to Montana, there was a correlation to when he had moved the war god in the direction of the shaman's position. *This could not be possible, could it?* he thought. From the heart of his core beliefs, though there may not have been a plausible explanation yet for every observable physical phenomenon, he was certain a physical cause would eventually be found. But this vibrating stone and the effect his movements toward the battle seemed to have in changing the outcome were beyond any parameter he could imagine.

Montana would therefore have been the last to appreciate that his experimental movement toward the shaman's side of the field had had an effect on the battle. His struggle as he sensed the progress of the battle was different. He had not heard from Elliot by the report of his gun, and his last observation of the battle had frightened him. Whatever this vibrating piece of stone in his pack meant, he was not about to put himself at risk.

So he stopped, thought about his options long and hard, and decided. He turned on his heels and headed back toward his side of the canyon, positioning himself so that he could escape if the battle went badly. It was at this point another unexpected event occurred. The vibration of the object in his pack suddenly stopped. Montana noticed, but had not a clue as to why or what it meant—if anything. He hurried back to his position at the foot of the left-side mount and hunkered down to wait it out and see what would develop.

Unfortunately for the Musquaeli side, this was a terrible choice. Urchuwa noticed his renewed strength begin to quickly erode, and he found it increasingly difficult to hold his arms in the position his warriors had interpreted as inspiration. Almost as quickly as his warriors in the field noticed the change, the ripple effect across the battlefield soon made itself apparent. The strength of the Musquaeli momentum began to fade, and the enemy warriors noticed it and reinvigorated their own attack.

A central core of warriors comprised of the enemy's initial advance guard was surrounded by the Musquaeli. But the Musquaeli found themselves surrounded in turn by the fortuitous arrival of the main body of enemy warriors that either by plan or accident had fanned out on both sides of the river valley to envelop the two inner circles of opposing warriors.

As the Musquaeli men's confidence faded, it was just too much to expect their fighting spirit to survive. Momentum had finally shifted once and for all against them, and they had a loss of heart as the enemy warriors closed in for the kill. The result was disastrous.

Montana decided to take one more look from his vantage point on the left hillock before deciding what he should do, and neither the climb nor the view did anything to bolster his courage. What he saw was sickening: the outer and inner rings of enemy warriors were closing in on the last great hope of the Musquaeli. They were fighting for their homes and families, the defense of their sacred canyon, and finally for their very lives. If they lost this fight, there might very well no longer be a Musquaeli tribe. The women and children would certainly succumb or be made slaves instead.

The fighting was vicious and hand-to-hand, as spears were no longer useful in the tangle of combatants. Montana took one final look at the battle and made up his mind. He was out of there! Having decided, the rest was easy, at least for the present. He slid down the little slope, gathered himself, and headed west, toward the village, where his remaining supplies were.

He had hardly taken two steps when a native warrior appeared, running in the same direction he was. It was Wanei, of all people, who had made the same decision as Montana and extracted himself from the battle after using his spear to dispatch the last enemy he had faced, opening a slight avenue of escape. He could see that his former tribe was going to lose, and he did not want to have his own head hanging from the hutches of some enemy warrior's village as a war trophy. He had been away from the tribe long enough to make this decision without a great deal of heartache. It was a matter of survival.

"Wanei, old friend, are you leaving too?" Montana asked breathlessly.

"Yes, Big Doctor, battle lost. Must run now, or too late," Wanei said, also struggling for breath.

"What goes with Elliot, Wanei? Is he still fighting? I haven't heard any gunfire lately."

"No, Big Doctor. Spear thrust by enemy—dead!" Wanei explained, heaving from exhaustion.

It didn't take Montana but a second to assess the situation and decide what to do. "Come on, Wanei, we go!" And he whirled around and started running toward the village. Wanei followed right behind him.

The battle lines truly had collapsed, to the detriment of the last surviving Musquaeli warriors, who had not the good sense to cut and run as Wanei had done. The enemy chief stood at the shore of the Pangria, surveyed his victorious fellow tribesmen he had successfully led into battle, raised his blood-drenched spear into the air, and emitted one of those characteristic grimace-faced, open-mouthed shrieks that men everywhere find a tension relief from the adrenalin rush of battle, sports, or any other contest in which all their emotion has been expended in the task. The men joined in the celebration, creating a virtual din of undifferentiated noise that reverberated down to the end of the sacred canyon and propelled itself like a giant megaphone. The sound reached across the sacred lake and into the Musquaeli kingdom like a town crier announcing the coming doom as the Visigoth hordes stormed the gates of Rome.

The enemy chieftain allowed the celebration to continue for a time; the men deserved that. But it wouldn't have mattered if he'd desired otherwise, for men will be men in such situations. After an appropriate period had passed, he made the "quiet down" sign with his arms, still holding the bloody spear, and the men obeyed.

He shouted, "Us tah leh shu gus taveah. Ough esta see lah meah, see lah meah!" (Ten of you go now to the enemy village so a vision plan may be put before us. Send back message of sight beholding.) And ten of his warriors turned downstream and headed at a fast pace toward the Musquaeli village. Their purpose was not to eliminate the last traces of the dreaded enemy, but to reconnoiter and report back so that a coordinated plan for that very purpose could be put together.

Montana and Wanei reached the Musquaeli advance camp in time to gather what supplies they could carry before launching their escape. Wanei stood facing back toward the battlefield in deep concentration as

Montana scoured the campsite for supplies. He stopped when he noticed Wanei in this strange posture.

"Wanei, what gives, man?" he asked, genuinely curious. At this point any aberrant behavior was noteworthy.

"We go, must! Enemy come soon. Great danger Musquaeli people," Wanei said with deep concern in the tone of his voice. Even Montana, preoccupied as he was with himself, could sense this.

"Musquaeli people in danger? How about us? They'll come here first! We go, Wanei."

Wanei nodded and headed out of the advance camp at a steady pace that could be sustained over time and put the greatest distance between them and the enemy. Montana tried his best to keep up. It would turn out to be a race for survival even though the enemy was not aware of their existence yet.

9

The Last Thing Is You Have to Leave

The escape route was shortened, as Montana made it clear to Wanei that he wanted to avoid the main village. He had rationalized this way to accomplish his main objective, which was far beyond what he actually expected to accomplish. The fact that the Musquaeli tribe was about to pass into the pages of history did not enter his mind. Also that his "old friend" Urchuwa, who had so graciously welcomed him on several expeditions, would soon be dead was not in his mind at all. He had not actually seen the shaman die in combat, but his death was inevitable, regardless.

He could only think of two things: one, he needed to survive by getting to that escape chute alongside the waterfall; and two, he must at all cost hang on to his prize. The "prize," as it were, had gone strangely silent ever since that fateful—if not fatal—moment when he had first realized that the little beast actually had some mystical powers and turned away from its apparent need to be reunited with its priest, Urchuwa. From that moment, all had gone downhill in an uncontrollable sequence of events that was to end in defeat. Montana had not weighed the moral, ethical, or historical significance on the scales of justice yet, but the decision had tipped in favor of Montana, in his mind, and not the Musquaeli.

Wanei approached the plateau where the escape tunnel to the lower reaches of the Rio Ucayali awaited like a pathway to Heaven, but going down in this case, rather than the traditional *up* in the religious sense, and as an access to someplace definitely better than this for the desperate duo.

Wanei stopped, and listened with his experienced ear for jungle noises, and raised the caution signal to his charge.

"Enemy us on, Big Doctor. Go now!" he quietly asserted, while forcefully pointing with his spear to the opening of the escape route.

"How can you be . . . Okay, Wanei, you know best, man!" Montana said, almost in passing, as he ran with reckless abandon for the opening and clamored down the hand-over-hand route as rapidly as he could. Wanei, true to his calling as an honorable warrior of the Musquaeli people, stood his ground and waited for the inevitable conflict that he knew would be his last.

He was born a Musquaeli; lived in slavery until he had the joy of returning to his kinsmen; fought with them in the last futile, desperate battle against extinction; and, in the final chapter of the book of his life, was prepared to give it all so that even an unworthy subject like Montana could escape. He had signed on for this job, and as a man of honor he would stick it out to the end, no matter what that end might bring. He didn't have long to wait.

10

THE HOME FRONT

It was spring again in the small town of Hedley, Florida, and what a lovely time of year that is. Many former residents of the Florida Panhandle follow the maxim "Never after April in Florida" for return visits. There is a practical reason for that, for by May each year, the humidity that smothers most of the southeastern part of the country for the rest of the summer descends like a giant blanket across North Florida until the first frost arrives, hopefully by November, and makes everyone miserable.

The home of Dr. Montana Blake was situated on the outskirts of Hedley, at the end of a long lane flanked by live oak trees, which by nature grow into beautifully sculptured shapes rebelling against any tendency to uniformity, their upper limbs draped with Spanish moss waving in the gentle afternoon breezes like an imaginary convention of gray-bearded dwarfs hanging by their heels.

On approach to the Blake place, surrounded by a sizeable lake, visitors would not find its design or structure unusual for that part of North Florida. The house was one story, its frame covered in white asbestos shingles, better to reflect the summer heat. In front of the property there were adequate spaces for parking for the occasional parties the Blakes had, usually in the summer months when the fishing was good. There was a simple carport for two vehicles on the right side and a small cottage to the right of that, where the Blake's cook and housekeeper could stay when the family had extended stays. The three bedrooms were adequate, with Amanda and Montana's twin sons sharing one, one for the occasional overnight guest, and the master bedroom for Montana and Amanda. Of course, there was a kitchen, where Mary, the cook, stayed occupied with her household duties. From the front entrance across the solid tile flooring—a cool-to-the-touch necessity in the hot and humid Northwest Florida climate—a spacious porch was available to sit on and watch activities out on the lake. Also visible were a dock with a covered cabin for fishing and, to the left, under the shade of the oak trees, a boat dock from which anyone could access the fishing boat for recreational boating or fishing.

The rear of the property before the edge of the lake had a respectably large backyard. All things such as heat and humidity considered, this was a typical North Florida lake, dark and mysterious. It was sprinkled with water-logged snags suitable for turtles and birds to perch on, purple-blossomed water hyacinths to gaze on, and an occasional alligator or cottonmouth to be cautious of. It was just the kind of attractive backyard nuisance that would drive an insurance agent bonkers but was a haven for kids to play and revel in. Montana's two boys were no different, because they loved this place.

If there were ever fraternal twin brothers completely unalike, Horatio and Averill were it. Although the boys' names came from their father, his first and second names respectively, their temperaments were so different they could have been grafted into the family from outside sources, or at least Averill could have.

From childhood until he picked up the Montana moniker years later, he was called Harry. This was not actually his given name since he had been named for his grandfather Horatio Averill Bissett, the last living grand old sage of his mother's husband's otherwise pathetic family. Horatio's ancestor George had made his money in one of the successful oil wells in rural northern Pennsylvania in the early days of the black gold rush that was destined to change America—and probably the world—forever. His wealth and strong personality had first made his mother's husband, Averill, attractive to her as a student at Gettysburg College those many years ago, when both were young, idealistic graduate assistants. She had yielded her natural tendency to dominate any situation when the time came for naming baby Bissett and agreed reluctantly to name the boy Horatio Averill Bissett after his grandfather. Yet she couldn't imagine calling the kid Horatio in front of her friends, so he became Harry.

Montana and Amanda's son Horatio was blessed with that rare combination of confidence and credibility you see every once in a great while but rarely in a youth. His special gift was that as soon as he made an appearance in a room of people, especially adults, he would find a way to become the center of attention.

He was, in a way, a carbon copy of his father: full of confidence and self-importance. But he had the ability his father lacked to make any adult who happened to come near him think they were the most important person in the room and love him for it.

Averill, on the other hand, although having shared the same womb and many of the same genes with his twin brother, was shy and unsure of himself. By a process no one in the family could explain or remember, the boys had picked up nicknames that echoed, by sound at least, their given names. Horatio, named appropriately for his father's first name based on their common temperaments, had become Ratio; and by an even stranger turn of events, Averill had picked up the name Average, which, given his temperament, was appropriate in a sense but at the same time unfortunate for his self-esteem and confidence.

Amanda Blake came out on the back porch and yelled to her sons playing down by the edge of the lake: "Boys! Come in here this minute. Your poppa's coming home today with some really big news, and I have to get this house ready for the coming-home party. That means perfect, do you hear me?"

"Yes, Momma," Ratio yelled back before Average had a chance to respond. They stopped immediately, in the middle of the war games they were engaged in behind some washed-up logs in the cleared area by the shore behind their house. This was the only area their mother would allow them to play in because of her inordinate fear of the snakes and alligators that inhabited the uncleared portions of the lakeshore.

"Come on, Average, Momma's calling. Poppa's coming, did you hear that, Average?" Ratio said, and grabbed his brother by the arm so that his mother would see him taking charge in something that mattered to her.

Average had grown up with this dominance by his brother in every situation that would benefit him, and although he rarely said anything, he dearly hated it—and his brother too, for that matter.

Amanda Blake was not a trophy wife in the usual sense, for she did have other abilities to accompany her stunning good looks. But her greatest attribute to Montana was her devotion to him and the gift of social organization. This lady really knew how to throw a party. For her, the twin goals of maintaining her social status in the small academic community of Hedley and promoting her famous husband's reputation were woven together like the strands of a rope supporting each other and stronger because of it.

11

Interlude in Miami

The plane for Montana's return trip from Quito, Ecuador, had flown nonstop to Mexico City, where he had changed flights to Miami. On arrival in Miami and before boarding after a two-hour layover for the last leg of his flight to Pensacola, the closest airport to Hedley, Montana was able to find a telephone and make several important calls. He placed one call to Amanda announcing his arrival time so that she could make the drive from Hedley to Pensacola and pick him up. He also suggested that a suitable welcome from his colleagues at the college could be held at their place on the lake if she thought it best. There was no chance she would think or do otherwise, for Amanda reveled in the publicity, attention, and fame her husband generated.

He also let her know that he had an important announcement to make about a discovery on his recent trip, and she might expect some additional professional and journalistic guests to show up at the event once word got out of his success. He placed another call to the Florida Museum of Science and Natural History in Pensacola to alert them that his expedition had been a success in the recovery of an artifact of significance, of which the anthropology world would be extremely jealous. He would not give any details over the phone, but offered to reveal his discovery at a welcome-home reception his wife was planning.

"And if any of my colleagues were to learn about this announcement, they might just want to be there," Montana said to the student teaching assistant who was manning the phones at the museum that weekend. He gave his estimated time of arrival in Pensacola, just in case word of his success should leak out in time for a press greeting on his arrival, at which he planned, if it were to occur, to reveal nothing but to add to the mystery accelerating to his dramatic announcement at his coming-home party. He also gave the date for the upcoming party and suggested that the student pass the word to the director by a call to his home, the number for which Montana was sure the student either had or could find around there somewhere.

That bit of business behind him, Montana decided he had just enough time for some relaxation and contemplation, so he headed for one of the bars located within easy reach of almost any tired passenger arriving from various ports of call and looking for a little adult-beverage refreshment. The first one he found, not far from where he had stopped in the concourse to make his calls, was inviting by appearance but intriguing in its unusual name.

At first sound, the Socratic Sojourner seemed like an odd name for a bar in an international airport, but the more Montana reflected on it, the more sense it made. Socrates, the famous Greek philosopher, made his place in history by asking questions to discover truth and a *sojourner* was one who stayed in a place temporarily.

The fact that Socrates's dialectical disputation habits got him executed and that most people don't really care enough for the truth rather than their own feelings, however derived, especially to risk that exposure, had not diminished the allure of the name of his method. The unusual name of the place was enough of a draw for this tired, discriminating traveler if the comfortable leather chairs and rich mahogany tables set comfortably apart for private conversations in a warm, dimly lit setting had not added to the ambience.

To Montana, this place was like a flashing neon sign to a lost traveler in the desert, signaling that civilization was ahead. For what he needed right now was a quiet place to think. After weeks in the jungles of Ecuador and Peru, civilization, with its comforts, was the place for it. He had to sort out his thoughts about the expedition that had just concluded and revel in the monumental accomplishment, notwithstanding the unpleasant things he had done to pull it off. So he welcomed the idea the name of the place generated.

Montana chose a table separated from the other customers in the lounge and signaled to the attractive, young cocktail waitress to come over and take his order. He decided he could think better with a stiff single-malt scotch straight up, however illogical that was, but he did it anyway.

Sally Foster was a college student at the University of Miami supplementing her student loans in the pursuit of her degree in engineering by pulling shifts at the Socratic Sojourner. But even though the pay was lousy, the tips were good. She could parade her obvious physical attributes in the comely attire the owner demanded of his staff, to encourage tips. And while giving the appearance of being fascinated by the patrons, she really didn't care much at all.

She approached Montana's table with her patent "here I am" smile and was surprised and pleased that he did not ask about the name of the place, a question that had been asked and she had answered so many times she was sick of it. It was sort of like a Las Vegas B-grade singer who told anyone that asked what it was like to play the same songs requested by patrons night after night: "If I had to play and sing 'Proud Mary' one more time, I think I would throw up."

Montana was in no mood for chitchat and was not in the least interested in hitting on this beautiful, young cocktail waitress. He had things on his mind that were far more exciting and stimulating than any imaginary sexual encounter that was never going to happen anyway, so he placed his order with the admonition that he had to board his flight to Pensacola soon. She brought his scotch promptly, asked if he wanted to run a tab, nodded when he said no, and went off to serve more financially rewarding customers.

He took a long sip of the scotch, kicked back in his leather lounge chair, and propped his feet on the seat next to him with memories of the expedition running through his mind. He relived each moment, especially the concluding ones. He could not will himself to forget the horrible moment when he had struggled with his dilemma of whether to aid the surrounded Musquaeli warriors and Elliot by delivering the war god to Urchuwa or to withdraw from the field to save himself and his treasure.

Even days later, resting comfortably in these pleasant surroundings, the debate raged on in his conflicted mind. *That was a strange vibration, unexplainable, especially to me, a scientist. Odd thing: every time I moved in the shaman's direction the vibration increased and he, and by the sound of it his war-*

riors also, got stronger. Makes no sense! But, hell man, it was fact: Urchuwa's arms were noticeably stronger and the Musquaeli war cries got louder. No doubt of that. I walked away with this little piece of stone for me, and people died! That is fact! Sad but true.

He took another deep drink of the scotch and cleared his mind for a few minutes, trying to watch the television above the bar, but it held no interest for him. The battle scene continued to play through his mind as if it were plastered all over CNN for the whole world to see. *But there is no certainty it would have made any difference, and I had my reputation to think of, didn't I? I must have been mistaken about that vibration. Stones don't vibrate without an external cause, and that is certain. Wanei was in the heat of the battle, and it was clear Elliot was dead, may eternal peace rest his soul, although that's not really possible is it? Besides, I never would have sacrificed my Musquaeli tribal friends for personal safety or personal fame. I would never have done that, would I?* There was no answer to his conscience.

He finished the last of the drink, waved across the bar to Sally for another, and when she came, settled the bill with a generous tip and dismissed her. She was surprised by that. Obviously, something had changed in this man's attitude, and it had nothing to do with her sex appeal, which was the reason most men tipped this much. *But no matter*, she thought. *Tips are tips, and that's why I do this.*

She was right about Professor Blake: something had changed. He had been engaged in a moral war of sorts between two sides of his conscience, memory and pride, and one side had won. The philosopher Friedrich Nietzsche summed it up well when he said, "'I have done that,' says my memory. 'I cannot have done that,' says my pride . . . Eventually, memory yields." That was as far as the philosopher took it, but experience observed shows that pride forces memory to be obedient until it crosses that line of memory and becomes a personal truth.

For Montana Blake, he had crossed over for good. No one, not even he speaking to his inner self, would ever say or hear it any differently. His thoughts were interrupted by a public address announcement: "Now hear this: last call for boarding Continental flight four two five seven for Pensacola at gate eleven A." He sat up, finished the last of the second scotch, carefully gathered his utility pack under his arm to prevent any possible harm to its precious cargo, and hurried toward his boarding gate.

12

TOUCHDOWN

The Continental Boeing 737 entered its approach in the traffic pattern, which circled the Pensacola area, giving passengers a panoramic view of Pensacola Bay, a deep blue mirror reflecting a dazzling sky surrounded by a seemingly endless flatness that comprises the Florida Panhandle coastal region. Montana gazed out the window of his first-class seat, courtesy of the Florida Museum of Science and Natural History, as any man deep in thought might, seeing nothing. This early morning his thoughts were on what was about to happen. He fully expected that the seed he had planted with the receptionist at the museum would by now have grown into a crop of hungry reporters from Florida's tiny intellectual press corps. He was not to be disappointed.

When the jet taxied up within walking distance of the Jetway and its wheels were chocked by the ground crew, the flight attendant in the first-class compartment opened the front side door to allow the rolling disembarkation ramp to be secured into place. Inside the plane, the passengers had waited impatiently while the sleek little jet found its way through the ground traffic. It is the same for travelers the world over: when they land at the airport of their destination they just assume they are there, in Pensacola or wherever they are, and the time spent waiting until the airplane stops, the gate is opened, and permission is granted to finally leave is a challenge to the human sense of time. If the mind is in one place, such as already in the terminal being greeted by their loved ones or in the rental car with their family on the way to SeaWorld or Disney World, nothing will convince them that their body is not there or shouldn't be there already. It is the time-compressed adult version of that eternal question by children "Are we there yet?"

Montana was a bit different today from most other passengers in this regard, for he did have an excellent sense of timing, or at least the desire to control it. He stayed in his seat while all the first-class passengers and most of the coach people had gathered their carry-on bags, wraps, and laptops and headed up the aisle as fast as the reverse accordion effect would allow them. As he looked out his window, his discriminating eye noticed the telltale sign of a group of too-eager young men having no discernable reason to be standing at the foot of the exit ramp trying to look disinterested when the opposite condition was patently obvious.

He smiled at no one in particular, thinking, *It worked. You can't keep a good rumor down*, and having decided that now was the time, got out of his seat. He stretched his arms and back to smooth out the kinks from the long flights from Miami and to Miami out of South America, and carefully extracted the utility pack from the overhead compartment. He opened it just enough to make sure his treasure was still there, cinched it down tight so there was no chance it would fall out, and placed it over his shoulder before methodically heading to the exit door. He reached the top of the ramp, looked out across the tarmac, and paused for a few seconds before walking slowly down the ramp.

The group of young reporters spied his exit and quickly gathered around the foot of the ramp with previously unnoticed cameras and microphones pulled out of nowhere, eagerly shouting out their questions to see who could score the first hit on the target that was Dr. Blake.

"Dr. Blake, Dr. Blake, is it true you have made the anthropology discovery of a lifetime?" Billy Dixon, eager young reporter for the *Pensacola News Journal*, shouted.

"Tell us about the expedition, Doctor. The scientific world wants to know," Josh Becker said, the most senior scientific journalist on the scene on assignment from the Florida Museum of Science and Natural History.

"Where is the rest of your team, Doctor?" asked a prescient third.

"Gentlemen, gentlemen, patience please!" Dr. Blake said with a broad smile. "This is not the time, my friends, to give my discovery its due. Come over to Hedley this coming Friday for my reception party. I'm sure you know where I live, and I promise your questions will be fully answered." Montana hurried on down the ramp, shaking the reporters' hands as he parted the crowd on the tarmac like a campaigning politician working a rope line. He left the tarmac for the terminal to reclaim his bags and meet Amanda at the front entrance for a brief embrace and departure for Hedley and home.

PART II

THE CONSEQUENCES

13

GREETINGS, WORLD TRAVELER

The boys stood on either side of the front steps as the car with their parents approached. All had been readied at home, and the welcome time was about to begin. Ratio had been mulling over in his mind, *There might be an opportunity here*, and timed his movement away from the steps so that he would be the first to greet their father. Average, in his normal state of reticence, waited by the stairs.

The car stopped, and before Montana could do it, Ratio rushed over to the door of the sedan and opened it, yelling to his father, "Father, Father, you're finally home! I can't wait to hear about your adventures in the jungle—they are always so fantastic!" From the front seat of the touring car, with his utility pack safely under his arm, Montana smiled at his young son appreciatively and then exited the car. He received the affectionate rush and embrace of Ratio as Average lingered in the back-wash of Ratio's aggressive wake.

As a consequence, Ratio got the only public display of affection that was available and Average, as usual, had to be content with the leftovers. There weren't many today, as Montana was totally absorbed in his own plans. He buried his resentment over that and moved on.

Montana disentangled himself from Ratio's aggressive embrace and nodded a perfunctory greeting to his other son. "Now, now, boys, great to see you, but enough of that. Help your mother with my bags," he said, ending the greeting as though he had fulfilled another item of his duty checklist.

"Tell us about the trip, Father," Ratio said, looking up into his father's eyes with that idolizing gaze only young boys can have.

"Later, Ratio, there will be time for that. Help your mother like I said. I have a lot of preparations to make; an important event coming up, yes indeed," Montana said, mostly to himself, as if greeting his two sons after a long trip to South America were nothing.

The house quickly resumed its normal routine, with Montana busy in his study compiling his recollections of the trip for a report to the museum and an occasional retrieval of the little stone relic from its secure location in his utility pack reviving his vivid memories of those cataclysmic events and reliving the tragic and—in his mind—heroic accomplishments on the Sangria. The boys returned to their play about the grounds, and Amanda steadily began her preparations for the great event.

The boys headed out to the lake, their favorite hangout for war games, and lost themselves in play by the safe shore, naturally. Ratio made an occasional glance toward the window of his father's study and decided now was the time for a diversion.

"Say, Average, you know that old bull gator that hangs out in the lagoon. Why don't we see if we can sneak up on him, maybe catch him in a snooze, and really spook him?"

"Okay, Ratio, that would be fun! But you know how Momma feels about it, right?" Average said with enthusiasm for any adventure out of the ordinary.

"You're afraid, that's what you are, Average. Forget Momma like we usually do or plan around her, right?"

"Well, all right, if you say so, Ratio."

"I tell you what, why don't you go around the lake to the north side and scout out for him, and I'll catch the other side. We then join up at the old snag, okay?" Ratio said.

Average nodded his agreement and dutifully headed around the north side of the lake. As soon as he got out of sight, Ratio spun on his heels and headed straight for the house. This was his chance to find out what really happened to his dad on the trip. *He might tell me more if we are alone*, Ratio thought as he beat a steady path inside the house and into the study, where Montana was busy working on his report.

"Hey, Father, Average is busy playing out by the lake, and I couldn't wait to hear one of your stories from the trip. Just one, please?"

"I'm busy now, boy. Come back later. There will be plenty of time for that. I'm working on my speech for the party, and that is the most important thing right now, you know."

"I know, Father, but if you let me be the guinea pig, you know, just sit here and listen as you practice, your speech is bound to come out better. You've always said practice makes better, right?" Ratio said, buttering his father up like a piece of breakfast toast.

"You have a point there, son. I would sound better with practice. Let me see . . . The Musquaeli nation was locked in the final struggle for survival. Their warriors had been engaged in hand-to-hand combat for hours and were losing. I had already lost my faithful companion, Elliot, to a native spear; what a terrible way to die! I somehow managed to escape with my life." Ratio listened with rapt attention to this marvelous tale that boys his age longed to hear. A live, true tale of war, heroism, and death in a struggle for survival—this was better than all the comic book tales he had ever read put together. He noticed his father looking toward his utility pack over on the floor as he spoke and stopped his reverie for a moment. "What's in there, Father? You've been looking at it an awful lot," he asked from pure curiosity.

"Oh, that?" Montana tried to just brush it off. "It's the little idol I was fortunate enough to bring home from my trip."

"Can I see it?" Ratio screamed with excitement. The Musquaeli war god had been well known in the Blake household ever since Montana had first reported a rumor of it that he had picked up on one of his early trips.

Just at that propitious moment, Average entered the room after having made the circuit around the little lake without any success of spotting Old Bull, as the boys called the old gator, or Ratio either, just as Ratio had planned.

Montana looked up as Average came into the study, and decided this practice idea was a bit too cumbersome. He didn't want too many eyes looking at the war god either, so he called a halt to it.

"Now, boys, now is not the time. This is just too distracting. I must prepare my report, so go now!" he commanded, waving his hand with that get-out-of-here direction.

"But, Father, I missed out on everything so far. Ratio's here and heard it. It's not fair, Father!" Average argued pointlessly.

"You do as I say, boy. Why don't you follow your brother's example? See, he knows me well, just when I need to be alone. He knows how to do it; follow him, Average!" Ratio had read the tea leaves and started out of the room before the disturbance of too many boys could disrupt his father's plans for a little tranquility. Average, crushed by the putdown as always, lowered his eyes and head before turning and—obediently as always—left the room.

14

GETTING READY

Amanda Blake got up early to make sure everything was ready. This was her husband's most important event so far in his already-illustrious career. She jumped out of bed and, after attending to necessary personal matters, grabbed her robe and hurried downstairs, where her checklist of everything to do was ready at the breakfast-nook table. There was no way she would screw this up; it was just too important. She turned on the preset coffee pot and sat down, ready to check off everything done on the list while the machine began its steady *bulerp, bulerp, bulerp,* and *perp.*

In spite of this appearance of thoroughness, she was taking no chances. And just to be sure she was thinking it right, she started her mental checklist out loud to the kitchen counters and cabinets and any secret mouse observers hiding inside the walls, Heaven forbid.

"One, caterer arrangements for food to be enjoyed with drinks before the press conference starts. Confirmed: standard barbeque pork with potato salad and pie, white and red wine, beer in the cooler; they supply all the goblets, mugs, forks, napkins, et cetera. Check. Two, security guard contract with parking attendants—three ought to cover it out front; the pasture across the street for overflow; Mr. Smeltzer agreed yesterday—and backyard security just in case the press gets rowdy—ha!—two is fine. Check. Three, microphone set up by Causeys' Music. Used Bill Causey before, good man; he knows how and can be trusted to do it right. Check. Four, final calls to Associated Press—we wish—local papers and TV, museum and academic connections, all done through surrogates to make it seem legit and not a pumped-up deal. Check. I tried my best to get Monty to use that press-agent guy he sometimes uses for university events, but no way; Monty just *knows* he can do it better than anyone. What arrogance! But I'm in for the ride this time, loyal wife and all that. Besides, I have too much of me invested in this gathering of the university folks and can't let this be a social flop or I'll never live it down."

The coffee maker did its last *bulerp, perp* and Amanda rose to fill her cup, leaving enough room for her favorite flavored cream, French vanilla, feeling great about her progress so far. She paused and stretched her arms to relax the tension that built up every time she got under stress, and looked over the remainder of the list.

At about that moment the boys came roaring downstairs in their usual manner and bounded into the kitchen looking for breakfast. "Momma," Ratio yelled, "eggs and pancake ready yet? I'm starving!" Average was right behind him and added his demand, belatedly but placing him squarely on the front lines in this encounter: "Yeah, Mom, me too, or should we—"

"Now, Average, you *must* remember what day this is and how important it is for your father. You boys will just have to get some cereal like you do on Saturdays, okay?" Amanda said, directing her frontal assault by way of defense against Average, even though Ratio had been first in the room and with the most specific breakfast order.

Ratio, knowing how the system worked in the preference and rejection departments of parent-child relationships in the Blake family, said without a moment's hesitation, "Yeah, Average, you know how important this is for Mom and Dad. The nerve of you asking for pancakes and eggs this morning of all mornings."

"But you said that first, Ratio!" Average shouted in his own defense, but Amanda quickly cut him off.

"Average, no matter who's first or last, I told you boys its cereal or nothing, so scram. You know where everything is. I have no time for this, *this* morning," she said, again directing her ire toward Average as if it had been his idea alone, because Ratio was already headed away from the breakfast nook. It was hopeless for Average, no matter how hard he tried; it was useless to complain as long as his favored brother was in the room. So he hung his head once again, then turned and followed his brother out of the room.

Without further hesitation, as if the interruption by her sons had not even happened, Amanda continued: "Five, calls to university wives just to be sure their sorry husbands will shuck their jealousy long enough to give Monty the cover he needs with his academic colleagues in attendance. That Sally Whitfield was the *worst* on the list, that bitch. Hugh Whitfield hasn't attended a university function in ten years because he hasn't published or done anything worth bragging about, that's why. That arrogant snob. Even without any of the usual stuff to his credit, he thinks he's too good to let people see him in public. He's the type that assumes what he's thinking is all that counts; just so long as he is convinced, it's enough. Oh tenure, oh tenure, whyfor aren't thou, oh tenure, for him at least?" she mused longingly. "But I finally tricked them into it, didn't I? Monty was counting on me, wasn't he? So how could I fail?" *You should have heard me, Monty,* keeping this part to herself, for there were limits to what even Ms. Machiavelli was supposed to do in polite university circles even when it was desperately necessary to have the whole scientific faculty there, as it was this time.

Montana had assured everyone he had talked to that the local university crowd would be here, and she could *not* let him down. *I appealed to her vanity, and that bitch, she didn't even catch on, bless her! I said, "Sally Whitfield, there are few university wives that add luster to these university social occasions, and you are one of them. Do you remember that time when you came without Hugh and everybody said, "Where's Hugh, dear? We wanted to see him too!"? Do you remember how embarrassing that was for all of us? You had to run across town and stir him out of the den and get his butt over there even though he wasn't dressed properly, and you said, "Never again will I let this happen, not on my life." I remember how much that must have hurt, really, Sally. Let's face it, Sally: Hugh is a social gnome at these things because he's always so busy solving the problems of the screwworm fly eradication, or something like that, and doesn't want to waste a minute of his valuable entomological career entertaining university wives and professors he sees every day. But this event, Sally, will top the calendar for the year, if not the decade. Monty's announcement will shake up the scientific anthropology world, if not the bug world, and it wouldn't hurt Hugh's career to be a part of it, with the national press in attendance with their cameras and all, maybe even TV. I have it on good authority—mine, bless me—that the* Associated Press *scientific reporter will be here, and Hugh's latest project, that screwworm thing, will be big news if they get wind of it. You know, just leaked out in social chitchat with the right person, maybe even me. Think of how you will look, my dear, in that stunning black outfit you wear to these things and the pictures alongside your important husband, nationally."*

I was tired after that was over, but it worked. That press lure was trolled right in front of her greedy face, and I could hear her on the end of the phone line, snapping it up like a big bass after a shad out in the lake. It was stunning, if I must think so myself. She will be here with Hugh in tow if she has to drag him. "Check!" she said out loud and defiantly just as Montana came into the kitchen rubbing his eyes after a night of limited sleep with visions of fame plums dancing in his head.

"Good morning, dear. How about breakfast? Would pancakes and eggs be all right?" Amanda said cheerfully as the boys in the other room laughed and grimaced respectively.

"Sure, dear, just what I had in mind," Montana said, scratching his bed-matted hair.

"Coffee's ready, sit over here. I know how tired you must be. Everything is ready for the big event; you can count on it, Monty."

"Uh, okay," Montana said without much enthusiasm, or appreciation for her efforts for that matter.

There are other rewards of his fame, and personal strokes from him will just have to wait, she thought as she got up to prepare a feast for her famous husband's breakfast.

15

PREPARATIONS

Tony Callaway had left Tallahassee the day before and spent the night in Pensacola at the Best Western, being careful not to stretch the *Tallahassee Democrat*'s budget too much. He had been against this trip out to the boondocks, as he liked to call every place west of the Apalachicola River Bridge, but his editor had insisted on it. What was so all-fired important about a party at some little-known anthropologist's digs that would make driving clear out this far from Tallahassee worthwhile? He had made a losing argument with his editor, who had some tip—probably based on a favor he owed to a press agent—that a story could be found at this thing, although for the life of him, he could not imagine what it might be.

The *Tallahassee Democrat* was the only newspaper in the state capital, except for the college weekly, but it was important for political purposes statewide, since it was the state capital. How this party fit into a political—or, for that matter, any other kind of envelope—was beyond him; but although not reasoning why, he would do his best even if he had to die, of boredom that is.

Reporting on the scientific exploits of a small-time university professor at a backwater school like Fangleer—no matter how famous he was in his own narrow circle, with a bent for headline-grabbing stunts on expeditions to Brazil, Ecuador, Peru, or some other South American place or the other—was hardly front-page material for his paper. But a job is a job, and he knew when it was time to shut up and do the story. He would just have to go out there and find something.

Tony was an athletic sort of older guy who had maintained his muscle tone and weight with careful eating practices and regular exercise. He was insightful, clever, and experienced enough with human nature to be a fairly good judge of character on the uptake. After all, he had made his career doing just that, working in a national news sinkhole after he first attracted national attention by reporting on some trial or other when he was just a fresh kid on the news scene, but there hadn't been that much notoriety since.

Like everybody else in Florida, Tony had wallowed in the mire of the 2000 election-count debacle, but because so many had had their hands in it, there hadn't been much of a chance to shine. Reputations were like hot showers in the panhandle: you had to keep taking them or you began to smell like everybody else.

The big event was supposed to start that afternoon at three o'clock, and he saw no reason to get out to Hedley much sooner. In the meantime, he put out a few feelers to the limited contacts he had in the scientific community.

"Hello, Barry. Tony Callaway here. How're they hanging in the pinhead set, man?"

"Tony, my good fellow, are you calling all the way out here to West FU just to chat, or do you have some devious ulterior motive as usual, like chasing a story nobody else has heard about yet?" Barry Gordon said good-naturedly to his old friend.

Barry was on the downhill side of fifty but fit for his age and now sedentary occupation. He had adopted the clothing style and personal habits of his fellow academicians, like tweed jackets with leather elbow patches and of course his sweet-smelling—to him anyway—briar pipe often in his hand. Walking across campus with a group of students, he really looked the part he had chosen to play—urbane, suave, and sophisticated. He had been a cub reporter at the *Democrat* when Tony first made his national reputation during the Bryant trial. Barry had been a decent enough staff writer in those early years, but as the years wore on he had gravitated back to academic journalism, bounced around a few specialty scientific magazines, and finally settled into Pensacola as an associate professor of scientific journalism—whatever that was. He was nearing retirement anyway and was coasting without having to publish much anymore to keep his faculty position now that tenure had finally arrived for him after a late start on his academic career. But he had never completely lost his touch and had kept his ear to the ground in the scientific arena.

"You know me too well, Barry. No, I'm actually out here in your neck of the woods this time," said Tony. "My editor—yes, I still have an idiot editor to answer to, and this one takes the cake—he insisted I come out here to cover the big splash over at Hedley, where that world-traveling anthropologist Professor Black or Blake—something like that—is supposed to have his big announcement to shock the academic world. Have you heard about it?"

"Yeah, Tony, but its Blake. Horatio Averill Montana Blake. And have I heard about it? This is the most staged event of this kind you will ever want to see. The trouble is it's so obvious, all the promotion and crap like that. This guy doesn't have a subtle bone in his body, except maybe his funny bone. If there has been any humor except the aura that envelops his enormous ego, no one out here has ever detected it."

"Well, fill me in, man. Is he a story, or is this a small-time academic hype exceeded only by his overestimation?"

"It's hard to say, Tony. He's been trailing hints of some great announcement in his field of primitive-tribe anthropology like a surface plug among the lily pads in a bass pond ever since his plane touched down in Miami coming back from Ecuador and again when he landed in Pensacola. But not enough to tell us what it is. It's like a Hadacol promotional buildup. You remember, don't you, back in the fifties? Advertise the hell out of it, with nobody able to buy it, and then, once the demand is sky high with none available, you dump tons of the stuff into a local market and it sells like crazy. But the fact that it was forty percent alcohol and not really a cure-all didn't hurt the long-term demand. But this guy doesn't have any long-term hooks. Apparently, he just wants to make a big splash and attract as much attention as he can muster and hasn't thought much about the afterwards."

"Are you going out there today, Barry? It would be great to see you again."

"Unavoidable, my friend. The professor's wife has contacted every faculty wife in the 'scientific community' at Fangleer and West FU and put enormous pressure on them to come and to have hubby in tow or else. The talent for persuasion at the Blake household is apparently not limited to the man of the house. She really knows how to pull in a social chit, even mine."

"What could this announcement be? I mean, what kind of expeditions has he been on and that kind of stuff?" Tony asked.

"Your guess is as good as mine, Tony. From what I hear, he has wormed his way into the good graces of one of the Stone Age tribes in some remote-as-hell region near the headwaters of the Amazon in South America. He has published numerous articles on Stone Age cultures and their war-making propensities in that region. There was even some mention of a certain artifact this particular tribe thinks is the cat's meow, you know, the secret of their war-making success, but he has supposedly never seen it. Maybe it has something to do with that," Barry said.

"Do you know the name of the tribe? Maybe I could do some fast research before this afternoon," Tony asked.

"Ha! Fat chance that. You could read every article he's ever published and still not know what his big secret is. But to answer your specific question, the name of the tribe he has cultivated is the Musquaeli, or something like that."

"I've already read his stuff, and I agree it must be that tribe and something about their war-making tendency. But what I can't figure is what could be so earthshaking in his little world. Could he have finally seen the little idol he writes about, and why would that be so darn important?"

"Beats me. But you are closer to it than anybody I've talked to. You always were that way, Tony, close to the heart of the matter," Barry said, giving a genuine compliment.

"I don't know about that, Barry, but thanks anyway. So, I guess I'll see you out there this afternoon?"

"Right, my boy, wouldn't miss it. Old Montana Blake, I'll have to hand it to him—subtle or not—he knows how to draw attention to himself. That must be a fascinating and frustrating place to dwell. See you there, okay?" Tony thanked his old friend again and rang off.

The Blake household had become a beehive of activity by lunchtime. At Amanda's explicit directions, the caterers, the security people with parking attendants in tow, and the music and microphone setups all had to be in place before the very first guest arrived, and they were so set by noon. She left nothing to chance. With a brief stroll around the grounds she could see everything from a facilities standpoint was coming together nicely. That freed her to do the important things, like her last-minute reminders to the university social set. *This is going to be perfect*, she thought.

16

THE BIG EVENT

Montana and Amanda had stationed themselves in their spacious backyard, with its commanding view of the little lake, so that as guests arrived they would not seem too eager. The pre-press-conference food and drinks were conveniently presented around the area, with ample staff to accommodate the guests while they had their drinks and engaged in chitchat, social maneuvering for position, and even obvious surreptitious intelligence gathering from colleagues while waiting for the main event.

Speaking of eager, the first car approaching the front entrance was that of the most astute and motivated scientific reporter likely to be present. Josh Becker took his assignment as director of research for the Florida Museum of Science and Natural History extremely seriously. He was a graduate of Harvard with a degree in scientific statistics and had worked for years with various scientific publications before moving to Florida as he approached retirement. He was an owlish-looking man with old-fashioned wire-framed glasses and an almost disheveled appearance given by the ill-fitting clothes he had the careless habit of wearing, such as bulky jackets worn the wrong time of year or sometimes T-shirts and jeans when everyone else was dressed up. Before taking his current job with the Florida Museum, he had published numerous articles in professional journals.

Becker's article that captured the attention of academics across the country had come out a few years ago in the prestigious *National Journal of Science*. It had reported on the statistical authenticity of double-blind scientific testing in medical research, and many protocols had been rapidly revised to catch the glitches Josh's studies had revealed. He had taken his position at the Florida Museum as he was nearing retirement, and actually enjoyed the heat and humidity many northerners could tolerate only in wintertime. Although he was an old hand in the scientific journalism field, and highly respected, he had never gotten the hang of appearing at ease and confident in a crowd like this one. He was shy and did his best work in research and fact-checking, not personal encounters.

Since the museum was located in Pensacola, it was easy for the institute to send Josh over to the airport to meet Dr. Blake when his flight from Miami had touched down. And it had taken no sleuthing on Josh's part to know to be at the airport in Pensacola—or here for that matter—since Dr. Blake had deliberately planned it that way from his first stop and phone calls to the museum upon arrival in Miami.

Josh Becker had mistimed his arrival because everyone concerned about appearances—as even an old hand like himself was—knows not to be seen as too eager, and arriving with not a single car on the grounds was inexcusable. But it was too late to turn back, and too embarrassing to turn around and go back since the house was at the end of a lane. So he pulled over, stopped his car, and got out.

The two parking attendants at the ready quickly asked for the older gentleman's keys and moved his car across the street, into the neighbor's pasture borrowed for the occasion. Seeing no plausible way to avoid the embarrassment of arriving first, he swallowed his pride and walked up the front steps and rang the doorbell. The maid answered and escorted him through the house and out into the backyard, where Montana and Amanda had been impatiently waiting.

Josh's early arrival and awkward moment did not last very long. A veritable stream of cars seemed to be converging on the Blake place as if somebody had held them back down the road like race cars at a NASCAR event and Josh had been the distant pace car. Included in the approaching motorcade were more scientific reporters as well as a collection of other guests. The reporters were an inexperienced bunch generally sent to this kind of event because their subject matter rarely lent itself to public events like this one.

Elizabeth Whartley, for example, was young, bright, and experienced in her field of reporting for *Scientific American* on rather mundane subjects. But regarding people, she had experience researching and writing about candidates for various academic prizes, like the Arthur S. Fleming Award for outstanding recognition in the field of entomology, the Fields Medal in mathematics achievement, announcements that rarely made the news of interest to the general public, but the candidates were usually interesting.

Elizabeth was short and slender and had a perky personality that endeared her to ready acceptance in public gatherings, especially a party scene, and even more so if young men were present. Even the older ones enjoyed watching her, if nothing else for she was attractive—even sexy—although attracting men was the last thing on her dedicated scientific interest list.

She had flown down to Pensacola that morning and picked up a rental car from the airport. This news of Dr. Blake's announcement—even if true as she had heard it—was hardly going to qualify for the prestigious annual Margaret Mead Award presented by the American Anthropological Association, an award Professor Blake had been nominated for but never won in the past, as a young scholar after his first articles written about the Musquaeli people.

She came anyway just to be sure because of the way she had learned about the announcement. So Elizabeth had done her typical, professional due diligence by reviewing the publications of Professor Blake. She had picked up one of the peripheral tentacles of the purposefully leaked news story, that an announcement of scientific significance was to be made this afternoon, from her office in Atlanta, and she would not have missed this party for the world.

Bill Dixon of the *Pensacola News Journal* didn't have as far to go as Elizabeth, but by chance he was in the line of cars approaching the Blake residence right behind her. He had been at the airport when Professor Blake's airplane from Miami had landed and had fired questions at him to no effect. He was determined to do better this time. Bill was far from young or inexperienced in this business, and the refusal of a news source to answer questions as Montana had merely whetted his appetite. This whole event had such a staged quality to it that his natural instinct was to see if he could find an angle to penetrate the plot and make the guy who was trying to manipulate him subject to his own manipulation.

The cars were parked in the pasture across from the Blake residence, in a pattern that would only have convinced John Nash, the eccentric and mentally ill mathematician, that it had a plan, contrary to the instructions of Amanda Blake; but the teenage boys hired by the security company had no experience whatsoever in event parking, and it showed. And considering how inexpertly this parking job was being done, the guests, whether professional, social, academic, or locals who just loved parties they heard about, filled this one rather quickly. As the guests exited their cars those who recognized their parking neighbors stopped to chat for a few minutes, while the others secured their vehicles and headed across the street to the Blake residence to join the party.

The Blake's maid escorted the guests through the house to the back porch, where Montana and Amanda were anxiously waiting—internally at least—for the party to start. They had been engaged in a desultory conversation for a few minutes with the dean of the scientific press corps, Josh Becker, much to the consternation of the Blakes. In one-on-one conversations, Josh could be dull indeed. But he had been persistent and had probed closer to the details of the mission than Montana had planned to reveal this early, so Montana's relief when the rest of the guests suddenly arrived was dually gratifying. They didn't have long to wait. Barry Gordon and the other colleagues from Fangleer and the other scientific journalists and their friends joined the crowd in the backyard gathering around the hosts, where they stood ready to orchestrate the proceedings so carefully planned.

Barry took up a position not far from the deck so he could see and hear everything that transpired. *This is curious*, he thought, *Too much of a buildup for some artifact he might have seen.*

Tony, on the other hand, had made a fast circuit around the party crowd and touched base with the other journalists in attendance. "Elizabeth, I'm Tony Callaway, *Tallahassee Democrat*. You've covered these scientific luminaries more than I have. What's your best guess for the big announcement?"

"Oh, hi," Elizabeth said as she extended her hand to shake Tony's. "I really don't have much of an idea, but my sources suggest it will be big."

"Has he been a player in the awards game—in the past, I mean?"

"Not really, but he has been nominated at least once for the Mead Award. He is one of those anthropologists that actually goes out into the field to meet and greet the Stone Age types, which among academic anthropologists is unusual but not remarkable. My readers actually like that kind of story, but it gets dull after a while, you know. Too much same old, same old. How many versions of the primitive folk habits can your average reader stand, you know? Straw huts, simple tools, communal habits, dressing habits, diet, even sex and all the rest? He needs something striking—really exciting—to set him apart from the group of anthropologists nominated for the Mead Award. Take the great lady herself. She not only wrote about primitive people but concentrated on the role of the woman, sex, and child-bearing in several different cultures that may have given some insight into how our cultures evolved."

Billy Dixon joined the little group of interested journalists within the gathering crowd to compare notes and jockey for position for the expected announcement. The key to being a successful journalist was to garner all the inside or leaked information your competitors might have, sharing little tidbits here and there—real or made up—to make them believe you're generous and really one of them, but to save your gotcha question for the precise moment when the luminary was most vulnerable. The question of the day for Billy and all the others was this last one. He really didn't have a gotcha question, or much of anything else, and no amount of schmoozing was likely to change that.

Becker had spent the most time with Montana and Amanda that day because he had made the mistake—he thought—of arriving early. But once he got there, he had rolled up his sleeves, figuratively of course, and pumped Montana for all he was worth. He had learned, for example, the basic story of the expedition, the war that wiped out the Musquaeli people and Montana's own miraculous escape. Montana couldn't stop talking about the little war god the Musquaeli people cherished, but stopped short, no matter how hard Josh pushed him, of admitting whether or not he had actually seen the artifact.

Montana had brushed Josh aside, like a veteran politician shaking hands in a receiving line, as soon as the rest of the crowd arrived, using the greeting handshake as a veritable steering tool to move each person along in the line to be seen by the maximum number of voters. Having mined that shallow vein for all its worth, Josh joined the others in the party, figuring he might as well have a few drinks and pick up what the others might be willing to share.

The journalism professionals clustered together near the bar to commiserate and glean each other's harvest, like so many vultures waiting for the beast to become a corpse.

Tony and Barry, the closest of the bunch to being friends because of their history together, were locked in close conversation as the others arrived at the bar and ordered their drinks.

"Hey, Tony," Billy Dixon shouted as he approached, "what brings you out west?"

"Same as you, buddy. Dead-end non-story probably, but you know editors," Tony said as he grabbed Billy's hand in greeting. He knew Bill Dixon vaguely from their occasional encounters covering news stories of interest to their readers at the state legislature in Tallahassee.

"Dixon, old friend," said Barry, not because he was close to the local guy on the *Journal,* but it was a professional custom among print journalists to pretend more than was real in relationships, and Billy played along as customary and returned the thrust with a parry of his own.

"How's the wife, Billy, and the kids?"

"Fine, fine," Billy said as they completed the ritual flawlessly. Neither cared a whit about the other personally, but a naïve observer would think they were old, close friends joining in the camaraderie of the event. The common-event part was true enough.

Josh Becker waddled over to take his place in the little crowd by the bar. "What's your poison, mister?" the young bartender asked over the heads of the small crowd in front of him.

"Scotch, rocks, thanks," Josh said. He turned his attention to the people around him and was astonished to find some with similar interests, or at least he assumed it was so as soon as he recognized Bill Dixon in the middle of the group. And this was quickly confirmed as he listened to the conversations.

"Hi, Josh," Billy said as soon as he saw him. Josh nodded, lifted a finger in recognition, and eased his way over against the side of the bar without stopping to engage the younger reporter in conversation.

"Just what could this mysterious announcement be?" asked Elizabeth, not having a clue herself and hoping to pick up a hint from the others. In fact it seemed that each one of them had about the same idea. Josh, who was the least adventurous of the bunch, ironically had probably the most information about the details of Dr. Blake's expedition to share. But he remained true to his form and stood silent.

"What I can't figure out," Elizabeth said expansively, "I mean, I've covered these prize seekers my entire professional career. Some have been really noteworthy, but most are fame seekers. It's a real paradox, kind of. The most notable, the ones who've made it by a lifetime of achievement, are the least interested in what it means to them—person-ally, I mean—and the rest are primarily interested in themselves and how winning this or that prize will add to their résumés for some future pro-motion or award. They don't come right out and say it, mind you, but you can just tell by how they act. They never talk about the real good their work is accomplishing for humanity, or whatever, or what we can all learn from it, but how they are reflected in it. The 'I did this and I did that' aspect, you know? On the other hand, the really good ones care less about what winning will mean to their careers—or so it seems—because they can't stop talking about their discoveries and why they're import-ant to others, not them. It's a subtle difference sometimes because the seekers, as I call them, will try to fool you with words, but their actions give it away."

"How do you rate Dr. Blake, Elizabeth, on your 'seeker' scale?" Tony asked.

"Yeah, Elizabeth, we never see the big-time science guys down here in the boondocks, the ones that really accomplish something worth-while, on a regular basis. How does our Dr. Montana Blake measure up?" Billy said.

"He's in the middle," Elizabeth said, revealing practically nothing.

"Yeah, just what went on with this expedition the great discov-ery was made on?" Billy Dixon asked, looking around the group. "Anybody know?"

Josh figured it wouldn't hurt to let some of his gold coins slip out of the bag, thinking that maybe some of these guys would have some ideas that might help him launch his "gotcha" at the critical moment once he figured it out himself.

"Well, I found out this much," Josh said as though reluctant to let out his secret. "He was down to this tribe in Peru on one of the feeder rivers of the Amazon, almost one of the headwaters, I'm told. It must have gotten messy, like he landed in the middle of a tribal war of some kind and had to get out by the skin of his teeth."

"What's the name of the tribe?" Billy Dixon asked.

"It's Musquaeli, or something like that," and he spelled it for them as best he could.

"What was the war about?" Elizabeth asked.

"Don't know," Josh said.

"Was he the only one from the expedition who escaped?" Tony asked, thinking about possible collateral damage that might not sound so good coming out at a press conference.

Josh spread his hands and tipped his head to one side in the traditional "I don't know" gesture.

"What was the war about?" Barry Gordon asked.

Josh only shook his head, pleading ignorance, which was true.

"Did you get the impression he actually saw the war god or—better yet—made off with it?" Tony asked, getting exactly nothing from Josh and figuring this well was about pumped dry. He was right.

The journalists looked at each other, refilled their drinks one more time, and drifted off into small talk. Then, like a clarion call, the group was startled by a loud squawk from the electrical equipment up on the porch, where the press conference was to be held, and all of them hurried to get in the best position to be recognized for questioning.

"Ladies and gentlemen," the speaker said, an unrecognizable functionary from the Florida Museum of Science and Natural History, which had sponsored and paid for the expedition, "can we have your attention, please?" Their attention was no problem because there was no conceivable reason for any of the guests to be there but for the press conference. It only took a few minutes for the crowd to gather in front of the makeshift podium.

"It is my privilege to introduce a man who needs no introduction. Dr. Horatio Blake is here today to make an announcement about the results of his recently completed—successfully, I might add—expedition sponsored by the Florida Museum of Science and Natural History. Dr. Blake, known affectionately to us at the museum and most of the scientific community as Montana, has called us here today for his report. Dr. Blake?"

"Good afternoon, ladies and gentlemen. Welcome to our home here on Crescent Lake in Hedley. I asked you all to come out here today to let you know the results of my latest expedition to study the Stone Age peoples of South America. As many of you know, I have made my reputation as an anthropologist systematically studying the culture of these truly incredible people. Those of you not from the academic community may want to find my articles published on the subject for further background, but for today, I have some more important news. Some years ago, I had the privilege to find and make contact with a village of the

Musquaeli tribe located on the Pangria River in Peru, one of the tributaries feeding the Rio Ucayali.

"For the geography aficionados in the audience, the Ucayali in Peru joins the mighty Maranon in Ecuador to make the headwaters of the Amazon River, which flows to the Atlantic Ocean in Brazil. The tribe is located in a pristine setting on one of the most picturesque river scenes you would ever want to see. It's a jungle environment for sure, and never has a better ecological balance between man and nature been demonstrated.

"The Musquaeli are wonderful people, but primitive by Western civilization standards, truly right out of the Stone Age. Their tools and weapons, for that matter, rely on stone rather than metal. I had made three, maybe four trips to the region and became personally acquainted with tribal members, including the shaman of the tribe, Urchuwa. This rather remarkable Indian was a real source of strength for these people and the one member of the tribe supposedly entrusted with the spiritual connection with the gods of their culture. I had the rare privilege to get to know this man and gain his confidence. The Musquaeli believe that the earth is the source of all things and that they are just a part of it. They were dependent on earth, for sure, and even threatened by forces of the gods of this nature.

"I discovered on one of my trips that the spirits were manifest in a small idol which they call their war god. I had never seen it before this trip, mind you, but from the way the villagers spoke of it, I was convinced it existed.

"Warfare is an integral part of the Musquaeli culture because the tribes that border each other are in constant conflict with each other to control territories that supply food and special places that represent the mystery and power of nature to them. They are willing to die to win or keep their territory. The tribe that gets the best territory gets the best food, and their population and power grow, and vice versa. So warfare is critical to the tribe's survival. These are basically hunter-gatherer people that do not cultivate any crops. They survive on the animals they can trap and kill, as well as various native plants that supply carbohydrates in their diets in the form of tubers, which the women make into a potato-like concoction. It's quite tasty, actually.

"On this trip, our expedition stumbled into a horrendous conflict. A nearby enemy tribe was in the process of launching an invasion to capture a sacred river valley of the Pangria that both sides claimed and revered as a special place to visit with their gods. This is all superstition, of course, as we of the scientific world of rational thought know, but these people don't know that. In fact, they believe fervently quite the opposite.

"My team was a very small one consisting of my able assistant Elliot Drake, a former US Army Ranger, and two Indian guides who happened to have been captured from this very tribe as children and were very familiar with the language and even related by tribe and blood to some of the older tribal members. We did our best to assist them in this battle, but sadly I must report there was a disaster that caused the loss of the tribe in a terrible fight to the finish for control of the sacred valley to both sides.

"Urchuwa, the much-revered tribal shaman, saw that the battle was going badly after Elliot, even with his firearm, was unable to prevent the loss. So he—Urchuwa, that is—entrusted to me the idol of the tribe so that the dreaded enemy could not claim it as a victory prize.

"After Elliot was killed in heroic defense of the tribe, I was able to make my escape with the help of one of the guides, who gave his life to permit me and the tribal idol to escape. I am afraid I must report that my dear friends the Musquaeli no longer exist on the registry of Stone Age tribes in that part of the world, as these people have no concept of negotiation once the fighting starts and no agency of the civilized world available to settle such disputes.

"I will be writing a book of my experiences on the expedition, but I wanted to have you all here to make my announcement that the Musquaeli war god idol will be presented to my sponsor, the Florida Museum of Science and Natural History, so that the public and other interested scientists may study it for the advancement of the study of anthropology.

"Are there any questions?"

There was considerable applause from the crowd as the exciting tale of science and warfare was so unusual for this conservative and largely sympathetic crowd, but not from all of them. The crowd drew closer to the makeshift platform where the de facto press conference was about to begin. Montana seemed eager to answer the questions he most assuredly expected to come as the excitement of the moment, with him at the center of attention, welled up in him with an admixture of anticipation and dread. Anticipation that his long-awaited moment of announcement was about to come, and dread that he might be unable to comfortably answer all the questions that came with it.

Elizabeth Whartley was the first reporter out of the gate. She shot to her feet with her shouted question even before Dr. Blake recognized her.

"Dr. Blake, Elizabeth Whartley, *Scientific American*, here. Do you expect the announcement of your recent success in Peru to gain you the Mead prize this year? And why is that, sir, if the answer is yes?"

"Uh, ah, no, Miss Whartley, is it? The prestigious Mead prize is 'The Award' every anthropologist respects, and far be it from me to even suggest that my humble efforts and accomplishments—as useful as they will be to the accumulation of scientific knowledge about these ancient people—would in any way qualify for the Mead Award."

Yeah, I'll bet you don't, Elizabeth thought.

Billy Dixon laughed to himself and stepped next into the fray. "Professor Blake, do you mind if we refer to you as Montana?" and, not waiting for an answer, proceeded with his loaded question. He had not forgotten how Dr. Blake had stonewalled the press corps upon landing in Pensacola. "Montana, now that you have announced that you did not come home empty-handed, can you explain to us, sir, what your thoughts are on the fact that you were the only one from the expedition or the tribe to get out alive?"

Montana was astonished, if not surprised, by the question. After all, he had orchestrated the attention-getting aspects of the announcement and had to take the bad with the good. But he was up to the challenge.

"It was the saddest moment of my life to lose my loyal, competent assistant, Elliot Drake, and our two trusted Indian guides, Wanei and Estova. But worse than that was to accept that I was powerless to prevent the loss of the Musquaeli tribe I had spent so many days and nights with, my people, the Musquaeli. And the only emptiness now is the space in my heart for this terrible loss."

Then why this grandiose press conference centered on you? Billy thought.

"Professor," Barry Gordon asked next, "you mentioned that you managed to come out of this scrape with the most precious idol these Stone Age people worshipped, you know, really believed in that they would be safe. Why would the shaman entrust that precious an item with you if the tribe was going down for the long count, forever?"

Montana had struggled with the deeper meaning within that question ever since he had stood at the opening of the canyon by the river sacred to the Musquaeli at that critical moment in the battle. He had felt the vibration of the seemingly lifeless idol, seen the glowing red eyes, and tried to pretend with all his will that there was no such thing as a nonphysical phenomenon in the universe. But the effects of the idol's proximity to Urchuwa's side of the battlefield had been undeniable. Now the realization of having acted for his personal safety—and, worse yet, to be standing in this place at this very moment seeking personal fame and glory as a consequence—was threatening his sense of self-worth more than he was willing to accept. He had to answer the question, though, didn't he?

"It was a complicated circumstance, Barry—Professor Gordon, that is."

Whether he was giving acclamation or seeking it was not all that clear, most thought.

"Warfare among those primitive tribes is an ongoing problem of cultural survival. One side wins and again it may lose, and they know that. They believe in their idols as a means to access their gods, whom they really expect to protect them; and this one seems to have, as the Musquaeli prospered, so to speak, by surviving for many generations in their village on the Pangria. We in the West who know better realize these primitive superstitions are real enough to the Indians. But really, Professor, there's not anything to it. The shaman of the tribe is the one who has mastered the appearance of spirituality; it's what we in the West call charisma, attraction, or leadership, nothing else, really. The ancients and many Westerners call it faith, the 'leap' as the philosopher Kierkegaard called it, or better yet a gamble worth taking as the philosopher Pascal claimed with his famous wager. Anyway, they believed in it and their shaman, who definitely believed in it, became the custodian, if you will, for the symbol of the attraction, the little idol. You see, Professor, that kind of belief is funny in a way. The idol became more important to Urchuwa than what it could do for him or the tribe. You understand?"

Barry Gordon shook his head, more confused than ever but not on the attack anymore as a result. Montana sensed that not-so-subtle shift in momentum and plunged ahead, seeing a way out of Barry's trap as well as his own.

"You see, Professor, it became more important to Urchuwa that the war god not fall into the hands of his enemies, even if he had to give it and the hope for his people up. Wouldn't you call that true devotion? Now that I think on it, you don't see that kind of devotion to any god—not even ours—but that question is above my pay grade. Anyway, it was clear to me that the Musquaeli were losing the battle; and discretion rules, as they say, right?"

Gordon didn't have a follow-up.

Josh Becker had been biding his time, or, more accurately, building up his courage to ask the right question. He was an intelligent man with a Harvard degree in scientific statistics and not a little bit of recognition in the scientific community, but he was a better researcher than he was a debater. He found his stimulation in numbers, which held their secrets, rather than in people. Josh came across as shy, being seemingly overprotective of his own image, as most shy people seem to be. But underneath his overprotective exterior was an insightful mind, able to see through the obvious and get to the heart of the matter, even if it took him a while.

"Professor, tell us, if you will, how you could tell from where you stood on the battlefield at that critical moment when the idol was passed to you that the Musquaeli were going to lose. I mean, in most battles, even in sports, momentum shifts back and forth before—before the outcome is certain. Weren't you willing to give this beloved tribe of yours the chance to win, or was coming away with this anthropological prize more important to you than their chance of survival as a tribe?"

This question stung Montana deeply because it was coming dangerously close to his dark secret. Deep down in his inner character he had a sense of truth telling, no matter how easily he could disregard it when it suited his ego's survival, which was, in the end, the most important thing to him.

"Uh, well, ah—you see, folks, it was a confusing situation and I could not really tell who was going to win. I knew that Elliot had bought it, and it sure seemed like the end was near, and Urchuwa had more at stake than me, and it was his suggestion that I save the idol, you see."

Had there been in the audience one of those rare people who can see the little facial twinges, the subtle, nervous hand motions that show that a person is being deceptive, the case would have been perilous. But that rare talent had not shown itself yet. Besides, Josh seemed to be mollified by the ambivalent response. Elizabeth shot up again and leveled another zinger at Dr. Blake.

"Dr. Blake, the Mead prize committee—and you will surely be a nominee again this year, or soon after your book is published, anyway—will want to know how the Musquaeli women and children met their fate and if there were any safeguards built into the battle plan for them; or did you have any say in the battle plan in that regard? You know that

Margaret Mead made her reputation studying the effects of tribal life on sex and procreation and what that might mean for moderns, don't you?"

Montana was taken aback by this line of questioning, for it was the very first time he had even thought about the women and children of the tribe; not during his manipulation of Elliot to devise the battle strategy or in his escape. He really didn't know if they had been killed or just taken as slaves, wives, or worse. He had to think fast.

"Well, you see, Elizabeth, and thank you for that very good question," he said, trying to use a little flattery to defuse the barb of her question, albeit unsuccessfully, "the Musquaeli, unlike some of the Stone Age cultures, and from my experience they are all different in that respect, didn't have a tremendous respect for the role of women in their culture, unlike we in the enlightened West. As you may know, even some modern civilizations in the Middle East have very little respect for the role of women in their societies. Maybe the genetic origins of that treatment are deeper than you might expect, but I don't have enough evidence on that as yet, so it is too soon for me to conclude one way or the other on that. But to answer your question . . ."

Montana paused, nervously touching his face with one hand and then the other, giving a clear sign of deceptive intent to any skilled and perceptive observer, if there were any.

"I was reasonably close to Urchuwa, who was the decision maker at that point," he continued. "If he thought—and I did know that Elliot was done for—that the battle was over, there was nothing I could do by myself to save the village people, so I took his instruction to save the idol from the enemy as more important and left. That was the way we saw it at that moment, and I have to live with that."

Tony Callaway had been taking the whole explanation in as one colleague after another had taken their best shots at the man on the hot seat, rising to every occasion so far. He had very little at stake since he was only here because his editor had insisted, and he did not see his role as an attacker, as some of the others had. But Tony was a clever guy and did have some gifts in reading people. He hated arrogance and detested deception even more when it was used to manipulate the press for personal gain. He had seen this type of subject many times in his long career and had developed a pretty good ability to catch the blatant liars, at least, in their little cover-up games with the Fourth Estate. He had heard Dr. Blake duck each of the questions using his esoteric position that no one could possibly know what had actually happened but him. He had watched the man carefully and noticed that his body language cried out, "Liar, liar, pants on fire," at key points in the story, although he wasn't instinctually confident enough in his conclusion to directly accuse him.

The part about deciding when to leave and that baloney about the idol's safety being more important to the Indians than what he could do for them were just not credible, especially because he gave the little tell-tale signs Tony recognized as deception. He had ridiculed the Indians' faith often enough, yet he was claiming to believe that they had believed, when an equally plausible motive seemed to be his own ambition. This was even more plausible to Tony given the way Dr. Blake had orchestrated the party and press conference for his own accolades. He also noticed the disdain some people in the audience seemed to have for Montana; they were probably jealous academic types and should not be taken too seriously in their angst. But the whole thing didn't pass the smell test to Tony, so he finally decided on his question.

"Dr. Blake, Tony Callaway, *Tallahassee Democrat.* I have some questions, sir, if you please?"

"Yes, Tony, fire away, my man," Montana confidently asserted, realizing he was nearing the end of the session.

"I notice you never answered Elizabeth's question about the battle plan. Was there a plan, and if so, who devised it? Was Elliot Drake a part of it, as an experienced former Army Ranger? How did the terrain figure into it? You know, it would help if you could give us a word picture of the terrain of the battlefield. Where were the set pieces—offense and defense—and where were you stationed all the while? For example, was the idol with the shaman during all phases of the battle or with you? How did it get there with him, and if it did, how did he pass it to you and what was your role in the whole process?"

Montana was struck with the danger of the questions. He could not be open and truthful, or his secret would be revealed, and he couldn't have that. *This guy is good, very good! Better think on this quickly.*

"Well, Tony—may I call you Tony? I guess I already did. Those are very good questions." He paused for a few seconds, which seemed to stretch on interminably to the others, but he had to think.

Don't forget, Big Doctor, you don't need to say too much, and nobody here was there, and nobody there can ever be here, heh, heh, heh, not funny, Big Doctor, not funny at all.

Then he spoke: "You will have a hard time imagining the battle scene, and my poor ability to describe it will not do it justice. But suffice to say, imagine an elongated bowl with a river running through it, open on one end and more or less plugged by small hills on the other. The mountains made the sides of the bowl, with a rather flat valley down the middle. Elliot Drake, as an experienced military man, conceived the plan taking advantage of the terrain. The plan, in essence, was to lure the enemy warriors into the bowl with the Musquaeli warriors positioned on both sides waiting to swoop down, as it were, at the propitious moment and administer the coup de grâce.

"Unfortunately, there is no perfect plan, and that rule applied here as well. The attack went well for a time, and Elliot's firepower, his gun, you understand, was administered at just the right moment. The Indians called the guns we had the 'smoke and punch,' and well named I'd say. The only problem was the fog of war, and all that, reared its ugly head in the form of a counterattack by the enemy with a totally unexpected force and awful timing for our plan. Elliot's well-designed plan devolved into a melee of hand-to-hand fighting. But even then, the success and failure ebbed and flowed for a time until the battle was lost. Only then did I manage to escape. Is that a good enough word picture for you?"

The journalists scrambled to make their notes, and of course none of them could imagine much of anything except in a general sense, which is exactly what Montana had in mind with his extemporaneous, dramatic story. Elizabeth for one wasn't fooled and picked up on one rather glaring, to her at least, unanswered question. After all, it was her question, even though until Tony picked up on it, she had missed it. But she wasn't missing it now.

"Excuse me, Dr. Blake."

"Yes, Elizabeth," Montana said.

"Where were you while all this hand-to-hand fighting was going on? Did you actually ever see the enemy warriors? And where was the idol?"

"Uh, ah, well, you see, Elizabeth, Urchuwa's people cared a great deal for the safety of their idol, and as I said, the safety of it was more important to them than their own survival. You know, Elizabeth, that philosophy is not really very different than Western religious faith. Isn't the idea of glory to God more important than what happens to you and me? Has there really ever been an answer to the question of pain in the world? I mean, is God responsible for it all, and if so, how do we give him glory in the face of all the suffering? When you think about it, given the admittedly superstitious nature of these people's beliefs, that position is not really too strange, is it?"

Well, he had her there; and Elizabeth Whartley, agnostic as she was, was not willing or able, for that matter, to meet this epistemological puzzle that had challenged philosophers for centuries, so she sat silent. But not everyone was cowed by Montana's brilliant counterstroke.

The antisocial entomology professor at Hedley, Hugh Whitfield, who had been browbeaten by his wife to come because she had been leaned on by Amanda Blake to attend this useless function, had only partially listened to the blowhard Dr. Blake's contest with the press. He had tuned most of it out and even dozed off for a part of it. But this latest exchange had wakened him and caught his attention. He may have been a very different kind of scientist from his colleague at Hedley, but in things religious he had some depth.

"Dr. Blake, how do you compare a pagan Stone Age culture's concept of devotion to their idols to what most in the West call a devotion to God based on our Judeo-Christian heritage? I mean, what tradition of devotion do these Muscalie people, or whatever you called them, have to compare with thousands of years of written and oral traditions in support of the one true God?"

Montana was taken aback again, partly because he had never heard Hugh Whitfield make a public statement in his life and to hear this challenge to what he had considered a masterstroke to silence that pretty, young reporter Elizabeth Whartley and the rest. He never dreamed Whitfield had ever spent five minutes outside of his beloved bug field of science, much less in the nuances of religious philosophical speculations.

"Well, Hugh, and nice to see you here at a social occasion for a change, it's what they call in literature an analogy—you know, comparison by illustrative example—not a case-by-case identity. More of an anomaly, actually, the more I think about it."

Tony had been listening carefully to this very gifted polemicist spar with each challenger and had decided Dr. Blake was not going to be exposed for the blowhard he appeared to be, so he shifted tactics.

"Professor, you mentioned that there was an ebb and a flow of the battle. Did that have any relationship to the location of the idol, either in your hands or Urchuwa's? You haven't yet answered our questions on that point."

Montana was stunned by the question because he knew this was dangerous territory. What bothered him the most was his seeming inability to have anticipated these barbs and to have avoided or deflected them with proper thought planning and strategies. This press gathering he had planned as a triumph was turning into something decidedly less. If he ever admitted that he had known that there had been a definite correlation between the strange vibrations in the little stone piece and the rather obvious changes on the battlefield, it would expose him as the fraud he was.

This is serious, he thought. *If I go down that road . . . disaster. Remember, self, they don't know any of this. Don't be lured into a stupid trap. Stick with the symbolism-and-analogy talk, or whatever comes out is usually best. Maybe now is the time to bring the little bugger out? That should divert attention away from these very sore points in my story.*

"Well, Tony, everything was very confusing, as it always seems to be in warfare as the historians tell it. I couldn't testify about that kind of history from personal experience before now, but I tell you, I saw as much of it as I ever want to. The expectation that a wild, spear-wielding savage might pop out of the jungle without warning, bent on running me through, is terrifying, I must confess. As a scientist, I have always left that sort of thing to the experts, and fortunately my work has been on the whole rather peaceful. I would have expected that the ebb and flow of battle, as you phrase it, is hard to read, and it was. I had no idea who was going to win at that point. As to the transfer, I can only say I ended up with the relic as Urchuwa desired. Where it happened on the battlefield is lost to me now." Montana had decided he had to do something dramatic to divert attention away from the awkward positions the skillfully placed questions had left him having to defend.

Montana stood back a few steps, taking a dramatic pause of twenty seconds or so. The crowd, in their scattered, eclectic groups, began to murmur among themselves quietly, the cumulative noise becoming a crescendo as they wondered what was coming next. What had seemed to all of them a dull and staged event had turned into a rather exciting challenge of wits, and Dr. Blake was becoming a lot of fun to watch.

Montana began to speak again, and the audience fell silent. "Ladies and gentlemen, the loss of the Musquaeli tribe is more important than the details of how it all happened. I had a tremendous respect for the integrity of the Musquaeli people and especially their spiritual leader, Urchuwa. I trusted him to decide what was best for them. If he thought the battle was lost, and that was how I was reading him—my direct interpretive skills are good but not that good, you know—it had to be good enough for me. The history of the Musquaeli people will be my judge, if anyone, and I'll leave it at that," Montana said.

With that dramatic statement, like a Greek chronicler recasting history to turn ordinary details of an account into an almost mythological framework, Montana turned, walked across the yard, and entered his home. But before the astonished audience could collect their thoughts and engage in an almost unanimous chorus of "What the devil, is he leaving?" Montana quickly reemerged from the house carrying a nondescript case and returned to the microphones. He put the case on the ground, opened it, and lifted out an object about the size of a small football, wrapped in a black cloth.

And for Tony, who had been waiting to bring this charade to an end with one final clinching question and maybe with an accusation, Montana had him there. He had answered enough of the questions to satisfy all but the truly curious and insightful, and the rest would have to accept that this was all they were going to get. Then producing what almost certainly was going to be the artifact that this whole thing had been about was a very skillful demonstration of critical timing. This guy was either a genius at deception or the luckiest fool on earth. The best politicians he had been dealing with in Tallahassee for years could not have handled it better.

Montana slowly and carefully unwrapped the little stone idol and held it up. There it was, in all its ugliness, for the audience to see. And of course it just sat there, apparently not choosing to vibrate or for its little beady red eyes to glow. He hoped he would never see that again, especially not now.

There was a mixed reaction from the crowd. Some were astonished, others curious, and others simply wondered to themselves, *Is this all this was about, a carved rock? Oh well, the food and booze were pretty good.*

Amanda Blake, standing near her husband's elbow, decided now was the time to intervene.

"Gentlemen, ladies, isn't this fun? My poor husband is exhausted after his trip, the tragedy, and all these questions, my goodness! We want you all to enjoy the party, and you media types can't have all the fun with your questions and all that, so, everyone, enjoy!"

She grabbed Montana's arm to usher him off the podium and toward the refreshments before any more deadly questions could be asked. He gladly welcomed the lead for once, and rewrapped the stone idol and safely placed it back in the carrying case. He would not open it again that day. Amanda had not been on the Pangria that day, *thank God for that*, but she had enough of a sense of timing to know that this grilling had to end. As usual, she was exactly right. And that was all there was to the Blake press conference except for a few more harmless questions one or another of the reporters could squeeze in, in the time remaining, but most of their weapons had been fired already, and after a close look at the artifact, not many questions were left.

17

LAUNCH

Average and Ratio woke up early the next Saturday morning in order to concoct their usual plans to avoid what they believed to be their mother's unreasonable fear of the snakes and alligators in the lake. War games were fun, and nothing would stand in the way of that.

"Do you really think we ought to without asking Momma, Ratio?"

"Don't sweat it. She won't be up for hours after that thing yesterday. Come on, Average, are you afraid or not?"

"Oh well, okay, if you think it's all right."

Things had settled down to normal after the party. Although the cleanup crews had done a decent job on the yard and grounds, there was still scattered debris, like a drink cup left in the edge of the bushes by the lake, where one of the guests had tossed it aside, and even a beer bottle floating in the water.

"The enemy has taken the house, Average. You sweep with a flanking attack on the side yard, and I'll sneak inside and cover your approach." Ratio hand signaled to his brother using a code they had worked out to keep their actions secret in the "danger zone," as their mother called it, reenacting one of their imaginary battle plans and pretending to be marines or soldiers of some kind.

Average enthusiastically did his crab-like sideways sprint, ducking and darting as if imaginary bursts of enemy gunfire would open up at any minute as he attacked the left side of the rear porch structure. Ratio darted right and then dropped into a crawling maneuver just as he approached the back steps and prepared to enter the enemy defenses.

Montana had risen later that morning after a sound sleep that came with the relief that the press attacks had done no real damage to his dignity, which was all he really cared about. He had felt trapped into finally displaying the little stone idol, and it was a relief there had been no immediate reaction to its simplicity. His fear: that the idol being held in his hands without the supporting artifacts he had managed to collect over the years and place in the museum would seem insignificant, unimportant, and even ordinary. *What a relief,* he thought. The story of it was far bigger and more important than the thing itself. To his way of thinking, having kept the reveal secret for so long had just heightened the mystery of the artifact. Although he hadn't expected to see its curious supernatural behavior when he unwrapped it at the press conference— or ever again for that matter—the little bugger might have lit up and started vibrating like it did that day back on the battlefield. While that would have caused a stir all right, he was relieved he did not have to explain that aspect of the idol's curious nature to the crowd of onlookers and press meddlers. He settled comfortably into his high-backed leather chair behind his deck in the study, where he did all his important thinking and writing.

Many thoughts went through his mind: *How do I report this in a way to call the most public attention to the discovery? That press grilling didn't do it. Some of them will write a blurb and bury it back in "section Z" or in the local news section, where it's guaranteed nobody will see it. Just turning it over to the museum will never do. They will bitch and moan about their rights and all that, but I can stall them for a spell if I can think of a good reason. Let me see. A wider audience, that's what I need, but how to do that? It really was an exciting trip, with the final battle and all, and that would make quite a story. What if I wrote a book documenting all my past achievements and culminating in a detailed account of this trip? Slightly revised of course to protect my ass, naturally. Hmmm, what if I made this trip like a novel? Could be quite a story, not completely fiction, and factual as far as I want it to go. It might even be an innovation in scientific report writing. Scientific fictionalization. Yeah, I like the sound of that.* The oxymoronic implications of this thought never occurred to him.

Meanwhile, realizing they risked their mother's admonition by staying out any longer by the "dangerous" lake, Ratio had come back inside and was slipping soundlessly down the hall in a pretend house-to-house combat patrol and had arrived outside his father's office when Average came running past him noisily, not realizing their father was even in the house.

"*Tad-a-dat, rat-a-tat-tat, boom!*" he yelled, as authentic a war sound effect as he could make, caught up fully in the emotions of the game.

"Average, you idiot, can't you see I'm working? Get in here, young man, and what pray tell are you up to?" Montana yelled at the top of his lungs. Average was almost bowled over by the ferocity of his father's attack and shut up immediately.

"Yeah, Average, don't you know not to yell in the house? You really are stupid, aren't you?" Ratio shouted, making sure that all the heat their angry father was about to vent at them would be directed away from him. After all, he was a part of the game too. It worked, too, because Average was always so easily manipulated. Average hated his brother for it, but out of habit obediently turned silently into the office to take the verbal thrashing he knew was coming, while Ratio would get off scot-free.

"I have had the most important event of my career just yesterday, boy. Have you forgotten that already?"

"No, sir. I'm sorry, Father, I didn't know you were in here, and we were playing war down by the lake and—"

Montana cut him off in the middle of his explanation, before he could pull Ratio into the picture, however hopeless that would be.

"'Playing war,' did I hear that right? I've just been in a war, and you boys—especially you, Average—ought to have remembered that and have anticipated I might just need some peace and quiet around here. And in my own study, too! Does that make sense to you, boy?"

Amanda, who had slept in this morning after the ordeal of arranging the party details and the people too, to some extent, was headed toward the kitchen when she heard the tirade by Montana down the hall. Recognizing the sounds of a family attack on the boys in the making and seeing Ratio skulking outside the office as if he were Mr. Innocent—as usual—she hurried to the door and quickly worked her magic on the scene.

"Now, honey, the boys were just playing. Come along now, Average. You and Ratio go outside to play. The weather is nice this morning, but stay away from the edge of the lake except where the shoreline is cleared. I've told you a thousand times to be careful out there, understand? So leave your father in peace. I'm sure he has some important things to do today after our wonderful event yesterday."

This last comment did the trick because Montana really did need to get started on his written account right away, and Amanda's subtle stroking of his ego was all it took to lose the heat of his anger, so he let Average leave without imposing any more punishment than the tongue-lashing he had just administered. Average needed no persuasion as he scampered down the hall with Ratio, giggling to himself, right behind him.

Montana resumed his seat as Amanda headed to the kitchen to fix breakfast for her family. He opened his laptop and began to make an outline of his work of fiction/fact from the materials he had filed away in his desk from his many trips to Ecuador. In his mind, the scope of the project, with the key last trip and its devastating and tragic battle scenes, began to dance around in his active and creative mind. He could see it all again: the beautiful scenery, the native people, their Stone Age culture, even the personality of each of the players in this life drama, especially Urchuwa, Elliot, and his guides, Wanei and Estova. He could see it all like a kaleidoscopic cyclorama spinning around the walls of his mind, over and over again, as if he were there now watching the tragic events unfold.

How can I make this record interesting but scientific? Just who is my audience, anyway? This last trip was a true venture, and it ought to be told. What if I tell that story and fill in enough data accumulated from my past ventures into that never, never land, or the land where time forgot? Might that not capture the general public's interest? Let me see now. He turned to his laptop and began to type. "The campfire was dying a natural death in the muggy heat of the evening, and good riddance, too, for the team I had built and headed . . ."

He labored far into the night, now tenured and safe from criticism or anything else against his plans and with two weeks' leave from the college built into his contract. The project would take much longer than that, but he had learned early in his career that the hardest part of a project was getting started. He would have to weave around teaching and other commitments, but he now had the motivation to stay with this until it was done.

In his mind the events were still lingering like an unpleasant dream that wouldn't obey the normal rules and disappear with the fading darkness and rising light. There were good things in this "dream" all right, like the capture of the elusive, ancient stone relic he had craved for so long and loved in a sense with unrequited love. Unrequited because he desired to own it so much despite never being able to cradle it in his possession, where his inestimable pride could caress it with thoughts of devotion, but it could return nothing on its own to him. It had frightened him when the thing seemed to take on a life of its own, blinking its insidious red eyes from its otherwise lifeless appearance, seeking to be possessed only by its rightful owner, as it was in that horrid final battle scene.

The little artifact had made its loyalties clear, in a sense, by the results. Montana had been able to see differences in the fighting when he carried it in the direction of Urchuwa and conversely when he made it withdraw. The moral dilemma over whether he should act to help the tribe or save himself reverberated in his troubled mind. But his intense personal desire to be recognized by those scientific colleagues he personally despised always overcame the guilt and shame he had buried as he came back to his default position of scientific discovery being paramount over any personal need—or so he told himself.

He sat at his desk and wrote page after page, reliving the experiences from the expedition. He thought about those two noble former warriors who had faithfully served his purposes, and wrote: "The two ex-warriors were a little past their prime according to Musquaeli standards since, by the time of maturity, most of their men either died from disease or found the wrong end of an enemy spear; but the guides were still able to heft a spear or run all day on the jungle trails, if necessary."

Those two guys were the best. Damn that they had to pay the ultimate price, but the greater good and all that, he thought, and continued writing. Capturing the beauty of the Musquaeli village setting, the primitive nature of its people, and their culture would have been a difficult challenge for any writer, and Montana was hardly an accomplished writer in that sense. He kept on in his tedious process of trying to capture the images memory had left him of these remarkable people and their jungle home. As the pages quickly accumulated, he got deeper and deeper into his story.

The really troubling parts were yet to come, but for now he painted a fairly presentable canvas for his scientific readers, displaying a panoramic vision of the recurring dreams he kept having each evening.

He could not get the image of Urchuwa out of his mind, that strikingly handsome and passionate disciple of the war god he now possessed. He wanted his readers to appreciate the qualities of the man, including the special sensation one perceived that seemed as though it was caused by an emanation from his visage, as he wrote: "There was almost a glow about him that made his skin radiate, not with light as such but with an aura that defied physical description." He captured as best he could the tension in the atmosphere created by the reaction of the natives to the war conditions that were underway.

For the record he was making, Montana thought it important to portray the beautiful river setting where the battle was to take place. He must be careful here, for the secret he was hiding could accidentally be revealed if too much of the positions of the opposing forces were disclosed. He had not anticipated that the battle plan he had instigated would lead to the wonderful opportunity to steal the relic. He recalled for his future readers how the Indians' original plan to defend the sacred valley man-to-man had been modified after Elliot had suggested that they reconnoiter the proposed battle scene from the natural observatory before committing to the final plan.

He described how the eagle's-eye view of the valley had caused the final plan to be incubated in the council of war. He was quite proud of the way he had subtly suggested to Elliot that the final plan had to be seen as his, and how adroitly his assistant had picked up on it by suggesting three plans and staging it in a way that the plan picked was his; but he could never write for the world to see that his ego may have manipulated Elliot too far and left the final plan, which failed, as his own alone. *Couldn't have that! No way; no, sir!* he thought.

This version of history would never do, so he wrote his account in such a way that Elliot's plan had been conceived by Elliot, accepted by Montana, relying on Elliot's obvious military experience, but carried out by Elliot because he was Montana's military advisor and thus the one to blame for the failure that happened. It could be no other way.

The most delicate part of this historical revision was next to come in the only written record of this ill-fated battle that had resulted in the destruction of the Musquaeli people.

At the time, Montana had climbed up on the little mountain at the plug end of the valley on the left and seen the retreat as planned in execution, but he had also seen the approaching disaster of the well-timed arrival of the enemy reserve. A commander of a modern army in that position would have called in artillery strikes to break up the concentration, and a gifted military commander would have seen this as a possibility and had a backup plan with reserves in place. Montana was neither of the above and had no backup plan, much less modern artillery.

But he had seen an opportunity to achieve the only goal that meant anything to him, to steal the war god, and the fog of war that was about to descend over the field created a golden opportunity. However, this written version of the tragedy could not be that truthful. He had started out that day with the noble objective of bringing the idol up to the battle scene to see if it would help his side in the desperate fight in which they were engaged—or at least he was telling himself that.

Every component of his complicated ego rejected the idea of there being such a thing as a spirit power, a scientific materialistic belief that dwelled indelibly in the marrow of every intellectual bone in his body—or wherever his deepest beliefs resided—but he could never imply that he had decided to steal the thing, no matter what happened.

His strategy for the account he was putting together allowed him to justify the retrieval of the war god from its hiding place in the small temple without any danger of revealing his true motive. His depiction of his attempt to give the Indians spiritual assistance—whether he believed in it or not—at the time would be applauded by his scientific readers. In a sense, it was an experiment to see what emotional effect a belief in the supernatural had on those simple people who believed it. But he could not argue that this alone was his purpose, for some of his more sensitive readers might take offense that he was playing with their religious beliefs.

But his bringing the war god to the battle scene could never be criticized, especially since he had created the story that Urchuwa had pleaded with him to go and get it. *Let the analysts discern that I was as surprised as they were that the little stone object may have some strange aspect. This will only add intellectual curiosity and elevate my fame in the process.*

Montana told—or, better yet, let others discover by his understatement—how by following Urchuwa's instructions he had found the hiding place of the idol. He wrote with excitement how he had hurried to the battle scene as instructed and discovered to his shock that the little piece of stone began to vibrate in his pack, an event totally unexplainable to his scientific mind, and had vibrated even more the closer he got to Urchuwa.

He had been careful not to mention the vibration at the conference, but that detail was too juicy to leave out now. He had also noticed at the time that, when he had reevaluated his chances and the prospects of the battle and moved back to his leftward position of safety, the vibration had stopped. It was only much later, after he had escaped with the idol and his life, that he had put together what had really happened and reluctantly came to the conclusion that his decision to leave Urchuwa's side of the battlefield had actually caused the disaster, but he would never expose this dirty little secret.

He would never admit to anyone that he had made up the story about Urchuwa seeing that the battle was lost and asking him to bring the idol to him for spiritual assistance and, when even that seemed to fail, persuading him to take the idol to safety.

As he told that false story to himself over and over again in a vain attempt to eradicate the unpleasant aspects, it had come no closer to being truthful, even to him. But he concocted a beautiful scene of Urchuwa seeking him out on the battlefield and pleading with him to leave the sacred grounds with the idol so that it would not get into the hands of his hated enemy.

The story's detail had grown with each mental recital, and he had perfected this song until it resounded like a symphony in his head. A dark and brooding one for sure, but music of a majestic kind nonetheless to his willing ears.

He now undertook to turn his memory's mosaic into a masterpiece on the canvas of the written page. No detail was left out of the shaman's entrustment episode he had created with such imaginary embellishment because without it his secret would be blown, and that would never do. He had confidently claimed in his press conference that Urchuwa had loved the idol more than what it could do for him or his people, and he was standing by that now in his writing.

The last of the extraction story was easy to write because it was comprised of none of the unpleasant things buried in his memory. He could not be blamed for the loss of the tribe since their warfare had gone on for generations, often with terrible consequences, and was well known to the scientific community. He confined the rest of his book to the truly anthropologically significant events of his many trips, for which he had a traveling library load of information to draw upon. This process took many months, but he was lost in the pleasure of reconstructing a career's accumulation of knowledge.

This was the kind of stuff the Mead committee loved to read about, and he knew it, so he left the battle scene behind and made that walk down memory lane with much pleasure. The process continued all through the fall, winter, and the next spring as he could fit it in with his teaching and other scholarly duties at the college. By the end of the next summer, he was nearing the end of his book and put off the dreary task for a few days, which itself would take more weeks of editing his own words he had so lovingly created and placed on paper. Killing any one of his accounts for reason of context, fluidity, or even the beauty of expression was painful to him, as with most writers, scientific or otherwise. But he finally steeled himself to the task and finished the manuscript and went about the business of getting it ready for publication.

18

Fantasy Impromptu

Life had gone on as usual that year on the home front. By the end of the next summer the weather was finally moderating in Hedley, the stifling heat and oppressive humidity of summer gradually replaced by cooler evenings and more pleasant days, much to the relief of the community. Montana sat at his writing desk with the finished manuscript in front of him, and the satisfaction of finally being finished gave him pause to reflect back on the road he had traveled. The memories of the choices he had made confronted by the motivation of scientific achievement and dreams of finally gaining the professional recognition he thought he deserved raged like a war within him.

First, the dreaded unpleasant memories he had tried so hard to suppress had gained the upper hand, and he wondered how he could go any further with this project and continue to live with himself. However, those awful demons of his lesser nature were pushed back by pleasurable fantasies of being nominated at last for the Mead Award, and that this time he might actually win it. Although he was rapidly moving out of the age bracket from which the usual crop of young scholars generally considered were drawn, he understood that hope does spring eternal within the heart of man, at least in his own vision of things to come. The contest within his psyche went back and forth, savagely at times, with the dark side gaining the upper hand before being repulsed by the light.

Where would this battle for his very soul end up, and more importantly, when would it end? His sanity demanded that it be soon. The angel of mercy finally gained the upper hand over the god of justice, and the more unpleasant spirits within his tortured mind receded into his unconsciousness, where they would not distract him again. It wasn't a perfect resolution, but as it always had been with him, it was a solution he could live with. He turned his attention to the next obstacle, finding a publisher.

Finding a publisher for a manuscript can be a challenge for any writer, especially an academic one. Every serious college professor well understands that his department head expects him to have published works out there for recognition of the department, even though much of this literature is rarely read. The pressure to do this may be ameliorated somewhat by the exalted status of tenure—very much the department head's bane—because it takes away the threat hovering in the background that gives him talking control in the little battles that go on over budgets, staff assistants, and student assistant allocations.

Although Horatio Averill Blake, PhD, was not a name on the lips of the scions of anthropology, he was published well enough in his field. However, he still—and often—fantasized it would be so at the occasional academic conference they all attended.

Let me see . . . Where did I put my copy of last quarter's AAA journal, the least read document in my library? he thought as he looked under a stack in his publications cabinet, that place where valuable but rarely used publications, books from his rivals, and other such materials were kept. Pretty soon he found it and quickly thumbed through it to find the publisher advertisements, a good starting place in compiling a prospects list.

He had been published almost exclusively by Routledge Press and, of course, out of loyalty would send one manuscript to them. But he was interested in a wider audience, so he would also submit to the usual players in academic circles, like Cambridge University Press, the University of Chicago Press, Oxford University Press, and University of California Press, where the big names in the association were published.

Commercial publishers, including Routledge, Palgrave Macmillan, and AltaMira Press, rounded out his list of publishers known to be interested in his type of work. But he was interested in a wider audience than the egghead set, so he began a search for publishers of more general reader interests. He happened to run across the name of a publisher in Los Angeles, Paragon Press, that had a prestigious address on Wilshire

Boulevard. Montana had never been to Los Angeles, but recognized Wilshire Boulevard as a street of commercial significance in that city. So he added Paragon Press, at 5055 Wilshire Boulevard, Suite 864, Los Angeles, to his prospect list alongside the usual big houses, like Penguin Random House and HarperCollins, that were into volume productions, who would get copies along with the others, but he never expected them to seriously consider it.

The next task was to take the manuscript to the local copy center and have fifteen copies produced, double-spaced for easy reading, and then arrange for the shipping parcels and address labels to make the application look professional. He knew from experience that most publishers had screeners who read the first few chapters for interest; and if they approved, the manuscript made its way up the chain of command, where more and more of it was scrutinized to see if this, among the many reviewed, was actually worthy of publication.

A nice presentation of manuscript and query letter was necessary to attract the first screener's attention, to at least give the book a chance. Most would reject it early on in the process, especially the commercial publishers, who had the profit motive as their overriding concern in the selection process. With staggering printing and promotion costs, publishers would not waste their precious resources on what they thought were losers.

Some of the academic houses were more tolerant of manuscripts written by recognized scientists and would give it more attention before rejection if the material was consistent with the publishing house's criteria for subject matter that publishing season.

The query letter was just as important as the first few chapters of the manuscript to make sure the attention of the screener was drawn to the story, so Montana doubled down on this part of the overall effort. He wrote the letter with care, revised it ten times over the next few days, sleeping on it for a few nights, and then late one evening, with a dramatic flourish no one could see or hear, stood with his arms outstretched and shouted, "Done!"

As far as he was concerned, the penultimate part of this enormous project was over. The final difficult task was to assign a title. He had actually given this matter quite some thought during the creation of the manuscript. The title that had been rummaging around in his head was "Containment or Consequences: A Search for Tribal Survival." It was a title with a note of mystery and a hint of adventure. With that, it was done. The next day, the bulky packages were dropped at the local commercial mail drops for pickup by UPS and delivery. All he could do now was endure the waiting.

19

Unintended Consequences

It was a busy day at the screenwriter's agency of Ansel, Livingston & Stone, located at 5055 Wilshire Boulevard, Suite 865 in Los Angeles, when the manuscript and query letter of Dr. Blake's arrived the next week along with dozens of other manuscripts of varying length. In the usual practice at the agency, the query letter and packaging were separated from the text by the receptionist girl, Anna Starke, who could fly through her assigned tasks with seemingly reckless abandon but nonetheless a thoroughness that impressed her employer.

As a regular practice to save time and having been trained to avoid all the self-serving pap that permeated these things, she discarded the packaging and letter without noticing both were addressed to someone else in the same building on Wilshire Boulevard. The agency was owned by the three named partners who had all made their reputations in Hollywood by finding that unusual book or screenplay and, by the creative magic of rewriting, often turned an apparent sow's ear into a silk purse.

They had a bright, young staff of wannabe screenwriters working as temporary employees—just waiting to be discovered by somebody—to review each submission, and carefully trained to reject all but the most promising materials, which were then passed along to the partners for serious scrutiny. The review-every-proposal philosophy had become ingrained at Ansel, Livingston & Stone ever since that fateful summer many years ago when John Ansel had stumbled across the manuscript of a first-time, then completely unknown author, Jules Strothers, whose opus one had been turned by Ansel into the screenplay that became a sensation at the Academy Awards a few years later.

Mr. Ansel's instruction to each new crop of reviewers was to read every proposal no matter how boring but reject without mercy if the story didn't grab and hold the reader to the end. "Pass along the best and trash can the rest" he was fond of saying. And each year a vast quantity of stories—some good, mostly really bad, and some just plain terrible—passed through the screening mill with only the very best making it to the experienced eyes of John Ansel, Bob Livingston, and Carol Stone.

The manuscript of Montana Blake—intended for Paragon Press at Suite 864 on Wilshire Boulevard—found its way instead to the screening floor of Ansel, Livingston & Stone at Suite 865, sans address label and query letter. The aspiring young screener Andrea Lester happened to be in the "stable," as the gang of twelve maintained by the firm called itself, when it arrived.

Andrea was a recent graduate of UCLA with a degree in English literature and creative writing. She loved the written word's ability to express emotion, describe things seen and imagined, and move readers to identify with characters in their struggles and victories in life. She hoped to someday find her own niche as a writer, probably in fiction, but was open to whatever the Fates had in store. She was convinced, with the enthusiasm and optimism of youth, that a career as a writer awaited her. She had taken the temporary job with the agency as a screener for the experience, and even though the pay was minimal, she was convinced she would find her own path to stardom, whatever that turned out to be.

Andrea was a fast reader with an uncanny ability to concentrate with almost a fixation on the manuscript before her so that she was oblivious to the chatter that went on around her.

"Hey, Andrea, get a load of this," the annoying scratchy voice of Davis Liberstram said from the desk next to hers. "This guy couldn't paint a word picture if it came to him in a say-it-by-the-numbers kit. Listen to this: 'The sun rose over Stillwater Creek again that morning as it had done for a million years'—what is that trying to say?"

She ignored Davis and continued with her reading. The opening chapter of the Blake manuscript caught her attention, especially his description of the journey into the headwaters country of the Amazon and his somewhat colorful description of the primitive natives and their culture. She flipped on ahead, scanning the story with her "see the big picture but spare the details" reading style to quickly pick up the action portions and see if the story had any potential for entertainment, before doubling back for a more careful reading and analysis.

She discovered, to her interest, the description of the battle scene near the end of the story. Its ebb and flow of individual combat was not unlike that of many movies where an escalation of tension leads toward disaster with a miraculous escape before building up again.

Then she spotted the description of the magnificent character the Indian shaman and how his presence on the battlefield was a kind of talisman that at times seemed to spur on the combatants to greater efforts. From her reading of earlier chapters, she had noticed the dominant treatment the narrator was playing and figured this might very well be somewhat autobiographical and not just another attempt at the great American novel she so often read.

But in the final battle scene of the story, the egocentric narrator was more understated and seemed to dissolve into mere spectator. This puzzled her. Especially puzzling was the mysterious scene at the end when the Indian shaman made a gift of the war god while his people were about to be wiped out. The narrator's escape with his life down the vine ladder chute, thanks to the sacrifice of his faithful Indian guide, was reminiscent of one of the Die Hard or Indiana Jones movies.

From her cursory reading and the passable writing style of the author, this story passed Andrea's test for handing it up to the partner level for more thorough scrutiny. It was odd because, as the first project of the day, it didn't seem right that she hadn't warmed up by rejecting a few miserable manuscripts, of which most submittals made up a stockpile, or ready rejectables before finding her first acceptable one.

She intuitively understood that she must meet the high standard of respectable skepticism the agency maintained, or she would be earning her livelihood teaching an elementary class or finding a survival niche in the personal service industry.

Her final task for a selection was to write up an analysis of the manuscript and make suggestions for directing this project toward the goal of becoming a successful screenplay. In the case of Dr. Blake's manuscript, if accepted—a very big *if* indeed—a skillful screenwriter would have to take this very raw manuscript and turn it into a project that could be pitched to a studio.

She concluded her summary report with this endorsement: "The story has potential for an action film in the Indiana Jones genre without being a mere copycat. I can't be sure, but there is a possibility this material is autobiographical, and an authentic experience reported. If a contract is placed with this guy, make it clear that someone with the gift for turning novels into screenplays will definitely be required with full license to alter details to make the story sellable. In my humble opinion, this piece deserves scrutiny at the partner level."

Andrea signed the report, bound the manuscript and her report with the Ansel, Livingston & Stone money-colored green ribbon, placed the bundle in the cart for that purpose, and picked up the next manuscript. *This next one is bound to be a dud, or am I just getting soft?* she thought.

20

ELSEWHERE

The fate of the Blake manuscript was entirely different at the more traditional academic publishers, and in these cases the query letters made it to the reviewers along with the correct address. The University of Chicago's reviewer rejected the manuscript because they weren't publishing anthropology texts that season. Oxford University Press already had two manuscripts from this category in the process of editing, so with the pipeline full, the routine rejection letter was coughed up and out to Dr. Blake in about a week. It had the usual "we were impressed with your contribution to the record of the study of ancient indigenous people, but unfortunately . . . yada, yada, yada" in a standard one-page letter without the return of the manuscript.

No publisher would ever pay postage to send rejected manuscripts back home. After all, they were the one doing the author a favor just by reviewing it. University of California Press took a bit longer, and Montana's book actually made it up the line to a final cut before it too joined the chorus telling Dr. Horatio Blake that his hard work to produce this tome wasn't worth the time and money of this institutional house in the cloistered set.

The commercial houses, like Palgrave Macmillan and AltaMira Press, always motivated by the need to actually make a profit on the sale of books, were tight-fisted with their rare approvals, and this offering was no different. It was a no go from both, and the polite letters saying so were soon making their inexorable way to Hedley, Florida, where they joined the daily unanimous chorus of "we do not accept this work for publication."

Routledge Press was a different story because of its history with Montana Blake. Routledge had published numerous scholarly articles in the field of anthropology, including his. A book like this was different because the financial investment was significantly greater. The review job was assigned to Alec Gustafson, one of the better reviewers. Alec had not been in the industry for long, but he had cut his teeth on one of Montana's articles, and in an effort to make a good first impression, he had done significant research on the subject of Stone Age cultures before tackling the article.

The investment had paid off too. He'd spotted right away the extremely close connection that Montana had built up with the Musquaeli people and saw that the fruits of his labors had yielded many anecdotal personal stories, and the richness of the accounts was impressive. The article had been published in one of Routledge's scientific journals after a lengthy peer-review process. For a first-time review assignment it had been—for Alec—a stunning rookie success. It earned him a permanent seat at the screening table, and he was careful to make sure that he stayed there.

So screening the manuscript "Containment or Consequences: A Search for Tribal Survival" was the task at hand. Alec tore into this assignment with reckless abandon. This was not the usual serious scientific effort with data exhaustively accumulated to test and hopefully prove the author's hypothesis. This offering was more like an adventure novel than the serious contributions this publisher normally considered.

There was all the more reason for Alec to really dig into this one. He could not afford to rely on the professor's past accomplishments to carry his load for him. It had to stand the more rigorous literary test and affirmatively answer the question of whether the reading public would find enough interest to buy the thing and, better yet, tell all their friends this was a book worthy of their time. That is what successfully sold a printing of this or any other type of book.

But Dr. Blake did not have the built-in following that successful novelists often attain. Once a winner has been distributed, promoted, read, and talked about and that lovely niche of eager expectation is achieved, the follow-on publication success is easy to predict. You can get away with one dud, possibly; but like a good restaurant, the taste and service have to meet expectations time and again, or the pent-up demand will fade like granny's cups and saucers. Alec understood this and was not about to be responsible for suggesting that this manuscript be accepted for publication unless he really thought it was of that repeat caliber.

As he read the manuscript, the story began to fascinate him. It was a curious mixture of adventure and science. The writing style was a bit labored, as many scientific writers tended to be consumed with their subjects. Better novelists understood that their interest was not as important as the reader's and performed accordingly. Most scientific writers had such a love of their subject that they couldn't conceive that everyone else didn't see the subject matter in the same way. But this story had a real mystery to it, and the author's emotional investment—although egocentric to the extreme—had the unanticipated value of serendipity to it. Even though the professor tried his best to camouflage his personal ambition in telling the tale, it showed through in verdant hues of desire and deception.

Alec thought the book attractive because it revealed its true purpose in spite of the attempt to cover it up. It had enough anthropology stuff to satisfy the scions that ran the old Routledge Press establishment, but enough excitement to liven up the stately old scientific publishing house. It just might be a winner. He pored over the battle scene chapters and noticed with curiosity the role Dr. Blake continued to assume for himself, pretending to care about the Musquaeli tribe all the while. It was the cleverest piece of rationalization given in the name of science he had ever read, and he found it amusing. It was not quite comic opera but close to it and cloaked in a serious purpose. *This may even be a new genre of literary art, self-deception in the name of science*, thought Alec as he finished his last reading and typed up his summary and recommendation for publication.

21

A FOOLISH CONSISTENCY

Montana received the steady stream of rejection letters with mild amusement, consternation, and then disappointment as one after another made its methodical way to the Blake household, and it finally began to sink into his self-absorbed brain that he just might not get any publisher to accept his beloved manuscript. After all, he only needed one, didn't he? But he had not given up hope entirely, for his old reliable friends at Routledge would not let him down. And on this issue at least, Montana was right.

The envelope from Routledge came three weeks later. He sat in his study and held the unopened envelope in his hands, staring at it as if he could divine its content without actually having to open it, find out the truth, and maybe discover that no one, not even his old friends at Routledge, had found his contribution worthy enough to publish.

At this point he had even stopped dreaming of an offer of a cash advance. He would almost be willing to make a contribution for publication costs. *But seriously now, I'm not that desperate yet, am I?* He was just about to summon the courage to open the envelope and overcome his fear of rejection when the twins came rudely bounding into the study.

Montana glared at the boys and said, "What, pray tell, is so important for you boys to interrupt me in what just may be the most important moment of my life? Well? Answer me."

Ratio saw that they had blundered, and turned to his old tricks.

"Average, I told you Dad was busy this morning, but you insisted that we come in here right now. See, I told you so. You really blew it this time."

Average was dumbfounded.

"Average Blake!" his father almost shouted, from the heart of his own intense frustration, a condition he would never acknowledge, much less admit, as long as there was a convenient scapegoat around.

"Sir" is about all Average could manage, for he knew that excuses and protests about his brother's dishonesty would fall on deaf ears. He instead fell back on the time-tested safe harbor: say nothing and take the heat until it passed. It didn't change his hatred for his brother because of it.

"You boys—and you especially, Average—have come into my office at the worst time. No! I don't have time for this! Get out, the both of you! Get out, now!" he shouted.

Ratio grabbed Average by the arm and said, "Later, Average, like I told you. Dad's busy; this will keep." And without further ado, the boys left.

Montana finally calmed down enough from his own fear and immense frustration and used his silver letter opener to carefully lift the flap of the envelope, turning it over so that he could read: "Dear Dr. Blake: It is with great pleasure . . ." The relief was so overwhelming, rolling over him like giant breakers at the seashore in wave after wave, each one greater than the last, that he hardly had the courage to read the rest, afraid that the ecstasy of the moment would end.

But in time, as all such raw emotion must do, his excitement subsided and he was able to complete the rest of the most delicious communication he had ever received from a publisher. Routledge wanted to publish and distribute not only to college libraries, as usual, but to the general audience market as well. The details had to be worked out, they said, but a contract with a substantial advance was on its way from their lawyers.

Montana could already envision a copy of *Containment or Consequences: A Search for Tribal Survival* in the usual booksellers, like Barnes & Noble and Amazon. But dreams of recognition in the *New York Times* Best Seller list as well as congratulatory calls from jealous colleagues danced in his head like so many sugar plum fairies in a Christmas fantasy land. It could not get any better than this, and no reality could match the dreams he was creating this beautiful summer afternoon. He could die right now and go to Heaven, if there was a God and a place like that, a notion he personally rejected, but it could be no better than this. The first rational thought he had was, *Who do I tell first?*

22

NEXT IN LINE

The partner review meeting was called to order by John Ansel as they gathered in the richly appointed room to discuss the collection of the best prospects recommended for their review. Each partner had been randomly assigned a few manuscripts for the necessary second review. No matter how gifted their young crop of literary geniuses really was, experience trumps inspiration.

"Carol, why don't you go first. What do you have that looks good this morning?" John asked.

Carol reached into her stack of materials and pulled out the summary of the manuscript somewhat amateurishly and melodramatically entitled "Containment or Consequences: A Search for Tribal Survival" and began her summary pitch to the partners.

"Well, gentlemen, in spite of a vainglorious title—in fact a good bit of this work is steeped in vainglory—it was written as a scientific piece in anthropology and authored—if you can believe the name—by Horatio Averill, nicknamed 'Montana' Blake. In this story, the professor returns to the headwaters of the Amazon to make a further study of the Musquaeli people, an isolated, primitive tribe hidden in the upper reaches of scenic rivers that feed the Amazon. Our narrator is the same Montana Blake, a professor from a small college on the Florida Panhandle.

"According to the reviewer, the story is probably autobiographical since it was supposedly headed for publishing by Routledge Press, a scientific house, until it somehow made its way here. It would not have been a fit for Routledge anyway, because they have never done fiction and would not have started with this piece. The name seems to be authentic, down to the Montana moniker, and not some Indiana Jones imitator, although it might be difficult to distinguish the two. Where the cognomen comes from is unknown at this point.

"Anyway, Montana and his team, comprised of Elliot Drake, a former US Ranger with considerable experience in guerrilla fighting, and their two Indian guides, whose ancestry is from the same tribe, reunite with the Musquaeli village located in the Andean Mountains of Peru near the headwaters of the Amazon River."

She continued, "Apparently Professor Blake has made his anthropology reputation by studying this tribe and others like it. He was a runner-up for the Margaret Mead Award a few years back, when he was much younger, based on his work with these people in a specialized study of how their religious beliefs fit into their history of war making. They are believed, according to Professor Blake, to possess a 'war god,' a stone image that is supposed to grant their warriors favor in battle.

"Blake has never seen the idol before this trip since it is guarded carefully by a rather magnificent physical specimen of an Indian shaman named Urchuwa, and none of the tribe—much less an outsider like the Blake team—has ever seen it. But they believe in its mystical powers, and so long as the Musquaeli have control of it, according to Dr. Blake, the Musquaeli win every battle.

"Apparently—unknown to the team beforehand—a war is brewing with a neighboring tribe that if not won would threaten their survival. Montana convinces Urchuwa to allow Elliot to reconnoiter the surrounding jungle and devise a defensive battle plan, which Montana, the egotist that he is, quickly confiscates as his own. While the tribe's warriors and Elliot are busy implementing their defensive maneuvers, he takes the opportunity to search for and finally gets to see the little black obsidian stone idol the tribe relies on for their survival. Somehow, by a process he will never be able to explain, Urchuwa learns of his violation of the secrecy rule, but entrusts him to bring the idol to him at his crucial location on the battlefield at just the right time. Although having finally seen the little idol and desiring to have it for his reputation as a cultural anthropologist, Montana has a loyalty to the tribe and resists the temptation. The plan, which Urchuwa has endorsed, is to lure the invading warriors down to the end of a mountain valley, where the Musquaeli warriors, with Elliot's help, can close the door of the trap and destroy them. Montana, as instructed, brings the war god with him to join Urchuwa, but the plan falls apart as Urchuwa's position is about to be overrun. Realizing that all is lost, Urchuwa makes a gift of the war god to Montana to save it from falling into the hands of the dreaded enemy.

"Our reviewer finds this odd, however, since the egocentric personality of the narrator, who dominates on all fronts, seems to suddenly become compliant and understated at the end. Montana humbly takes his gift, which was his main objective of the expedition from the beginning, and somehow manages to escape with his life.

"Andrea thinks if we try to market this book with a decent screenplay, some literary license needs to be employed. I think a gifted screenwriter could do a lot with a supernatural war god that, to a Western scientific mind like Blake's, seems to be just a stone art object. Montana is shocked when the little idol actually appears to have supernatural powers, and works its will on the battle as he moves toward and away from the shaman's side of the field.

"It could either be a great struggle of conscience between loyalty to the tribe and scientific skepticism, or some other plot twist that only these guys can create, or a seismic tremor in his core belief system that anything supernatural just could not exist in his world of scientific materialism, which leads him to get out of there. It would be a personal crisis either way.

"Andrea advises—and I think she shows great promise as a judge of talent and a shrewd strategic thinker—that any contract we may write up should guarantee us the right to change the facts of the story to make its chances for sale to a studio more likely. We don't want this guy, with his enormous ego, trying to control the script or the plot anyway, agreed?"

The others nodded their heads without yet having made a commitment to this selection.

Carol continued, "Gentlemen, I like this story and think it worthy of getting the professor under contract. The mixture of scenic beauty, Stone Age culture, scientific discovery, action adventure, superheated ego, and the shattering of comfortable beliefs and crude religious mysticism can be woven together into a stream of nonstop excitement that could be a real winner at the box office. I'd call it *Indiana Jones and the Kingdom of the Crystal Skull* meets *End of the Spear*."

"Wait a minute, Carol, isn't this just another Jones imitation? Could this guy really be named Montana Blake? It sounds too showbiz to be real to me," Bob said.

"We could check it out, Bob, but as Shakespeare said, 'The play's the thing,' and you have to admit it's a great drama story. I mean, it has it all. Action, adventure, war, blood and guts, breathtaking scenery, the questioning of basic beliefs over materialism versus religion, character development, you name it; in short, it has everything."

Carol continued, "I mean, guys, can't you just picture this magnificent native Indian shaman who believes with all his being that this little war god will save him and his tribe from extinction? He is one with his element and can't imagine that will ever change; then along comes one he believes is his friend, who manages—despite his scientific skepticism—to ruin everything he holds dear.

"Montana comes in as 'the Big Doctor,' which he insists that all the Indians call him, with his Western superiority hanging all over him like a Joseph's coat of many colors, and proceeds to ruin everything he has been studying for years as a scientist. A tragedy comes out of this for sure, but what an unenviable one to expect. Usually a tragedy celebrates goodness indirectly when the one who suffers does so unjustly. This one turns that myth on its head because Montana, who probably should suffer, if the truth were known, comes out winning academic fame on the corpses of his supposed friends. I mean that if the Big Doctor had left these people to their traditional methods of fighting—with or without spiritual assistance—they might still be there in all their noble, savage glory to this day. Won't the Hollywood crowd love that little twist and turn of moralistic thinking they so easily criticize in the rest of us?" Carol concluded, and sat down waiting for John's reaction, for his was the one that counted.

John sat there for a few minutes mulling over the two stories and internally comparing them to the one he had to pitch. It didn't take long to realize which one would carry the water because success with Hollywood was more important to the agency than his ego. There would be other days, and it was to some extent the luck of the draw.

"I'm sold. Let's sign the guy up and then assign the containment, or whatever you called it, to Bill Springer for a screenplay effort. Bill's the best, and this one needs his special talent for finding just the right mix among these varied elements." Carol tried to contain her excitement because a win was a win no matter what the contest, but she knew better than to rub it in this time.

"Where is that Florida town, Carol? How do we get this guy under contract the way we have to?" John asked.

"I checked on that. There is this guy our contract staff found down there who may be just right for this rather clandestine job. We can't deceive the professor, but we need to reserve the right to change the story if we have to, considering how convoluted the plot- and pride lines are. It's near Pensacola, a really small town by the name of Hedley, where his college is located. Anyway, Horace Finder is his name, if you can believe that name for a private investigator. Hails from Chipley, another country town, but operates all over that part of the Florida Panhandle, real redneck country, I'm told. Our contracts people say he is a frustrated actor and really loves this type of assignment. A very smart guy, like so many others who went to one year of law school before he decided to return to life, but understands that we can't mislead the guy and have it come back to bite us with a breach of contract lawsuit right after the studio signs on and is in the middle of an expensive overseas movie production."

"So you've talked to this guy, Carol?"

"No, not me, John, but our contracts people have. They think he's just the man for this job."

"So we offer him the standard package of a sign-up bonus and a contract for movie rights. He must agree to go on location just in case there's anybody left in the industry making movies on location with all the digital technology available these days, however the producer decides to do it. So tell him he can bring the family along as, you know, a fun and exciting trip. It has to be contingent on profits, you know? Many of these deals—no matter how good they sound—never turn a profit at the box office. But if it's a true winner, he'll do all right. It's usually enough, though, because every author has dreams of seeing his precious baby in lights. If he's the egocentric bastard you depict, he'll go for it. But I like the undercover angle just to be sure it's sold, but not oversold, if you get my drift."

"Then I can turn the contract boys loose?" Carol asked.

"Yeah, go for it, but I want regular reports, both financial and informational, from our Mr. Finder, you hear?"

"Yeah, I hear you, John. Consider it done."

With that the partner meeting was over for this round.

23

From There You Can See It

Chipley was a place a hound dog would love, and many did, if love was one of those things dogs thought about. It wasn't far from anywhere in town to where a deer, fox, or raccoon scent could be picked up on a cold December morning. But Horace Finder was not into deer scent or scent of any kind this morning, except the one wafting up from his fresh, hot cup of coffee, because he had just received a call from a new client—not just any new client, but one that had real possibilities.

He was sitting in his office on Main Street with an unrestricted view out onto downtown Chipley with its unoccupied parking stalls and empty meters on Saturday morning, the weekend shopping crowd having not arrived yet, if *crowd* was a good term for the few who straggled into town to buy groceries or hunting supplies this time of year. The city council hadn't figured out that parking meters didn't make any sense because they kept the shoppers away.

He was leaning back in his leather executive chair with his feet propped up on his credenza and his lovely young assistant's attention dutifully focused on him.

"This is some Hollywood book or movie agency that wants me to sign up some pinhead professor over in Hedley for a movie contract," he said in Sally's direction, knowing how much she loved movies, Hollywood actors, or anybody famous or soon to be.

"Who is it, Horace? Anybody we've heard of?" Sally asked enigmatically, as if there were anybody west of Chattahoochee that Horace Finder, the only private detective in West Florida east of Pensacola, didn't know all there was to know about.

"Yeah, Sally, we—that is, I—know him. It's that bag of wind on the faculty over at Fangleer College, Dr. Montana Blake."

"What's the big deal? Didn't you say 'movie contract'? Wouldn't a college professor jump at the chance to have his name in lights? Why do they need you to get a contract signed?" Sally pointed out.

"Now, Sally, don't go getting sensible on me, at least not where the client could possibly hear you. This is my kind of case, and I don't have to crawl around at night snapping compromising pictures either. All I have to do is smooth talk this guy into a standard contract that gives the studio and the agency the full right to alter the story without restriction. Usually the money makes it attractive enough with authors, especially first-timers; they could care less what shows up on film. But this one is supposedly different. They suspect he's hiding something and may be protective beyond the typical pride of authorship. The book is already being published by an academic publishing house, without much expected circulation beyond colleges, libraries, et cetera. You know, a very limited audience. The client wants me to come up with a plan, and the contract documents will arrive here tomorrow, priority mail. They're in a hurry. Any suggestions?"

"Let me see. What if you pretend to be a potential investor in the proposed movie based on his book, who got a tip from an inside source in Hollywood that his book was up for consideration, and you won't invest in the project unless you know it will be a winner, and from your experience in making hit movies you have learned the hard way that unless the studio has full control of the script and story line, the project rarely succeeds? You can tell him you won't invest in the movie unless that feature is in the contract, and that's why you've come all this way just to see him: to be sure he agrees to that and insist that it be written in the contract whenever it comes from Hollywood so you can be comfortable putting up the dough for the film. You can be lying through your teeth, but he will never connect you with the agency, and you will have deniability. The client will write that in the contract and just send it out by FedEx or UPS, and the good professor will be looking for it. But they need to be subtle and clever by having the control language in fine print somewhere so he won't see it at first, or—better yet—have him be the one to insist that it be so and then they add it. And of course they sign only after he has signed. What do you think, boss?" She drew in a long breath.

"I wouldn't be that clever—the last part, I mean. The guy may just say no, or he forgets or fails to ask. It has to be there from the start. But it's a good plan, Sally. Let's go for it. Write up a proposal, add my usual fee doubled, and we'll see what happens. Be sure there's enough in the budget to create the illusion of wealth, with the appropriate dress, car—rented, naturally—and accoutrements. He won't believe me as a high-roller investor in the Chipley style; I have to make it look good, if you know what I mean. Can you have it ready today?"

"Sure, boss."

24

TRAP FOR THE UNWARY

Average had been on his own all morning. He was tired of games with Ratio by the lake or anywhere. It was more accurate that he was tired of Ratio's antics, period. Not so much his brother per se, but the continual put-downs, the incessant manipulation to make him the fall guy, and the inferior status in the family he was forced to accept every day were beginning to wear on his usually submissive temperament. It was not that this condition was unusual, for he had learned to live with it. But with his father's preoccupation with his book project, Average seemed to keep stepping into it more than usual, and he was tiring of it. He didn't really hate his brother, he was just tired of being the brunt of every mistake, especially when he wasn't the one at fault—most of the time. Besides, something important had arrived that morning by delivery from the FedEx truck, and their father had made a special point at breakfast that he was not to be disturbed.

So, with nothing else to do after breakfast, he took a walk down by the lake. Ratio was off doing his own thing, so he had slipped quietly outside on his own. It felt good to be there alone in the early morning with the mist rising, watching for the gator eyes that occasionally popped up surreptitiously here and there across the surface of the lake like parallel periscopes. The memories of too many episodes in which he always seemed to bear the brunt of their run-ins with their father were heavy on his mind.

What is to become of me? he thought. *I am just no damn good. That's it, isn't it? It can't be me every time, but it sure seems to be. Ratio always gets the credit and I always get the blame. It's that simple, isn't it? But he sure seems to find a way to blame it on me, no matter that we both screw up. Father is just too easily upset by kids, but I always seem to be the one responsible or at least the one that gets blamed. Why is that? Am I just so clumsy that it really is my fault? How could I always be the one? I am just no good. I must have a screw loose or something. I wonder if Ratio just uses me or manipulates me to take the blame. Father is really easy to upset when he's preoccupied, like now with his precious book project, and I should be aware of that. But Ratio seems to find a way to dump all of the blame on me, and Father loves him more than me and he knows it, isn't that what it's all about? I should never have been born, and none of this would hurt so much, right?*

Average asked himself these questions but got no answer, as usual. His deep inner journey of self-pity was interrupted by the noise of a car approaching the house, so he turned away from the lake and hurried back to the house to see who was coming. Naturally, Ratio was there ahead of him.

Horace Finder arrived unannounced around midmorning at the Blake household in his rented Jaguar, which had been hard to find even with all the rental car agencies in Pensacola. Sally had found a way to have the agency change the Florida plates to avoid the telltale tourist label that showed on most rental car company license plates. A set of hastily obtained vanity plates stating MINE, shipped by FedEx from Tallahassee for this occasion, adorned the front and back of the Jaguar. It's amazing what one could do for an affluent client willing to pay all expenses and who's in a hurry. He had waited a sufficient amount of time before his arrival to allow the agency to approach Dr. Blake with a written contract proposal. They had told Horace when it would arrive so that he could time his arrival as he thought best. Having the proposal in Hedley at the Blake household for four days sounded about right to Horace. So much for planning since it arrived only that very morning, but he couldn't have known that.

He was dressed as he thought a movie investor might dress: business casual but expensive. Not too extravagant to maintain a planned under-statement, but rich looking nonetheless. He opened the door of the dark green Jaguar and turned to do a survey of the house and grounds as if he wasn't sure he had the right place. Ratio hurried over to greet him and find out what his business was so he could report immediately to Father and get the credit ahead of his brother.

"Hello, boys, could you tell me if I have found the residence of Professor Montana Blake, the famous anthropologist?"

"Yes, sir," Ratio said, "You have found him, mister, and who might I tell him wants to see him?"

"Here's my card, boys. Fred Wilson, at your service. Do you suppose I could have a few minutes with the great man?"

"Why don't you come on up to the front porch and have a seat while my brother and I go tell him."

The boys left their guest and hurried into the house to find their father.

"You go tell him, Average. I'll wait here and run the message out to the man. And that way if he's upset or too busy, since it sure sounded at breakfast like he would be—"

"Okay, I'll tell him," Average said, and ran down the hall to his father's office, which as usual was closed.

Ratio waited in the front room, where he could get the benefit of being there if it was a good interruption or let Average take the blame as usual if not.

Averill stopped at the door, pausing to decide whether to knock first or just to enter and take his chances. The door had an ominous if ordinary look in its closed position, saying in effect to him, "Keep out unless this is really important." *How can I really know what's best? Knock and have that sound interrupt his concentration, or just open it and plunge in. Either way it's a risk. I think I'll—*

Average hesitated for only a moment longer and then knocked on the door softly.

For the past hour, Montana had been deep in evaluation of the documents on his desk in front of him. He had read the letter accompanying the contract proposal many times before delving into the complicated language of the document that had come in the FedEx envelope delivered early that morning. Montana was conflicted about it, to say the least. One part of him was thrilled at the very prospect that his beloved book was even being considered for a film project, but another part could only imagine the consternation and jealousy it would bring from the academic community.

He had little regard for his university and college competition, who he thought hated him anyway, but being made a public figure in that sense was a little more than he thought he would want to tolerate. But the advance fee was very attractive, and the terms the agency offered to draft a screenplay and sell it to a film production company were beyond his wildest imaginings.

He was dreaming about the scientific expeditions he could take without the usual prostitution of his intellectual standards and arm wrestling over budgets to sell a prolonged visit into the primitive tribal areas of South America when he finally heard the persistent knock on his office door.

He rose from his chair and walked to see who this could be interrupting his precious study time. It could not possibly be any member of his family on their own since he had made it clear to everyone at breakfast that he was not to be disturbed in his study today. When he opened the door and saw Average standing sheepishly waiting for him, he said, "And what, young man, could possibly be so important as to make you forget my explicit instructions this morning at breakfast that I was *not to be disturbed?*" in a tone and at a volume that left no doubt that he was thoroughly agitated by this interruption.

Screwed again, Average thought. "I, I, that is, Father, I came to tell you that—"

Ratio waited no longer and rushed past his flummoxed brother and announced, "Didn't you tell him, Average? Father, a Mr. Wilson is here from Pensacola just to see you. He's driving a really nice car and looks like he might have something important for you."

Bastard, Average thought. *How did he get that out of what the man said?*

"Well, show the man in, boys. Average, why didn't you say so? You need to explain yourself better, son."

Average just dropped his head.

Finder was shown into Blake's study by the boys, who closed the door and left knowing full well they were not included in any of their father's business discussions.

"Dr. Blake, I'm Fred Wilson, and I'm here because in my business one has to find leads wherever he can get them."

"Are you selling something?" Montana said. "If you are, you have wasted your time, for I am interested in the least, especially today."

Finder perked up at that comment, which only meant one thing to him: Blake had just received the proposal from his client.

"Well now, Dr. Blake, we all sell one thing or another, even you, but that's not why I'm here, not exactly."

"Then what is it?" Blake demanded impatiently.

"Well, sir, I am an investor of sorts, so I am more like a buyer than a seller," Finder said.

"I don't have anything to sell, sir. So if you don't mind, please get right to your business and then leave, you hear? I'm busy today," Blake said.

"I'll get right to it, Dr. Blake. You see, I make it my business to find out who has something to sell, and unless I'm sadly mistaken—and I rarely am—you have something I am very much interested in buying, in a sense."

"I'm afraid I don't understand you, sir, not in the least," Montana said.

"Listen, Dr. Blake, I happen to know from my reliable sources that you have been offered a contract for the screenplay and movie rights to a story you have just had published with Routledge Press. Am I right?"

Montana was astounded by this disclosure because he had only received the contract offer by UPS that very morning. This guy was clairvoyant, lucky, or worse, but Montana was now curious all the same.

"I see. So how is that any concern of yours?"

"I am not interested in investing in these movie projects unless there is a real chance they will be successful."

Montana mulled this over for a moment and went on the attack.

"Mr. Wilson, is it? You must understand that my interest in this work is more than profit, so whatever you thought might persuade me one way or the other is a hound treeing the wrong coon, as we say down here."

Montana cocked his head to the side a little bit as if to decide if a different angle on things might reveal the right course to follow. Finder caught the not-so-subtle shift in the wind and, in the mode of a true professional, quickly changed his approach.

"Please do not misunderstand me, Dr. Blake. I am an investor, and it's true I will not invest without a significant prospect of a suitable reward, but my interest in the project goes further than just money. I have read several of your scientific works before this one, and your work with the indigenous peoples of South America is truly astounding."

"Oh, which ones, Mr. Wilson?" This was intended as a curve ball to this possible imposter. For what ordinary movie investor would have done that kind of research? But Horace Finder was not even close to being ordinary in the roles he played.

"Well now, let me see," Finder mused, as if trying to remember some titles he might have read several years past, but instead, he was recalling the list his assistant had prepared yesterday and that he had committed to memory. "I especially enjoyed *South American Stone Age Tribe Cultural Identities*, and there was one other one . . . Oh yeah, *Cultural Evolution among Primitive Tribal Groups*, both published by Routledge if my memory serves." Before Blake could quiz him further as to the actual content of either, he quickly went on to say, "In that account of yours, the shaman Urchuwa was a truly remarkable character. What intrigued me most of all was the devotion he had for his people and the way they reciprocated. I had always thought those tribes were such simple people, you know, Rousseau's noble savage and all that. But your work shows their society was—in its own way—as complicated as ours, from a societal perspective, I mean. Then, to cap it all off, you were able to gain his confidence, and by doing so, were accepted directly by the people, even in the middle of a war for their very survival. That being said, and with the disaster that caused the loss of the tribe, the modern world would never know how that complicated social process really functioned. It was an astounding report. And that is why, Dr. Blake, you must make this movie possible. It's in your hands, literally. The story of their little world needs to penetrate the consciousness of the wider outside world."

Finder paused to judge how his performance was going and noticed with glee that Blake was buying it, so he pressed on. "You see, Dr. Blake, you have to let this story be told. Not enough people get to read your truly remarkable books in the cloistered academic world. The story of the Musquaeli people will be told, at last, for all to see! But I told my sources that if you turned this project down—as sad as that would make me—I have to move on, even today unless I actually see you sign that contract. What shall I tell my connections, Dr. Blake? Is it a go?"

Montana Blake was not easily manipulated, but the appeal to shared scientific objectives, not to mention his enormous vanity, had worked. He paused for a moment longer and then sat behind his desk and pulled open the contract ready to sign.

"Thank you, sir. You won't ever regret this, but one more detail. I am told you will be the scientific advisor for the film, which would require you to go with the production company to the site and help with societal relations with the indigenous people, if necessary," Horace Finder said with a glow of appreciation showing all over his face.

Blake held the contract in his hands and paused for a minute, thinking about how this aspect would fit into his concept of things, and finally nodded his head in silent agreement and signed the document. Finder thanked him profusely again, shook hands and left the Professor's home office.

Satisfied with his morning's work, Montana placed the original contract in the return shipping envelope provided and called for Ratio to come and take the thing out so the public carrier could find it. He then sat down and imagined his name on the reader board of theaters all over America, taking pleasure in the jealousy and envy his academic colleagues would feel to see him become famous in public as well as in academic circles. And realizing that at least one financial sponsor of the project had the same interest as he did was something to think about too.

As Horace Finder drove away from the Blake residence, he looked in his pocket calendar for Carol Stone's cell number, which Sally had dutifully saved there for his convenience. After three rings, she picked up.

"Hello, Carol Stone here."

"Ms. Stone, this is Horace Finder on the Blake matter down in Florida you asked us about."

"Are you reporting already?"

"That's right, Ms. Stone. It doesn't take me long on an assignment like this."

"Well, Mr. Finder, we can't wait to hear. How did it go with the contract? Did he sign like we needed him to?"

"Yes, that's right, he signed it as is. And you know what? I don't think he even read it!"

"Way to go, Horace," came the reply, much to the satisfaction of both ends of the conversation. "You'll have to stop by if you're ever in California and give us all the details."

"Just send my check when you get my bill; that will be enough."

"You've got it," Carol said, and rang off.

25

IN SEARCH OF GOLD

"The pond had almost a mirrorlike surface this morning, when I got up to start a new day writing again," Bill Springer said to his colleague and friend, a feature writer for the *L.A. Times*.

"Sure does. Coffee's great, by the way. I could enjoy this aroma and the scenery every day with no trouble, buddy," Ed Heather said as he sat comfortably in Bill's study, with a view across the pond ringed by the tallest evergreen trees he had ever seen. Ed had made the long trek by rental car from the Spokane airport into the far reaches of northwestern Washington just shy of the Canadian border on scenic Lake Crescent, where his friend and phenomenally successful screenwriter, Bill Springer, had a sizable, well-appointed cabin to do his work.

Ed had come all this way trying to find his own way to fame by writing a biography of the great man. Bill and Ed had been friends since high school at Highline, a South Seattle high school. They had left Highline with ordinary middle-of-the-class academic standings but, with Rotary Club scholarships and generous use of student loans, had matriculated to the liberal academic enclave of Reed College in Portland, Oregon, where they had both discovered a love for creative writing. Or was it that the love of great literature had found and awakened in each of them a talent for putting ideas into written form?

From there Bill and Ed went their separate ways. Bill's degree in English—considering he was determined not to sign up for twenty years as a high school teacher—took whatever thankless and career-euthanizing job he could get just to sustain his addiction to travel and avoid the establishment of roots, whatever the cost. He managed to take whatever short-duration job he could get, including teaching in private schools, where a teaching certificate was not required for a one-year contract, and filling in the summer break with odd jobs while he tinkered with his writing style nights and weekends, ending up in LA in the process.

Ed had gone a more traditional route by getting a job writing special features at a community weekly newspaper in Salem, Oregon. With no small natural talent and a dedication toward making his mark in journalism, his baccalaureate major, one break after another had made it possible to land his dream job of being a feature writer for the *L.A. Times.* It was in this pursuit that he had honed his skill, writing about both the underside and upper side of life in LA. A breakout biography was next on his agenda, and there was no one better to start with than his friend Bill Springer.

Bill left college with lofty ambitions, but it was by chance that he stumbled into a handyman's job on a grip's staff at a movie production company in Hollywood. Bill had a mechanical knowledge and considerable skill in fixing things. His father, a career machinist at Boeing, could fix anything, and as a child of the Great Depression, had left home and high school to sign up for a machinist union apprenticeship program. Bill's father was indelibly marked by that social cataclysm with a frugality that he never lost even when his seniority in the shop provided a decent blue-collar wage. Those mechanical skills rubbed off in generous proportions on his son.

Getting a job, even as a handyman, on a Hollywood grip's staff was no easy accomplishment since those spots that occasionally came open usually went to friends and connections of fellow union members. But Bill was young, social, and a joiner and always on the lookout for new friends wherever he worked. He was keeping the wolves at bay that summer in a dead-end job working as a legal messenger. But in the course of making deliveries, he did get well acquainted with the Los Angeles County courthouses, the clerk's personnel at the various filing counters, the bailiffs for most of the superior court judges, and operations personnel at larger law firm clients.

One night after work he had dropped into a blue-collar bar by the inauspicious name of Darryl's Days End Tavern, or DDT to the regulars, including him, for a few beers before taking the bus from downtown LA back home to Pasadena, where he rented a studio apartment as a wall-bed month-to-month special, about all he could afford as a legal messenger. Occasionally he would get the higher paying job as a fill-in process server and be flush with cash for a few days, as he was that week. He sat in his usual spot in the bar, at a side table with a good view of who might come in, with the hope to find someone interesting to talk to and commiserate with over his terrible luck finding a suitable job for someone of his inestimable intellect. After all, he had a degree from Reed. But realistically, with career dropouts in abundance in the area, sporting degrees from UCLA, USC, UC Santa Barbara, and even Loyola waiting for their big chance in Hollywood, why should a Reed alum bum like him expect any sympathy from the hangers-on at DDT? "But you never can tell: luck springs eternal," he liked to say, butchering that tired old cliché just for fun.

Bill was well into his first six beers when she walked into the bar and looked around the dismal place like a newcomer that didn't know where to sit. She was about Bill's age and strikingly beautiful in a one-piece close-fitting dress as she stood there with arms akimbo as though waiting for the right seat to tell her "this one is it."

Bill could not take his eyes off her as his mind churned through the usual mental algorithm of the pickup lines suited for this precise situation. As usual, nothing came to him that made any sense, so he just got up and walked across the room to within a decent distance, close enough to show he was brave and serious but not so close as to frighten her into thinking he was stupidly aggressive.

"Hi, I'm Bill and a regular at DDT. Haven't seen you in here before. What's yours? Would you like a drink and some intelligent conversation? I might be able to find either or both for you," he said with his warmest "I'm safe, trust me" smile. She wasn't frightened or bothered, which he could sense right away to his relief.

"Oh, I'm Melody. You know, like the part of the song everyone recognizes and tries to sing along with? Works great when you're alone in the car with a Beatles' tune or whatever exit music you like real loud on the radio, but never works with karaoke," she said in a lilting voice, as if whoever named her had had some modicum of prescience before she said her first words.

"Great to meet you, Melody. Why don't you join me? It's over here on the side where you don't miss anything, if there is anything to miss, but safe enough from the occasional bar brawl that breaks out up there," he said, gesturing toward the crowded bar where a few of the regulars were in a heated discussion about some aspect of the Lakers-Spurs game on the bar TV.

"I'd love to join you, Bill," Melody said as Bill turned to lead the way over to his table.

They did the usual exchange of personality conversation, telling one another just enough to be at ease but not enough to open any wounds they had and assiduously avoided disclosing. They covered the safe subjects, including the weather, the latest nonpolitical and nonreligious news, a sketch of family background, and matters of personal interest.

As it turned out, they found a common interest in literature, he with his degree from Reed as an English major and a passion for the Romantic poets and she as a graduate of UC Berkeley with a major in psychology and a passion for Freud and Jung's delving into the underbelly of man's reason for being what he was.

"I've never really found myself since college," said Bill. "In a career sense, I mean. And it's hard to explain probably because I don't understand it myself. My dad is a union machinist, lifer at Boeing, and all that I brought away from home, other than a love for my parents, was this uncanny ability to fix things. Anybody we visited always saved up their list of everything that needed fixing. He was dynamite on that, you know, never saw a mechanical failure code he couldn't break, and I suppose I picked up most of that kind of stuff from just watching. He would always explain the problem and then let me do it. He would kibitz but let me do the actual work of the repair, so I learned a lot.

"Don't know how I ended up in English at Reed; maybe should have been an engineer rather than spend all those hours reading and thinking about Coleridge, Burns, and Wordsworth. But I loved it; couldn't help myself, it seems."

She held his gaze with those beautiful blue eyes that made him feel as though she not only cared about what he had just told her but that he was the center of her interest whether that was true or not. It was a real gift she had with people, he would discover, but right now he had taken the bait, hook, line, and all.

"Look, Melody, I'm running on too much about me; you haven't told me about you. Come on now, your turn, okay?"

"Well, there's not much to tell, really. I graduated from Berkeley on time with a degree in psychology. I was fascinated first with Freud, but Jung captured my real interest. I found the concept of the unconscious mind fascinating, you know, dreams and the archetypes explaining human behavior when reason offered no clue, but the pain of it all being real enough. I went on to get my masters and then my PhD from UC Davis. It was close enough to home in Vallejo, so I was familiar with Davis all right, but my grades and GRE scores weren't that great, and the competition to get into Berkeley's grad school is withering.

"But then I got lucky. After my doctoral dissertation on the Christian life and the unconscious was published, a Christian movie mogul—if that's not an oxymoron, huh?—who controlled Register Studios, at that time an up-and-coming movie production lot, happened to read it and called me after to offer me a job as an evaluator on the set. His idea was that if he understood the complex personalities of actors and directors as to what made them tick, you know, what pushed their emotional buttons, he could run a smoother ship.

"It turned into a fascinating job for me. All I had to do was get to know the crew on the movie set and behind it and keep the boss informed of what moved them. It's been fulfilling and fascinating. Like being licensed to have them lay on your couch and spill their emotional beans. The Hollywood zeitgeist is a curious mixture of elevated egos, deeply wounded pathos, and exaggerated or understated hubris, so it helps the boss clear the air. So even though I'm sitting in this dingy, smoke-filled bar risking my health to secondhand smoke in downtown LA with a complete stranger, I am a Christian who somehow escaped most of the atheistic influences at Berkeley with my faith intact. How about you?"

"Gee, Melody, most people avoid the R subject on the first meeting, but to be perfectly truthful with you, I've never really thought about it," Bill said, finishing off the last beer of his ironclad "six" rule and wondering how he could change the subject. He turned the conversation back to her.

"So what brings a doctor of psychology to DDT on a weeknight, then? I mean, for a Christian, isn't this a little out of bounds? Or are you slumming—psychologically speaking—Doc?"

She thought about that comment for a moment and said, "I find human personality fascinating. Take you for instance. And there are a number of 'yous' scattered around LA. Call it slumming if you like, but I find it interesting to discover what makes people tick. For example, you? You tell me you love great literature, and yet you are content to eke out an existence as a legal messenger. I mean, what are you waiting for, lightning to strike?"

And strike it did for lonely Bill Springer. That chance encounter in a working-class bar led not only to a close personal relationship with his intellectual equal but the remarkable opportunity of a job as a grip on a Hollywood movie production company. One thing led to another and Bill Springer wormed his way into a chance to edit a friend's screenplay. Before he knew it, his talent blossomed into recognition, and his career at his true calling as a screenwriter was born.

One success after another led Bill to the pinnacle of screenwriting success, and the rest was history. At Lake Crescent that day, Ed could not wait to get his friend's permission to write his biography and achieve his own version of critical acclaim. Bill Springer had become the best, and Carol Stone could think of no one else to write the Montana Blake story for a hit movie.

26

TALK ABOUT DIFFICULT CHALLENGES

I wonder where the next project will come from, mused Bill to himself as Ed started his SUV and backed out of the driveway at his Lake Crescent cabin. Within a day or so, his phone rang and to his delight it was his old friend Carol calling with a paying proposal. They wanted an original screenplay written for a very unusual scientific manuscript by a professor in anthropology from an unknown college down south somewhere.

There's one aspect of this project I like, he thought. *The original screenplay stuff has terrible odds, even for me, with so many wannabes flooding the market with the next "Great American classic" for film. But the Ansel firm has bought this one in the adaptation category and has the resources to pay me to try, even though it sounds dumber than a lamppost to make a profitable film out of some pinhead's scientific documentary. As the chronicler of the Charge of the Light Brigade said on an equally impossible mission, "Ours is not to reason why, but to do or die," or something like that.*

Some people find they understand themselves better if they speak out loud what muddles others' thoughts. Bill was one of these people, probably as the product of his profession as a screenwriter. Some of these folks believe that what isn't written down—of their best thoughts, in a journal of sorts—is lost. Bill's method, learned from his experience with and loving the expression of words for the pleasure of others, was, whenever possible, to speak his thoughts out loud with the same care that he reserved for his customers in the movie industry. Working alone as he primarily did, this became comfortable and rewarding.

He spoke into the recorder on his desk: "FedEx delivered the manuscript within a few days. I let it sit for a few more so it could seep into my conscious mind before tackling the unenviable task of making it my own. Melody was gone on one of her shopping trips for a few days, so I had the cabin all to myself.

"As I usually do with these projects, I curled up in my favorite chair with a comforting view of Lake Crescent and began reading the damn thing straight through without any analysis. The first reading is the toughest because the author still owns the manuscript and too much of his ego lies encrusted on every page like mold on a pie accidentally left out too long after Thanksgiving. I have to make it mine. Only seemingly endless repetitions will do that. All of them are like this because, with human nature being the self-glorifying phenomenon that it is—especially for writers—they just can't help themselves. The writing project is their baby, and each word has been labored over longer and with more pride than a mother giving natural birth, but without any of the pain.

"I finished the first reading in record time despite the subject matter. The book had obviously been written for an academic audience concerned with the nuances of how primitive people function in their cultures. I mean, how can a movie audience get interested in crude cooking utensils, or even weapons of personal destruction, the same way a collection of eggheads can while sitting around in discussion groups at the annual conference of the anthropological society?

"The second reading went slower, as I forced myself to absorb the geographic details, like the hand-over-hand access trail up the waterfall; the towering tree canopy; the abundance of chattering birds, monkeys, and other wildlife; and—most significantly—the picturesque lake scene where the war that destroyed this tribe would take place. Even Blake couldn't seem to help himself in describing the awe and mystery that emanated from it.

"Before I began any kind of individual character analysis, I looked for the basic archetypes, such as the white explorers or scientific investigators, the Indian guides, the local people and their habits, the postulated hated enemy tribe, and the local witch doctor or shaman. Now, right away, I found this shaman character interesting. Not only his unusual name, Urchuwa, but the complimentary descriptions Blake gave him, not only physically but also his courage, presence, and charisma. He was going to play a key role in the screenplay, that was a given.

"The third reading began to open up the story and make it mine. I began to think in terms of how I would write this story and even paused for significant periods there, by my own lake, to imagine myself living the experiences of the story. The long trek up the river, the tenuous climb up the unknown access route, the scene by the campfire, the buzzing of mosquitoes, and the anxiety of the unknown dangers.

"I could almost see in my mind's eye the first encounter with Urchuwa, standing tall, stately, and magnificent and trying to imagine what must have been going through Blake's mind. He was obviously on some sort of quest to extract the war god idol for himself as an archeological artifact. Right away the moral conflict started to become apparent.

"Try as I might to keep an objective attitude, the huge conflict between Blake the scientist and Blake the egocentric overachiever could not be put aside in my mind. Something was wrong here, both in the plot and the outcome. What must Carol Stone and her firm have been thinking? How to make a screenplay that would appeal to the typical movie audience out of this piece of self-serving garbage? 'Don't forget, Bill, old boy,' I told myself, 'you are the best. Read it again.'

"On the fourth reading some interesting insights started to emerge. Blake, the unredeemed egotist that he appeared from his writing to be, was covering something up. And the character Elliot Drake had to be more than what Blake portrayed him to be. He was an ex-Army Ranger, and yet Blake claims the flawed final battle plan is Drake's and blames him for the loss? How convenient. Who is this guy Elliot Drake, really? Poetic license suggests a different background than what Blake portrays.

"What if Drake is an ex-mercenary with an unsavory personal history? That would really play well into the story. Why is he doing this rather tame job of escorting an anthropologist into the jungles of scenic South America unless he is hiding from something?

"Questions, questions, only questions deserve answers. Carol said I had an expense account for this project. I think I need to learn more about this character Horatio Averill 'Montana' Blake. Hollywood will want to know whether this is a pandering imitation of Indiana Jones or a legitimate scientist in search of truth and the American way, so I had better find out more. As the great American novelist Henry James wrote, 'Character determines incidents, and incidents illumine character.' I could accept that axiom as appropriate for my task.

"I made a quick call to Carol, and she told me they have the rights to alter the story in their contract with the author and that a private detective in West Florida had scoped Blake out. She told me that if I needed to go see this guy to make the screenplay more salable, go for it. As soon as I could call to make a date with this Horace Finder, I got a flight out of SeaTac to Pensacola, Florida, the nearest city down there. Then I rented a car for the redneck trek to—what was it?—Chipley, Florida? Yes, Chipley.

"This was the most interesting part of the project because Finder not only had the psychological goods on Blake as an egomaniac, he had the whole nine yards of his reputation and personality. He described Blake as an ego looking for a place to take up residence and reign supreme from the throne of the kingdom of his own importance.

"Finder did me one better. He said since I was this close, I might as well drive over to Tallahassee and talk to one of the reporters who attended the press conference when Blake announced his 'big recovery.' 'An interesting guy, that Tony Callaway,' Finder said.

"Tallahassee wasn't that far from Chipley, so I headed over there and caught up with Callaway at the *Tallahassee Democrat* where he was the senior reporter. I asked his impressions of Blake without telling him of my suspicions, and he said, 'The guy seemed a phony to me. Not that he wasn't who he said he was, but that it hadn't happened the way he said it did.'

"I asked him what he meant, and he told me that he had been listening to Blake and it didn't make sense what he was saying about the Indian shaman deciding in the heat of battle to give Blake the idol that the Indians believed could win all battles for them.

"He said he asked Blake if the location of the idol had had any connection to the ebb and flow of the battle he had described, and he said Blake seemed stunned but that he recovered nicely. Callaway didn't think he could expose what he sensed was a lie, so he left it there. But it had always stuck in his gut that something strange had been going on with that idol. 'Blake knew it,' Tony said, 'but he took advantage of the circumstances and stole it to the detriment—no, to the death—of the tribe that he supposedly loved.'

"I thought I had mined this local vein for all it was worth, so I thanked Callaway, made a call to thank Finder, and drove back to Pensacola to catch a flight back to God's country.

"The more I thought about this project, the more interesting it became. From my reading of Blake's account through his own egocentric eyes, the outline of a screenplay began to appear. Blake manipulated the truth to justify his own egotistical rationalization by claiming the shaman Urchuwa asked him to save the war god at the expense of the very people the war god was supposed to protect. Poppycock! Drake, the supposed mastermind of the battle plan designed to fail, is made the fall guy for—guess who?—our author in chief. So how can I show this magnificent story of ideology, treachery, and personal ruin in the usual screenplay context of setup, conflict, and resolution?

"What are the inciting incidents, the plot points, and the key incident? I decided that Drake was the key to the story because there needs to be an inciting incident. I decided that, since the screenplay-and-movie-rights contract gives me the license to do so, I would create Drake to be an Army Ranger all right, but also a mercenary soldier of fortune. I built his character as a former soldier drowning in guilt over having abandoned his squad mate still alive, and violating the Rangers' code that nobody is left behind, nobody!

"In my screenplay, he joined the Blake scientific expedition seeing it as a safe harbor from his guilt as a mercenary. What logically followed in the plot points of the screenplay was that Drake was clever enough to propose alternative strategies for the battle plan that Blake was able to choose as he, Blake, designed it, and the disaster that followed would automatically fall on Drake's shoulders as Blake writes it.

"So how to resolve this conflict in Hollywood terms? That is the question. And what is the key incident? That much is easy: the key incident is the struggle that our unsavory protagonist goes through. Blake's intellectual side told him to use the vibrating idol to spur the tribe to victory. But the defeat of the tribe could afford him an excuse to steal the idol away. But how to resolve the conflict? As Shakespeare might have said, that is the question.

"I had to draw upon all my creative skills to solve this one. All the participants—Elliot, Wanei, Estova, Urchuwa, and the tribe—were dead except the prevaricator-in-chief, Montana Blake. Why not a mystical solution by having a numinous appearance by Drake or the shaman at the Oscars that only Blake can see but believes somehow is real or that the others see it also, real or not? Would that be plausible for Hollywood even? There is precedent for it in *Ghost*, and that plot sold.

"What would that do to Blake, the ultimate scientific materialist? But he has had a taste of the numinous with his own admitted experience with the vibrating idol and the corresponding changes in the tide of battle as he approached the vital incident. Maybe that would sell, but maybe not. Would it be wishful thinking for a screenwriter to suggest his own nomination or that this film might seriously be considered for an Oscar in some minor category? You're getting off track, Bill. Probably should reject that idea. Do I want to manipulate history? What do I care? This guy would deserve the exposure his fraud has hidden. I think I will write the best screenplay I can, earn my fee, and let history, justice, and the director take care of themselves. How's that for rationalization?

"All that being decided, I put pen to paper and began to write the opening scene of the screenplay. But first there was the matter of title. As I had constructed the story, every character had something to hide: Drake, his guilt of the past sins of war and mayhem; and Blake, his secret to cover up his betrayal of the tribe he was supposedly studying to protect and preserve. That left no doubt as to the title of the screenplay and hopefully the eventual movie: "Hidden." I then wrote the first scene with the initiating incident."

HIDDEN
by Bill Springer

FADE IN:

EXT. CAMPSITE - NIGHT

Jungle setting with a campsite alongside a scenic river. All MEMBERS OF AN ANTHROPOLOGICAL EXPEDITION asleep under mosquito nettings.

Men SNORING

DRAKE
(cries out, dreaming)

DISSOLVE TO DREAM SCENE:

EXT. BATTLEFIELD - DAY

ELLIOT DRAKE is flattened out in a hole, in a position of cover, with bullets zinging overhead, barely missing him.

BATTLE SOUND EFFECTS

>   NARRATOR (voice-over)
> Ranger Chalk Four—dropped in the wrong place on an ill-fated mission to capture a warlord in Mogadishu, Somalia. The survivors of the team were eventually recovered, which is well known to history. But the secret Elliot Drake, one of the rescuers, has carried deep in his conscience ever since is not.

>   DRAKE
>   (crying out)
> What the hell? Come on, guys, we have to get out of here!
>
> That's not good enough, Clark. Rangers never leave anybody behind, so get off your ass and follow me to cover.

>   CLARK
>   (yelling)
> I can't, Sarge, I'm hit. Can't walk. Shot to pieces, Sarge. Can you come get me? I'm going to die if you don't!

                    DRAKE (V.O.)
     Time's gone, man! Any fool can see
     that, right?

Sound of an RPG ROUND EXPLODING nearby

                    DRAKE (V.O.)
     If I wait any longer, we're all dead.
     But Rangers *never* leave their men,
     never, and that's gospel.

Drake crawls out of his hole and over to PFC
DARRELL CLARK's position.

                         CLARK
                   (in desperation)
          Thank God, Sarge, you came!

                    DRAKE (V.O.)
     No way to get us both out, no
     way! Dammit!

Clark lies unconsciousness. Drake quickly checks
for vitals.

                    DRAKE (V.O.)
     It's me or none of us. Seems clear.
     I'll say he was dead; no one will
     ever know.

MACHINE-GUN FIRE SUBSIDES

Drake makes his move. With one last check on
Clark's status, he hauls ass for safety.

                    NARRATOR (V.O.)
     And no one ever knew—not even the re-
     view committee that recommended Staff
     Sergeant Elliot Drake for a medal
     for bravery.

INT. HOTEL ROOM - NIGHT

Drake paces the room, sobs, then turns and rams
his fist into the wall, kicking over a nearby
chair. He starts to sob again, shaking his head
in regret.

                       DRAKE
                    (crying out)
     I could have hauled him out, dammit.
     I'm done with this. No more, dammit.
     Money isn't everything. Got to find
     some peace—somewhere! Somehow!

INT. TENT - NIGHT:

WANEI wakes, gets up from his cot, and shakes
MONTANA BLAKE awake.

                      WANEI
     Wake up, Big Doctor. Day come soon.
     Night fires done. Path above soon come!

Blake awakes, quickly surveys the scene, pushes
the sleeping Elliot into alertness, and issues commands.

                      BLAKE
     All right, men, everybody up and
     at 'em. Elliot, aren't you supposed

                    to be in charge of logistics? Where
                    are we, man?

                              DRAKE
                    (Hurriedly regaining composure from
                          the effects of his dream)
                    Right, sir, all hands alert! Wanei,
                    Estova, get our rations ready. All on
                    alert, men; the access is ahead. We
                    have to be up top by noon, men!

"From there it was a matter of stagecraft. The Elliot Drake dream was the inciting incident, and the scenes where Blake finally gets to see the war god, and his appetite for recovering it, set up the conflict. The conflict was the battle scene that Blake manipulates Drake to come up with. If it succeeds, it will be Blake's claim for glory, but if it fails, Drake's responsibility.

"Of course, as I constructed the plot points, Blake could not envision it happening as it did. Blake is a scientific materialist of the first order and cannot imagine that the little idol could actually have mystic powers. And to make matters worse, when he discovers without question that the idol not only has supernatural powers but that those powers could actually save the tribe, the final drama and vital incident are thrust on the audience. He wavers between duty to the tribe and his own ambition, but ambition wins out.

"Telling the story in the book is a marvelous covering of his guilt from having betrayed all that is honorable. Blake creates out of whole cloth the lie that Urchuwa pleads with him to save the idol from falling into the hands of the dreaded enemy tribe."

"I thought long and hard on how to end the screenplay. After thinking about the mysterious appearance of Elliot Drake or the shaman at the Oscars, I decided it was a bit contrived and would ruin whatever chance I might have for an Oscar on my own.

"But didn't I read somewhere that Blake was nominated for the Margaret Mead Award in anthropology at one time in his career as a scholar? So why not use that as an ending for the movie? The plot needs a traumatic climax; otherwise, what is the point of the exposure? The awards scene just might do it. I would change the name of the organization presenting the award, obviously; no reason to disparage that organization for having chosen what the movie script will expose as a fraud. Let me see, I think I will call it the Lucius Larksburger Award instead.

"It could end there, but I think I'll wait for the decision by Carol's firm about whether to create the juicy ending that would satisfy my taste for justice, if nothing else. Instead, I'll have the camera fade away from this emotional scene of an aftermath of the betrayal and refocus in Ecuador at the final battle scene as Blake is shown selling out the Musquaeli tribe by running away from the battle to save his life and taking the war god with him. All have something to hide, and I'll bet that Blake will be one surprised puppy if this movie is ever made, which I sincerely doubt. Since this story actually happened to some extent, it would not surprise me if the tragedies for all the survivors are worse than even I have envisioned.

"I finally wrapped up the story in my best screenplay form, checking to be sure I achieved the best visual effects, and shipped it off to Carol Stone for the Ansel firm to do its magic of trying to actually sell the beast. Good luck. I have to say it was a challenge, but the money was good."

27

THEN YOU HAVE TO SELL IT

The partners met to review Bill Springer's work product, which had arrived the week before. Their investment so far in the project was manageable, and all three had confidence in Springer as an accomplished screenwriter. Now the hard part was selling the thing.

It was an unusual project, so the typical approach of pitching it to several studios would not work. So why waste the effort? Carol's suggestion was to reverse the odds by going to a producer who would dearly love this type of product. And it was important to find one who had the desire and the money to make it work. After all, the partners understood how Hollywood worked. None of the usual blather around town of artistic creativity or market appeal made any difference with this type of producer. They called them "talk and walk" guys. That is, money talks and the way you think it works walks.

Bob, Carol, and John had already read Springer's screenplay before meeting and had mixed reactions. Carol thought it was right on target with the scope of the assignment as they had laid it out to Springer, and was prepared to defend it. Bob, on the other hand, had reluctantly gone along with the partnership vote and the expenditure of their funds. He had serious reservations about how it would be received not only in Hollywood but also by paying viewers, the ultimate measure of the worth of a film project. The very idea of a major motion picture filmed on the headwaters of the Amazon was a stretch, let alone with an egotistical anthropology professor manipulating primitive people he claims to care about. That was the way that Bob saw the effort.

John, as mediator for the firm in disputes like this, pointed out what he thought Bob was missing in the value of the story and said, "Audiences will read into the ending what they wanted to see. Screenwriters like Springer are just the start. They set up the story, create the conflict, and resolve it. Yet he has left it up to the audience to fill in that part of the individually desired results. You can't ask for more than that. They build the skeleton, but by the time the producer and director hang the meat on it with cast selection and cinematography, the audience loves it. And besides, movie projects with secret political or other agendas, some subtle, some not, are not unheard of. Remember *Wag the Dog, All the President's Men*, even *Bowling for Columbine* or the more cause-driven *An Inconvenient Truth*? There is plenty of room left in that genre for a movie like *Hidden*."

"But how on earth, Carol, can you bring this guy down to where the film is being shot as a scientific advisor and not have him blow the whole thing up when he realizes he is being made a fool of for the whole world to see?" Bob said with a puzzled look on his face.

"Don't worry about it, guys, we have a plan. He'll never know what hit him until it's way too late. Trust me," Carol said confidently.

They nodded approvingly, in respect of her devious methods for getting things done.

"But how will we be able to pull off the funding for an unusual project of this kind?" Bob asked.

Carol, sensing that she and John had the majority and were in the process of winning their partner over as required since a unanimous approval was the voting rule they employed, said, "I have in mind the perfect producer for this project—Roger Farnsworth."

"*Farnsworth*, the billionaire currency trader?" Bob and John said almost simultaneously.

"What interest could Roger Farnsworth possibly have in film production of any kind, much less one like this?" Bob asked.

"A very keen interest, a very keen interest indeed," Carol said.

"You may not know it, fellows," Carol continued, "but before Farnsworth got rich trading in international currencies, he was an assistant professor of sociology at New York University, and I happen to know that he lost his full professorship application before he earned tenure at NYU because one of the senior men at the university bullied the committee to reject him. It seems that Roger's published research papers were in competition with the chairman on the review committee and in fact criticized him by implication. Apparently the guy had a huge ego and could not stand the heat of published criticism, so Roger was denied tenure by delay after delay, using politics, with several members of the committee voting denial after denial, until the tenure application period expired. Roger never got over that insult by a real bastard who had power over him, and he left the university and teaching in anger. You may also not know that after Farnsworth got rich in his financial career, he invested in an occasional movie project."

"Carol, how do you happen to know all this about Farnsworth? He has to be one of the most private men in America," John asked.

"Well, I know this because it's my business to know things about the movers and shakers in this business, guys," Carol said. "Actually, one of my sorority sisters from UCLA is a literary agent who repped the biography of Mr. Farnsworth several years ago, and she shared the anecdotes with me knowing I am always on the lookout for film projects and fascinating stories. I have a good memory for personal history details, and you never know when it just might be useful."

"Okay, I get your point, Carol," Bob replied. "Farnsworth just might be the right guy to act as producer of *Hidden*, if we can get to him the right way. The comeuppance for Horatio A. Blake, an actual pinhead professor—and undeserving bastard in my opinion—just might strike a chord and resonate with his psyche. I guess I'm in. How about you, John?"

"Yeah, I'm there, and good job as always, Carol. Why don't you set it up and see if you can sell him on the project? Then we can hook him up with a suitable director and all the other logistics to make this one a success. He doesn't have to know the mechanics; just have the money and the desire. He might enjoy this project. Isn't sociology the study of society and how people relate to each other? What difference does it make if the Musquaeli people would probably still be living in their Stone Age society if Blake's antics hadn't done them in?"

"Well then, that's it; we are agreed and project *Hidden* is off and running. Regular reports will be forthcoming as usual?"

"I'm on it," Carol said, and the meeting was adjourned.

28

How Do You Find a Loner?

Carol was able to reach Gail Grissom, her Kappa Alpha Theta sister, by phone in Gresham, near Portland, Oregon, where she had married and settled down while maintaining a few good writer clients as she swam in the good life. Carol asked Gail if she could stop by for a visit with a special favor to ask as she was passing through Portland on her way to Seattle for the Northwest Film Festival.

Carol Stone rarely attended film festivals, but it was better to have an authentic purpose for stopping by even though she and Gail had been close friends in the sorority at UCLA and on many occasions shared secrets together. That was the easy part, however, and she knew it.

Gail, as a literary agent, was the one with the past contact with Farnsworth, but that was a bit dated as his biography had not really become a bestseller. There were no sequels or follow-up stories to tell, and as a super-rich guy who valued his privacy, he didn't much care for publicity in the first place. Carol would have to use all the personal charm and cleverness she could muster to talk Gail into reaching into her fading bag of tricks and concocting a plan to gain an audience with Farnsworth.

Carol suggested that Gail meet her for dinner at the Hotel Lucia on Broadway, where she was staying. It was in the downtown corridor of old Portland, and Gail could catch the MAX transit system in Gresham, exit near the hotel, and return home the same way after dinner.

The Lucia was a modern hotel that was somewhat out of place in old Portland, with its stainless-steel and fabric interior and furnishings that looked as if they had been selected for a futuristic air terminal rather than the older European style of the surrounding buildings. But it had a charm that made visitors comfortable in its own way.

Carol checked into her room, not particularly paying attention to its richly appointed modern furniture or eye-catching art pieces that matched the modernistic décor. She didn't notice the Picasso print collection placed tastefully around her suite, or wonder how such valuable paintings—even if they weren't originals—came to be there, as she dropped her single bag on the bed and hurried into the bathroom to tidy up.

It was six thirty and Gail was due to arrive downstairs in the lounge soon, where they had agreed to meet at seven. Carol had made a reservation for two in the Lucia's fine restaurant for seven forty-five, which—if Gail was as punctual as Carol remembered—would give them time for a glass of wine or two and some preliminary girl talk. Carol looked at herself in the bathroom mirror, nodded her head in approval of her attire, made a self-congratulatory touch kiss toward the image, then turned and headed out.

The lounge was reasonably quiet for a weeknight, and she took a table near the back, where they could have some quiet to recall old times before commencing her mission. Carol had always intuitively understood that the hardest part of a task was getting started, but the timing of this one would be critical. Comfortably seated, she took in her surroundings. There were only five customers in the lounge, two couples at tables widely separated from hers, and the fifth: a single man seated at the bar with both elbows propping up his head over the drink placed in front of him as though he were praying to it. Carol looked up to see Sally, the waitress, coming over with a winsome cocktail-hour smile and asking what she wanted to drink. She ordered a glass of Château Ste. Michelle Chardonnay, 2006 or older, in honor of the Northwest from her new "friend." The waitress returned quickly with the order.

Carol sipped the wine and thought, *Hey, this is a pretty good year, and a Washington wine, even though not from California's wonderful wine counties of Napa, Sonoma, or Mendocino, is a good substitute. My all-time fave is La Crema, but oh well. How will I do this? Chitchat, let it drop, play it by ear? Oh, how I hate this deception crap—maybe just pop the question for old times' sake!*

But in the midst of her musings, desperately trying to come up with a plan, a familiar voice from the past wafted across the lounge.

"Carol Stone, as I live and breathe, could that stunning beauty from my past and Hollywood's present and future talent creator really be seated sipping wine in the Hotel Lucia bar in *my* hometown?"

Carol turned and, with genuine delight, jumped up, ran across the lounge, and threw herself into Gail Grissom's welcoming arms. They hugged, spinning around like long-separated fraternal twins reunited. In a sense, they were since college had been the dawn of new and different days forever for both of them.

Gail had left UCLA, done her stint as a single gal lit agent, flying all over the place, chasing the right book contract, until she married her beau from her freshman year in high school. Her husband, after his college days at Oregon State and law school at Columbia, had become a litigation attorney in their hometown of Portland, where she was happy to back off from the career thing and settle down.

Gail never seriously considered any career for the long run except that of being a loving mom to some number of kids. Meanwhile, Carol majored in English literature and had developed a passion for writing, with one thing leading to another and eventually Hollywood. But in any event, it had all started for her at the UCLA campus at Westwood too. It was their mutual birth window to the world, though with different destinations.

Gail and Carol finally stopped spinning, stood back from each other, and drank to the dregs of the image glass without a pause, following up with another round. It seemed they could not get enough of each other, and for the moment Carol's master plan seemed to be slipping away. The memories of college parties, the endless hours of studying together, and the sessions of shared dreams and solving problems for one another came flooding back into their collective consciousness.

The dorm room their frosh year had been the place of ignition as friends. The sorority house came next and their friendship had never looked back.

"What have you been doing with yourself, Gail? I want to hear it all. Sit over here. I've already started with a glass of wine. Sally, come on over; my friend needs a drink. What are you having, Gail?"

"Oh, something red maybe. What do you recommend, Sally?" she asked as the waitress arrived.

"Well, there are many fine local wines. We have a lovely 2001 Solera Cabernet Sauvignon by Dimmick Cellars, a Columbia Valley—Oregon side, naturally—wine, or a very interesting Hinman 2000 Rogue Valley Red from our scenic Oregon Rogue River area. You will love either," Sally said in her best imitation of a *Sideways* wine aficionado, picking up from the overheard conversation that she had upscale folks in front of her who would not be satisfied with the cheaper house cab sauv, and she was right.

"Oh, wonderful," Gail said. "I'll take the Rogue Red." Neither one asked the price or even cared.

Sally left to fill the order and the girls sat down side by side, anxious to begin the old ritual of meandering down memory lanes. The stories of the three kids that were the delight of Gail and Tory's life, a sampling of Tory's courtroom successes that the guys liked to call "war stories," an endless account of the most successful of the projects of Carol's partnership with John and Bob. They talked through a montage of domestic, community, and social club relationships each had as only truly good girlfriends can do.

The wine and the one or two replacement glasses were gone before both suddenly realized they were late for their dinner reservation. Sally came by to make one final sale, but Carol said, "Whoa, girl, we have to run. Reservation for dinner in the Lucia restaurant and we're late. Check, please."

"Right," Sally said, and quickly came back with the check, which Carol paid over the good-natured protest of her friend. *I can't tell her it's a business meeting, can I?* she thought. *That would be telling too much, wouldn't it?*

After the food was served and enjoyed in the dining room, the girls waited for the coffee that was welcome about now with all the wine they had consumed. Carol decided if there was ever going to be a good time this was it. But before she could cleverly weave the conversation into a moment for an innocent question that just might lead to "what is old what's-her-name up to these days?" Gail launched into an account of their friends—some mutual, others not—over the years and asked Carol, "Tell me, Carol, what interesting projects are you working on these days? And you did say you had a favor to ask? I've been dying to ask but didn't want to pry. Many of Tory's friends love to hear his client stories, but due to confidentiality as a lawyer, you know, he can't discuss the juicy details, and most of my little things are dull as sloe gin, but you must have some exciting ones you're working on. Well, how about a couple?"

Carol marveled at her good fortune. Here was the chance she had been waiting for, and she didn't have to manipulate Gail at all.

"Well, there are several the firm is working on, but one unusual one we have is an adaptation of a published scientific account of an anthropological expedition to the headwaters of the Amazon—Ecuador, actually. The firm got this manuscript and managed to get the author—this Dr. Horatio Averill Blake, known as Dr. 'Montana' Blake, if you can believe it—for a scientist. Make you think of anyone?"

"Not like Indiana Jones?" Gail asked half jokingly.

"Not exactly, Gail, but similar."

She began her almost-rehearsed presentation of the plot. "It seems our Dr. Blake has been going to Ecuador to study a Stone Age people and manages to get in the middle of a tribal war. He's the only member of the expedition to escape with his life but manages to return with the cherished stone relic from the shaman of the tribe. His account of the expedition has brought him the nomination for the Lucius Larksburger prize for anthropology—made-up name of course.

"We hired Bill Springer, the best freelance screenwriter in the business, to write a script for the movie. He dissected the professor's story and figured out that the old professor is either lying about the shaman offering him the idol as a gift while the tribe is about to be wiped out, or that he stole it and the tribe perished.

"Dr. Montana Blake is—even by the accounts of his own writing— an egotistical fool that needs to be exposed as a fraud. My job is to find the right producer for the project."

Gail was intrigued by the story and wanted to know how Carol went about putting a script like that into an actual movie, not being familiar with what a producer of a movie even was. Carol explained the process and then blurted out without any plan at all, "Gail, didn't your friend you repped for—I can't remember her name, darn it—author the biography of Roger Farnsworth, the old gentleman who made a fortune in currency trading?"

"Oh, you mean Elaine Gregory, the biographer. Yeah, I handled that account some years ago, but it never sold well. Farnsworth is too private and would never open up to reveal the interesting stuff that sells a biography. That guy was amazing though; came out of an academic background as I recall."

"I remember that. Roger's story, if I remember right, was one where he was treated badly in academia in some manner or another but managed to leave the whole business and strike out into something entirely new."

"Yeah, new indeed, like money. How's that for the flip side of struggling for tenure—finding some real safety like being filthy rich?" Gail asked.

"What was he like, I mean as a person?"

Gail sipped her coffee and sat back, trying to remember details about the guy. Carol's attention was riveted to her friend as if this was the most exciting story she had ever heard, and in one sense it was, for finding the way to an introduction to Farnsworth was the only story that mattered at the moment.

"He was quiet, really, not given to talking about himself, and a good listener. It was as if he really cared about Elaine's project, which for her was everything; but for him, probably not that important, or so it seemed. Although, he was really analytical in his approach, whether he really cared about the result or not. He took Elaine's manuscript apart like an engineer would take a gadget and figure out how it worked and then run off with the idea for himself. But this was about him, so he didn't have to steal anything. That just sort of explained how he delved into the subject at hand. I had the feeling he did that with his currency trading too, and that's why he was so stunningly successful. I mean, I learned from Elaine's research that he started with just a few thousand and turned it into billions! How do you suppose an egghead professor of sociology—which I never thought was a particularly academically challenging field—had that kind of decision-making skill and brains to dissect the secrets of the international currency markets and blow them sky high? Go figure."

"Sounds fascinating. Say, do you suppose you could help me get a meeting with him? Would that be an imposition on your relationship with Elaine?" Carol asked, tilting her head slightly to the side for emphasis.

"What on earth would your firm expect to have in common with Mr. Farnsworth, I mean if by some chance Elaine would help me find him?"

"Well, Farnsworth has the bucks, and I happen to know he has funded a couple of movie projects before."

"I never heard that before. Are you sure?"

"Uh-huh, it's true, my dear. And with him behind us, *Hidden*—that's the name of the screenplay—would bypass the crapshoot that selling screenplays to studios is. Once you start down that road and don't sell it on the first try or two, the word gets out faster than wildfire in a broom-sage field and you're dead meat. Might as well toss your investment in that script in the trash instead of continuing to beat your head you know where. We've taken flyers before, Gail, don't get me wrong. But this one is so unique—with the protagonist being an egghead egotistic professor with a hidden agenda—it stands little chance of being sold unless the skids are really greased."

"I see," Gail said, thinking of how she could even find Elaine Gregory. And if she found her, what chance would she have of talking her into doing it?

"You know, Carol, my contact with Elaine is really a bit dated. And like I said, that biography never really sold well, and I seriously doubt she would have any pull in getting a meet with Mr. Farnsworth."

"I have it!" Carol said excitedly. "Forget old what's-her-name. Let's do it together!"

"Carol, what on earth do you mean—do what together?"

Carol jumped from her seat in the uncrowded restaurant and spun around like an impresario with her arms outstretched, oblivious to the stares of the patrons in the Lucia. "You take a leave of absence from motherhood and rep the screenplay with me to Mr. Farnsworth. The firm will find him, wherever he is—Hong Kong, Bern, London, wherever! Set up a meeting under some false pretense or another, and you simply introduce me so I can sell the script. You earn your usual cut, and the numbers could be really large, especially if the movie is made like we're counting on. What do you think?"

Gail sat back in her chair in shock. She had never repped a screenplay before, and did she really want to leave home, even for a week or two? What would Tory and the kids do without her? Hadn't she sworn off a heavy lit schedule after the kids started coming? But this was her old bud from Theta days and she seemed to really need her.

Carol was watching and waiting expectantly, hoping she had not oversold her hand.

Gail thought about it long and hard, and finally said, "If Tory and the kids are okay with it, I'll do it. But this is a one-time thing, Carol—I mean it. You promise on a Theta oath?"

This threw Carol for a loop; the Theta oath was never to be taken lightly. But she had never intended to manipulate Gail into a career sort of thing, so she said, "Done!" and rushed over to hug her old friend with such a warm embrace she thought she might stop breathing for good.

When it ended, Gail pulled away. "First, I tell Tory and the kids, and if they are okay with it, what's next?"

"I can tell by your face, it's a done deal, so here's how we proceed. I return to LA—forget the Northwest Film Festival—set our sleuths to work, and I'll call when we have located him, and we do a conference call. If the guy's as analytical as you say he is, he'll be intrigued by this story. You let me handle it, just get me the intro."

"Okay then," Gail said, "let's celebrate! I want another one of those Rogue things. I loved that wine."

"And I'm having a Sonoma County La Crema—my California roots are stirring within my soul."

The wine arrived and they toasted their deal and spent the rest of the evening in the reverie that only the best of friends can have when nothing is hidden and all is gain.

29

ANALYZE THIS

It didn't take Carol's research department long to track down Farnsworth, who happened to be on a skiing vacation in southern Germany at a magic mountain bordering the Austrian Alps called the Zugspitze.

"You just get there and run into him. We'll set it up and text you the lead-in. Gail never has to know, trust me, boss. You'll look like a genius," the super sleuth had said.

That'll be the day, she thought. She had learned to trust these guys from their experience in such things, though. There was no way that Gail would be able to pick up the phone on her own and call old Roger to say, "What do you say, Roger? How are things? Remember me? I'm the dude who got your biography by old what's-her-name. You know, the book that sold about three thousand copies to business libraries and maybe ten thousand copies in bookstores? Do you mind if I drop in on you in the middle of your vacation for a little business that will take up a mere ton of your time, destroy your privacy, and make one of the richest men in the world even richer? Aren't you just dying to buy another island somewhere, maybe a small country?"

In fact, Carol had to fight to sell herself on the idea of going to Germany without an appointment, traveling by rail into the mountains, and making it look like they just happened to randomly catch Farnsworth on the hotel veranda enjoying a spectacular view, while finding a way to horn in on his privacy and sell him on the idea of producing a movie. *That would be some selling job*, Carol thought as she called Gail to give her the trip details. Gail had agreed to the plan after twisting Tory's arm and promising she would never do this silly kind of thing again. Carol instructed Gail to catch a flight in Portland and meet Carol in New York before boarding a flight together for Munich.

Even though the task was daunting and it frightened each of them in different ways whenever they thought about it, the bond they had was even more powerful. It was extremely important to Carol's firm—and her reputation among her partners—not to mention the film community in Hollywood that never liked to pick a loser. Without the financial backing Farnsworth could bring to the project, it would never get an intro meet with that greedy crowd. There was no such thing as a quiet failure in Hollywood, and Carol was not about to let this one out of her grasp and fuel the gossip mill among those who mattered in her industry that her agency had picked a loser. Gail sensed that, and as they talked and plotted together on the long trip overseas, she fell into line with her own brand of outward optimism, her hidden fear never showing.

Bavaria is beautiful in the early spring, and the village of Garmisch-Partenkirchen is a classic example of the Old World brought back to the future. The women landed at Munich International Airport and took a cab to the *Hauptbahnhof* for tickets by rail on the Deutsche Bahn. It was tempting to stay a day or so in Munich and stroll down the Marienplatz and enjoy an eclectic voyeur experience among jugglers, American college kids performing covers, and string quartets, or spend an evening at the Hofbräuhaus. But both of them were too scared and excited for the mission, so they settled into their seats for the seventy-five-minute scenic ride to Garmisch-Partenkirchen.

The travel experts at the agency had suggested they could, depending on the time of their arrival, connect right there in the train station in Garmisch-Partenkirchen and arrive at the resort later that evening, or they could stay overnight and catch the morning train out to the resort. As it worked out, the train they were on was delayed due to an electrical short in the train's main cable feed, much to the consternation of the passengers accustomed to relying on the typical German efficiency. Nevertheless, they would finally depart for the resort only two hours behind its original schedule. This forced Gail and Carol to use the backup reservation plan the agency's travel office had suggested, and stay in the lovely Bavarian town, with time to have a nice dinner after checking into their hotel.

After dinner they walked along Helmen Strasse in front of the Wittelsbacher Hof, where they were staying for the night, toward the main part of town where the shops and other places of interest to locals or visitors were located. One of the bakeries they passed had such delightful aromas holding in the air even this late in the day that Carol stopped for a minute to take in the ancient architecture that had either survived WWII or been artfully recreated in accordance with the original plans. After a moment, Carol said, "Gail, I know we just ate, but how about a strudel with an espresso?"

"I was just thinking the same thing." They turned into the shop and found a cozy table near the back where they could freely talk. The room was dark any time of day, but especially this late in the evening. The heavy woodwork, rich brocaded wallpaper, and romantic lighting made the women feel it was the perfect place to plan their attack.

Earlier in the day, the strategists at the agency had texted a plausible plan, almost in the form of a screenplay. It was entirely too detailed for Carol's taste, like trying to memorize the text of a magnificently written speech only to have clumsiness, anxiety, and poor memory ruin the effect of it all when she would inevitably lose her place, then look and sound like a puppet on a string with one or more connectors broken.

In this case, it was worse than a speech. At least with a speech she could have controlled the chaos by not allowing a Q and A at the end. But here, Farnsworth would never sit quietly like a college sophomore when a congressman or the secretary of defense came to speak, no matter how badly he mauled his text. Carol, with her experience and nerve, could probably handle rejection of any kind no matter how rude the response.

"What's the plan, Carol? Should we rehearse a little, or at least go over it enough times so that we don't stumble pathetically?"

"Okay, Gail, here's the outline our people came up with."

The waitress came over with a tray of pastries and asked the women which they would like with their espresso. Even though the women were not very hungry, the pastry presentation was beautiful, and the rich aromas inviting. Having made their selections and taking the waitress's suggestion for Bavarian espressos, they could return to the plan. Carol had hastily handwritten two copies so that she and Gail could follow along together.

THE SETUP — As we see the scene, the best approach is to find the subject alone, or, worst case, with guests in a public place. Carol leads, with Gail a short distance behind, and boldly approaches in her best fearless manner.

CAROL — "Mr. Farnsworth, I'm Carol Stone from Los Angeles. I'd recognize you anywhere. Although finance is not my trade, I do read the journals and your picture is there often enough. Isn't the scenery up here magnificent? Is that Austria over there?" Your demeanor is to be that you just happen to be there and he is another member of the human species enjoying the scenery like you; nothing more at this point.

THE COLD-SHOULDER REACTION — Expect any number of brush-off techniques, from just ignoring you, a polite nod of the head and a return to whatever he is reading at the moment, to a "please don't bother me, I'm busy." Worst case, he says, "What makes you think I talk to strangers without appointments?"

THE REGAIN THE ADVANTAGE TECHNIQUES — Try either "Oh, I'm sorry if we bothered you. We thought as a fellow American you would at least be polite and pretend to be a gentleman instead of the jerk you seem to be. Why don't you make up for it by taking our picture with the Austrian Alps in the background?" or turn to Gail and say, "Gail, is this the man you promoted a biography about? I thought you said he was always pleasant, even when you had to listen by the hour to stories about when he was denied tenure at NYU. Could it be he was mistyped in that bio?"

THE GOAL HERE — Our personality research shows that no matter how rich this guy is, he is gentle and friendly even to strangers. So we don't really expect the hostile brush-off. Anything you can do to engage him personally will allow his past relationship with Gail, no matter how tenuous, to engage him in conversation. Once Gail is recognized—and she will be—Gail takes it from there, listening at first; and then bring in your pitch as you think best. We were unable to make contact with his money man and let him introduce the project, so this is the best we could come up with. Good luck, Carol.

Thanks a lot, guys. I really appreciate it, Carol thought as she listened to Gail reading the script with a deep frown. She looked up and said, "This is the plan that is supposed to break the ice? I can't wait to tell Tory I came all this way to play this part cold turkey."

"Look at it this way, Gail. What's the worst that can happen? You get embarrassed and we lose a bundle and we all go home. So let's enjoy our espresso and strudel and go get a good night's sleep, fair enough?"

"I'm sorry, Carol, I just hate rejection, no matter how irrational it is when the stakes are high enough."

The espresso arrived as if on cue, and the girls settled in to enjoy the food, drink, and companionship. The rest of the evening was spent in telling old college-days tales over and over again with as much joy, laughter, and fun as two old and close friends could enjoy.

30

Ascent into Heaven, or Is It Hell?

The next morning, Carol and Gail checked out of the Wittelsbacher Hof and caught a taxi to the local Deutsche Bahn station, which allowed passage by single cable car to the Zugspitze Resort. They selected a seat near the front to get the best view. The train traveled through a dark, thickly grown coniferous forest with not much to look at from a tourist's perspective, with one exception.

Along the way they passed a lone walker on a trail alongside the track. He was an older man, probably in his late sixties, dressed in a way that would have made a Bavarian tourist brochure proud, complete with heavy boots, home-knit wool socks that came to his upper calf, dark green lederhosen supported by suspenders over a red wool shirt, and a face surrounded by an expansive full gray beard that reached his shirt collar. A Bavarian-style hat completed the picture they would never have expected out in the countryside and not in a Munich Bavarian costume competition. Gail and Carol both snapped numerous pictures and almost forgot the impending rendezvous with either destiny or destruction.

The picturesque train ride continued across the southern Bavarian countryside and gradually gained elevation as they approached the entrance to the mountain resort. The unusual feature of the Zugspitze is that there is only one way to reach it. There are no roads or trails up there, as the resort sits across the face of the Bavarian Alps facing Austria, accessed only through a dark tunnel by a train whose journey ended at the entrance to the resort.

Carol and Gail walked up the stone steps to the lobby and checked into a beautiful room with a southern exposure, its view unparalleled for beauty of a natural kind, as all the rooms had. It was late morning and Carol checked by email with her investigators to confirm that Farnsworth was in fact checked into the resort with a single guest.

As planned, the panoramic scene out of their room included a good view of the veranda, where almost all the tables were occupied by guests enjoying the view and a glass or two of the fine wines available in the well-stocked wine cellars of the resort. After a quick change into comfortable clothing, Gail studied the guests on the veranda and concluded Roger was not yet present.

"Must be out skiing, I don't see him yet. Nothing else to do up here except ski and look at mountains and skiers," she said.

"It's just as well. Let's go on down to the veranda so that when he comes in from skiing we'll already be positioned as regulars on the veranda," Carol said, and Gail agreed.

In the category of snowcapped mountain ranges, the scene from the veranda of the Hotel Tiroler Zugspitze was unsurpassed. The girls picked a table strategically located to give a view of all persons coming and going from the hotel or the ski slopes. The young and handsome Bavarian attendant Frantz came to their table as soon as they were comfortably seated.

Carol and Gail ordered chilled local white wines and sat silently, taking in the view. There was a slow stream of patrons coming and going from the hotel and slopes, busily engaged in chatter in an eclectic mixture of German, English, and Italian, even uninterpretable, to most, Farsi.

Gail was demonstrably nervous as she shifted positions, crossing and uncrossing her legs, and took rapid sips from her wine. Any observer—especially one trained to notice such things—would have wondered about this pair, one very noticeably jittery and the other cool, calm, and self-assured.

"What will we say when Roger shows up? Are you really sure about this? When will this tension end?" Gail asked without allowing any time for an answer, as though expressing her fear and frustration was answer enough.

Carol looked around and focused her attention like a laser on a man and a woman dressed in ski gear who were coming up to the landing adjacent to the veranda, laughing and obviously concentrating on each other, oblivious to the seemingly disinterested crowd.

"There, Gail, look there, that couple coming on the veranda. I think that's our target."

"Oh my God, it's him, that's Roger!" Gail exclaimed. "What do we do now?"

Roger and guest were headed right at them and in a minute would pass right by them.

Carol got up hurriedly and started across the rapidly diminishing space between them. And a terrible thing happened. In her excitement, she tripped over a small stool well below her line of vision and fell spread eagle right in front of the man himself.

Farnsworth—startled as everyone else in the area—did the noble thing: he dropped his ski gear and carry bag, stepped around his guest, and reached over to help Carol to her feet. Gail, with no time to think about their grand plan, or anything else for that matter, rushed to Carol's aid as well and found herself staring right into the face of Farnsworth. Roger recognized her immediately and cried out, "Gail! Grissom, is it? I'm terrible with names—you were the literary agent for Elaine Gregory, who did my biography, weren't you? What in the world are you doing here?"

By this time Carol had recovered her balance and her composure and professionalism kicked into gear, leaving her well-thought-out strategies lying hopelessly in the dustbin.

"Mr. Farnsworth, I'm Carol Stone, with Ansel, Livingston & Stone, Los Angeles. We develop and promote movie scripts. Gail and I are old friends, and she agreed to come with me halfway around the world to see you, no matter how graceless our entrance was. Please join us for a drink?"

Roger, not one to sit down with strangers, and being a very private person with the personal wealth to keep it that way, was caught unawares. His instinctive, chivalrous reaction and the presence of an old professional acquaintance left him feeling as if he had no choice but to accept, though he'd try to keep it brief.

With introductions made all around and Frantz on the spot, taking orders from everyone at the little table, Roger turned to Gail and said, "You know, Gail, I was never happy with that book. You tried your best to get Elaine and me to include some personal stories to make it appeal to all but my competitors, unfortunately for book sales at least, a very limited group, but I am used to getting my way and kept it all out. Nobody would care about that stuff anyway, would they, really?"

By this time Gail had recovered from her shock, and all the scheming and planning to have just the right approach for this, along with her top-notch lit-agent savvy, kicked into play.

"What you failed to grasp then, Roger—may I still call you Roger?" He nodded. "The reading public needs a villain. That's why your book never sold very well. It's sad to say but they need someone to hate, to get even with. Whether it's a psychopathic killer in a cop novel, a dishonest politician who abuses his power, or better yet someone who seems to get away with what everyone deep down knows is wrong and then gets exposed and stepped on where it hurts, in the public venues he values so highly. You had that kind of story to tell. I'll bet you really don't care all that much about accumulating wealth trading in mere money, the symbol of value, not value itself when it doesn't add a thing to the improvement of ordinary people's lives. Something you told me really was your passion back then and the opportunity you were denied—unjustly I might add. That was a story worth telling, but I couldn't convince you to do it."

Carol was shocked. The only reason her mouth wasn't gaping open was that her professionalism was always in control. Here her shy, frightened, and distanced-from-the-game sorority sister had found her A game right on the spur of the moment. It couldn't have been a better lead-in. The real question was how the man would react.

Farnsworth sat silent and listened to Gail's speech, not realizing it was not prepared at all but coming from her heart. His knack for seeing through any kind of game to make a money play for him was on high alert. He had heard Carol Stone say that she was from a script agency in LA, and could quickly see this as a play for some pitch to him, however cleverly pulled off with that accident that sure did look authentic. He had invested in movie projects before and wasn't against making money but hated losing it. And Hollywood losers could be spectacular in a negative way too. But something Gail had said touched a spot deep within him. She had said the public desired or had an insatiable appetite for revenge, and it did something to him he could not quite put his finger on and stirred his interest. This was true internally at least; he would never let anyone see that part of himself in the public face he maintained. He had really hated that bastard who chaired the tenure committee at NYU and denied his chance to produce—from a secure academic platform—solutions for some of the troubling aspects of American society. Where he sat now, even as one of the wealthiest men in the world, no one cared what he thought about the average man's societal problems or that a solution might in fact exist for some of them. No matter how clever the suggestion, the universal and visceral reaction would be, "Good enough for *him*, but it would never work for me." Now, getting even with that jerk personally was beneath even him, so why did it draw him to what this woman was saying?

What is really going on here? he thought. "Why are you two here, exactly?" he finally blurted out.

"Carol's firm in LA has a really interesting script, but it's one of those stories the typical Hollywood studio won't touch, no matter how successful it may eventually be," Gail said. "Let Carol tell you about it." She handed the floor to Carol.

Carol began as though her speech had been rehearsed for months—and conceptually it had been—though the actual words she spoke were completely unrehearsed, rising from the unexpected opportunity of the moment, that unlimited source of creativity everyone is endowed with, if it could ever be released from those inner realms of dreams, experience, and fantasy.

"This true story is about one of the most successful academic frauds in history. It is a fraud because the ego of this anthropologist is so large that he was able to steal away the spiritual power of a Stone Age tribe in the Amazon he had supposedly devoted his career to studying, and paradoxically managed to get the tribe destroyed. They were slaughtered to the last man, woman, and child so he could win the Mead Award for anthropology and publish a scientific account that would have made him the academic hero in a terribly narrow field. When in truth, he is lying about his role in the whole thing. We have the movie rights with the guaranteed freedom to tell it the way we want, and maybe even how it actually happened. The guy's ego is so large, the idea of seeing his name in lights allowed us to manipulate him into total—and I mean total—literary freedom.

"It's amazing what greed and clever approaches can accomplish, but more on that later. The script we've had written has everything that the public will respond to: jungle exploration, anthropology, Stone Age culture, blood and guts, war and peace, and the contest between truth and mystery."

"What do you mean a 'contest between truth and mystery'?" Roger asked.

"I'm getting there," Carol said, and continued, "I'm sure you are aware that many are conflicted in their beliefs on whether this material existence is all there is. Some believe there is more to it than what we see or can understand, while others will not unless science or philosophy can explain its existence.

"This story accurately shows a microcosm of this controversy when our anthropologist, one Horatio A. Blake, aka Montana Blake—yes, that is actually the name he's known by—discovers that this Stone Age tribe he has been studying has a so-called war god that is supposed to be their survival totem in tribal warfare. It is a stone idol carved or made from obsidian that only the shaman of the tribe has access to because it's so sacred.

"As our story develops, Montana Blake actually gets an opportunity to see and take possession of the object right in the middle of a tribal war. He discovers to his horror that the little stone object actually has mysterious powers. He is forced to decide between aiding the people with whom he claims a friendship and leaving them to their doom. In the middle of the battle, he discovers that when he moves in the direction of the friendlies, the battle goes their way, and when he moves away they begin to lose.

"He elects to escape with the idol, abandoning the tribe and his expedition party. He then wins academic acclaim with publication of a scientific report recounting the episode. One of the reputable scientific houses publishes a sanitized version of events, in which he claims to have been asked by the shaman in the heat of the battle to protect the war god. We never would have heard of it except for the fact that it was mailed to us for some reason. After review and discussion, we thought enough of the story to create a screenplay. All we need is the right producer to make the project happen, and for that we have come to you, Mr. Farnsworth."

Roger stared into their faces, saying nothing, as he mulled over the story. He examined its content to decide whether it could possibly be true as represented, weighing its implications on him, and most of all questioning whether he had any business investing in a project of this kind for the silly personal ego-driven reasons these two women had detected and played him with so well. He took a disliking to Dr. Montana Blake and saw him for the intellectually dishonest, egocentric fool that he truly was, or deeply troubled at best. All his business and human instincts said no. But something about making a public spectacle of an academic figure taking credit for a lie would be a sweet revenge against those bastards on the NYU review committee that had denied him tenure.

It wouldn't be the same as exposing that guy to the public hanging he deserves, but even that delicious thought is best reserved for my fantasies and never given a public airing. But to do it to someone else—that would be a kind of vicarious pleasure that only I and these two would ever recognize. No matter that the asshole may never see it, and even if he did, would never understand, he thought.

Finally, he spoke: "Tell you what, send me the manuscript and screenplay for my review. If I like the story and my own due diligence checks out, I'll get back to you. But I can tell you this much—I'm leaning toward a go. There is one condition I'll lay out up front. If I decide to do it, it has to be done by the people at Star Wisher. I know what you may be thinking, that I am setting an impossible condition as an easy way to say no. But Star Wisher is a winner and I only play with winners. So there, if you are still interested, send me the stuff.

"Now, why don't we have dinner together in an hour, okay? There's only one choice of restaurants up this high, but the food is good."

Carol recovered from the shock that they were still in the game and quickly accepted the offer on behalf of herself and Gail.

They finished their wine and left to be reunited for dinner, and the second round of game plan B that had evolved seemingly all on its own, which is usually the best kind.

31

CHAMPAGNE AS A TOAST

The trip home to LA was delayed a week as Carol stayed with Gail in Portland to celebrate their success. When Carol did arrive back in LA, the celebration continued at the Ansel firm.

The whole staff was there with the usual accoutrements for an LA celebrity party. She walked in the door to cheers all around. She didn't bother to ask, "How did you know?" because she had known that her phone call from Germany would trigger this inevitable response. These guys—the partners, that is—loved it when it turned out like this, even though two very large remaining unknowns were whether Farnsworth would actually pop for the project or not and, more importantly, whether Star Wisher would take it on.

"Don't start a celebration just yet," Carol said over the din of the genuine shouts of appreciation. "He hasn't given the okay yet, has he? Or did I miss something?"

"Yeah, he said okay after reviewing the screenplay and talking it over with his lawyers. You guys really must have done a number on him—and took forever getting back here," Bob said.

"You're kidding, right? He really bought it? But what about the conditions? He was very careful to say there would be conditions. And Star Wisher—I know those guys and they don't take on losers, if they see it that way, no matter how easy the financing is."

"There are conditions all right, Carol, but we can live with them."

"Well, what conditions?" Carol asked skeptically.

"There are two. One, the filming has to be done on location, somewhere similar to where the fraud was committed; and two, as you said, Star Wisher has to provide the production. If we meet those, Farnsworth will finance the whole venture with Star Wisher."

"Great! No wonder you're celebrating," Carol said sarcastically. "But didn't Blake cause a wipeout of the entire tribe of the Musquaeli people? How could we possibly risk a production company's assets and people to set up a shoot in such hostile territory? And when did Star Wisher ever risk its reputation on such a project?"

"Settle down, Carol. Your skepticism is expected, but we have both covered. Farnsworth owns a significant stake in Star Wisher. I'll bet you never knew that, and he probably wanted to know whether you did or how good of an actress you were. That was the easier condition to meet. And while you and Gail were saying your farewells in Portland over the last week, our research department, in conjunction with Straight On Films, the outfit that puts the boots on the ground for Star Wisher, went to work on the other. They will find a way; you better believe it. And old Montana Blake agreed to go along and act as consultant for the scientific aspects of the film. So for now we are in a celebrating mood, and you deserve most of the credit, Carol."

She was stunned, to say the least. They actually could pull this one off, though it had seemed almost impossible from the start to her.

"Here's to you guys, way to go team!" Carol said as she lifted a glass in salute. Clink went the glasses and the chorus of cheers was a veritable surround sound of acclaim.

32

AN UNEXPECTED CALL

The day had begun normally for Professor Blake, and by midmorning he was situated comfortably in his spacious office at Fangleer College with his ritual first cup of coffee in front of him on his desk. He was preoccupied with his class schedule for the week with occasional thoughts on just where his next research project should go. The blinker on his phone set was on so he picked up the receiver and heard the familiar voice of his secretary say, "Dr. Blake, you have a call waiting. It's a Carol Stone holding for you from California."

"Thank you, Liz, I'll take the call." He pushed the button and said simply, "Hello."

"Dr. Blake, this is Carol Stone, a partner in Ansel, Livingston & Stone in California. Remember us?"

"Yes, Carol, is this about our contract for movie rights on my book?"

"Indeed, and the purpose of my call is to let you know we now officially have a movie project. And I say 'we' purposefully because when the project becomes profitable both of us are going to be very happy. As you recall, Dr. Blake, you agreed to go to the production set as a cultural advisor on primitive native cultural aspects, such as hierarchy relationships in primitive tribes, how their living arrangements should be portrayed, and any other such contributions to the director and staff on the set."

"Yes, I agreed to all that, but where is this set you mentioned? They aren't going back to Ecuador to the place where the Musquaeli people used to live on the Pangria tributary of the Rio Ucayali are they? Surely not."

"No, of course not. The producers are counting on your cultural advice to make the film an authentic portrayal as your marvelous writings describe them. The film will be shot in Brazil, actually, west of São Paulo, on the Pinheiros tributary of the Tietê River. It is an area with similar geographic features to those in your book. The film is a joint production of Star Wisher and Straight On Films in Hollywood. I'm sure you have heard of them, Dr. Blake, haven't you?"

He hadn't, but Blake was unwilling to show his ignorance of any subject, so he nodded his assent even though Carol couldn't possibly have been able to see it. Regardless, she took his silence either as ignorance or as an indication that he was impressed.

"But the important thing is that we expect you to be there during the setup and the filming sequences so that the production is authentic. Can we count on you?" Carol asked.

"Wait just a minute, Carol. There are a few points I would like to clear up. I know that I agreed as you say, but how long will I be required to be there, what compensation do I get? I mean, I do have a job here at the college, you know?"

"Sure, Dr. Blake. You will be paid just like it says in your contract. You did read it before you signed, didn't you?"

"Yes, of course, but refresh my recollection on that, will you? More important is the matter of my time and my family, if I am sitting down there for weeks on end."

"It's the standard part of your contract as the author. The details are in section three, on page three. We already paid you the fifty-thousand-dollar down payment; the rest will be paid on a monthly basis, plus all expenses, once the project begins as identified in that section. And yes, that includes your family. We like families, Dr. Blake, and it will be a great experience for them too. Especially your two sons. You do have two boys, don't you?"

He wondered how she knew that, but he was too embarrassed to admit he hadn't thoroughly reviewed the contract, so he let the other go.

"So how long is the set development and shooting schedule going to take? To put it bluntly, how long must I be away from my work?"

"Well, Dr. Blake, the first phase, the set construction, will be this coming summer, when you do not have teaching assignments, anyway—we checked on that. Filming starts after the sets are finished, and you will be required to be there for at least the first month of filming to consult on the script development, casting, and the inevitable plot refinement that always happens in the actual filming of the movie. They will use native Indians as extras, and we know you have much experience in interacting with those primitive people. The producers will provide interpreters if you are not up on any specific dialects of the Tupi Indians.

"We have been told it was a common language even though the tribes hated and killed each other. That's the past, of course, but you get the picture, right? You don't have to worry about being away from your job, Dr. Blake; we have already talked to the Florida Museum of Science and Natural History, and they are excited about the publicity the film will bring to the institute. And get this: our research team has discovered that there are primitive tribes of native Indians in the region, remnants of the Tupi tribes that dominated the region before the arrival of the Europeans way back in the sixteenth century. They have never been visited by a scientist of your reputation, so while you are consulting for the film, you can use much of the inevitable down time to make contact with these tribes for possibly starting a new scientific study the institute is very likely to be interested in funding at a future date.

"That is what the people I talked to at the institute indicated was their potential interest. I am confident Fangleer College will love to give you a leave of absence. Just think of the publicity this project will bring to the college. How does that sound, Dr. Blake?"

He sat silent for a time, mulling over this latest disclosure. As an anthropologist he was familiar with all indigenous groups in South America, including the Tupi people, who had populated what is now Brazil for untold centuries. He also knew that the Portuguese explorers and their descendants had, by the deliberate polygamous practice called *cunhadismo*, melded the native Indians' gene pool with their own, eliminating most of the unique features of the native Tupi population and resulting in the current mixed race. But he had often thought there might be pure samples of the original Tupi genetic strain in isolated tribal areas, and the prospect that he might be able to discover and—more importantly—get credit for it excited him.

But never let them see you sweat or gloat, he thought. After what seemed like an interminable pause, he said, "I see. There's much to think about in all that. But I want your assurance that I will get to review the script for this movie."

He had to admit she had done her homework, but he was not taking the bait. Unbeknownst to him, Carol has used Horace Finder's research about the man and personality of Dr. Montana Blake to touch all his decision buttons but the script. She had read the screenplay and knew that for Dr. Blake this was going to be a huge problem. Screenplays don't always end up as originally written, but this one as written had a time bomb ready to distort this professor's reputation. She didn't have the courage to face this now, so she prevaricated. "The screenplay is to a movie what a script is to a stage play, Dr. Blake. It is filled with coded descriptions to tell the director how to present the script and plot, and will change a hundred times before production shooting is finished. So there is no completed script ready to review at this time. That is a key part of your role in this process. As the actual actors portray their parts from the screenplay, the script is continuously rewritten for each scene sequence. Understand?"

"I think so, but I will get to see it down there before the final version is finished and have my input in the choices made in the story?"

"Yes, of course," she lied. She didn't want to risk blowing the deal. There would be no gain in exposing what the script revealed about him now and forcing a lawsuit for specific performance of a reluctant but necessary consultant. You can lead a horse to water, but you can't make him drink, she instinctively understood. She waited hopefully for a positive or at least a temporarily neutral answer.

"Well, Carol, who do I coordinate all this with from your firm, like travel plans and arrangements for São Paulo this summer, that is if the family agrees?"

She breathed an inward sigh of relief. The explosion had been delayed until he finally read the script. Though she didn't know enough about Mrs. Blake's influence, she very much doubted it could affect Blake's ego if he really wanted something. "You can start with me, Dr. Blake, but I will hand you off to Anna Starke, the girl Friday in our firm. Fair enough?" Carol said.

"That's fine, Carol. Call me at the next stage of this thing." And with that, he hung up.

"Whew, that was close. Good to go so far!" was the only thing Carol could say after hearing the dial tone. *He won't know what hit him.*

33

The Ground Game, the Start

The lion's share of the set location selection and development fell to Straight On Films in the deal Farnsworth put together with Star Wisher, the top-name partner for publicity purposes. As soon as the ink was dry on the contract, Straight On Films released its technical team to scour the Western world for a suitable site for the project.

Many rivers in Central and South America had bits and pieces that fit the true story that birthed the book and this film project, but not enough for their selection. Farnsworth had insisted that since he was paying for most of this film, he wanted an authentic portrayal of the geography for movie audiences. The mountain-sourced rivers of the Amazon in Ecuador, where the actual event took place, would have been nice, but the access and cost to pull this off were prohibitive. The perfect site, the Pangria where the Musquaeli tribe had lived for centuries until history and Dr. Blake had decided otherwise, could not be selected for obvious reasons. The team settled on Brazil, near the fairly modern city of São Paulo, because the location satisfied the transportation and communication services requirements for the support teams.

A suitable river, the Tietê, had location prospects fairly close to the São Paulo metropolitan center that were not found elsewhere. The river flowed through the city and out into the river drainage system, where it joined the Grand and Paranáiba Rivers to form the headwaters of the

Paraná water course, winding its way south to eventually empty into the Atlantic Ocean between Uruguay and Argentina near Buenos Aires. The Tietê itself was hardly a pristine water course since it flowed through São Paulo. As with many modern metropolitan areas, unchecked pollution had turned the once-clear freshwater stream into a brown drainage system.

However, the Pinheiros tributary feeding the Tietê, not too far from São Paulo, had the right vertical drop from its source in an unusually small but photographically spectacular mountain range. Almost by serendipity, the research team found a site very similar to the one described in Dr. Blake's manuscript.

One of the geographic team members had been experimenting with some modern satellite photographic programs on his computer and happened to spot the little mountain range with the lovely Pinheiros tributary to the Tietê nestled within it. It wasn't an exact match with the two small humps at the end of the river valley where the final battle scene was to be shot, but that could be easily remedied with subtle enough CGI. The team member was so excited by his discovery that he literally ran into the team meeting scheduled that day and startled everybody with his announcement. Although some were skeptical at first, the computer images of the terrain sold the point. The team was ready to implement "Plan Musquaeli."

The site selection decision was passed along to all concerned and eventually made its way through convoluted channels to Montana.

34

A Fateful Decision

Montana sat for a long while in his office, mulling over all he had heard from Stone and her assistant. He tried to work out what was in it for him, what the downsides were, and how he could turn even those to his advantage. He had pulled out a Richardson's Guide for Brazil, replete with an appendix showing terrain contours, and intently studied the Tietê basin from São Paulo to where it joined the Paraná. His closest examination was of the Pinheiros River, a tributary of the Tietê, which had the best geographic potential for the film.

As a well-informed anthropologist, he was aware of the location of all indigenous groups in South America. The idea of finding an isolated tribe from any of the well-known Tupi tribes, such as the Tupinambá, the Potiguara, or the Caetés, untouched by scientific study, seemed fanciful to him. History clearly showed how the Portuguese had pretty much wiped out all isolated strains of the Tupi people by intermarriage with their women since AD 1500.

Oddly enough, the phenomenon of *cunhadismo* was borrowed from the Tupi, who had an old Indian tradition of welcoming strangers into the tribe. The Portuguese were offered young maidens by the Tupi in order to form a bond with them. However, the clever Europeans turned the tradition on its head and claimed dozens of Indian wives per man, which created a breeding matrix that effectively dissipated, or at least diluted, the Tupi gene pool over time.

But Montana was fascinated with the idea primarily because the Tupi tribes, though united with a common language, were territorial to a fault and constantly warred with their neighboring tribes for territory, women, and more. This had also applied to the Musquaeli people he was trying to forget. Unlike the Musquaeli, these particular Indians had in their ancient traditions the horrible practice of cannibalism as a part of their ritual of war. It seemed they believed that to eat one's adversary after capture in a ritualistic fashion would transfer the strength of the enemy to the victor.

But all the same, the possibility for developing a study—if an isolated tribe could be found—or studying the sociological effects of the decimation of the pure Tupi gene pool on the remnants, just might, with the right approach to the institute, open the next horizon for his career. *I might as well use my fame from the book and movie to jumpstart really interesting things, as far as that's concerned*, he thought.

"Yes, this year has some interesting prospects, if I play my cards right. Now, to just convince Amanda. She'll love it. Always wanted to go on one of my jaunts, and this one is on somebody else's dime. Come to think of it, they all are. I'll do it! By Jove, I will!" he said to the empty room.

35

A Package Deal

Montana left the office early that day and headed home, his manuscript published and making its way around the academic world that he cared about. The fact that his competitors would be poring over its pages looking for errors that might be dropped casually to his embarrassment at the next annual meeting of some anthropological society that he attended was not worthy of his concern at this point.

He was headed to São Paulo, Brazil, for a double blessing. Assisting in the filming of a great commercial venture commemorating the scientific publication of his soon-to-be famous study and the delicious prospect of starting a new venture in his chosen field of interest were two blessings indeed. Bringing his family along was just icing on the cake, for them at least. He had never done this before, and the restriction on his time would just have to be tolerated. His wife was a very manipulative and careful person, but she always erred on the side of furthering his career, not her personal preferences.

When he arrived at home, Amanda was busy preparing dinner and the boys were playing by the lake.

"Father's home, boys. Amanda dear, it's Monty back from a hard day at the college," he said loudly as he came in the front door with no one to hear him. He looked around and noticed the boys weren't in the house, so he stopped by the family bar to mix his favorite drink of bourbon and

Coke and hers of gin and tonic before heading into the kitchen, where he felt sure Amanda would be at this time of day.

"Hello, Amanda dear, I'm home. Here, I fixed your favorite G&T. How was your day?"

"Oh hi, Monty. It was all right, thanks. I could use a drink. You know I get so bored with the college wives' committee assignments. There's the homeless relief project, the annual gala planning committee, and it just goes on and on. I get so sick of this pretense of caring we go through. Do you understand what I'm saying, Monty, really understand?"

"I hear you, darling, and I have a surprise for you—if you are willing, of course—that may change all that for the next few months anyway."

"Surprise? Any change in my humdrum existence would be a surprise, so don't keep me in suspense."

"Come over here and get comfortable. You and the boys will really like this." Montana walked into the den, took one of the chairs, and pointed her to the sofa. She dutifully followed his lead and sat down, sipping her G&T all the while, patiently waiting for the news he seemed to be dying to tell her but was holding back for some reason she couldn't determine.

"Well, darling, good news—got it today. The movie deal has been signed and we are off for the summer to Brazil. How does that sound?"

"Brazil!" she exclaimed. "For the summer? And who is the 'we' you're speaking of? And the *whole* summer? How could that be?"

"Now calm down, Amanda, and I'll explain. First of all, don't forget, Brazil is in the southern hemisphere, their winter is our summer, and quite pleasant you know. But more importantly, you remember the contract I signed for us with the California agency to make a movie of my book, if they could put together a deal with a producer?"

"Of course I remember, Monty. So why don't you just tell me and stop beating around the bush?"

"I'm getting there, dear. The production company is called Star Wisher. I checked it out today and they are big-time folks in the movie business, well funded and all that. The contract between the agency and Star Wisher requires that I consult on set construction and during filming on Indian culture, housing, relationships in the tribe—you know, all that stuff. And I agreed to do that if and when the agency found a willing producer, and they have. Another company called Straight On Films does all the site selection, setup, logistics, and all, and they found a location in Brazil.

"Apparently, the money guy the agency found has connections or even owns a piece of Star Wisher, and he insisted that the settings be as authentic as possible as outlined in my manuscript, and that's where I come into the picture."

She interrupted his description with more questions. "Where in Brazil? You said for the summer, and again I ask, Monty, who is 'we'?"

"It's in the interior from São Paulo on a tributary of the Tietê River. The 'we' I am referring to is you and I and the boys. We spend the summer in Brazil, when I don't have classes anyway. And get this, the institute has been contacted and they might have an interest in a new study if I play my scientific cards right. How does all that sound, my girl?"

"What on earth will I do for two whole months, Monty? You'll be heavily involved in your advisory role, handling Indian extra relations, advising on the script, and all that fun kind of stuff, but what is in it for me?"

"Remember, Amanda, people are people wherever they are, whether culturally advanced or primitive. Not all communication is by language, my dear, and you are the best people person I know. Besides, the agency wanted the family along for some unfathomable reason, so I aim to please these guys. They're paying for all this, you know. So you plan on keeping the boys occupied and out of trouble and the campsite organized and functioning, and you will be a tremendous help to me to see that the boys don't get the Indians stirred up. You are the best at all that, Amanda, and I'm counting on you. Am I right or am I right?"

Amanda was thinking it all over so didn't answer right away. The time away from home and avoiding the social life of Hedley, Florida, for the summer—that was a plus. The heat and humidity in the southern hemisphere couldn't be as bad as in North Florida, with or without air conditioning, so that also was a plus. The boys' hanging out in jungle rivers with snakes and alligators was about like their playing in the lake out back, so that was a neutral. But living in tents with no bathrooms, camping out for three months—*that* was a big negative. But she had always supported her man in his academic and professional pursuits, and this was no different. Watching a movie being made would be different, maybe even fun. She was about ready to announce her decision when the boys came bursting into the house from out back, where they had been playing.

"Boys, come in. Father has some news," Amanda said calmly.

"News, what news?" Average asked, not able to curb his insatiable curiosity.

"Now, Average, you know better than to spoil Father's announcements by asking before he's good and ready," Ratio said in his usual impertinent manner.

"Boys, I was telling your mother that Hollywood is going to make a movie from my book on the Musquaeli Indian disaster, and we all are going to Brazil for the summer so that I can assist the producer and director to make the film as authentic as possible. A summerlong camping trip in the jungles of Brazil—how does that sound, boys?"

Ratio and Average could not at first believe what they had just heard, but looking into their father's face and seeing the smile of contentment on their mother's made the case for authenticity. They smiled and began jumping up and down with an excitement they had not demonstrated for some time. They ran to their normally impersonal father and hugged him with glee. Even Montana was smiling as he looked over at Amanda and saw her approval. She had not answered Montana, giving her approval, but it would have been wasted words. The Blake family, it seemed, was headed for an adventure in Brazil this summer.

36

FLY, FLY AWAY

The Boeing 757 lifted smoothly into the humid air above the runway at Miami International Airport after a two-hour layover for passengers from feeder flights like the one that originated in Pensacola that day. The Blake family was comfortably seated in the first-class cabin that Dr. Blake had arranged through his friend Anna Starke, who also provided window seats for the two boys. A flight like this was a first-time experience for them, headed out of the country to exotic Brazil.

The United Airlines nonstop flight to São Paulo, Brazil, was to take eight hours. A travel coordinator selected by Straight On Films had arranged the family's packing for the trip. Their personal gear had been scrupulously designed, specified, procured, and packed by their personal travel coordinator. Amanda loved every minute of this because normally she had to shoulder this part of the preparations for their infrequent trips. All the gear for their support on location was provided, including tenting, sleeping cots, insect screens, cooking equipment, and food and drinks. With this kind of extensive support, the Blake family needed not trouble themselves with anything, a desirable condition indeed.

All the Blakes had to bring was their personal clothing suitable for the wilds of the Brazilian outback in the middle of what was summer in Florida, but in the southern hemisphere was the more pleasant rain-free autumn and winter. Naturally, the set experts at Straight On Films would appreciate this advantage.

"I can't believe we are finally in the air out of Miami, Monty," Amanda mused meaninglessly.

"There you have it," Montana said, gesturing out their personal view port toward the seemingly limitless blue expanse of the beautiful Caribbean Sea.

37

IF WE BUILD IT, THEY WILL COME

The construction site on a level piece of land alongside the Pinheiros River had virtually destroyed the natural habitat that it had been for centuries, possibly, but not permanently. The deal made by Straight On Films with the Department of the Interior of the São Paulo State government required a full restoration after the filming was completed, down to a replanting of native materials as close as possible to the preconstruction state. A careful film inventory from every conceivable angle had been made and preserved. The skeletal frames of the fictional Stone Age huts were spread around the site, unfinished, waiting on the arrival of Dr. Blake so that the finishing touches could be applied with an authentic look, taking the eventual audience to an imaginary visit to primitive times in an area seemingly so isolated that it could coexist with the modern world and remain unnoticed. The construction activity had from the first day attracted the attention of the local inhabitants.

The site selected was far enough up the Pinheiros River into the picturesque mountain region that the spectators were almost exclusively native Tupi Indians. There were a few tribes of this kind, such as the Tupinambá, in this particular region.

Communication was difficult since none of the construction crew could speak a word of Nheengatu, the common tongue of the native

Tupi tribes, a language introduced by the Mamelucos, a mixed race of Europeans and Indians under the name of Bandeirantes, in the seventeenth century and that had been retained in these isolated areas where there was little contact with the Portuguese. Not even the local language expert hired by the production team was much help since the inevitable changes that creep into language had left this particular tribe with a unique dialect unfamiliar to the expert. Sign language therefore became the lingua franca crudely utilized to keep the observers pacified.

The small security team hired by the production company stayed close by to protect the crew but remained unobtrusive so as not to upset the curious native spectators. However, after a few days, the native observers pulled up stakes from wherever they stayed in the jungles nearby and no sign could be seen of them. The language expert packed up his gear and left, not willing to hang around and watch the work, having accomplished nothing anyway.

Dr. Blake was due on location any day now, and the team was counting on his knowledge and experience of dealing with primitive peoples, as well as his reputed language skills, before beginning the cast selection from the local Indians. If the natives could not be lured back, this was going to be a big problem.

The professional actors would arrive later to supply the speaking parts of the script, but the number of extras required for the battle scene would be large, and the production crew was counting on a local supply of volunteers. The living quarters consisted of cooking, eating, and other necessary facilities as well as the best tenting for sleep and work that money could buy.

38

A TRIAL RUN OF SORTS

After landing in São Paulo, the Blake family stayed a few days in a plush five-star hotel to adjust to the South American culture. The Calinister was selected for this part of their adventure by Anna Starke, and of course the tab for it was included in the budget for Straight On Films.

Montana and Amanda would have preferred to sleep in the first morning, but the boys would have none of it. Ratio woke up first and explored the suite they were staying in and then went out into the hotel complex to explore. Finding it no fun alone, Ratio ambled back to the apartment to roust Average out of his sleep.

Shaking his brother, he said, "Average, Average, wake up, bro. This is a way-cool place. It's got pools, lots of them. Let me show you." Average felt the shake and heard the noise of his brother, but tried to ignore both and return to his pleasant sleep. Ratio only shook him harder and said, "You have to see the jungles out there, Average. Come on, bro, don't you want some fun?" The mention of jungles finally worked, and Average got up on the side of his bed and asked, "Jungles? Where? I thought we landed in some big city."

"It's like a big park, but it's like a jungle sure enough—streams, big trees, and all that," Ratio said excitedly, trying to motivate his brother to join him in further exploration.

"Okay, you have me. Let's go see this jungle of theirs," Average said as he jumped out of bed and grabbed his shoes and clothes.

It really wasn't much of a jungle that Ratio had found but rather a facsimile of one created by the hotel owners to manufacture that South American ambience for those who didn't want to leave the relative safety of downtown São Paulo, where all the shopping, theaters, restaurants, and other entertainments could be found. The South American version of the outback was not really that far away, but inconvenient and possibly dangerous.

The boys walked out of the hotel and into the tropical garden for some serious exploration. The paths meandered through a canopy of tropical trees and ground-covering grasses, shrubs, and other plants, and they walked slowly, taking in this new scenery. The North Florida flora they knew was nothing like this.

A small stream flowed in an elegant man-made curvilinear pattern throughout the park, with numerous beautifully designed deep, crystal-clear pools, each populated by an array of colorful tropical fish swimming up, down, and around to entertain the eye and generally titillate the senses.

"This is cool, but it's so fake, I mean, like Disneyland—you know—made up," Average said.

"Yeah, I agree, but it's a taste of what's to come. I hear we're camping out for the summer in some real jungles."

"Do you think we will see alligators out there?"

"No, I think they're likely to be crocs. Dangerous too, I hear. This is South America. You know, they eat dogs and deer and stuff like that and maybe even kids, if they're not careful" Ratio said, trying to scare his twin brother.

"You can't scare me, Ratio. I think it will be great. Are you hungry? I'm starved. How 'bout you?"

"Yeah, me too. Let's go wake up the folks and get some chow."

"Okay, lead the way."

39

THE BIG DOCTOR COMETH

"All your gear is loaded in the trucks, Dr. Blake. You and the family will ride in truck number two," said Frank Custer, the logistics and supply person for the expedition, leaving the Hotel Calinister. The sun was out and the atmosphere pleasant by comparison to Hedley, Florida, this time of year, where the humidity and temperature were usually high and equal.

"No, Frank, we'll ride in truck number one. I want to be the first to arrive at the location," Montana said with emphasis, falling rather easily into his usual position of command in any situation. He may have gotten that from his upbringing, having a dictatorial father whose family inheritance had made it possible to attain his education and later his reputation on his own as an anthropologist. But he had resented the way he was made to do everything his father wanted. His father was not particularly talented, but he had managed his inherited money well. His birth mother had the brains of the family, but she and his young sister had been killed in a tragic car accident that he, as a survivor, may have been partially responsible for. He may have inherited some of his mother's qualities as evidenced by his ability to overcome the lack of certainty in every situation.

"That's not a good idea, Dr. Blake. The security team goes first on these trips, just to be safe. Where we are headed, civilization has been left behind by history, and these native Tupi once practiced a ritual capture and cannibalism. I have been given the responsibility for the safe arrival of you, Mrs. Blake, and your two sons, so I must insist we follow protocol."

"Follow protocol all you want, Frank, but I am riding in that first truck! You hear? Amanda and the boys can be safe and secure from all alarm in number two, but I *will* be the first one to arrive on the scene, get it?"

Frank was not used to handling such a strong-willed person, but since there was no higher authority to appeal to and getting the team of his charge out to that location was his highest priority, he caved.

"Okay, Dr. Blake, have it your way. It might even be better to have an armed security guy in the second vehicle too. But it's a risk you must realize you are taking, okay?"

"Sure, Frank, whatever you say. Let's get going," Montana said, smiling inside, knowing he always got his way.

The caravan made its way out of the congested, mostly paved streets of São Paulo, and soon found itself moving into the interior, where the practice of paving roads suddenly vanished like a stage setting when the final curtain falls. The vehicles were well equipped, with four-wheel drive and carrying adequate hydraulic jacks, winches for as long as battery power lasted and come-a-longs for when they might run out, and chains to get out of any conceivable difficulty.

Montana had chosen the front passenger seat over the objection of the security team. As the caravan got deeper into the interior, the rough flatlands surrounding São Paulo were replaced by low-level but sharp-peaked mountains cut here and there by streams feeding into the Pinheiros tributary of the giant Paraná River system. They drove for hours on the well-packed roads—gutted from traffic in the rainy season but dry this time of year—jostling everyone.

"How's the ride, sir?" the driver asked, looking over at Montana, who had remained silent, apparently deep in thought.

"It's fine," Montana said, choosing not to engage in chitchat.

The driver suddenly slammed on the brakes, throwing them both forward. "Geez, what was that?" he shouted.

Montana recovered nicely and calmly looked at the driver and said, "'That' was a snake, probably a young boa constrictor. Harmless if you stay out of his reach."

The driver quickly recovered from his embarrassment, and the journey resumed.

In time, the caravan reached the encampment, much to the relief of everyone—from security to the Blake twins, but especially the driver of vehicle number one. By then he had endured quite enough of the famous Dr. Montana Blake. The construction crew came over to welcome the Blake family and got them comfortably settled into their tent quarters. Their timing was perfect, as the evening meal was just being served. Tomorrow the team leader would discuss the problem of the vanishing extras, but for now, the first night in camp for the Blake family, there was peace.

40

What on Earth Can We Do about This?

The sun came up the next morning, shining bright into a clear sky. All was peaceful in the camp as everyone slept well into the morning, until the camp hands brought to prepare meals rang the bell hung up high on a bamboo stalk just outside the dining tent, giving an adequate warning in time for all hands to get ready and make their way over for a hearty breakfast.

The Blake family filed in and took their seats at the camp table designated for guests and were served bountiful helpings of pancakes, eggs, and bacon. Nothing South American in this diet, as all hands were from the States.

"Well, Dr. Blake and Mrs. Blake, how was it, sleeping in a tent? Get a good rest after your trip in?" Camp Director Ray Stephens asked pleasantly.

"It was wonderful," Amanda said quickly, knowing that Monty did not like to engage in much social chat, and for him, sleeping in a tent was not a new event after many expeditions in primitive conditions unlike this rather plush set of accommodations. He kept eating, basically ignoring Stephens.

But that was just a prelude, for Stephens was ready to deal with the serious problem of finding extras from the native population that had fled the encampment, whether Blake was ready or not. The production team was counting on him to act as liaison and, in effect, as recruitment officer for the casting director, who should arrive any day now.

"Dr. Blake, when we arrived a month ago, natives from the nearest village gathered around in curiosity mostly, I figure, but they didn't hang around long. We brought a language expert with us to reach out to them, make friends if possible, but mainly to recruit volunteers to act as extras. It was going to take a lot of them since the battle scenes you described indicate that. We'd pay them, of course, but we got nowhere fast with the language. Our language guy, Dr. D'Souza from São Paulo University, was supposed to be fluent in Nheengatu. It didn't do any good, however, because these Indians either had a different dialect or just didn't want to become involved with us. So we were stuck. He tried for a few days, but it did no good. In a week they vanished into the jungle, and we haven't seen hide nor hair of them for a month. We sent Dr. D'Souza back to São Paulo. I don't think they're coming back, Dr. Blake. So we need your help desperately. The investors that financed this project wanted authenticity, and casting a crew of Brazilian look-alikes won't do. To put it bluntly, Dr. Blake: we need those authentic Tupi warriors. So, sir, can you help us?"

Montana sat quietly and listened as Stephens explained the problem. He intuitively understood how native Indians would react to a virtual invasion of their territory. He had studied the history of the Tupi people. The Portuguese colonizers had done a fair job of melding their settlements peacefully with the Tupi, and over time adjustments had been made. However, for the villages out in the hinterlands like these, a separation had become more or less isolation. They weren't as isolated as the Musquaeli people had been, but he understood the problem well enough. If truckloads of men and construction equipment rolled into any such native people's territory, they would be very curious at first but would not trust any of these white Europeans. Vanishing into the jungle would be the expected reaction. It would take his best efforts, applying the things he had learned in communicating with such people, to bridge the gap. It was in his best interest to try.

"Mr. Stephens, I completely understand your problem. Your planning people should have consulted with me in advance and we could possibly have avoided all this, but that can't be helped now. It will take some time, but I will give it a try. I suggest that in a few days, after my family gets acclimated here in camp, I go alone upriver and contact these people. Maybe I can succeed where Dr. D'Souza failed. I often do."

"Splendid!" said Stephens excitedly. "You can go whenever you think best, Dr. Blake."

"Very well, I will let you know," Montana said.

"Are you sure you want to go upriver alone, though? Is that entirely safe?"

"Of course it's *safe!*" Montana said loudly, with mocking emphasis. "Let me inform you, Mr. Stephens, I have spent my entire career studying and living with primitive and—for that matter—warlike indigenous people far more dangerous than the Tupi, for extended periods, often alone. These Tupi descendants of the once-primitive indigenous people of Brazil have been so domesticated for several centuries by interbreeding with their European colonizers that there could hardly be a warlike bone left in them, no matter how currently isolated this harmless tribe's village is."

"Now, Monty," Amanda Blake said, calmly trying to placate her impetuous husband's outburst, "everyone knows you are probably the world's foremost expert on native people, but Mr. Stephens and his team have actually met these Indians, whereas you haven't, isn't that right, Monty dear?"

Stephens ignored Mrs. Blake's effort to calm her husband down and diffuse the controversy. "Well, Dr. Blake, I defer to your obvious superior experience in these matters, so have a good—safe—expedition!" Stephens said, in obvious mockery of Blake's own declaration. "Now if you will excuse me, Dr. and Mrs. Blake, I have production chores to which I must attend." He got up and left the dining tent.

Amanda stared at Montana with as much disgust as she could manage and returned to her meal with no further comment. He returned her look, thinking, *This little expedition might relieve my boredom for a while, if nothing else. That would turn out to be a surprise.*

41

First We Have to Find or Be Found by at Least One

A few days later Montana donned his jungle-probing gear, consisting of heavy trousers, a plain long-sleeved shirt, and an expedition jacket, along with his hiking staff, a selection of small tools in a satchel strapped over his shoulder, where he stashed his canteen, water testing kit, and a few days' provisions. He had spent the previous two days evaluating the partially constructed huts the preproduction crews had built as described in his book and compiling a detailed list of suggested tasks to complete them, and spent the remainder of each day with his family.

"Boys, you mind your mother as you do at home. This could be a dangerous place, so stay close to the camp."

"But, Father, what can we do around here?" Average asked.

"I told you not to ask him that, Average. Father has a busy day; we can entertain ourselves," Ratio said.

"You listen to your brother, Average. He knows what to do; follow his lead, son," Montana said. Average lowered his head in a sign of obedience and kept silent. Being satisfied with all those arrangements, Montana shoved off on foot into the jungle, following the rough road in some places and a mere well-used, narrow trail in others, along the banks of the Pinheiros River that flowed by the construction site for the movie.

The path followed the course of the river but meandered up and down around natural obstacles, such as rock outcroppings, large trees growing near the riverbank, or fallen trees. Montana made his way easily since his experience allowed him to instinctively sense changes in terrain and upcoming obstacles. This stretch of the river was clothed in lush tropical foliage growing profusely from the rich soil and ample rainfall, with large deep-green leaves that provided adequate cover for predator and prey alike.

Montana was fluent in many language groups common to indigenous people in South America, especially those tribes he had visited on his research projects, but he was not fluent in the various Tupi languages and definitely not in the varying dialects found from tribe to tribe. He had studied and brought along a copy of Jean de Lery's Tupi phrasebook, which transcribed entire dialogues and was the best available record of how Tupi was actually spoken. This was his assignment today, so he drew upon that book with his capable memory and began rehearsing basic greetings. Beyond that he would have to trust to luck.

The jungle was free of the sounds of human presence after he got away from the noisy encampment, and the canopy overlapping the riverbank also made his a dark journey. His hearing was excellent, as was his ability to detect intrusions by their secondary effects on bird life and, more importantly, their noise or the lack thereof. The river current was strong, and small waterfalls here and there made a delightful understated symphonic chorus that, to the untrained ear, would have been an intermingling background sound of gurgling, popping, and fizzing. Montana could hear the chirping songbirds and the racket little monkeys made in the canopy as they went about their everyday lives.

He had been walking along the trail for several hours with no detectable blips in the noise radar detection. The first anomaly he noticed was a sudden cessation of the chatter and monkey racket and movement noises high in the canopy overhead. That was followed by a hush in the bird noises, which left the gurgling river as the only noise in the immediate area. Even the wind seemed to still suddenly, as if some unseen hand were orchestrating near silence all around.

Montana picked up on this change immediately and became more alert, looking for telltale movement in the foliage around the path. When he finally spotted the reason for the change it was too late. Native Indian faces became visible on all sides of him away from the river. Recognizing the danger, his first instinct was to escape, but that was impossible. At this point on the trail, the riverbank was near but steep, with sharp out-croppings ten feet below him, staring up from the surface of a deep pool in the river, like the spines of a giant stegosaurus with the body of the beast submerged and invisible below the water's surface.

The spot for the ambush, if indeed it was an ambush, had been well chosen. But his experience with indigenous tribes told him this group was not necessarily hostile. He could not see the glint of spear points, and from his own study, the evidence for there being remnants of tribes in the region still practicing cannibalism was unclear. He had read of the accounts of Hans Staden, a German soldier and mariner captured by the Tupi, who was able to win the friendship of the local chief and survived to publish an account of it in 1557. So he was wary but not yet frightened.

The Indians closed in on him, fifteen males of varying ages. The youngest in the group was a mere boy, and the oldest, a wizened gray-beard probably near the end of the normal Tupi lifespan. With the ex-ception of one who appeared to be the leader by the ornaments he wore, they wore virtually nothing.

Montana held out his hands, palms open and away, in the universal sign of *wait, peace, stop,* or whatever. The Indians stopped their advance, and the leader stepped forward as if to speak but remained silent. He just stood with a look of part curiosity and part suspicion.

Montana considered the Tupi phrases he had practiced, and said, "Taba abá-etá?" (Are you men from the village?) There was no answer—not even a head motion—so he said it again, louder, as if that would im-prove their understanding. Still there was no answer or other sign. The leader remained silent and expressionless.

"Xe pysyka abá takûarusu. Îande ñeenga?" (You have caught me a man by the bamboo tree. Now can we talk?) he tried to say in Nheengatu. There was no answer. They were either waiting him out or the dialect of this village was so different it might as well have been Latin.

Montana tried other languages, but nothing was working. The leader was stone-faced and completely immobile. The rest of the group were about the same, although they started to move around a little as if they were getting excited or maybe just restless.

Montana grew desperate. Fear was starting to creep into his emo-tions and undermine his normal front of bravado, for he was at a loss as to what else to try. One of the Indians near the back of the group raised his arm, and to Montana's horror it held a crude spear, the first outward sign of hostility from the group.

In desperation he spoke out to the men in his rendition of the Musquaeli dialect of the Quechuan language: "Aes coolah etram. A lous seelah becanni fooleousia maaau. Seau cumlaepha?" (What else can I try? I mean you no harm. I bring you good news for this day. Please say something, anything.)

The Tupi leader backed away from this stream of sounds he could not comprehend at all. If he had understood the other, he never showed it. This truly was a stranger among them. The other men also withdrew a short distance and said nothing.

Then, to Montana's shock and surprise, there came a response in the Quechuan language from a man in the back row.

"Istu sshlamaneaah, ug shallno petulanah?" (How do you speak the language of my people?)

Montana recovered quickly and was smart enough to take advantage of this deus ex machina, however improbable it was that an Indian in the outback near São Paulo, Brazil, could possibly be speaking Quechua. He was thinking, *When at first you don't succeed, as the saying goes, try and try again.* He launched into a tentative but eventually fruitful conversation with the Indian, whose Musquaeli name he discovered was Estabinha, although the tribe had given him some unpronounceable substitute.

This remarkable exchange between the white stranger and one of their own had a calming effect on the other tribesmen. They gathered closely around to listen to what the white man was saying, though they couldn't understand one word of what was being said until Estabinha would stop Montana by a hand signal and a comment—"Wait a minute while I explain this"—and translate into Nheengatu. His fellow tribesmen nodded in enthusiastic appreciation of what was explained—if they agreed—or with equal excitement when they didn't. After a lengthy and intense discussion between Estabinha and Montana, the group took Montana to their village, where the matter of the tribe's participation in the project could be considered by their chief and ruling council.

The Tupi people, in their rich tradition of honoring the elders of the tribe in any important decision, would first explain the questions to their chief and elders and wait for a consensus to develop. This was all the more difficult because the tribe had already abandoned the area the noisy white construction crew had invaded in the first place, so somebody's decision had to be overruled regardless.

Montana learned over the next few days that Estabinha, with whom he was developing a rapport, had been brought to the construction village as a boy by Portuguese mining engineers working on a project for an international consortium in the Rio Ucayali Valley of Peru. Estabinha, on the point of starvation, had wandered into the engineering camp one night and gladly remained. What had put him into that condition and how he had abandoned or been banished by his Musquaeli tribe could not be ascertained.

Estabinha was taught the Portuguese language by his adoptive male fathers, though they made no attempt to accomplish the reverse. When their design portion of the venture was finished, the engineers returned with the youth to their home base in São Paulo, Brazil.

After maturity, the strong pull of the jungle and childhood memories, however painful, left him increasingly unhappy and out of place. His de facto adoptive parents, two old, experienced male mining engineers, had encountered this particular group of the Tupinambá tribe on one of their many adventures into the countryside and left him there as a token to gain acceptance, in the ancient Indian tradition called *cunhadismo*, whereby strangers were incorporated into their communities and favors were given to the donor in return.

Their job was to search for new mining sites, and having a good relationship with a key tribe in the area was a plus. It practically killed two birds with one stone. So, though Estabinha had been raised as a Tupi, he had never forgotten his original Quechuan language, which for Montana was like a gift from the Heaven in which he never believed.

Now that he had a way to communicate, all he had to do was convince them that helping him make this film was a good idea. No small task, that.

42

MEANWHILE BACK AT THE COMPOUND

The set preparation site was buzzing with activity. The film director, crew, and actors with speaking parts had arrived with much excitement. The village scene was practically complete even though Dr. Blake was still gone on his mission to find native Indians to play the supporting roles in the battle scenes.

Amanda, with nothing useful to do, had struck up acquaintances with the food-preparation and provisioning teams. There were no faculty wives or social events around, so she had to do something. This left the boys free to explore.

"Average, why don't we shove off and do some exploring. I'm bored."

"Shove off to where? It's a jungle out there, Ratio. We aren't supposed to leave the camp without Father's permission and he's not here," Average said.

"Oh, Average, don't be stupid and act like your name. Where's your sense of adventure?"

"I don't know. We get in trouble every time we wander off without telling. Why don't we ask Mom. She's around here somewhere, isn't she?"

"No way. She'll only say no and we'll miss out on all the adventure. I'm going whether you come or not. And if you tell on me, I'll say I told you where I was going and you promised to find Mom and ask her but you didn't. We'll be back before dinner anyhow. They'll never know," Ratio said.

Average was thinking, *I'm screwed either way. He'd do it too, and they always believe the glorious one, Ratio the Magnificent, over me, Average the imbecilic one—always! I really get sick of this. Okay, you talked me into it. Let's go find those crocs. Maybe they'll eat both of us.*

The boys slipped out of camp unnoticed and followed an animal trail they had discovered on the outside of the clearing. They soon found themselves deep in the jungle. It was just like the movies, they thought. The trail, with the indomitable explorers walking briskly along on it, meandered deep into the jungle. It wasn't long before they began to see and hear wildlife. First, birds chirping and shrieking everywhere it seemed. Large, colorful parrot-like creatures and many other smaller birds flew noisily from limbs in the canopy overhead, announcing their presence to the rest of the animal kingdom, and who knew what else, like a town crier in Pompeii.

The first animal they saw was a marmot-like rodent that scurried off the trail, disturbed by their progress, at the last minute. The path followed a small stream flowing behind them toward the Pinheiros, as one of the hundreds of such tributaries did to make it a major feeder of the Paraná system.

"No crocs yet, Ratio?" Average asked mockingly, getting braver the farther away from the camp and parents he got. He had been dominated and used by his brother for so long; he relished the chance to get a little dig under his skin when they were outside the retributive reach of their favoring father.

"Shut up, stupid. Crocs don't live in such pissant streams; there's nothing to eat there. You just wait until we get really deep into the jungle, man. Then you'll see, just wait."

"Yeah, yeah, I hear you, Ratio, I'm waiting."

When they were a mile or so further, the boys heard a tumult of falling water up ahead and stopped.

"Big water up ahead—hear it?" Ratio said.

"Uh-huh, I hear it. Let's go look." The boys pushed faster up the rapidly inclining trail above the main river until they came to a breathtaking overlook. Down below them on the trail was a valley cut deep into the little mountain they had been climbing and a large stream coming from an even higher mountain that created an intriguing and beautiful pool of significant dimensions.

The collected water was blocked on one end with a large rocky protuberance across the valley as if a giant hand had been raised and said, "Whoa there, Mr. Watercourse, stop here for a while!" The best the boys could estimate as they discussed the apparition was that the pool or small lake was a half mile or so long and fifty yards across in its middle, though wider on each side, making a rough hourglass shape. The area of the watercourse at its narrowest point was girded like a waistband by a barely visible walkway made of stones. It was hard to tell from this distance, but the boys thought they could see fish in the shallow pools. The lake was surrounded by deep and lush vegetation, making the whole imprint look like a tropical garden in the middle of which someone had dug out this shape and filled it with crystal-clear rushing water.

"Wow, look at that," Ratio said.

"Yeah, beautiful, man!" Average echoed in sentiment at least. "Let's go down and see if there are crocs. Look, the trail makes it way down there," he added.

"I don't know . . . Look how late it's getting. Father is bound to be back soon, and we'll catch it for sure if we push our luck." Ratio was playing the responsible one now.

Average knew he was being set up. *Ratio will enjoy the excursion and risk but blame me for staying and probably lie and say the whole thing was my idea, when the ultimate decision—as always—was his*, he thought.

"Let's go on back then," Average said, "before it gets too late." Ratio nodded and turned to head back down the trail in the direction of the camp. Average dutifully followed.

43

BEFORE THE SUN SETS

The boys made it back to camp in time for dinner. Their mother had missed them earlier in the afternoon and had searched frantically everywhere, but no one in the camp had seen them. Ratio and Average walked briskly into camp with Ratio in the lead.

"Boys, where the hell have you been? I've searched everywhere in this camp for you, and nobody has seen hide nor hair of you all day!" Amanda cried out angrily the minute she saw them enter the compound.

"See, Average, I told you we shouldn't have gone without asking, but you insisted. 'Ask Mom,' I pleaded, but no, you were the great explorer looking for fun in the jungle. I told you we'd get in trouble, didn't I?" Ratio said.

"It was your idea, Ratio. Remember, I told you this would happen," Average meekly said.

"Average, you know you should have listened to your brother," Amanda said, ignoring his explanation.

Average responded in resignation, "Yes, Mother, I'm sorry, I should have listened."

But before the tongue lashing for his "mistake" could be carried out, an unexpected cry arose from the other side of the compound.

"Someone's coming! From out there in the jungle! People are coming!" various compound workers shouted out, quickly stirring up everyone in the small encampment—including Amanda and the boys. The admonishment and punishment of Average would have to wait and would probably be forgotten.

"It's Father! It's Father and maybe the tribe!" Ratio yelled and ran with everyone else in the direction of the commotion.

The excited crowd moved en masse in the direction the lookouts pointed, and promptly collapsed to form a viewing ring, with the jungle trail's entrance into the encampment like the main stage of a melodrama.

The first actor to make his appearance—center stage—was none other than the Big Doctor himself, Horatio Averill Blake, PhD, followed by several Indians in native dress. As he strode confidently into the ring of curious admirers he stopped, lifted his head in triumph, and said, "Ladies and gentlemen, may I present to you the honorable Cacique, chieftain of the Tupinambá tribe, and representatives of his council of elders at your service." Montana Blake took an anticipatory bow. Out of an abundance of caution, with the future of the movie project at stake, no one made a sound. It was fortunate, too, because the Tupinambá had no experience with the Western practice of expressing appreciation by applause. Montana gestured to the audience to sit, and he spoke in Quechua under his breath to Estabinha, who was standing silent in the back of the Tupinambá group, behind Cacique, who in turn whispered in Nheengatu the instruction for the Indian contingent to sit. They did as suggested.

Camp Director Stephens, who had angrily sent an unchaperoned Dr. Blake on what he thought would be a fool's errand, stepped forward with a broad smile to offer his greetings.

"Well, Dr. Blake, who is this Tupi chieftain and company you have with you? And do you bring good news in connection with our native extra problem? For the film, I mean?" Stephens asked.

"Mr. Stephens, I remind you I am a recognized expert in primitive Indian tribes for this region of the world. And as you know very well, Mr. Stephens—can I call you Ray?—before my arrival this production company had managed to clumsily frighten away the Tupinambá tribesmen, situated for centuries—genetically speaking, at least—on the Pinheiros tributary of the magnificent Paraná water course system.

"This tribe is a vital part of those ancient peoples you were counting on to provide extras for the battle scenes in our destined-to-be-famous film; and they have agreed, after several days of my assimilation into their language, customs—and friendship, I might add—to assist my humble self, as the author of the published account of the culture and sadly, regrettably, the end of the Musquaeli people, in any manner required. So, Ray, is that good enough news for you?"

"That's marvelous, Dr. Blake. How on earth did you manage to pull it off, where Dr. D'Souza utterly failed?" All the sarcasm was gone from his voice and demeanor, replaced by a genuine admiration.

"Oh really, Ray, it was nothing, really nothing. A lot of the credit goes to you for challenging me to go with an armed guard. Had I given in to that demand, these people would still be spread by the wind. All in a day's work—or was it a week's work? It was a simple matter of solving the language mystery this particular tribe's dialect posed, and from there a matter of gaining the tribal leaders' trust, something I have become expert at over the years. You see, Ray, the Tupi Indian groups are quite hierarchical in their organizational nature. You sell yourself to the chieftain and his leadership council and the rest will follow along. So when you picked me to solicit their help, you were in luck. None better for that, I'm afraid. We can go over the arrangements tomorrow. But for now, could you arrange some food and sleeping accommodations for my new friends? They have agreed to stay long enough to digest the plan as to the schedule and the number of warriors and village people required, and will return when we are ready to start filming their part in the production. It will take a lot of explanation from me through those I have become closest to in the tribe to make this work. And by the way, Ray, when can I get a copy of the screenplay? It will be essential for that planning, you know. Has everybody you need for the project arrived?"

"Yes, Dr. Blake, we have tents set up in preparation for them in an adjoining area—close but not so close we'll frighten them—and I think they will all fit. May take some selectivity for food, but it's all edible anyway. The director, his staff, and the professional actors are all here and comfortably situated. We can go over all that tomorrow and provide you a copy of the screenplay at that time," Stevens said.

Montana rose from his seat on the ground and signaled for Estabinha to come closer. When he came within hearing, Montana whispered to him in Quechua, telling him to explain the arrangements to Chief Cacique so the Indian men could get settled in for the evening. This being quietly done, the Indians rose and moved in a group behind Stevens's assistant, who led the way.

The rest of the audience had drifted back to their tents by now, and just to be sure they were settled, Montana walked with the Tupi representatives who were acting as liaisons with the production people through his interpreter. Afterward, he eagerly returned to his own family. By then the sun had set and darkness had returned to the encampment, except for lanterns carefully placed here and there for everyone to find their way.

44

FAMILY NIGHT

"Here's Father," Ratio shouted as Montana stuck his head into the Blake tent.

"Uh, hello, all," Montana muttered to Amanda and the boys, who rushed over to embrace him. He was exhausted, physically and mentally, from the combination of days spent trudging uncertainly through the jungle and the narrow escape he'd had, which was balanced by the delight of the accidental discovery of the Musquaeli tribesman and his rescue thereby from what could have been a deadly and final encounter with Indian tribal groups. He gave a quick summary of his trip.

"Monty, that was marvelous! How on earth were you able to talk the Indians into cooperating?" Amanda said.

"There's not much to tell. Luckily, one of the tribesmen could understand my rather poor use of the language of the Musquaeli people, and I was able to persuade him to act as a translator to sell the idea of cooperating with the making of the movie.

"I knew I had to sell the chief on the benefits to the tribe, and once that was done, he did the rest. The Tupinambá people apparently operate on a kind of consensus government, but the Chief position is inherited and what he says carries a lot of weight. They debated the thing for days and finally came around to see cooperation as better than adaptation to a different territory, if running away from all the commotion was a necessary affair. Apparently, the memory of past encounters with European guns made a lasting impression. I was able to convince them that was a real threat and that strangers would be brought in to play their parts and the territory would never return to normal. You see, I told them, 'Help the white men out and they will be gone sooner,' and I was able to convince them the area would be ecologically restored after it was done. Don't misunderstand: they'd never heard the word *ecology* before, but they do know what normal is. Normal to them is all for them and none for us, so to speak. Logical or not it, worked and there you have it. Mission accomplished. Now, can you show me the way to my bed? I am so tired I could sleep a week."

"This way, Big Doctor," Amanda said, borrowing the moniker he treasured on all of these scientific expeditions, without even a hint of sarcasm in her voice, and she led him to the inner chamber of the tent, where a warm and inviting cot awaited.

45

A Pause for Reflection

The production meeting called by the director and his production staff began in a virtual whirl of activity. In the typical fashion of preproduction, much of the planning had been accomplished. The production had been visualized and storyboarded with the help of illustrators and concept artists. All those materials for *Hidden* were on hand and ready to be displayed to the team.

The large meeting tent in the center of the encampment was filled with property masters, the script supervisor, the assistant director, the stills photographer, the picture editor, and the sound editor. Because it was a compact foreign location, the camera crews, the scene and set coordinator, the costume designer, and various assistants were also on hand. The grip, electric generator crews, and production design crews had previously assembled, and the first day's scene was ready for rehearsal and shooting. The professional actors who had been brought in from the States to play the parts of Dr. Blake, Elliot Drake, Urchuwa, Wanei, and Estova were gathered as well and ready for costuming, makeup, and first walk-throughs.

Montana stood in the back of the assemblage with one purpose in mind this morning: he was determined to get his hands on the screenplay he had been demanding since his arrival. Something about the apparent reluctance of the director to release it until now made him suspicious. He was determined that the account of his actions be followed as written in his book, and had a nagging fear that it might not be.

"Listen up, people," Director George Fox said loudly. "We have a movie to make."

Never shy about anything, especially when his image was at stake, Montana stood and said rather loudly, just to be sure he was heard, "Director Fox, Montana Blake here, sir. I have repeatedly requested to see a copy of the screenplay. Since you are about to get busy scheduling your scenes and shoots, could I have a copy now? I was brought here supposedly to offer scientific anthropological advice on the scenes, sets, costumes, and the like, and I can't make my contribution without it."

Fox looked startled and bothered at Montana's request. He hadn't dreamed it would come up this soon and so blatantly. These so-called technical advisors were brought to the production set primarily as a token honor for their contributions to the story, and in his mind, Dr. Montana Blake was a hindrance to controlling the shooting schedule, not to mention the well-conceived plan to delay this conflict to the end of the shooting sequence, when not even the famous Dr. Blake could alter the inevitable.

He looked at Dr. Blake long and hard as he processed this latest challenge. Forget that Blake had singlehandedly saved their bacon by somehow convincing the local Indians to return. Fox could only see the potential disruption of his production schedule by some silly "advice" or insistence that scenes be changed, which often happened with "writers"! Been warned about that by the producer, right? Time for plan B.

"Oh very well, Dr. Blake. Alice, get a spare copy of the screenplay for Dr. Blake. You know, the *writers copy* I told you we would need about now."

"Yes, Mr. Fox," his chief administrative assistant said with a knowing look as she turned and left the tent.

She returned in minutes with an envelope containing a copy secure in a plain manila envelope embossed with "Writer's Copy" on the cover. Dr. Blake took the envelope and turned around to head to his tent.

Montana checked first to see that his family were otherwise occupied with camp duties or play, then settled into his camp chair to read through the manuscript. Although still light outside, the tent was too dark for reading, so Montana fired up the portable lantern he had brought along just for such occasions, hung it from a hook overhead, and began reading. It was a tedious task because it contained so much more than just the story he had written. But he had to be sure that the Hollywood syndrome had not converted his version of the truth into the real thing. He could never allow that. *So might as well start at the beginning*, he thought, and opened to page one.

Okay, Montana thought after reading the first part of the screenplay, *nothing surprising there. Interesting speculation about Elliot's background. Probably made that up. Moment of caution here: creativity sells scripts, but have to watch for the critical scenes—about me, that is. If he did that job on poor Elliot, what will he do on me?*

Montana continued to read, skimming the harmless stuff. Didn't matter to him if the film made money or not. After all, what did he know about making movies, successful or not? His check was already working away in his investment portfolio, unlike what he was doing here.

Okay, the entrance scenes check out. Wanei and Estova's roles just like I wrote them, the village description, meeting Urchuwa. Then we went to the battle site, right. He read on faster now, not finding anything to alarm him—not yet anyway.

Okay, the council of war where they meet the warriors. Now the battle plan scene. Elliot takes initiative just like he did back then and is led away by Urchuwa and the two warriors on their expedition; good, good. Then he reports back with a plan; have to read this carefully and see whether Mr. Creative gets it right. Let's see, how did they handle that?

                    DRAKE
          (tone is even and professional)
     Dr. Blake, Urchuwa, men, the valley
     is a natural setting for a trap. We
     lure the enemy into it by a thin line,
     call it a "thin red line." The enemy
     scouts will see it as a logical posi-
     tion but vulnerable to a frontal as-
     sault. We stage the bulk of our men on
     the slopes on either side and when the
     enemy attacks—the weak appearing cen-
     ter in the style I was told was typ-
     ical of them—the line folds, fighting

> backwards to lure the main body into
> the trap. Wanei and Estova will follow
> me into position to act as interpret-
> ers for the men, Wanei to the left,
> and Estova and I on the right slope.
> Be ready to spring the trap. On my
> command, signaled by a flare, the two
> sides will envelop and attack the in-
> vading force and hopefully finish them
> off or weaken them so that the tribe
> will no longer be a threat to the
> Musquaeli. Questions?

>   DR. BLAKE
>   (calm and complacent)
> Okay Elliot, if you are sure this
> is best, I rely on your profes-
> sional judgment.

That's good so far. The writer didn't read anything into this part. Montana read on, anxious to find out how the writer treated the battle scene's development and, more importantly, how he dealt with the idol's part in this drama.

He has me watching from the left hillock with a clear view of the battle; that's right. The tide turns after Elliot springs the trap and it backfires. Damn clever of those native warriors or just dumb luck to divide into two groups. Anyway, that's what happened. He has me deciding to go over to see Urchuwa once his charisma and whatever the long-distance effect of the little war god was have been tried and have obviously failed. We meet in the valley central. Good. Urchuwa takes command—good! Here it goes—the key part.

EXT. VALLEY BATTLE SITE - DAY

Urchuwa and Blake meet to confer.

CRIES OF VICTORY AND OF THE ANGUISH OF
DEFEAT AND DEATH

234

Urchuwa stands tall, head erect, but resignation shows all over him like a fading lightbulb. The radiant glow is gone. He remains proud and steadfast, but confidence has been replaced by resignation.

URCHUWA
(voice is steady but soft, in broken
English this time)
Big Doctor, we lose great battle. Tribe will be defeated, our people destroyed. Only honor tribe left. Go, Big Doctor; take war god to safety. Urchuwa stay to die. War god must be saved.

BLAKE
(incredulity in his voice)
Urchuwa, my friend, surely this is not the end. Tell me where the war god is hidden and I will bring it to you. With its presence your warriors will sense it and still emerge victorious. Let me serve you in this way.

URCHUWA
(resignation resonates)
No, Big Doctor; all lost. Idol must be saved for the spirit memories of my people. You take. You leave; tell rest of world we fought valiantly for our people. Musquaeli people remain in spirit if not in this life. You go now! Before too late, or all truly lost.

I don't know what I was worrying about. This is a very fair treatment. I can live with this. But how do they end this sad tale? He read on faster now, skipping over huge sections about the return trip, the public announcements—which he cared nothing about because he had nothing to hide there anyway. They even had him making the finals of the Mead Award, although that hadn't been announced yet. *At least they don't try something stupid there with so many witnesses when it does happen. And then the final scene. The Academy Awards?*

```
INT. ACADEMY AWARDS - EVENING


            NARRATOR (V.O)
The lights are always bright in
Hollywood, but no brighter than on
the night for the Academy Awards.
The best and the beautiful, not neces-
sarily in that order, cannot be kept
away. Personal achievement is suc-
cess's greatest reward, but public
recognition is the cream at the top,
and sometimes running over the top.
It might even be considered ecstasy.
Many strive for that status of winning
the Oscar, but not many ever make it.
Can you say junior high football play-
ers with their eyes on stardom in the
NFL? The award ceremony is an evening
of ostentatious glitter, full of par-
ticipants nominated for an Oscar who
could not possibly be anywhere else
this night of all nights.
```

For Bill Springer, this condition was nothing new. He had dutifully sat in that great audience of egos many times before, but had never been granted the ultimate prize. He had given up preparing his acceptance speech in advance, having been disappointed so many times before, so he just put on the obligatory tux and entered the hall with his wife, Melody, by his side, taking their seats in a modest, not-expecting-too-much row.

BILL SPRINGER and MELODY SPRINGER enter the hall, proceed up the aisle, and take their seats near the back.

> NARRATOR (V.O.)
> With a name that almost defies pronunciation, Clifton Ruggelsby, the master of ceremonies that night, was, oddly enough, a literary critic with a flair for public presentations. He made the rounds of celebrity shows and other programs that showcase talent of one kind or another, and an adoring public could never seem to get enough of his humor and charisma. Tonight he is no different as he's at the pinnacle of his own particular tower of success and definitely on his game.

RUGGELSBY appears on stage from a distance.

APPLAUSE

> RUGGELSBY
> Ladies and gentlemen, let me welcome you to the eighty-seventh Academy Awards. Tonight is our lucky night.

TRIUMPHANT MUSIC

> NARRATOR (V.O.)
> Ruggelsby began and droned on in that melodious manner that is his trademark. The show began with the usual

entertainment acts and finally got into the preliminary awards that hardly anyone but the nominees or true movie aficionados are even vaguely interested in, like costume design or sound-effects editing.

Bill and Melody Springer were fast getting bored until the MC finally got to the screenplay awards. The Academy has two categories for these awards to recognize the changing reliance on original screenplays over time to capture the imagination of the voting public at the movie theaters. These folks at the pay stiles are ultimately the only voters who count. But possibly for historical reasons, the Oscar for writing an adapted screenplay remains an award. This was Bill Springer's category this year, but he gave himself no chance of winning. The title of the academic tome, if nothing else, was sufficient to turn away any voters in the Academy, yet even *Containment or Consequences: A Search for Tribal Survival* had not closed the door on his nomination.

MUSIC ENDS

Bowing slightly, Ruggelsby waves his right arm across the view of the vast audience as if conducting.

                    RUGGELSBY
To present this prestigious award welcome two-time Oscar winner in the same
category, Eric Roth.

ROTH makes his way to the microphone from
stage left.

APPLAUSE

Roth takes the envelope containing the nominees' names.

                      ROTH
          (unenthusiastically due to his disap-
          pointment at his own screenplay hav-
            ing been left out of contention)
The nominees are: *Escape from
Hamburger World*, Elias Anderssen,
from the novel *The Other* by David
Guterson; *Treasure of Another Kind*,
Esther Herndon, from the novel *The
Alchemist* by Paulo Coelho; *The Scrolls
among Them*, Truance Stillbinder, from
the novel *The Last Disciple* by Hank
Hanegraaff and Sigmund Brouwer; and last
but not least, *Hidden*, Bill Springer,
from a nonfiction account of Stone Age
peoples by Horatio A. Blake, PhD,
*Containment or Consequences: A Search
for Tribal Survival*.

And the winner is . . .

                          FADE TO BLACK:

By the time Montana finished reading the screenplay, it was dinner time, so he packed it up and headed over to the communal tent where all the meals were served. As expected, he found Amanda and the boys seated in their accustomed places and joined them to learn what their activities of the day had been. There was no way he could truthfully share what he had been up to, so he put on his face that hid all the important stuff from his family. He actually liked it that way. As he joined them in conversation, he didn't notice that he was being watched from across the tent.

46

LET THE CAMERAS ROLL

The next morning, Montana rose early, before the rest of the family, and made his way to the dining tent, carrying the bulky screenplay. He was already satisfied that the writers had not seriously distorted his description of the events. In the important areas, that is. One final review was his intention as he sat at one of the tables, having his first mug of coffee. No one else seemed to be around, so he was free to spread out the screenplay notebook before having breakfast. Except he wasn't alone.

The man sat across the tent, sipping his morning coffee in the quiet morning as well. He had noticed Dr. Blake when he came into the tent and was not surprised when Dr. Blake didn't even scan the area and notice him sitting there, watching.

He's still reading it. Amazing! Doesn't he see we put everything into that script that he expected to see? Man, that is one serious ego sitting over there. If it were me, knowing what I know he knows and reading that script, I would see it as a fake in a New York minute. Hell, no self-respecting screenwriter would put that stuff into his script. But, take a gift when you find it, I say. Better play out the hand we've been dealt. Yes!

George Fox rose from his seat and made his way across the tent to the coffee urn, where he refilled his own mug and got a fresh one for Dr. Blake before approaching him from the front.

"Good morning, Dr. Blake. Did you have a good rest?"

"Oh, Director, good morning to you, sir. Yes, I rested fine. I have just finished reading the screenplay—good work. I approve of the way it's written."

"Glad to hear that, Dr. Blake. Now we can concentrate on planning the early shoots. As you undoubtedly have read, the script opens with the dream scene, but that will be filmed elsewhere—the wrong setting here. We'll shoot the opening scenes today down by the river and take it from there. I anticipate that we'll do the battle scenes in a week or so, and for that we will need you to help us tell the natives what we expect, okay?"

"Sure, I can do that. Just tell me how many you need, et cetera," Blake said, not wasting any energy or words in his reply.

Good enough for now, Fox thought. "We'll start the first shoot this afternoon down by the river." Fox arose and left Dr. Blake sitting at the table, apparently deep in his thoughts, reading once again the touchy parts of the screenplay.

47

Round Them Up

Montana, along with key members of the production crew, had left the previous morning on his sojourn to select and recruit the movie extras. They needed the Tupi people primarily for the final battle scenes, but some would be selected based on size, build, and aesthetic appeal for use in close-ups. The Tupi people had the good (obedient), the bad (troublemakers), and, worst of all, the ugly (unpleasant to look at to Western eyes)—never acceptable in a film.

The trail to the village was easy walking, and he knew the way from the numerous trips he had made while finding the Tupinambá village on his first trip. Hopefully, nothing had happened to his new friend Estabinha, for without him to interpret, the project was doomed to failure.

He needn't have worried since Estabinha had found a new revered status among his tribesmen. There is nothing more useful than being needed. The hard part would be in telling each Indian exactly what he was expected to do and hoping that they could remember at shooting time and, better yet, perform on cue. Extras in most American-produced films were largely actor wannabees, and the biggest challenge was keeping them from overacting, always looking for a chance to be discovered for a greater role. That, at least, would not be a problem with the Indian extras.

The village was approached with caution, but there was no surprise in this encounter. The sounds of the forest had announced their approach, and the Tupinambá people were seated in the pecking order of the village when the group arrived.

Montana, spotting Estabinha right away, standing toward the back of the group, beckoned him to approach. He explained that the film crew needed approximately thirty of the warriors to make up the reenactment of the final battle, and possibly many others, including the village women, for other scenes.

The Indians would have great difficulty understanding what was expected of them, and a round of councils would be necessary to get the foreigners' wishes across and—more importantly—the final approval. Montana had expected this process to be long and arduous, but after a few hours Estabinha, Montana, and Earl Singer, the crew chief, were able to reach a general agreement.

The session completed, an evening meal was presented by the women of the village. The film crew had come prepared to stay overnight. Estabinha led Montana and the others to an area where they could pitch their tents and get settled.

In the morning Montana and the others, seated around a small fire, brewing camp coffee, were surprised to find the village men suddenly standing there. No one could remember afterward for how long, but there they were. The chief and other leaders were bedecked in colorful bead-and-feather headdresses, in stark contrast to the rest of the tribesmen, who wore little of anything and stood to either side.

The outsiders jumped to their feet and huddled to make a plan.

"Why don't you suggest to the villagers that they stand there as they are situated," said Singer, "and let me quickly go down the line and pick out the cast of warrior extras. You and your guide work out some way to identify those selected, and since these names are practically impossible to remember, much less pronounce, we can use a number system that cross-references to the names, which the guide can hopefully remember. I doubt they will agree to wear number tags, although that would be best. Try it and we can remove the tags for the actual shoot."

Montana thought for a few minutes, ensuring he was a part of the decision, and replied, "I'll suggest to Estabinha that these warriors are being selected because their build, postures, and attitudes show the greatest warrior capabilities and the foreigners want to let the others know who the best are. They will love the recognition and proudly wear the banners. So here is what we'll do."

He continued, "Have your costume staff make up some ribbon-like collars to fit loosely around the neck of each man selected, that can be clipped or, even better, secured with a snap, for ease of removal and re-installation from scene to scene. Go ahead and prepare titles, like East Side, West Side, Center Warrior, and so forth, based on where the men will be positioned in each scene. They won't be able to read it anyway. Use a distinctive font of some kind, the fancier the better so that they will feel important. I'll have Estabinha explain that each man was selected for his unique size and appearance, portraying the most warrior-like appearance, and they will love the distinction. Pride knows no cultural boundaries, men; trust me in this. As to any men selected for other scenes, let me know what you want."

Singer and the others nodded in agreement. Montana, pleased with himself, signaled to Estabinha to come over for a consultation. He did his best to explain to his friend that the selection process was based on the qualities that the Tupi considered relevant in any of their bestowments of honor and that the appearance of the warriors in the scenes to be filmed was a reflection on each warrior's honor. The concept of filming a picture of themselves was strange enough for them to comprehend, much less to even try to imagine that they should pretend to be someone else to create an image of reality. This little deception was necessary to accomplish the goal of fulfilling some future viewer's deception that this was reality—or so close to it the imagination would rule over the knowledge that it could not be.

Singer and the casting crew made their way down the line of Tupinambá men, looking for telltale signs that only men engaged in a career like theirs could spot. General build, musculature, variation in size and appearance, the way the head was held, even shades of color difference, facial features, hair and—most of all—attentiveness and focus on what was going on at the moment were the objective and subjective factors being considered.

Most professional casting experts couldn't or wouldn't say, even if they wanted to be completely candid, how they made these choices. But as it is said, cream rises to the top in any endeavor, and these men were the best from their years of experience in making these selections.

Before long, the selections were made and Montana was asked to have his interpreter tell each one that he had been selected for the honor of representing the tribe in the venture. The casting crew, prepared for almost any eventuality, came up with a set of tags fashioned into neckwear to get by until they could return to the main camp and come up with a more durable style that would last through the shooting schedule. The adornments were given in an impromptu ceremony, and each man proudly walked among his fellows showing what he believed was the special honor he had received.

After a plan was devised for telling the men when they were to assemble, the tribesmen scattered to their own pursuits for the day. There was enough daylight left for the film crew to return, so they packed up and headed back to where the real work would begin.

48

ROLL 'EM!

A day or so after their return, the camp was a madhouse. Lighting and camera equipment had arrived and was strategically placed at various locations on the ever-fluid set. One team was set up at the cataract for filming the approach of the expedition, and another in several locations near the reconstructed village.

The approach scene was a special challenge because the cameras had to be mounted at both ends of the precipice on which the actors would have to climb. The small waterfall that the crew located on a tributary feeding the Pinheiros River was nothing in size and grandeur to that of the falls on the Pangria where Montana, Drake, Wanei, and Estova had approached the fateful location of the Musquaeli tribe in Ecuador, but that was only a small obstacle for the capable film crew. Distance, size, and sound could be manipulated to create the illusion of grand size if needed.

While Montana managed the Tupinambá people for the role of extras, the parts for Wanei and Estova were filled by professional actors brought in from São Paulo. Director Fox would not risk failure by trading the authenticity of Tupinambá tribesmen for the reliability of men accomplished in the trade of illusion making.

The actors were in place at the foot of the waterfall, with camera crews on both ends and lighting banks where appropriate.

"Roll 'em!" Fox yelled from his position on top of the falls, and he watched the actors below begin their ascent. Up they climbed, hand over fist, stepping carefully on the disguised footsteps installed for safety, not visible to the camera's eye but nothing like the perilous ascent Blake and the others in the expedition had once climbed.

Montana stood near Fox and wondered how this miniature setup, in comparison to his vivid memory of the access up from the Pangria, would appear on film. He could still remember how each step seemed uncertain at best and perilous for the rest. The actors made it look easy and hard all at the same time, without much real risk to their safety, but creating the illusion that they were on the verge of falling to their deaths at every step.

As the actor playing Wanei climbed out at the top, he crouched in a semi-hidden posture and viewed the landscape as if watching for danger. He turned to assist the actor playing Elliot Drake out onto the plateau.

"Wanei, is it safe for the others?" 'Elliot' asked.

"Yes, Soldier Man, safe for Big Doctor to approach," 'Wanei' said.

Elliot eased back over to the edge of the precipice and gave the pre-arranged low whistle signal and the others scrambled out onto the rocks.

Dr. Blake stood tall, surveying the scene ahead as if getting his bearings, and said, "All right, Elliot, men, we head upstream from here, so pull up the ropes tied to our gear below and we can get organized."

"Cut!" Fox yelled, and the cameras stopped. "That's a take. I think we can use it after sound editing. The next scene is closer to the camp where Dr. Blake and his team arrive at the village and encounter the Indian shaman Urchuwa. Good work, team!" he shouted, and he leaned over to whisper a private message of encouragement to the cameraman and gave a thumbs-up to other key people. "Let's get back to camp for the next scene."

The next scene was the expedition team approaching the facsimile village and their first encounter with the tribal shaman. A runner had been sent to the Tupinambá village to gather together a selection of the village women to be used in the scene. In the story, the men were away preparing to defend the sacred territory, so only the women and children were left at home when Dr. Blake's team arrived, escorted by the older warriors who had been left behind as the rear guard. They now had the honor of escorting the foreigners and their guides into the village, where the wiser heads could decide how to treat the strangers. Within a few hours the set was prepared.

What am I going to do all day? Average thought. *The action is down by the river and then up at the make-like-it Indian village. Ratio has been a pain all day, as usual, and we were told to stay away from the shooting. That's just great! The only fun thing going on and we can't watch it. What if I got Ratio to come up with the idea of sneaking out there against the rules? Hmm, how can I do it this time? Misdirection? Opposites? Let me see . . .*

"Hey, Ratio, what'd you have in mind for today?"

"I'm just hangin' out, Average. You?"

"Well, I tell you what I'd like to do, but that's already out: I'd love to sneak out of camp and watch the film shoot today. I hear it's over by the fake village. But Dad was quite specific about staying away from there, and I for one don't think we could manage to sneak out, watch the filming, and sneak back before he could catch us. I could never do that, so boredom it is, I guess." *I see that look he gets every time.*

"You know, Average, for once you may have just come up with a bright idea. Let's blow this joint; follow me."

He's starting to leave without even waiting for me to gripe about it, just knowing I'll come along anyway. Guess it worked. Here we go, out into the world of film-making adventure. I better hurry to catch up.

"What's the plan—sneak up within a safe distance so we can't be seen but can still hear?" Average asked.

"No way," Ratio said. "That's too lame—as I might expect from you. We'll follow the trail down to the fake village, sneak up to the edge of the camera equipment area, and watch from there. Haven't you seen how they show it on TV? The director calls all the shots, but he's totally focused on the scene and the actors and all that stuff. He'll never see us. Come on."

He's so predictable, and still an ass. Oh well, here goes. I'll stay respectfully behind as Ratio surveys the crowd and equipment.

With the village as the backdrop, the women were seated out front of the fake huts as if it were any other day in the life of the village people, complete with cook pots and assorted utensils brought forth for meal preparation. Ratio decided where they should be perched and started his low-profile approach like an army scout sneaking up on an enemy position behind their lines.

Play along is best, even if this is really stupid, thought Average.

Ratio found a large clump of grass to hide them from the movie company's view and plopped down, signaling with his palm down for Average to follow, like a veteran Army Ranger would.

"What are you two doing here? Did I not make myself clear that I didn't want you bothering the film crews?" their father shouted. "And, Ratio, I expect more leadership from you in these things—so don't tell me it was your brother's idea. It's no excuse, so get back to camp *now*!"

Ratio looked over at Average and shrugged as if to say, *See what you got us into again?* Average rolled his eyes as if to accept the inevitable and quickly got up and headed back to camp. Ratio followed, and when they got out of earshot of Father, said, "I thought I had the perfect spot. What went wrong?"

"Well, you don't want to hear it from me, but when you left camp ahead of me and decided exactly how we should approach the set, I recalled that the first scene was being shot down by the waterfall and the expedition was to come back from there by the river trail. That would bring them right up behind us, and naturally, Father would wander over in that direction to report on his activity, and voilà! we're nailed."

"If you had it all figured out, why didn't you say something for once, stupid?" Ratio said, looking at Average with that "it's all your fault" look like he always did.

Average laughed inside, hiding it behind the "poor me" look he was famous for, especially since he hadn't figured it out ahead of time at all. *Gotcha, huh?*

49

"The Man" Cometh

The "expedition" slowly approaches the encampment set through some of the lushest jungle scenery found anywhere in the world. The strikingly handsome actor playing Wanei, acting as scout, leads the way, with the others close behind, trying to walk as though they are making no noise, although for filming purposes it makes no difference. Wanei steps cautiously, pauses to listen for imaginary jungle sounds, looks back to the team members, and signals that all is clear. The lighting is perfectly adjusted to show fingers of sunlight streaming through the vast overhead foliage, like the ribs of a giant fan rippling gently across the faces of the actors as they stealthily approach the village, emerging one by one into a jungle clearing until the entire team is shown crouching and moving as signaled by Wanei in scout-like fashion.

"Cut!" shouted Fox. "That's another take. At this rate, we'll stay on schedule for once; bound to be delays later, though."

The next scene was the approach to the village, which was all prepared thanks to the second photo shoot team. Montana, after shooing the two boys back to camp, could concentrate on his primary function of communicating through Estabinha to the Indian women what the film crew expected. No small order, that. After much preparation and conversation between Montana and his interpreters, the scene was ready.

The actor playing Dr. Blake arrives at the village, leading the expedition team, with Wanei by his side. He spots one Musquaeli tribesman who appears to be the leader among the group of warriors standing guard while the rest are supposed to be away having their council of war. After approaching him for a private conference, using the dialect selected for the Musquaeli people, he converses with Dr. Blake in an excited tone. The film will show subtitles so the audience can follow along.

Dr. Blake is told that the tribe is in a state of war for their survival, that most of the warriors and their leader, the shaman of the village, are at another location, planning the defense of their territory. Dr. Blake nods as if he understands all this fully, but in reality he doesn't, his body language on full display so effectively a viewer could almost follow the dialogue without the subtitles. He is surprised by the news but also pleased by the opportunities that might be presented. Of course, he is not saying that to anyone, always vigilant to be the curious scientist eager for discovery of new data to interpret for the world's benefit.

Meanwhile, having been warned by their home guard of the expedition's approach, the village people are excited about the foreigners' arrival yet have much trepidation as to its significance.

That being said, the little bit of stage business the actors portraying the village people engage in make it apparent to the viewers that something significant other than a first encounter with the expedition team is about to take place. They are undoubtedly asking each other, "What are these foreigners doing here at such a critical time?" The scene effectively portrays a moil of action and excited chatter.

In the midst of this confusion, the engineered surprise event unfolds. While Dr. Blake and Elliot are wrapped up in the discovery of the crisis about to engulf the tribe, a stillness settles over the scene as all the villagers suddenly cease their chatter and motion. All heads are turned to the clearing as if drawn like iron filings toward a magnet. The shaman has arrived.

50

The Trouble with Doing Nothing Is Not Knowing When You Are Through

Meanwhile, having been banned from watching the only action around, the boys sat with their mother after breakfast and grew bored with inactivity. Amanda soon left the tent to engage some of the film preparation crews in conversation.

Average was deep in thought. *I'm sitting here twiddling my you-knows and tired of it. This was supposed to be fun, a real adventure, yet all there is to do is watch the camp do nothing. Father wouldn't let us watch the filming, darn it, said we would be in the way. Caught in the act of sneaking out there is more like it. That old cook tent over there—what a boring thing to watch. It's covering the place we eat and serves no other function as far as I can see. Ratio is bored with it all too. He's sitting there waiting for what? Just like me, waiting for nothing.*

"Hey, Ratio, aren't you as tired of this place as I am?"

Ratio nodded and looked around as though he was thinking.

That's when my brother is dangerous. Thinking stirs him into action at least, and I usually suffer from it, but right now anything, even suffering, would be a pleasant change. I think that enchanted pool upriver would be fun to explore. All I have to do is get him to think it's his idea. Let me see now, how can I plant the idea in that large head of his?

"Hey, Ratio, that magic pool we saw upriver—I'm glad we left that sucker alone; could have been really dangerous, don't you think?" *He's looking at me with that know-it-all look he's especially good at. He's smiling like a mischievous idea is forming in that devious brain of his.* "I'd be scared to walk across that underwater footbridge, wouldn't you?" Average prompted.

"Scared? Not me, man. In fact, let's split this joint and go check it out, whaddaya say, live dangerously for once in your life, okay?"

"I don't know. You heard what Mom said when we were caught sneaking up to watch the scene being shot. I don't want to get on her bad side again. Once is enough for this trip."

"Oh come on, Average. Let's do it. She won't care. And if she does, what's she gonna do, sell us to the Indians as slave children?"

Let him rant on for a while, I say. If he makes his mind up, we're out of here, and anything would be an improvement over this nothing-to-do stuff. That's it, Ratio: you figure it out and I'll reluctantly agree and we're in business.

"Average, I'm tired of you being a chicken about this, so I'm going. Are you coming or not?"

That's the way, Ratio. You are so easy to manipulate. There he goes. Wait a few minutes and follow.

51

ARMAGEDDON REDUX

The shooting of the final battle scene went easier than expected. The Tupi men selected to play Musquaeli warriors in individual scenes were set up all across the mountainous terrain. Dr. Blake and Estabinha were kept busy hurrying from scene to scene, communicating what the director wanted each man to do. The whole thing was nonsense to the Tupi, but they enjoyed the attention and did their best to stand, look, squat, and hold their short throwing spears menacingly or actually throw them as required ad infinitum, or ad nauseam as it seemed to them. But eventually they got the hang of it, and hand signals and body language were largely successful in communicating what was desired.

Professional actors would have relished the opportunity to add their own show business to each scene, but these men were content to do just what they were told or shown. Fox liked this but had to do many more reshoots than he normally would have.

This process went on until late in the day. They were down to shooting the Elliot Drake parts in which his signal that was designed to save the day and bring victory to the home team instead triggered the disaster that would usher in their doom. Blake was content with this as he observed the shoot from a safe distance but stood ready with translations should hand signals become ineffective.

Any observer would not have had a clue as to the overall plot based on the shot order, but the magic of Hollywood editing would put the story in order for the audience, and that was all that really mattered to the production company, Fox in particular.

52

IT'S SO BEAUTIFUL, IT HURTS

The expedition of boyhood made its way up the trail discovered on the last trip. The morning sky was clear and free from rain so that the forest trail was a pleasure to walk along.

I'll let him stay ahead the way he likes it. It's been how long, an hour?

"Are we there yet, Ratio?" Average asked rhetorically, like every kid asks the older and wiser sorts—usually their parents—on a trip, but all he got was a wave of the arm behind his back in a dismissive gesture. "Do you still think we should cross it, the underwater footbridge?" he asked innocently, catching up alongside Ratio where the path was wider and level.

"Of course, stupid. Why else are we trudging up this steep mountain path?" Ratio said with a glance.

"I think I remember this part of the trail—it's right around the next peak on the trail that we reached the overlook from, remember?"

"Sure I do, Average. I was here the other day too, remember?"

"Just trying to be helpful."

"Yeah, thanks a lot!" Ratio replied sarcastically.

Average walked on and gained a little ground so he was a few yards ahead on the trail. It wasn't long until—with an altitude gain of a thousand feet—they broke out onto the plateau where they had been before. Below was a panoramic view of one of the most beautiful scenes on Earth. *Of course, I haven't seen that many, but it's my number one for now. Even Ratio, who arrived alongside me, has taken it in and remains strangely silent.* They took in the mountains surrounding the alluring hourglass-shaped deep blue crystal-clear lake with its stone walkway just beneath the water across the middle.

"Let's go," Ratio said, and headed down the trail ahead of Average, toward the edge of the lake.

"We better be careful. There could be crocs hidden in all that foliage," Average said from his position several yards behind Ratio as he plunged recklessly on ahead, determined now to see for himself and not bothering to answer. *He's at the edge now and I know he'll cross the thing, crocs or not.*

On their side the lake was surrounded by a rock shelf of sorts. Without looking back, Ratio took a tentative step out into the lake, finding his way onto the first flat rock that astonishingly enough was just under the surface and secure enough for him to stand on as he paused and looked back at his brother triumphantly.

54

THE BETRAYAL

I, Montana—the only one to please—am up earlier this morning than usual, before dawn even, because this is the day they shoot the end of the battle scene when Urchuwa selected me—who else?—to save the pride of the Musquaeli for the spirit world, apparently, because the tribe was about to get wiped out. The script is just the way I wrote it in my masterpiece, but strikes too close to home as I face this experience all over again.

Of course, looking back on it, taking the war idol was the right thing to do. Those poor primitive folk were going to get wiped out regardless. Anyone could see that. So what if I left the scene of the battle to go get that little piece of stone they believed in so highly? I brought it back to them, didn't I? Boy, that sure was a surprise when the damn thing began to vibrate in my satchel. I mean, I am an original scientific materialist, and this, according to my lights, is not supposed to happen except in legend and myth, but it was happening right next to me.

It was even more of a surprise when the closer I got to Urchuwa, standing there like a fool on top of that little promontory and raising his arms out like Moses holding his staff with the Israelites fighting against the Amalekites, the more the troops began to rally. Then, as I pulled away, the little bastard suddenly stopped vibrating in my satchel and momentum of the battle shifted.

Can you blame me, self, my conscience, that I made the choice I did? I mean, what fool would stay there and let the tribe and me get slaughtered? By then Elliot was dead and there was only Wanei and myself from the original expedition left alive. There would have been no one to tell the story, no one to record it for posterity; and that, in the end, is what the whole expedition was about. It was bigger than me, more important than who won or lost. It was scientific sociological history in the making, wasn't it? I could not let that chance be lost. But not to worry today. I read the script, and they have Urchuwa asking me to save the war god for their spiritual posterity. And it did, in a way.

"Dr. Blake? Dr. Blake, come here, please." I can hear the director's voice, but I can't see him in this early morning light.

"George, is that you? You need me for a translation or something? What scene is this?" I say with just the proper tone of irritation in my voice.

"Yes, yes, Dr. Blake, the scene for the next shot is ready, and we need you to stand by as consultant. This is the part of the script where you bring the war god to the battle, so come over and stand by me so if I need you, I won't have to call."

"Okay," I tell him, and walk over to his station at the set.

We are at a place not unlike the actual battle scene. That little hilly promontory over on the right is where it should be. I can see the actor that is Urchuwa standing there in his role as the spiritual leader.

"Action! Roll cameras," Fox yells, and I see the actor playing me coming from the left with a satchel. Can't hear the vibration, but that is expected. I wonder how they will manage that for the film's audience. He's coming cautiously like I remember it. There he stops to ponder for a long pause, eight or nine seconds, then—wait, what is he doing turning around and running back the other way, leaving the battle scene?

He still has the pack and the idol in it. Where is Urchuwa? Where is the entrustment scene? I turn to Fox. "George, this is all wrong. I read the script, and you are leaving out the key scene where Urchuwa realizes the battle is lost and entrusts it to me for posterity. What gives with this crap, George?"

He looks at me, locking eyes with me. No embarrassment, not a smug look either, nothing.

I speak up again: "George, I read the script, and this is wrong!" I am shouting by now. "Betrayal, that's what it is! You tricked me, you bastard. I'll sue you for this! You are defaming me, George."

Fox calmly smiles and says somberly, "Dr. Blake, we have changed the script since you read it. This is the way the production company wants to do it."

"I'll sue you and the producers. You will regret that you did this to me!"

Fox just looks at me, smiles once again, and says, "You say you read the script, Dr. Blake. But have you reread your contract with the production company? It gives the producers—and I am their representative in the field—the full legal authority to make any changes in the script. You signed that contract, Dr. Blake. I suggest that you calm down, go back to camp, and reread it. If you didn't bring a copy of your fully executed contract along on the trip, I will have Alice drop one off at your tent. You better leave now, Dr. Blake; we have to finish shooting this scene."

I stand there fuming, but realizing I have no choice for the present, spin on my heels and leave.

54

A BRIDGE TO DISASTER

Ratio looked sort of noble out there on that first stone, proud of himself for risking it, but, with only me, his ill-favored brother to watch, kind of disappointed as well. He looked at me for a rather interminable time, and all I could do was stare back incredulously and jealous as always that he got the first shot at whatever it was, watched by others or not.

He then turned in what I swear was kind of an unnecessary and risky dramatic gesture and leapt to the next stone, a fairly short jump away. He landed there, sliding a little but regaining his balance, and turned again to make a fake bow toward me in his typical lord-it-over-me gesture no matter how dangerous it really was.

As I watched, admiring his courage and balance but keeping silent so as to not distract him, he stepped across the next three stones and turned once again to boastfully yell, "See, Average? It's easy for one so nimble, so quick," and bowed again as though he had actually jumped over Jack's famous candlestick. By that time I was down on the ledge as close as I could get, preparing to follow Captain Courageous onto the seemingly safe footbridge across the lake. He was twenty yards ahead of me and literally skipping from stone to stone. Then, suddenly, the inevitable happened.

Not all of the stones were free of moss and slime, and I watched in horror as Ratio landed with his right foot on one of these slippery rocks and began sliding off his perch into the deep lake. But I didn't worry. Surely, he would grab on to the rock, but if not, my brother's a good swimmer and we had seen no crocs so far.

Ratio's right leg flew out in front of him, and I heard a loud crack as his head struck a glancing blow on the very stone that moments before had seemed so safe to him but had now led to his terror—and mine.

It's okay, I thought. *I can jump in and save him. But do I really want to do that? The little bastard is getting what he's always deserved. Let him swim out on his own.*

I started to turn back to shore and made it two stones away, this latest temptation having risen up from somewhere deep inside me. *He'll wake up in a couple of seconds because the water is cold, isn't it?*

Then, behind me, I heard a scream of an intensity and fervor I'd never heard before and will never forget. Too late, I looked back at Ratio in the water, and his body was sinking, immersed in a sort of red cloud like a bucket—no, a barrel—of red paint thrown into a swimming pool with a solid object in the middle and some smaller specks moiling around his disappearing body.

"Ratio!" I yelled with all my might, but what had been the body of my hated brother Ratio Blake was disappearing before my eyes in the red cloud and in seconds he—or what was left of him—was gone. The red cloud flowed with the current downstream to a waterfall on the other end of the lake, and in minutes it, too, was gone.

Was I so paralyzed with fear and guilt that I could not have moved? "What is happening?" I asked no one, because there was nothing but the mountains and the flowing water to listen.

This silent enemy had taken my brother, and I, stupidly, had turned my back on him from the start. It's true I hated him, I still do, but what will Father and Mother think? What could have taken him like that? I saw no crocs. The few fish we saw—what could they have done? Unless . . . Those dark specks in the red swirl—what could they have been? No fish could—Wait a minute, aren't there fish some places that shred the flesh of animals, leaving only the bones? I read that somewhere. Aren't they called piranhas, or something like that?

"Oh God, what have I done?" I yell in my despair, and even he doesn't answer me. I have to leave this place. Too late for Ratio, and is it too late for me too? No one will ever forgive me, even me! I climb onto the ledge around the lake and head off into the forest, seeking the darkness that grips my heart like a powerful vise.

55

I Signed It, Didn't I?

What can I do now? Fox made it plain he has the authority to make the damn film however he wants to. It's clear now I was set up. They even had a fake script prepared for that scene so I would cooperate while thinking I was in the clear. They needed me to talk to those native people which good luck dumped in my lap, that refugee from the Musquaeli who still remembers the language.

No wonder they wouldn't show me a copy of the script until we got down here and until after I had set them up with a native Tupi population, which even their language expert from São Paulo couldn't understand. When I get back to my tent I can look at that contract, but I'm betting Fox is right and I can't sue them, much less stop the production or make them alter the script back to the one he showed me.

So what can I do? This will ruin my reputation. They will make it look like I sold out an entire group for personal fame. My memory says I did that, but my pride is too important for that. So what can I do, what can I say, what will become of me to live through another day? How about a life? What will I tell Amanda? She has a piece of this too. Should I just leave and trust to luck? I've never faced this terrible a situation before, except maybe once.

God, I hate to think of that time way back when I was betrayed the first time. I didn't have any choice then either, did I?

56

Lonely Is the Only Path of Despair

What can I do to face this, brother gone? I'm to blame. No excuse will do. Can't hide, can't run, can't face it myself even. Where to go? This forest isn't black enough for my thoughts. It's too quiet out here. Where are the animals, the birds, even a breeze to stir this terrible air I breathe? I put one foot ahead of the other, testing to see if time will be the cure. It won't; stop fooling yourself! Why did I turn back after he slipped? I can't live with this!

Maybe I should look for his bones. Don't piranhas leave the bones at least? Have to do something even if it's hopeless. Is there a way around the waterfall? This trail doesn't go there, so if I push through the under-growth—it hurts when the brush slaps my face.

I reach the end of the lake and see the waterfall, but no bones could have made it out of there. Only the water clouded with his blood could make it out. Better climb up the other side and see if they are visible. There's no need to be stupid and dive into the lake; it would only add my blood to the stream and my bones to the bottom.

Damn, this water is clear! But it's so deep, just a bottomless blue pit, and somewhere down there is my brother—or what was my brother, is more like it. The forest was better than this; at least it's a quiet place where I can condemn myself without interruption. More of the same, death ahead somewhere, and will that bring peace? I have to have it, can't live with or without this shame.

57

None but the Lost Can Be Found

Later that day, after all the production shots were in, the filmmaking crews returned to camp and gathered in the dining tent for the evening meal. Although despondent, even Montana was there; he had to eat.

Amanda had raised the hue and cry with him about the missing boys. He had looked all around the camp and had asked everyone, but no one had seen them. *Where are those rascals?* he thought, assuming they had simply been up to mischief. Boys will be boys, and as an anguished parent will do, he clung to the hope that they must have taken off on an exploratory adventure and would eventually return. Amanda sat nervously, looking all around every few seconds, hoping to see them return. Montana's search and interrogation of every worker in the camp finally found a kitchen helper who thought he could remember the boys leaving earlier that day but couldn't recall when nor where they went.

So the boys had taken an exploratory hike. The question was: where? It was too late to search tonight when other dangers lurked in the darkness. But Fox, Stevens, Singer, and Dr. Blake put their heads together and came up with a plan. Tomorrow at daylight Dr. Blake would use his interpreter to interview some of the tribal leaders and the group would organize a search of every trail leading from the camp.

Tonight, then, had to be one of those terrible nights for Montana, but especially for Amanda Blake. The meal was hurriedly eaten, and they all returned to their tents to at least try the hopeless task of sleeping.

58

Somewhere out There
Is an Answer

After regaining the forest trail, Average walked on in the near darkness, wrapped up in his thoughts, reliving the day's events over and over, as if retelling them to himself could explain the way things had happened. It didn't, of course, and his despair only deepened.

The part of the memory he couldn't shake or alter by the retelling was that hesitation he experienced when he first heard the cry and the crack; the decision for a brief moment to do nothing to rescue his brother. No amount of rationalization—*he deserved what he got, it wouldn't have mattered anyway, there was no time to do anything*—would rid his memory of the horrible thought that he'd let his brother die and been glad of it.

The long history of insults, the innumerable times his brother used him as an excuse with their father, who always accepted everything Ratio did as golden and justified, while everything Average ever did was rotten. The memory—no, the terror—of that set of images played through his mind.

Even when he thought of a new excuse or rationalization, it was drowned in an ocean of guilt as he struggled unsuccessfully to reach the clean, peaceful air of the surface, as though he were a hopeless scuba diver out of air in the depths so long that only the light of the surface could be seen, with the realization flooding his mind, *I can't make it!*

His despair and despondency were so great he could only stumble down the forest path, one foot ahead of the other, in darkness as black as the guilt in his heart.

How much longer can I take this? Is death the only way to make the pain stop, or would that even stop it? he thought. *If anybody who ever lived deserved eternal punishment, it was him. What eternal punishment could be worse than this? Being dipped eternally in an emotional pit of burning oil would be no worse than this. Alive to one terror or dead to another—what's the difference? Stumble on is what I must do, even in this dreaded darkness of the soul and the forest.*

When he thought he could take this self-condemnation no longer, he began to think of ways to end it all. *I have no gun, no knife, yet lots of blood would be a fitting way to join Ratio in hell. I don't even have a belt to hang myself with from a tree. How about a cliff to jump off? A river to drown in? I could go back to the lake with its infernal countless miniature jaws, just waiting to make us even. That seems fitting.*

But instead, I'll curl up here on the ground and try to sleep. So what if it's cold? I deserve that too. Then first thing tomorrow, I'll go join Ratio in the bottom of the lake, fleshless in a fluid ossuary, where no one will ever find us. Brothers still, forever in torment.

59

A Dream Is a Dream, or Is It?

Average slept more than he thought possible, but was awakened during the night by an unnatural bright light. The light sliced through in a cone above him and reached nearly to the ground. All around the light remained black, as it was when he had cuddled for warmth in the middle of an old stump and fallen asleep. As he looked into the cone of light, he arose, thinking falsely that height would give more clarity. Average peered up into the glare and was surprised that the intense light did not hurt his eyes. Was he awake, as every sense of awareness he possessed cried out that he was awake, and not in a dream?

Dreams were funny. Average had never observed himself in a dream, or at least he couldn't recall a dream in which he could look at his hands or his clothes and recognize them as being his. And now, he could see debris from the rotted tree stump still clinging to his clothes and body. He was awake all right, that much he was sure of.

He had read somewhere about what are called lucid dreams, in which a person is in the dream and aware that he is observing himself in it and able to interact with the dream sequence or even change it, but this experience was nothing like that described. He looked around and saw the indentation in the rotted stump material where he had lain and saw a portion of the trail he had walked on to get there, at least as much of it as was illuminated by the cone of light.

Then, if this experience were not shock enough, he was totally unprepared when the intense light suddenly dimmed, expanding his view of the forest surroundings, and somehow a figure stood before him where before there had been nothing.

He jumped at the realization he was no longer alone. The figure appeared to be a man, though his body was as luminous as the light in which he suddenly appeared. The figure was no person he recognized, but the image seemed to be intently focusing what appeared to be eyes at him but in silence as if waiting for Average to speak.

Average worked up his courage and blurted out, "Who—who are you and what are you doing here, sir?"

The figure said nothing at first and then smiled before speaking in words so clear, so peaceful, and with so much empathy for him that they flowed over to him and into his perception almost without a sound. But still Average heard or sensed it just as though it had spoken normally.

"I am Elliot Drake, Average. Or at least I was Elliot Drake until I took a spear in the final battle for the survival of the Musquaeli people your father and I were trying to save. Though he had lost his way or purpose at the end. I am now in the world of the spirit, sent back to you by my master to help you find grace, mercy, and peace in the dilemma you find yourself in over the loss of your brother. My instructions are to lift you up from the pit into which you have sunk, to explain why you did what you did, and to reveal a remedy other than the two options you feel resigned to choose from."

Recovering somewhat from his shock on seeing the ghost—angel—whatever it was, Average replied, "I have heard of you from my father and was saddened to learn that your plan didn't work and you forfeited your life for it. He says he relied on you for the plan, and placed all the blame on you. Is that so?"

"It doesn't matter now, Average, but the plan was mine from the start. I knew your father well enough to manipulate him into thinking it was his decision. But neither of us anticipated what the attacking warriors would do in dividing their main force. From where I was stationed, I could not tell the first attack was not the main force, but that is hindsight."

The voice continued, "The real lesson for me was deeper than that. For you see, Average, I had a greater guilt that I carried around with me like a dark cloud. As a soldier of fortune, I took assignments in the past that required me to kill, often innocents.

"One time in particular, I was asked to kill the heir to a potentate over some oil issues—money, really, no matter what you call it. When I crept into the bed chamber where the heir was sleeping, I discovered a young boy asleep on the floor next to the heir's bed. The child suddenly awoke and started to scream, so I killed him. I don't know what made that death different from any of the others, but I carried that guilt to my death. I abandoned my career as a hired killer and ended up helping your father with this expedition. The invasion of the Musquaeli territory was totally unexpected by any of us. Anyway, that is not important now, only where you are, in facing this terrible dilemma."

He continued, "First of all, you could not have changed the outcome even if you had willingly and immediately gone to your brother's aid. Because you didn't, and because you have borne hatred for your brother's manipulation and senseless conduct toward you in the past, you have not been able to deal with the guilt of his death and your conscious decision for a brief moment to let him suffer and die. But my master has asked me to convey to you that he will forgive you if you ask and take away all the burden of your guilt. He understands that you do not understand this and do not yet know how to trust him in all things. He has asked me to convey to you that your true nature is to give love from yourself to even those who, like your father and brother, abused you because you were compliant or submissive to their wishes and power over you, and whom you hated for it. For this purpose of yours, Average, to give love, forgiveness is necessary for you to continue in it. This process of giving—from this and only this do you have worth in your life. My master is the source of all things, and he has given even me that precious gift."

"I don't understand Elliot—er, Mr. Drake. You say you were a killer for hire in your past life and even killed an innocent young boy. How did you lose this guilt?"

"Part of it was my own choice, Average, to leave that life of killing behind. The other part was my master's, the one I now serve. In my youth I had known about him, the Savior of mankind who gave his life for all and was brought back to make his Spirit available to any who would ask and trust him. My problem was I had made that decision but abandoned that trust to become a person who was a taker of precious lives, not a giver. But I discovered my master again later, after I had abandoned the killing for hire."

"But weren't you killing in the defense of the Musquaeli people?"

"Yes, Average, but I was giving all—even my life—for them and that is the difference. The invaders started the conquest; I could accept what I had to do. You never forget what you have done, but you can accept that you are forgiven."

"What do I have to do, Mr. Drake, to have this same peace you describe? Because I sure don't have it now."

"If you are sincere and repent of your trust in yourself and not my master, then tell him so and watch and see what happens."

"I'm ready, sir, because I can't live this way any longer."

"Then ask him, Average, ask him now."

"Do I get to see him as I am seeing you, sir?"

"No, Average, that's the way it is with trust. You have to act precisely when you can't see."

"Okay, but what is his name? Is it just Master, or does he have another name?"

"He is called Master now, but when he lived as a man, just like you do and I did, his name was Joshua, or as some called him, Jesus."

"You mean the Jesus in the Bible? Is he really real, not just a bunch of religious talk and show time at revival meetings?"

"Yes, Average, he is the only real eternal thing you will ever encounter."

"Okay then, I'm ready. Jesus, I was never a believer in you, but with this guilt and the offer that Mr. Drake has convinced me is real, I accept it now and ask for your forgiveness for letting my brother die. Even though Mr. Drake has shown me that it wouldn't have made any difference in the end, I knew in my heart that I had done the wrong thing, and for me that was unforgiveable because I intended however briefly that he would die. You have to understand, Jesus, in my heart I let him die because I hated him. You see, Jesus, he dominated and manipulated me all my life, and I have to tell you it brought me a kind of pleasure when he was in trouble. It was wrong, but that was what was going through my mind. But I can understand that if you forgave Mr. Drake for the deliberate murder of an innocent child, you can forgive me for my hatred of Ratio and my decision to let him die. Especially because, looking back on it, there was really nothing I could have done. That doesn't help my feelings about it, but could you forgive me for that possibly, maybe?"

Then a voice came out of somewhere in a form that Average could later not describe no matter how hard he tried. It may have been just a thought put into his mind, but it was just as real as if spoken out loud.

"Averill Blake, you are forgiven for all your past transgressions, even your unbelief in me. They are wiped as clean as if they never occurred. I impart my Spirit into your consciousness, and you will have it forever."

Average was stunned by this and said, "But how can that be? I will never forget what happened, what I did, and the memory of that awful red stain in the water. I could never forget that!"

The voice continued, "I know this is hard for you to understand, my son, and you are partly right in that you will never forget what happened, but in spite of that, accept that your forgiveness by me is only possible because I paid that price for you long ago. What I had to pay for were all the lapses in judgment; the selfish, greedy acts; the indelible pride, murders, and monstrosities beyond your comprehension that mankind has committed and still does to further its own ends or in emotional reactions. With my death I took the spiritual effects of all that into hell and left them there when I returned to life. I did it for you, Averill Blake, and would have done it if you were the only one.

"My love for you and all like you is the only reason for my creation. I desire a love relationship with each of you. But alas, you make it difficult when you separate yourself from me by bad choices, such as reserving the critical choices in your own mind for yourself and your interests alone. But remember this, Averill: all of the choices my children make to separate themselves—including yours—were offenses against my love, which is my unchangeable nature and why only I can forgive. What you have done to others can be forgiven by the other. But the acts separating you from me, only I can forgive. And because of that, I alone can forgive that terrible malice you bore toward your brother. The forgiveness and the resulting peace I offer you if you will accept it."

"But how can I accept? It seems so terrible to me, Master. Each time I think about it—and the memory is ever present now—I won't be able to forgive myself, even if you do. What do I do about that?"

The voice replied, "You don't understand, my son. Only I can forgive those things done deliberately that bring offense to me. You have to trust me in this and let this self-condemnation go. This memory will try to drag you back into blame. Remember this, that sin is gone because of what I did long ago for you. I had to do that, you see, because it was the price I had to pay for giving the free choices that inevitably would lead to the great separation. I had to make that choice because it was the only way I could have a love relationship with you, the one who is able to choose. That is the only enduring thing in my creation for which all was worth the price."

Average thought about this, and said, "But how can I be changed with this gift you offer? Won't I be the same boy after you leave me?"

"Remember this, Averill, my son: I will never leave you nor forsake you. You are now a new creation with my Spirit, which is deeper and stronger than you could ever imagine, within you, and all those that I caused to come into this life who have made this same choice have it too. You can converse with me whenever you like. From now on, your nature is to give my love to others, and it must start with your earthly father. He carries a deep guilt within him, and from you he can be led to me to be made clean."

The voice continued, "One of my prophets, Isaiah, one who spoke my truths, said, 'In a future day the wolf also shall dwell with the lamb, and the leopard shall lie down with the kid, and the calf and the young lion and the fatling together, and a little child shall lead them.' You shall be that child in your father's case, Averill, for forgiveness for his guilt when he repents of it is where he must start. Will you go now and do it? Give my love to others and believe you have value in my sight, the only kind of value that will last into eternity. And by the way, my son, from this moment on you will be known as Averill Blake, for you are no longer Average. Can you remember and act on that promise, Averill?"

"Yes, Master, you have my promise, and somehow it seems real to me now as never before because I can tell that your words are spoken as truth and your presence is in me, although I can't begin to explain how I know that. It's just different now and I'm filled with a presence that is something I can't explain, but I hope it never goes away from me."

"Go now, my son, and call on me when that time comes. I will always be there inside you, waiting to guide and direct you in this important task, even in things you won't understand and which may even seem impossible to you. Live in my presence with your conscious awareness, and I will be there with all my love on your side. Elliot, it is now time for us to return to other times and places."

"Yes, Lord," Elliot's image replied, and with that the voices and the cone of light were gone.

In the absence of light there was only darkness, and Averill found himself standing alone next to the crumbling stump. He settled back down, covering his chilled limbs with the debris from the rotted stump, and returned to a sleep that would restore him for the task tomorrow. How he would do it he was not sure, but that he would do it was never in doubt.

60

Return from Where I
Had Strayed

I somehow know I'm awake after a long night of secure and restful sleep, and that is the easy part. The hard part is telling exactly what happened to me last night. I've had dreams before, lots of them, but that was no dream. I was in it, clearly, but this exact place was in it, down to the minutest detail, the old stump, the stuff on my arms and clothes. No one or doubt will ever take that memory or the sense of reality away from me.

Now what? Guess I better head back to camp. The trail is right here and I know the way by now, so here we go, Averill. Yeah, Averill. My name is no longer Average. I hated that name and having His presence within could never be average.

So where or, better yet, how do I go from here? I have to tell Mother and Father that their favorite son was eaten by fish and I somehow walked away unscathed. I have to tell them that they can't call me Average anymore and make it stick. Most importantly, I have to be the means by which my father gets delivered from some guilt he has that I don't even understand the existence of, much less how I can possibly be the means to his deliverance from it. If I were to try to measure that task and my role in it and have the confidence that the Master has in it for me, I would say that reaching the moon in one leap would be a mild accomplishment in comparison.

But I will say this, self: there has never been a person in your life with the calm presence and absolute confidence like the Master. Considering the way I felt in the glow of his presence, there was no way I could say no.

So here we go, Averill Blake. The camp is up ahead. I just have to trust in the one now inside me and act on it.

The camp was in an uproar as Averill came within hearing distance. Amanda had been frantic since the day before, when she realized both boys were missing. Montana had come back from the film set in a huff, mad at something, but he'd quickly lost that attitude when Amanda told him Ratio and Average had left the camp that day, according to witnesses, and had not returned by nightfall. They had frantically searched the grounds before deciding that it was too late that day to mount a meaningful search, so one was organized for first light the next morning. But as all well-made plans of mice and men are led astray, the organizing was still going on. Among much shouting and advice giving after a regular breakfast, they were ready to shove off up the main river trail right about the time Averill arrived at camp.

Averill felt like he was walking into a disaster, and from all normal thinking about such things, it was. When the first person spotted him at the edge of camp that morning, the cry was deafening as every person thought it their verbal duty to raise the hue and cry of discovery. Almost immediately, Averill was herded by Montana and Amanda into their personal quarters for what a military contingent would call a debriefing. The rest of the camp waited impatiently for news.

"Average, honey, where is your brother? Tell Momma, won't you?" Amanda crooned soothingly.

Averill felt strangely at peace and quite frankly could not understand his own temperament at this moment, but remained silent.

She tried again: "Average, where is Ratio? Everyone says you left together yesterday," a little less soothingly.

He sat silent.

Montana had had enough. He walked around in front of Averill, who sat without expression, his head held high, but in stony silence. "Ratio is your brother, Average, and you and he went off together yesterday," he began, but his "aren't you your brother's keeper" pitch was interrupted.

"First of all, Father—and you too, Mother—you have that part wrong. The name you gave me is Averill Blake, and he's not average, so don't ever call me that again," As he spoke his gaze remained locked on the eyes of his parents, first his father, then his mother, never dropping his head in the shame they might have expected.

"Second of all, I'm sad to say, in answer to what you were probably about to say, that I am my brother's keeper, but I didn't keep him well." Averill started to cry, sobbing uncontrollably for a few seconds, but caught himself before his parents could react and continued. "You see, he slipped on a stone crossing a sunken trail under water across a lake upriver and he fell to his death, a horrible death. He was eaten by piranhas, so there's no use looking for his body because there isn't one, except maybe some bones at the bottom of the lake or washed into the Atlantic Ocean by now. He's dead. Gone forever."

Montana and Amanda were shocked beyond belief, not wanting to believe their ears. All Amanda could do was drop her head and walk away, anything but face this news. Montana wasn't much better, for despite how he acted most of the time, he really did love or at least feel some affection for his sons, especially Ratio. But Averill's demeanor was so calm and peaceful that any anger they may have felt instinctively to blame someone—even their own son—left Amanda and Montana speechless. Averill simply waited them out. They had to recover and speak eventually.

Amanda responded first, reaching out to embrace Averill, and he responded with heartfelt emotion. Although he had been absolved of his feelings of guilt as a result of his mystical experience, he knew his biggest task was ahead of him: to somehow help his father find deliverance from his own guilt, despite not fully knowing what it was. He had accepted the assignment although he had no idea how to carry it out. As he stood there, he couldn't help but see his father's eyes, looking seemingly at nothing as he stood by watching the emotional scene in front of him with a detached, almost disturbed look. His mother's emotional energy almost drained, he broke free and turned to his father, who hardly noticed him.

"What's wrong beyond the obvious, Father? You look disturbed about something. Tell me, is it me or something else?"

Montana blinked for a few seconds as though he was coming out of a trance and then turned to Averill and said, "Averill my boy, don't concern yourself with that other stuff, just get yourself together. We'll do the obligatory search for Ratio's body tomorrow, but you are probably right that it's hopeless and we must move on. Amanda, your assignment is to get the family ready; we are going home to Florida. My job is done here."

Amanda said, "How could you even think of packing and leaving, for God's sake? Our son is dead up there in those mountains and you talk about packing to go home! Where is your sense of shame, Monty?"

"Don't get maudlin on me, Amanda. Of course I'm devastated by the loss of our son. We will make that search, and a thorough one too, but it's probably hopeless based on Averill's account. There is something else of a tragic nature going on here, Amanda. This movie has turned into a disaster. You haven't been out there for the actual filming. These people tricked me, Amanda. They even wrote a phony script to lure me into helping them talk to these Tupi people they had no chance to reach without me."

Montana turned away, totally absorbed in the disaster he was facing with his reputation as a credible scientist on the line. He truly was shocked at the death of his favored son, but it paled in comparison to the shock that the deeply held secret he had almost managed to banish into the recesses of his subconscious mind was about to be exposed. He was, after all, a realist. The death tragedy was not changeable, but the consequences of the movie disaster might have a solution; he just didn't know what it was yet. What room was there for grief about something he had no control over when he was faced with something he was accustomed to having under his control?

Amanda could not believe what she was hearing. She was livid. Averill sensed it too and returned to hold his mother. He leaned over and whispered into her ear, "It's okay, Momma. He has a heavy weight on his mind with this movie thing. Trust me, there will be nothing to find tomorrow out there, Momma, so let the search teams go with me and you get packed like Father said. It's best in the end, don't you think?"

Amanda looked at her son with new eyes. There was something different about him. He was no longer the shy, submissive one, the butt of his dominant brother's jokes that, sadly, she had to admit, even she could see through most of the time. It was wrong, but she'd never had the presence of mind to do anything about it. He was definitely different in some way, but she could not put her finger on what it was. His advice to put things into perspective, given in the heat of the moment of her anger, was wisdom beyond anything she had ever noticed in him before. There was a glimmer of pride welling in her somewhere about this young son of hers, a sane voice of wisdom in the midst of this crisis of multiple proportions. Anger at her husband, grief over the death of her other son, uncertainty about her husband's future, although she had no inkling of what he was talking about, and the chore of getting them all ready for the trip home—all were warring for attention in her mind. That was her burden and no small task.

He is so different, she thought gazing at Averill sitting calmly on the floor of the tent. *Maybe this will become clear with time. It usually does, doesn't it?*

"We better get started, Averill. Packing for the trip home will be a chore. And you're right, son; you'll never hear the name Average again from me."

61

There's No Trip like Heading Home

The trip home was uneventful, if you call riding in a Land Rover over impossibly rough trail for a seemingly endless trek, then arriving in São Paulo for a few days' rest before boarding the return flight with connections and a ride by cab out to their home in Hedley uneventful.

Montana was quiet and absorbed in his own thoughts. He was deeply in sorrow over the loss of his son but equally worried about the consequences of the cruel way, as he saw it, that his secret had been exposed so brazenly.

Amanda got this picture quickly from the time they first boarded the Land Rover. Knowing her man as she did, she decided to use the time on the trip home to develop a more meaningful relationship with her remaining son and his new self-assured but oddly humble demeanor. She could not get the loss of Ratio from her mind either; it hurt so badly. She was conflicted by the two demands. When the conversation lulled between them, Averill just sat there in calm reflection, with no explanation to his mother of what it was he was thinking.

Those unspoken thoughts included a reliving of the horrible experience at the lake. But every time he ran those memory tapes through his mind, he jumped ahead to the terrifying yet wonderful experience with Mr. Drake.

The fact that the experience happened while he had been sleeping made it seem to the rational side of his brain as a dream. In a sense, Averill longed for it to have been a dream and that he could just forget about the assignment he had been given and, in that weakened moment, freely accepted. But calling it a bad bargain or a dream just wouldn't do, would it? It was so real to him.

Then there was that unexplainable experience with Mr. Drake and the Master. Averill had looked into those eyes and found them to be an opening into the depths of his own mind, his psyche—or was it his soul?—that gave him a feeling of love, peace, and comfort directed only at him at that moment. He'd had the unmistakable feeling that he was the only person in the world that mattered. He still felt it. Averill couldn't explain it, certainly not in an earthly sense, but there must be a spiritual sense that is merged somehow with the physical. But Averill really liked knowing it's there, that feeling, but more than that, like He was a part of Averill, fancy that.

From time to time Montana would awaken from having nodded off and gaze fixedly at the overhead compartment while replaying in his thoughts the events of the past weeks. *What will become of me when the whole world sees me portrayed as a fraud? Where can I go to get away from those sly looks, and the quirky smiles on my colleagues' faces? There will be politeness, of course; academia is so proper with its social graces. There will never be a word in public about the incident. They will smile as though they really like and respect me, yet they will be thinking otherwise; and when outside my presence at the club or bridge or at golf, I will be the butt of everyone's version of the dishonest fool story. It will grow and grow until the hints become more flagrant, and finally, when it becomes intolerable, I'll have to leave Fangleer College, but where would I find any other anthropology department willing to take me on faculty? And the arrangement I've had with the Florida Museum of Science and Natural History will never be duplicated. Even my masterpiece will never make it into the better libraries. Selection committees will always find a reason to exclude me from speaking assignments at anthropology conferences once this horrid movie is released. And if that isn't bad enough, how do we continue without our son? I try not to think about that, but it hurts too. They all hurt, these dilemmas. Maybe I can repair some of that damage with Averill and Amanda. Can I? Could it be that I am only getting what I deserve?*

When he tired of this exhausting exercise, sleep would rescue him from it for a few hours. Eventually they landed in Miami, went through US Customs, and boarded a local airline to take them to Pensacola and home. Home is the hunter, as the poets said, home from the hill. *What do we do now?* Montana thought as he helped Amanda arrange for their bags to be packed into a cab for their short trip out to Hedley and their home by the lake.

62

IN THE DARKNESS AN EMBER OF HOPE MAY GLOW

What will become of me? Montana thought. *What good will come to us even in the sanctuary and solitude of home? I'm not sure when that awful movie will be edited, promoted, and released. There is strong money behind the production, so it's bound to be released eventually. Although my colleagues in anthropology don't partake in such entertainment, if I am shown in a bad light, the news is bound to get out that one of their competitors is being made famous, or infamous in this case, in the public eye. And wait until they see that story! Sense and reason, study and academic fame, why have you abandoned me? How could I have risked my reputation by stealing that little artifact, and losing a whole tribe of indigenous people to boot?*

Damn, Montana, you were really stupid! As Henry Kerr so famously said, "All wisdom is plagiarized; only stupidity is original."

"Averill, time to wake up, son," Montana said, shaking his son gently as they rolled into the driveway.

"Oh hi, Father, are we home yet? I'm tired of all this traveling, Momma; how about you?"

"I'm awake, Averill. I'll start unloading our gear; your father will pay for the cab and go inside to open up the place. Is that all right, Monty?"

"Yes, Amanda, good plan."

Montana took that as his cue to retreat to his study for some serious thinking. Amanda knew him better than anyone, and she knew he needed his space. He paid the cab driver, who had just finished unloading their baggage, and turned to walk up the drive to the front porch to open the house. The mail had been held at the post office at their direction so the mailbox would not be jammed full over their absence. He thought, *I could pick that up in Hedley tomorrow. Or maybe now would be a good time. In fact, now would be a perfect time rather than sitting in my study, brooding.*

Montana returned outside in time to help carry some of the luggage inside.

"I thought you wanted to be alone, Monty," Amanda said.

"I decided to take the car and run into Hedley to get the mail—should be quite a bit," Montana said.

"Well, okay, but it could wait until tomorrow, couldn't it?" she replied.

"I think it's best," he said, and walked past Amanda and Averill to the garage. The car roared to life with no difficulty despite their long absence, and he headed to town.

By the time Montana returned, Averill and Amanda had put everything back in its place. He said nothing to his family as he carried the large bundle of mail into his study, closed the door, and sat in his chair to review it. Most of it was junk mail, and quickly tossed into the trash can nearby. Those things of interest to Amanda, like magazines and advertising for things she might want to review, he set aside for her while looking for anything to catch his own interest.

One envelope did catch his eye. The return address was the Southeastern Anthropology Association in Charleston, South Carolina. He held the envelope in his hands and stopped to think a minute. He knew the organization well enough. It was a less significant professional association in his field, one he had never submitted articles to for presentation or publication, but definitely an organization whose correspondence he would review. He opened the top drawer of his desk, took out his letter opener, slit the envelope open, and took a three-page letter out addressed to Dr. Horatio Averill Blake.

He scanned the letter and absorbed its contents in amazement. "Dr. Blake, congratulations. You have been selected to receive the first annual Lucius Larksburger Award for a contribution to anthropology for your work in the study of Stone Age peoples in South America.

"The awards committee has reviewed your recently published book, *Containment or Consequences: A Search for Tribal Survival,* which calls to mind the late Dr. Larksburger in whose name the award endowment was created for having made his own contribution to the body of scientific knowledge on the factors that permit such indigenous groups to survive as their cultures are encroached by modern civilizations. Your own study, Dr. Blake, on how the ages-old survival systems sometimes fail these tribes when different groups among the same basic cultural limitations go to war with each other for territory, women, or food, has made an invaluable contribution to the anthropological body of knowledge available to us all.

We invite you and your family to attend our annual convention in Charleston on September 30th this year. We will cover expenses, of course. The award will bear a grant of $75,000 for your next expedition plus expenses if you can meet the criteria set forth in the attached documents. Please let us know by September 1st. Very truly yours," et cetera, et cetera.

Montana turned the envelope over and noticed the postmark. It had been mailed from Charleston, South Carolina, on August 1 and arrived in Hedley on August 8. He glanced at the calendar on his desk and saw that tomorrow would be September 1, the deadline for accepting the invitation.

Then, running through his mind was, *How can I accept an award with this damn movie coming out? It might be embarrassing! But surely the movie won't be ready by then; that's less than a month, and they will barely have finished the Brazil footage, not to mention the editing process, which might take even a year. But what do I know about that kind of thing? Either way, they can't take it back once it's awarded, can they? Odds say, go for it.* Montana rose from his chair and hurried into the kitchen where Amanda was busying herself preparing the evening meal, a task she had not had to do for a long time.

"Amanda, good news. The Southeastern Anthropological Association has selected me for the first annual prize in anthropology from that august organization," Montana said excitedly but with a hint of sarcasm, still not absolutely certain the risk was worth taking. *New academic associations hardly register on the Richter scale of academic reputations*, he was thinking. But in Montana's mind, an award was an award no matter how new the grantor, even with the specter of that movie hovering over his consciousness like an ash plume after a pyroclastic volcanic eruption. Anything positive met his need for distraction for the moment.

Amanda stopped what she was doing, turned her head in his direction, and said, "The Southeastern Anthropological Association? I never heard of them. New kids on the block, eh? Hardly the American

Association that gives the Mead Award, is it, Monty? What do they call this one, the 'Mead Lite Prize'?"

"Actually, it's an award given in honor of the late Professor Lucius Larksburger, world-famous anthropologist in the field of indigenous-people survival studies in the face of encroaching development, an area in which my book is a significant contribution. When I think about it, Amanda, it is very appropriate; fitting, actually," Montana said with pride, quickly forgetting all the self-flagellation in which he had been engaged.

"But, Monty, what about this movie that makes you the goat of history for one particular group of indigenous people?"

That startled him, but he recovered quickly. "Nonsense, Amanda. No one in academia that matters will ever see that movie, and they won't believe it if they do. Hollywood makes up such ridiculous crap parading as reality that no one even thinks in a million years it's real-life history. So pack your bags, girl, for the end of the month. You and Averill. Yes, our son is coming too. It's in Charleston. It will still be hot in South Carolina by then, but they have air conditioning. It should be fun for you and Averill after the disaster of the Brazilian jungle!"

In her usual submissive manner, Amanda tucked her chin and returned to her work in the kitchen and left Montana to his imagination.

Satisfied and fortified by the experience, he turned on his heels and headed back into his study to call and accept what was not the best award he had hoped for, but it was an adequate ego stroke that was available that morning. Montana tried to put the whole moviemaking fiasco completely out of his mind. There was simply no room left for such unpleasant things in the mind and ego of Horatio Averill Blake, PhD.

63

INTERLUDE

The Blake family arrived at Charleston International Airport on September 27 to allow time for them to tour historic Charleston before the big event on September 30. The association had arranged for rooms at the French Quarter Inn, one of Charleston's finest, and transportation by a personal car. Their driver was waiting at baggage claim, holding up a sign that read, "Blake Party."

Averill spotted it first. "Look there, Father, Momma. That guy is holding up a sign with our name."

"That's expected, son. The letter from the association said they would provide for all arrangements. Go tell him we're getting our bags, and find out where he's parked," Montana said, and continued his search of the luggage carousel for their bags. The organizers were going out of their way to entertain and honor their guests.

In just a few minutes they were comfortably seated in a limousine and, for Montana at least, uncomfortably listening to a regular patter on the sights and sounds of Charleston on the way to the hotel, in the French Quarter no doubt. Amanda, on the other hand, was eating it up and met his expostulations with her own pitter-patter. Averill, more like his father in this respect, quickly dozed off in the comfortable, air-conditioned limo.

Upon arrival, Montana left it to Alfonse—Montana's nickname, spoken under his breath, for any of those in the servant class—to bring in the luggage. The French Quarter Inn was a relatively small hotel of fifty rooms, and even had a wishing well. But they didn't have to wish they were there together, as the song went, because they were there together in the Historic District of old Charleston. Antebellum architecture was dripping from the rafters, columns, and awnings of the place.

In the next couple of days, according to Alphonse, tours had been arranged at all the scenic and historic spots, including a boat ride out to Fort Sumter, where that cataclysm, the "War for Southern Independence," began in 1860. At least that was what Charlestonians, like most die-hard Southerners, still called the American Civil War. Averill, like most boys no matter where they hailed from, loved military history—the Civil War in particular. Since his father was a westerner and had no particular interest in the Southern pride expressed by the fathers of other boys he knew in West Florida, Averill had only a smidgen of Southern pride in his instinctive reactions. But the Fort Sumter trip would be fun, he thought.

Their suite of rooms was plush and comfortable. Montana and Amanda busied themselves unpacking their bags, hanging the dresses for Amanda and the tuxedo for Montana in the spacious closets. Amanda had even purchased a tuxedo for Averill so he would not be out of place at the award ceremony. After unpacking his own things, Averill excused himself from his parents' business and took the elevator down to the lobby to explore the place as he and Ratio would have done before.

Amanda gave strict instructions that he was not to leave the hotel and said that they would join him in the lobby soon because it was time for lunch. Montana had already asked Alphonse where they should go first in Charleston for lunch, and Alphonse had responded that he had a surprise destination for their first day of sightseeing in old historic Charleston. Montana wasn't sure he liked the idea of Alphonse deciding anything about their trip, but Amanda had pooh-poohed his objection with a "Come on, Monty, live dangerously just a little bit. It's just a surprise lunch destination, and he's trying to make our trip eventful. How about it, big fella?"

He could tell she was in a playful mood, and he had no idea where to go for lunch anyway. The guy did live and work in the place after all, so he called Alphonse to let him know they would be in the lobby at noon to leave for the surprise destination.

The place they went to wasn't that much out of the ordinary except for the parking lot. Alphonse explained that it was paved with old ballast stones from a sailing schooner long lost to active service and that the restaurant had young people to assist them in so they would not trip and fall. It protected the customers and the liability of the owners. It was a typical Charleston eating place with seafood predominant on the menu. However, the food was good and plans for the rest of their trip leading up to the award ceremony were carefully laid.

64

STAGE FRIGHT

The special day for Montana had finally come. He was the first of the family to wake up that morning and used the time while Amanda and Averill lay sleeping soundlessly to get his thoughts together for the presentation ceremony. He had been there before, though not in this venue and with this sponsor. In a way it was better to know in advance whether you had won or not: already knowing allowed a sufficient focus to at least sound organized, even if it was supposed to seem extemporaneous. But the anticipation of not knowing how you would fare was exciting too. He knew this from prior experience. *Everyone has a part*, he thought.

He went into the small sitting room of their suite at the French Quarter Inn so as not to disturb Amanda and the boy while he practiced.

"Thank you, Sarah, for that wonderful introduction. Or, it gives me great pleasure to be here—damn, that sounds prosaic and boring. Why not open with a greeting of a few words to the audience in Quechua, the language of the Musquaeli people? No one will understand a word, but it will get their attention—and give me a chance to brag a little—by sounding exotic and *anthropological*, like I just flew in from the dig site or the great outback somewhere or other. How about, Kem sei leah qhelia umtra keesta, I am so pleased to be in your village for this occasion, and then bow in my best imitation of the Musquaeli greeting ceremony.

Yeah, that'll work. Then how about, Ladies and gentlemen of science and guests, it is my pleasure to truly be among the friends of our profession dedicated to the study of—and more of that stuff. Then I do a quick summary of the goals of the expedition, being sure to give much praise to the Florida Museum of Science and Natural History. No reason to shy away from that source no matter what comes of this venture. They have been good friends in the past and—who knows?—maybe again."

"Monty, are you up?" The sleepy voice of Amanda broke through his rehearsing.

"Yes, dear, I'm out here, just going over my planned remarks for the award ceremony tonight," Montana replied, and rose to go in to talk with her and shake Averill out of his sleep.

Several hours later, banquet-goers mingled at a cocktail party in the spacious garden sunrooms of the Charleston Convention Center adjacent to the dining area where the festivities would be held. The rooms were well lit by the late afternoon sun and carefully air conditioned to combat the humidity plague in September prevalent almost anywhere in the Southeast.

Montana—himself no shrinking social violet—was at home among the few colleagues he knew in attendance and faked familiarity with the rest, just in case his memory was failing him. Amanda was in her element with the women accompanying these men of science, and yes, that was still the gender bias in the field of anthropology, Dame Margaret Mead notwithstanding, who, alas, was no longer among them.

For Montana, the fun could only last so long because at the back of his troubled mind was the magic moment ahead when he would discover whether any of his colleagues in the audience—the only ones he was concerned about—had heard of the movie disaster and, worse yet, might ask him about it. He had been safe so far, but he would never underestimate a jealous colleague, who would likely pick his moment for maximum embarrassment and of course the maximum damage to Blake's reputation.

The public address system broadcast the summons to the banquet, which to Montana seemed like the town crier in Atlantis announcing ruin and degradation before that mythical city slid into oblivion. The guests made their way toward the banquet hall in a rolling amalgamation of chatter, mirth, and anticipation. Montana sat with Amanda at the head table, and an aide to the meeting director was assigned to escort and entertain Averill near the front of the audience.

After several glasses of wine at the head table and extended private social conversations that quickly ran out of verbal steam, Sarah Covington, young, smart, and vivacious mistress of ceremonies, walked to the center podium and called the meeting to order with an oversized gavel, pounding its brass head on the podium.

"Ladies and gentlemen, honored members of the Southeastern Anthropological Association, welcome to the first annual awards ceremony. I know you all are as excited as I am for our main event, the awarding of the first annual Lucius Larksburger Award. As most of you know, the late Dr. Larksburger, the founder of our association, did groundbreaking work in the study of how modern survivors of indigenous groups handle encounters with emerging modern societies. But before we get to all that, let's enjoy a performance by the local Charleston Philharmonic Association. Let me introduce the string quintet, accompanied by Leon Stranati on the piano, playing a lighter selection of Frédéric Chopin's Impromptu number four in C Sharp Minor, opus sixty-six, better known to us all as 'Fantaisie-Impromptu.'"

The beautiful music began, and the audience quieted down to enjoy it. Montana endured that and the other lighter selections that followed as well as he could despite classical music not being his favorite.

Finally, they've finished, and we can get on to the more interesting events, namely me. Here comes that lovely MC, Sarah what's-her-name who will introduce me. Finally.

Sarah rose as the applause faded for the last performance and made her way to the podium. The crowd, sensing that this was the moment they all had been waiting for, hushed with expectation.

"Ladies and gentlemen, it's my privilege this evening to introduce the recipient of the first annual Lucius Larksburger Award. As most of you know, our beloved Dr. Larksburger blazed the trail of science in the study of the effects of modern civilization's growth and incursion into areas that for centuries had been the private domains of some ancient cultures. Dr. Larksburger made contact with these groups in various parts of the world and recorded for posterity how they coped with the expansion of modern civilizations into areas that hundreds of years ago would have been untouched by modern man."

She continued, "Tonight we have the famous-in-his-own-right Dr. Horatio Averill Blake as recipient of our award and generous grant from the Southeast Anthropological Association for his continued contribution to future discoveries in this field. Ladies and gentlemen, join me in welcoming our honored guest, Dr. Blake."

The audience offered a rousing applause as Dr. Blake left his seat and made his way to the podium to give his acceptance speech.

Montana opened with his carefully rehearsed opening remarks in the Quechuan language, but before he could get the English translation out, he was shocked as he looked out into the audience. He could not believe what his eyes—or was it his mind?—revealed before him. Seated in the front row of the audience, wearing his native garb, was the magnificent figure of Urchuwa.

How is this possible? he thought. *Doesn't everyone else see him? He's so out of place in Charleston's convention hall. Worse yet, the figure appears to be smiling and ready to stand up and renounce me as a fraud.*

Montana was speechless for once in his life. Then the image he was observing spoke.

"Us quelia umtra lesti, Gesto Wa? You come here back, Great One?" Urchuwa said, first in Quechua and then in his fairly accomplished version of English. Montana was stunned. He could understand the language, of course. What he couldn't understand with a belief system grounded in science was what it was he was experiencing.

Urchuwa was dead and that much was certain. His scientific materialistic philosophy did not allow for paranormal or metaphysical experiences by sane men. Was he losing his mind or was it already lost? He frantically looked out at the audience and quickly glanced from side to side at the head table to see if anyone else besides him had seen the apparition or, worse yet, heard Urchuwa's words that were so loud and clear to his hearing. How could the others not see and hear him?

It was as if Montana had entered a vision experience that no one else had entered, because it was apparent to him only, by a process he could not understand, much less explain. The audience sat there as before, attentive, excited, in anticipation of the speech he had prepared, but completely oblivious to the phenomenon he was experiencing at the moment, or the fact that time, as he was experiencing it, had somehow stopped. He stood there with his mouth open, not able to say a word, as he looked down from the stage at the well-recognized visage of the Indian shaman. Urchuwa began to speak, this time in his crude version of English.

"Big Doctor, dead come I from the people—challenge you! My people in spirit world send me with message. You, Big Doctor, betrayed Musquaeli people. Offend memories, history, value of my people."

Montana, reverting to his own defense, said, "Urchuwa, your battle was lost; you knew that. I had to save myself and your war god. Science had to preserve the history of how it ended, didn't it?"

Urchuwa replied, "Confuse your tribal history, Big Doctor. You save self and refused bring war god to battle scene. Self-love kill people, Big Doctor!"

Montana was stunned by the obvious truth of Urchuwa's statement, which entered his heart like a cold shaft of ice and twisted back and forth for its full deadly effect. His head dropped in an instantaneous sign of admission and surrender. There was no denying it, and even he could think of no way to rationalize it.

But Urchuwa just stood there as if impervious to the moral capitulation. Montana finally shuddered and shook himself back to reality, raised his head to look at the shaman, and said, "The Musquaeli people and you, Urchuwa, have every right to condemn me for my selfish and cowardly act. I tried to convince myself that the cause was lost anyway after my, er, ah, uh, Elliot Drake's, that is, plan of counterattack was foiled by the enemy forces and tried even harder to justify what I had wanted to do all along. How can you and the Musquaeli people ever excuse my unconscionable actions back there?"

Urchuwa replied, "'Excuse,' Big Doctor? Urchuwa understand not meaning you."

Montana struggled as he tried to explain the unexplainable to the man. "Well, it's like this, Urchuwa, and if your people in your spirit world, can, er, uh, hear me—a wrong was done to you by me. If you allow me to avoid the, er, consequences of that wrong, it excuses it in the scale of right and wrong, so to speak. It explains away what happened to you in a sense so you can be comfortable in your heart with the memory that it happened, but it hurts less and the other, me for example, has less pain over having done that terrible wrong, don't you see? We both feel better. Do you understand that?"

Urchuwa stood silent for what, to Montana, seemed an interminable period, mulling that strange explanation over in his mind, and then replied: "Excuse but keep memory of wrong? How two opposites stand together? Face each other in same forest? Big Doctor must lose memory of loss to Musquaeli people. Spirit world far better than struggle to live, fight, and die in forest. Pain of that memory faded now. But even betrayal of this one, Big Doctor, not greatest offense, even after my people and this one 'forgive' as you say. Big Doctor betray Great Spirit, creator of my people, origin of what right and what evil as Big Doctor say it. Great Spirit know you sold truth for self and grieves dearly for loss as much as loss of my people living in world Great Spirit intend before. You, Big Doctor, must make sacrifice and surrender to him, not this one!"

The words stung Montana to the depths of his being but in a different way than before. *If I understand the shaman's meaning, he and his people are better off now and can live, as it were, with the faded memory of the loss; but that does not excuse the wrong and, more importantly, let me off the moral hook. They seem to be accepting my apology in a way, but the offense to their Great Spirit, God or whatever he is, remains. I was selfish and rationalized my way out of a tight spot for my personal gain at the expense of the tribe I had studied and made a reputation with, trying to save them, but they are willing to forget that, but not the Great Spirit. Intuitively, sort of that is, I understood that. But the challenge as Urchuwa has phrased it is raising this to a new level. Offend others and rationalize for my personal ambition as I have done—I can handle that, and apparently they can also. That damned movie is about to make mincemeat out of my reputation as a scientist and academic scholar anyway. I could face that and maybe even recover something of it. But having betrayed this Indian's Great Spirit—I can't go that far. Something in me rebels at going that far. I have never believed in a god being responsible for creating the cosmos and can't now even with this horrible experience. A natural or imbedded moral law to all of reality is impossible for reasons I can never explain, even to myself. It just can't be, can it? Trusting a superior being—any being—after having studied the scientific findings made through research and analysis does not fit within my idea of the meaning of life and is inconsistent with how I have lived my life since I was a boy. I just could not trust anyone in authority to decide anything that really mattered to me! They always let you down! Still can't!*

Urchuwa, having spoken the words of his commissioned task, turned back toward the rear of the convention hall and disappeared from Montana's view as if he had never been there at all.

The apparition gone, the time lapse seemed to have ended and Montana found himself standing speechless in front of the audience. *Did anyone else see him? Did anyone besides me hear those damning words? How long has it been? Seems like hours.* He tried his best to pull up what he could remember of his prepared remarks, but for once his thorough preparation and quick thinking failed him. He sputtered and somehow managed to finish his remarks, but no one in the audience, much less his son and wife, who knew him better than anyone on Earth, could begin to understand his miserable performance. Amanda could only bury her face in her hands and cry.

Averill was equally depressed by his father's lousy performance, but surprisingly, he had been able to hear parts of the dialogue his father was having with what he assumed was an apparition, although he could not see the vision, if that was what it was. As he sat there thinking about all that had transpired since his own vision experience, his new confidence in who he was, and the desire to help his father in his embarrassment, there arose within him an impetus he could never later fully explain. Was he to go backstage so he could be with his father after his ordeal was over and try to help? How, he was not sure. When should he go?

When the rest of the painfully slow and boring schedule of events concluded, with all the laudatory words expressed, the plaques presented, the entertainers having entertained, Montana sat in a stupor, running the tapes of what he had experienced over and over in his head like an old never-ending movie reel.

Just before the final presenter began wrapping up the program, Averill finally decided to leave his mother seated in her sorrow and headed behind the stage area to comfort his father. How he could possibly do that was beyond him, but he had to try. Something was driving him to it.

65

A Little Child Shall Lead Them

The lights had dimmed in the convention hall, and the guests made their way out into the same area where the pre-meeting cocktail party had taken place and the post-meeting round of talk and after-dinner drinks began. Montana, deep in his disappointment, could not join what he had expected to be a joyous time of celebration. He withdrew into the dimly lit anterooms behind the stage, which matched his emotions.

Averill found him standing in a corner with his back to the open room. Many thoughts went through Averill's head as he paused to decide how best to proceed.

Help me, Master. I need your counsel now. I don't even know where to begin. What do I say, what do I do? You said to call on you when I need you, and I need you now!

In a still, small awareness inside his consciousness, as clear as if it were a spoken voice, he absorbed the following revelations: "Averill, my son, this is the task I said I gave you. Your father is in the hour of his deepest sorrow and need. You must embrace him in love and lead him into one essential truth: that I hold the only answer to his quest, a journey he has been on most of his life though he knows not what he seeks, or why he has been unable to find it, or even that he has been searching. He has put all of my creation and his place in it into a small vessel; he knows not how it came to be that way, or that it was even caused at all, and foolishly thinks he understands what on his own he cannot know. He thinks—as many of my creatures of this higher nature do when they find themselves in an almost limitless cosmos and believe it is all there is to existence—that man's reason can explain its source. It is so because it is so, he argues, to convince himself that I could not exist or demand anything from him. Not all his fellow scientists are so crippled in their reasoning, but your father is for a reason. You, my son, had a similar obstacle to clarity of thought about me because the pain of your guilt was so oppressive. But you did not have the guilt that your father has."

"But how do I proceed, Master? I don't know how to even begin with this."

"You sat in the audience tonight, Averill. You heard your father in a conversation with the Indian shaman when no one else did, isn't that so?"

"Yes, Master, and it was confusing too. I could tell no one else knew, but cannot explain that."

"I understand this is difficult for you, my child. But just as I permitted, by my spirit, your father, the shaman, and you to hear each other, this time only you will hear my words."

"But how will that help, Master? Will he not be confused by the silence as you instruct me in this, as I sure am?"

"Just as the audience was held out of this experience, he will not realize the lapse occurs. You have to trust me in this, Averill, my child."

"Okay, Master, my trust will be solely in you because I sure wouldn't know where to begin."

Averill walked as softly as he could up behind his father and stopped. Speaking softly and still unsure, he began, "Father, I came to be with you." His father turned around slowly and saw genuine sorrow and empathy in the eyes of his remaining son.

"It's all right, son. I know my speech didn't go well, but there were reasons you wouldn't understand."

"I understand more than you think, Father, and—can I call you Dad?—Somehow 'Father' sounds so formal."

"Yeah sure, son, whatever you like, but don't worry about this, okay?"

"I could hear, Dad. During the speech."

"Of course you could, son. It just wasn't pretty, was it?"

"Not that, Dad. I mean I could hear you talking with someone else, an Indian maybe by the sound of it? Nobody else could hear it, but I could. You were talking with someone about the battle and the loss of the people and things like that."

Montana almost jumped back as he heard this. *Could this be possible, could it be happening to me? Did Averill hear all that stuff? Was it even real? But if he heard it too, how could that be a dream or a vision thing as the mystics call it?*

"Averill, son, listen to me! What could you hear? Tell me, son!" he almost shouted. Fortunately, the after-dinner party was so loud that no one outside the room could hear him.

"You were defending yourself. I couldn't see the Indian you were talking with, but I could hear you both and he wasn't very happy."

"Don't concern yourself with him, Averill. Spirits like that are just dreams. It's not real, son!"

"If he wasn't real, how come you got so upset? Especially when he started telling you that you had sold them out to save yourself, rather than helping the good guys win. I saw your confession, Dad. You can't hide from that, can you?"

Montana was struck once again by the horrible guilt he had experienced when Urchuwa exposed his deceit. Learning that his son had heard it too made it even more painful. He could only hang his head in shame.

"But what could I do, son? He wouldn't even accept my apology."

"It was worse than that, Dad, wasn't it? It wasn't really an apology; more like an excuse. That's different, isn't it? What did he say? That the greatest offense was against the Great Spirit; that his people were okay now in the spirit world but that you had wronged their spirit god. Was that it, Dad?"

"I'm so sorry you had to hear that, son. It was a horrible dream, that's all it was. My beliefs won't allow me to accept that experience as reality. It just can't be. Not possible for a rational mind to accept such nonsense, like life after death, a spirit world, and all that."

At this point the Master gave Averill some guidance.

"Averill, your father is trapped in a misguided belief that only things that are material exist. That allows him to be the final arbiter of his choices, unimpeded by the wisdom I have made available in the ancient texts that you call your Bible. But there is a deeper reason than his experience with the numinous, and he has had more of that than most of the scientific ones who reject me have. Your job today is to break through the barrier his history has created."

I don't understand, Master. What barrier, what history? What do I tell him?

The instruction began, and Averill absorbed it in an uncanny, restructured way that later he could never explain, even to himself. Averill continued to speak to his father, standing there before him, as if this had instantly formed in his mind, and his father was unaware of the intervention and instruction that led to his words.

"Dad, I understand why it's so hard. That Great Spirit, whom you were told you offended and needed to ask forgiveness from—maybe you can't even believe he was real. Is that the problem?"

The Master spoke again to the consciousness of Averill: "His natural father betrayed him as a youth when he lied to rescue his father, who was accused of the wrongful death of his natural mother. Someone close to him who should have loved him let him down. Your father didn't think he could ever trust a father figure again. So why a great spirit or me, a heavenly dad, or anyone in authority over your father? Do past betrayals hurt so much that he cannot accept any higher authority?

"This problem goes deeper for him, Averill, because his next father tried to mold and make him into his own image. That's how he became an anthropologist. His adoptive father regretted abandoning that path himself and was living through his adopted son. Your dad resented it tremendously but had to pretend that path was his and finally adopted it in his own thinking. It came to a head when Horatio had to select his dissertation theme in graduate school and he used a religious theme to get even with his adoptive father. Like your dad now, his adoptive father totally rejected the supernatural in any respect and thought he had his son indoctrinated that way. When that father later died holding resentment against his son's betrayal of his philosophy, the wounds were left indelibly in a confused and conflated way. So you see, Averill, your father can't sort all of this out, as these themes of guilt and betrayal reverberate in his soul as his own choices have done the very same thing to others. The confrontation with the shaman and his final admission that he had acted wrongly, even by his materialistic standards of morality, brought him to the point you see him in now. Those reasons explain why he is so terrified by these numinous experiences."

Averill nodded as though he understood, but he had not a clue as to how he should speak. He just opened his mouth and began, somehow trusting that his spiritual guide would give him the right words should he falter.

"Dad, I sense there are deeper reasons why you fight the idea that the spiritual experiences are real. You never told us about your real father, how he betrayed you. But it's true, isn't it? And the man who adopted you was someone you resented for trying to remake you in his image, so you got even when you wrote your disser-something or other, didn't you?"

Montana heard the words, but they were nothing compared to the shaft of guilt and confusion that pierced his heart. *How could this be? I haven't thought of those horrible times so long ago in years. How could my son know about any of that?* He struggled to control his emotions and then finally responded.

"Averill, I don't, uh, understand what you mean, son. What could you possibly know about any of that stuff?"

"I must confess, Dad, that I didn't tell you and Momma everything that happened to me when Ratio died. I was so upset when I let him go without even an attempt to rescue him, I felt like I was to blame. I wanted to die—to join him in death. Can you understand that, Dad?"

Montana nodded.

Averill continued, "Well, I was a coward, I guess, and didn't want to jump in that lake and be eaten like him, so I ran away into the forest. I ran and ran and ran until I was exhausted. After it got so dark that I was tripping on roots and falling every few feet, I crawled into an old stump and buried myself in the rotten wood for some cover from the night air and finally fell asleep. Then the strangest—no, the weirdest—thing happened. I can't begin to explain or even understand it, but I had a visitor from the spirit world who helped me."

Montana stared at his son in skeptical disbelief and said, "What do you mean by 'spirit world,' Averill? There is no such thing."

Averill tried to calm down and draw from his memory all that had happened that night, and said, "I call it being from the spirit world because I know it wasn't real in an ordinary sense—you know, Dad, like rocks and water and human arms and legs, like that. It wasn't a dream either. I've had plenty of those, and scary ones too. This was different. I was standing there bathed in a cone of light, and this figure appeared out of it and spoke to me."

Montana interrupted him: "What do you mean, Averill, a figure appeared and spoke? Was it a human figure? How do you know it wasn't a dream? They can seem real as life sometimes, you know."

Averill continued, "It—the figure, I mean—didn't seem human like you and me at first, but the voice was clear and speaking so I could understand the words. I'm certain about that, and I know it wasn't a dream because I was not only in it but I could see the rotten wood stuff I had been covered in while sleeping all over me and it was still there after the figure, uh, man, or whatever it was, left. But it all came clear before that when his image finally became clear and by what he said."

Montana was intrigued, although everything he was hearing was so foreign to his beliefs.

"The man or spirit became more human the longer he spoke, and it all became plainer when he told me who he was or had been before he was killed in the final battle. I knew the name right away, and you will too. He said he had been Elliot Drake in his former life."

Averill and Ratio had never met Elliot Drake, so Averill couldn't recognize his image, but he knew enough about his dad's trip to Ecuador and had read his book about the expedition.

Montana was stunned by this revelation. It was so dreamlike that it couldn't be real. He had read all those near-death experience stories and had never believed any of them. But the part about Elliot was so shockingly true, and there was no way that Averill could have known this. Then his experience at the awards ceremony with the same exact kind of interactive image, this time with the deceased Urchuwa, which the boy also had at least heard. Montana just stood there, stooped, with a blank look of despair. *It had to have been a real experience the boy is telling me; he knows too much. These things don't just happen, do they? Not like this*, he thought, waiting for the next revelation.

Averill continued, "Mr. Drake said that he had been forgiven for his terrible crimes after the Spirit introduced himself as the Master. Elliot had confessed all his crimes long before and had turned away from being a professional killer. He said he had met the Master early in his life but had drifted away from the confidence of his final place after death. He later returned to those beliefs and it was all made right somehow, which I still don't pretend to understand.

"And what was more important, Dad, was that Mr. Drake introduced me to the Master and his voice spoke to me just like we are talking even though I could not see his presence like I could with Mr. Drake. Anyway, he forgave me for what I had done in abandoning Ratio and took that pain away. It changed me too, Dad, because it no longer hurt and still doesn't. It's wonderful to be at peace about something so terrible.

"He gave me a new name too. Well, not really new—because I already had it. He gave me my name back and said I was no longer average and was never to call myself that again.

"Also, he gave me an assignment. That's why I'm here, Dad. He said that I should tell you that you can be forgiven, too, for all your lies.

They've helped bring you fame, but it's led to more manipulation and dishonesty in your life and has made you an unhappy man. I certainly experienced the effects of it, but I forgive you for all of that. He told me that once you stop the lying, including to yourself, you will be free to be the real Horatio Averill Blake you always wanted to be and couldn't."

Montana grew more despondent. *How could Averill know all this stuff? I've never told any human being what lies I have lived with. They could never go away anyway, could they? I don't know about this "spirit world" business. Could any of this he is telling me be real? I can't abandon my beliefs, but what do I make of these experiences that are just as real to my perceptions as earth, wind, and fire?* He brooded in silence as Averill waited patiently.

Averill was prompted by the Master to begin again. "How about it, Dad? Wouldn't you like to be free of all the effects of those lies and the manipulation of others and start over?"

Montana finally spoke. "Averill, I don't see how that is possible, and I can't believe all this spirit world stuff anyway. It goes against my very philosophy about life."

The Master told Averill, "One of my servants from long ago, gifted in your language and in the understanding of the nature of man, said, 'There are more things in heaven and earth, Horatio, than are dreamt of in your philosophy.'"

You want me to say something like that?

"Not something like it; say it exactly like that."

"Dad, I am supposed to tell you this as the Master is speaking it to me: 'There are more things in heaven and earth, Horatio, than are dreamt of in your philosophy.'"

Montana could never explain later—not even to himself—the effect that statement had on his confidence in his beliefs. He had studied the basic sciences; the theories of Einstein; the puzzles over time, black holes, and M-theories, with their multiple dimensions; and Darwin's theory of evolution that could not explain the symmetry, order, and complexity in the cosmos. Possibly deep underneath all the lies that he had told himself over the years, there had always been the nagging questions: How could all this just happen on its own? What accidents upon thousands of accidents could turn nothing into something and a simple something into the marvelous complexity that even he as an anthropologist could not deny? He had buried those questions while building his reputation as a scientist. But these undeniable experiences with the

Urchuwa spirit and the long-buried events his son had revealed could not be denied.

If there is more in the heavens and on earth that my philosophy permits, and there sure seems to be, am I left with anything in my life to stand on?

Finally, he began to speak in a tone of authenticity and honesty the likes of which had never crossed his lips.

"Averill, I admit that what you say, or have related from this Master as you call him, has shaken me to the core. You have uttered things about me you could not have known, and they are true—all true. Admitting them is the hard part, even to myself. My life has been one lie upon another. I have made a mess of my life, and yours and Ratio's too.

"That whole movie didn't expose the half of it, but the part it did expose was truthful and painful enough. I wanted that Musquaeli relic and saw enough of it in the battle to know it had some mystical power.

"I got my friend Elliot Drake killed, and you have no idea how relieved I feel to know his spirit is all right even now. My problem is I don't know what to do about it. If the Master or God or whatever name he really has can forgive Elliot for his murders and you for abandoning your brother, maybe he will forgive my duplicity, guilt, betrayal, and all the rest."

Averill turned inward and found the words to say. "The Master says that you have done the hard part, by admitting it all happened as you have stated. The rest is up to him if only you quit saying no and—most importantly—ask him. Will you do that now?"

Montana looked into the eyes of his son and said, "How do I do that? Has he told you that?"

"Just ask. He's here now and hears you if you mean what you say." Averill stood by in amazement as his father asked an unseen presence to accept him despite his lies, his manipulation of others, his failure to believe.

The light of a revived life came over Montana's countenance, and he seemed to have heard, understood, or at least accepted the change. Montana turned to his son and embraced him with an authentic hug, which his son returned enthusiastically. Finally, they separated a short distance, looked at each other, and Montana spoke. "Averill. You will always be called that by me for you are no longer average in my eyes, son. You're the best and I love you."

"I love you too, Dad!" Averill replied.

"I guess there is more in heaven and earth than I ever dreamed of after all."

Averill grabbed his father again in an enthusiastic hug that lasted longer than either believed possible as they merged their emotions into a permanent bond that no crisis, no disaster, no ruined reputation, or even uncertainty in the future could break. Life for them wouldn't be perfect, but it would always be theirs, together.